I0788464

CIRQUE OBSCURUM

K.A KNIGHT

KENDRA MORENO

TELL ME YOUR NIGHTMARES

Cirque Obscurum

This is a work of fiction. Any resemblance to places, events or real people are entirely coincidental.

Copyright © 2024 K.A. Knight & Kendra Moreno, all rights reserved.

All rights reserved.

No part of this book may be reproduced in any form or by any electronic or mechanical means, including information storage and retrieval systems, without written permission from the author, except for the use of brief quotations in a book review.

Written by K.A. Knight & Kendra Moreno
Edited By Jess from Elemental Editing and Proofreading.
Proofreading by Norma's Nook.
Formatted by The Nutty Formatter.
Art by Dily Iola Designs.
Cover by The Pretty Little Design Co.

READER CONSIDERATIONS

Cirque Obscurum is intended for audiences over eighteen and features adult situations, please check the TW list before reading

This is a dark book.

Non con, dubious consent, sexual violence, sexual assault, physical violence, abuse, child abuse, imprisonment, violence, murder, torture, depression, PTSD, gore, kidnapping.

HA!
CIRQUE OBSCURUM

PROLOGUE

"Oh, come on, Marie. It's not that weird," my dad mutters, tightening his hold on my hand as he meets my mom's disapproving eyes—eyes that are the exact same shade of green as mine.

"She has been going on and on about seeing this circus for weeks now," my mom hisses. "Most girls want to get their dresses ready for the school dance, but not our little girl." There's disgust in her voice, as if wanting to go to the circus instead of wearing frilly dresses is the ultimate sin.

"So what? I don't want her to be like those snooty girls anyway." My dad winks down at me. I grin in excitement as his eyes land on the scene before us. "If my little girl wants to go to the circus, then we're going to take her." With that declaration, he begins to walk toward the gate, and I almost scream in victory.

For weeks, Mom told me I couldn't go to the circus. I've pleaded, begged, and bribed. As soon as I saw the vivid green flyers posted around town with stark black words stenciled across, I knew I had to go.

Something in me demanded it.

CIRQUE OBSCURUM: ALL ARE WELCOME.
OCTOBER 1-31ST.
FIND THE DARKNESS WITHIN.

Mom had been understandably horrified when I came home from school holding it. She almost had a stroke as she clutched her pearls and begged me to toss it in the trash. That didn't stop me from telling my dad about it, though, and now we're here. I can hardly handle my excitement.

I skip at my dad's side as we approach the elaborate entrance before us. The arched entryway is shaped like a yawning mouth with fangs hanging down, the face of some sort of demonic clown looking down on all those who dare enter. It's done in reds and blacks with a top hat perched on his head. At night, I have no doubt the lights will add to the eerie display, but in the daytime, it's almost comical.

Beyond the opening, I see the tip of the big top with red and white stripes—the signature look of every circus. It almost appears cute during the day, like a joyful mirage meant to beckon children in.

Grass crunches under my feet, the brisk autumn breeze making me snuggle deeper into my coat, even as I grin widely when we pass under the archway and into another world.

Tents and stalls line the walkway to the big top. Some are closed, but some remain open, serving food or offering carnival games where you can win a prize. There are caravans and old wooden houses parked throughout, all painted in the red and black color scheme with monstrous figures and drawings across each to announce who is inside.

Men and women in costume dance throughout the thin, early afternoon crowd. One tumbles by on a large ball, making me giggle. I gasp when a man in a black suit on stilts leans down, a giant, grinning maw painted on his white face and fake blood dripping around his red eyes. He gets right in my face, and I stumble back, briefly terrified, before being delighted with the strangeness of it.

"Welcome home, vindica." He chuckles before lifting one giant foot and ambling away.

Giggling, I spin to soak it all in before yanking my dad over to the closest booth. "Face painting, come on!"

"Alright, alright," Dad says with a smile before tugging some bills out of his slacks. I glance back to see my mom daintily holding her purse against her chest, clutching her cardigan shut as she looks around at the performers in horror. Ignoring her, I throw myself into the black wingback throne set next to the table and grin widely at a man dressed like a skeleton.

"Well, well, well, little darkling. What can we turn you into?" he purrs, his paints spread out before him.

"Oh, a skeleton! No! A clown! Oh, anything really." I almost jump up and down in my excitement. There's no way I can pick just one, so I let the man choose.

Smiling widely, he takes the money from my dad and grabs a palette and a brush, dragging his chair close. "Trust me, I know exactly the thing. Close your eyes, little darkling."

I do as I'm told, trusting him. I wiggle in my chair, but the man is very patient with me as he paints, and when he leans back, finished, my mother screams and turns away. My father just grins at me.

"Very scary," Dad says.

"Let me see," I beg, and the man hands me a mirror. My mouth drops open at the art he created on my face.

There are bright red devil horns above the arches of my eyebrows with a jewel at each tip. My mouth has been extended on either side in the same bright red with more jewels at each tipping point. Diamond's also frame my face, making a heart shape that ends on my chin and arches between my brows. My eyes are black with smoky tendrils trailing down onto my cheeks.

I look amazing.

"I love it," I whisper.

"Good, now go have fun, little darkling," the face painter says with a smile. "Enjoy the darkness you find."

"Thank you," I tell the man before taking my father's hand and letting him lead me away.

We spend the next hour exploring, eating, playing games, and enjoying a small juggling show. "Only one stall left, thank goodness," Mom whispers as we pass between two tents. I ignore her in favor of my cotton candy, but still, her words make me sad. It's almost over? Already?

Turning my head, I glance between tents as we pass to see a young boy in a black waistcoat and slacks. He's speaking sadly to a huge clown, his hands moving fluidly with his storytelling. He looks so normal but feels anything but. He's strange. I miss a step at the sight of him, and my father catches me so I don't fall. I don't know how, but they must sense me watching. When they turn, and I meet the black eyes of the boy so close to my age, my heart nearly stops. He's beautiful, but he turns away before I can study him closer.

"Ember, keep up," Mom chastises when I trip again.

Turning away, I focus on my steps, not wanting to get in trouble or for the day to end prematurely. We stop outside the last tent, and even my dad looks dubious at its appearance.

"Maybe we should just go home," he suggests, scratching his graying hair. "What do you think, squirt?"

"Not a chance," I declare before handing him my cotton candy, then I push through the closed flaps. The sign above the door announces that the psychic is in, as well as some other words I don't understand.

Fata manus

The decor inside the tent makes my eyes widen. The chill from outside is gone, and it's replaced by a spicy warmth that surrounds me as I step deeper inside. It's dark in here, with candles and lanterns strung from the ceiling and placed out on every available surface. Brightly colored material hangs along the walls in strips, and in the middle of it all is a round table with a black cloth draped over it. Upon it is a deck of cards spread out across the top.

"Hello?" I call boldly.

"Well, aren't you a brave little soul?" comes a smoky voice. A woman appears as if from nowhere, despite me not seeing any of the curtains move. Unlike the other performers, she doesn't wear face paint. Instead, she has lots of dark makeup on that only adds to her mystery. She's dressed in a long black gown that catches the light, and rings adorn every finger. There's a tattoo of an open eye on the middle of her forehead, and I'm mesmerized by it. "Aren't you afraid?" she asks as she studies the soft pink dress my mother insisted I wear. Clearly, I don't fit in here—not dressed like this.

"Not really," I admit. "I don't tend to get scared."

Smiling, she sits at the table and gestures for me to do the same on the opposite side. "Then come have your fortune read, little one. Let us find your fate."

I sit happily as she shuffles through the deck of cards before placing them on the table, then she lays her hands palms up around them. I place mine in hers, and her eyes close as she focuses on whatever it is she does. I see her mouth moving, and the lanterns and candles around us seem to flicker before they go out and we're doused in darkness. My heart speeds up, but I don't let go, and when her eyes open and a single candle comes to life on the table, I jump. Her eyes are no longer soft brown. They are bright white.

I stare in awe, my heart in my throat, as she releases my hands and spreads the cards out. She flips one, two, then three of them before looking back into my eyes.

"Oh, my brave little soul," she murmurs, but her voice is deeper now, darker, as if coming from behind her. "Life will not be kind to you, not in the beginning."

"I'll fail my tests." I sigh in understanding. "Mother won't be happy, but I hate studying."

"I wish that were all," the voice says. "Darkness encircles you, but remember that those who hide in the light can carry just as much evil as those in the shadows."

I frown, unsure what she means until she turns her hands over and grasps mine. She presses her palms to mine, and I feel something materialize between our fingers. "Take this. It's our card. Once given, it belongs to you. When you call, we will come. You'll know when the time is right."

"Why?" I wonder out loud as I tug my hands away to see the black matte card with red engravings. It's a joker, but the joker has a knife gripped in his hands and a heart lies across the edges.

"We always come for those who need to be saved. Remember that." She leans back, and the candles suddenly flicker to life, her eyes fading back to brown. "Your parents are getting worried. You should go."

"Ember?" I hear my dad's voice from outside, and I scramble back to my feet.

"Coming," I call as I clutch the card to my chest. "Thank you," I tell her, curious about who she is.

"No, thank you, little one." She stands, sweeping her skirt behind her. "One day, you will understand just what your purpose will be."

Nodding, I head to the tent entrance before my parents can come in after me. There are already enough rumors about how strange I am, how different. I don't need any more. Mom already worries for my future and how I'll marry and have a family if I'm an outcast.

I don't care about any of that, but I hate how she worries, even Dad.

"Remember, little one," the fortune teller calls as I stand half in and half out of the tent. "The darkness will always come when you call. Cirque Obscurum's doors will always be open to you should you wish for it."

Ignoring the strange feeling inside me, I nod and head back into the sunlight.

I clutch the card where my parents can't see, and it seems to burn in my palm.

CHAPTER
ONE

EMBER

Fifteen years later . . .

"Ember," Roger chastises, peering at my face. "No, we're too old to play dress-up."

"But it's almost Halloween. We should pick our costumes for the block party—"

"I said no," he snaps furiously, his eyes sparkling with darkness. There's hatred in his gaze that makes me shrink back. He was a kind man when I married him, or so I'd thought. At nineteen, I didn't really have a clue, but women don't have much of a choice besides finding a man to marry. Not many can get a job, at least not a good one, and we certainly aren't allowed to attend college like Roger did.

We are homemakers, wives, and child bearers.

Despite my vehement protests growing up, I married. I succumbed to the American dream to save my mother. She was sick, and Father had died five years before in the war so we didn't have any money for medicine. Roger came along like a white knight when I'd been scrambling for some sort of plan to purchase the medication. Roger came from money, and he was going to college to be a

9

doctor. He was also older and handsome and everything a proper woman should look for in a husband. Mother loved him, thought he was perfect, and so she pushed me to accept his first offer to go steady. He took me under his wing and showed me kindness, and we fell into the illusion of love.

When he proposed a few months later, he promised to take care of me and my mother forever. I had no choice but to say yes, so it seemed an easy decision.

It has been six years since we married. Mother passed six months ago, and it's like with her death, the bindings Roger placed on himself went with her. All shreds of humanity disappeared in an instant, and the kindness and softness I had been used to during the day vanished completely. Now, there is a cruel hatred that I'd only seen in very concerning moments between the sheets. I hate those times. I hate that he no longer keeps those emotions in the bedroom.

Roger is anything but a kind man, and I learned that far too late. I'm trapped with nowhere else to go, and he knows it. I have no money of my own, no family to fall back on or protect me, and no job or hopes of getting one. In the tiny town of Lost Springs, I'm nobody, just the strange wife who always seems a little out of sorts. Roger is their amazing, perfect doctor, and they worship the ground he walks on.

I play the game he wants. I learned the rules fast, but it seems like I struck a nerve over the Halloween costumes because he suddenly grabs my throat and slams me into the wallpaper behind me. My head cracks audibly against the wall, making me whimper, but I swallow the pain, used to it by now as I hang in his grip, struggling to breathe.

I don't even fight back anymore, and I hate that the most.

I did at first, but it only made things worse. If anything, me fighting back seemed to excite him, and at five foot one to his six foot five, I don't stand a chance. He knows that, and he takes pleasure in reminding me anytime I push back.

His boring brown eyes gleam as he glares at me, his perfectly coiffed blond hair pushed back. I used to think his hair was perfect and neat. Now, I see it for the illusion it is. He's still in his suit since he came home early from his practice without warning. "I let this foolishness go while your mother was here, but no more. You are not a child, Ember, and it's time to grow up. You will be submissive and beautiful. No more stupid makeup or costumes. No more games." He rips the one I was making, the leotard I sewed for days, away from my chest, and I close my eyes to keep the tears from falling.

I know what will come next. It always comes after.

"If you want to dress like a little whore, then I'll treat you like one."

I barely have time to gasp as he spins me and slams my face into the wall. My eye immediately echoes with pain, and I know it will bruise later. Black spots dance across my vision, my awareness fading, and I wonder idly if he will finally kill me. I almost yearn for it, wanting to join Mother and Father again, to be free of him and this house.

When I come back from the darkness to hear his grunts in my ear and feel the pain in my hips and groin, I know I wasn't so lucky. He thrusts harder, brutally ripping my insides because I'm dry. I cry out in pain, and he presses my face harder against the wall to silence me. He likes it when he hurts me.

He enjoys that he makes me bleed, and as tears slide down my cheeks, I force myself to go somewhere else and remember happier days.

When he's done, he throws me to the floor, and I can't even catch myself, my head slamming against the hardwood yet again. "Clean yourself up. You're a mess. The Carlsons are coming in an hour, and I expect dinner to be on the table for all of us, something they'll be delighted by. The wife likes pie."

I lift my head to see him zipping his pants before storming away, not even bothering to help me up. Swallowing hard, I reach down between my thighs, my fingers slipping in the blood there. I lift my fingers to the light and eye the red drops coating them before I bring them to my lips and suck them clean.

A perfectly placed scarf hangs around my neck, bangs cover the cut on my head, and the right amount of powder on my face makes sure the growing bruise isn't even apparent. My groin aches all night, but I smile through dinner, laughing at Roger's jokes and kissing him, playing the perfect couple so the Carlsons don't notice.

All the while, I'm dying inside.

More than once, I debate picking up the knife from the roasted chicken and plunging it into his chest. I'd be committed, but it would be worth it to watch his shock fade to horror as he bleeds out. I don't, of course. How uncouth. Instead, I listen to them blabber on about shit I don't care about, like frustrating patients, sports, and which mower is best for the perfect lawn.

When Mrs. Carlson asks when we will have children, I see the true Roger shine through. I cover my stomach protectively while forcing a smile in hopes I don't cry despite the echoes of pain.

No one knew, but I'd been pregnant not too long ago—until Roger became angry at the thought of having to share me with a child. Despite that being the dream, and despite it ruining his reputation, he strung me up and beat my stomach until I had a miscarriage. I bled for weeks and screamed in agony, but every night, Roger came home and still expected me to tend to my marital duties. I went numb the moment he decided to brutalize me completely—the final step.

He laughs at Mrs. Carlson's question, but I can tell it angers him, and I know I will be the one who pays for it later.

After dinner, he walks them to the door. I don't even realize I'm still covering my stomach until he turns to find me watching from the base of the stairs as he bids them goodbye. When they reach their car, his mask drops.

His expression becomes cold and angry as he slams the door behind him. "What do you say?"

"I'm sorry, Roger," I reply automatically.

"For what?" he demands.

I hesitate. If I say the wrong thing, it won't end well. I must hesitate too long because the next thing I know, I'm hitting the floor from a backhand I didn't even see coming.

"Pathetic. You can't even do what you were made for," he spits before stepping over me and heading to the kitchen.

I force myself up, ignoring the ache in my cheek, and follow him. I know that if I play the docile wife, this will end faster. I watch him pour himself a glass of whiskey.

"Stupid fucking woman. She makes me do this. If she just had the fucking baby—"

Anger ignites within me at his accusation. I blink and look down to find the carving knife in my hand. I don't even remember picking it up, but as he turns, he sees it.

"Ember, what are you doing?" he asks, his voice dangerously low.

"I—" I glance at the knife and then back at him as his eyes cloud with fury.

"Put it down. Now," he orders, one finger pointing at me over his glass.

I hesitate, and he doesn't like that.

Before I can use the knife, I'm thrown into the wall again. Groaning, I slip to the hardwood floor I loved the moment we stepped foot in this house. Now, I detest it because I've spent so much time hurting on it. He isn't holding me, so I claw my way to the stairs. If I can make it up there, I can hide and lock the bathroom door until he's over his anger, but I don't move fast enough.

I'm flipped over before I make it two feet. The next punch has me seeing stars, my head lolling back.

I feel my nose break, and it's suddenly hard to breathe.

I'm almost numb, the pain fading into the darkness as if this is happening to someone else. As I stare into his eyes, I know he will kill me tonight. I feel it in my soul.

I refuse to beg or plead, so I keep my mouth shut, and he hates that more, his dark orbs filled with manic glee.

"You want a baby, Ember?" he sneers, spitting in my face. "Then let's give you a baby."

Gripping my hair, he drags me up the stairs. I scream as my body hits each and every step, and the numbness fades in favor of excruciating pain. I feel bones break, my skin bruising and splitting, but he doesn't relent.

He throws me onto the bed. I can barely lift my head as he kicks the door shut, sliding his belt off with one hand. I'm too tired to fight, but when his hands rip my dress up, I struggle out, ignoring the pain and my inability to breathe. I land a decent blow to his shoulder, but it's not enough to stop him.

Grabbing my face, he presses it to the bed, ignoring my flailing. I can't breathe as I suck in mouthfuls of blanket. He holds me in place as he slams inside me, the agony unbearable since I haven't healed from earlier. I start to choke, but he presses my head harder against the bedding.

The slap of his hips is loud as he rapes me.

I must black out because when I come to, my movements are sluggish and I'm coughing. I feel his cum sliding down my thighs and for some reason, that makes me want to cry.

I don't know why. He's done much worse before.

Much, much worse.

Somehow, I find the strength to roll over. He's lighting up a cigarette as he glares at me, and for the first time, I open my sore, bleeding lips. "Kill me," I beg.

"What's that?" he murmurs, leaning down and pressing the lit cigarette into my thigh. I scream at the agony, the smell of my burning flesh filling the air.

"Kill me!"

"You want me to kill you, Ember? Tough shit. I'm going to lock you in here forever. I'll fuck this tight little body every day until you're pregnant again, and then once the child is here, I'll kill you. I'll say you died in childbirth. The mourning widower will be the hit of the town. I'll find another woman who is more obedient and better in bed. No one will remember you. No one will even mourn you." He drags me into the attic and slams the door, sealing me in the darkness.

TWO

EMBER

I don't know how long I lie in a heap in the dull attic. The pain in my body and heart is too much, and my head throbs. I must have a concussion, which isn't surprising considering the number of blows. I drift in and out of consciousness until I wake up shivering from a bone-deep cold so brutal, my teeth begin to chatter. It's dark, the only light coming from a small window. The dust motes float and dance before my eyes in the moonlight.

With a groan, I force myself to my knees, running my hand along my side until I gasp in pain. Yes, I definitely have some broken ribs, and my wrist feels like it might be fractured. I've read through enough of Roger's medical books to know that none of that is going to heal correctly on its own. Shivering so hard I have to clench my teeth, I drag myself over the uneven wood toward the cluttered boxes I hid at the back.

I need to get warm.

He's right. I'm not dying yet.

Not today.

I won't let him get away with his plan.

I search through the boxes with shaking fingers, barely able to read my scribble on the sides due to the low light. I don't dare turn on the lightbulb in case Roger sees and comes up after me. They are full of all my old stuff from my parents' house. Roger didn't want this crap in his house, so I hid it up here. There has to be something I can use to bind my wounds and keep myself warm.

Anything will do. I refuse to die here.

I will not die here.

I repeat it like a mantra as I search, my body aching everywhere.

I will not die here.

The first box holds nothing useful, so I push it gently to the side, panting from the effort as I rip open the one underneath. I have to take a moment to breathe through the pain and dizziness assaulting me.

I will not die here.

My hands hit something hard, and I blink, squinting as I try to see the contents. When I finally can, I realize it's a picture from when I was younger and happy. The sun is shining down on my friends and me, our bikes forgotten to the side. We were so carefree and happy, it hurts just to look at it. With a pitiful scream, I use some of the last of my strength to pick up the frame and throw it. I hear it crash and shatter where it lands, just like my soul as I risk Roger's wrath. Hopefully, he went to the bar to drink.

I'm not that girl anymore. He killed her a long time ago, but I won't betray her memory.

I will not give in that easily. *I will not die here.*

With a renewed sense of urgency, I tear into another box, and another, until I find an old forgotten shawl. It's lacy, probably my mother's, and eaten through with moth holes, but it's better than nothing. I drape it over my shoulders, shivering in the chill. I pull it closed with one hand while I continue to search with the other. As more time passes, the pain only seems to increase, and I know I don't have long before I pass out. Black dots start to dance and twirl across my vision, my breathing becomes labored, and my skin is too hot and cold all at the same time.

There's more useless crap inside, and I toss it aside with an animalistic cry of panic as I blink rapidly, trying to bring my vision back.

I won't die here. I won't die here. I won't die here.

At the bottom of the box, forgotten and alone, resides a black card. Frowning, I pick it up and shift up to my knees as I bring it closer, trying to make sense of it as my brain shuts down.

It's a playing card.

The joker grins from ear to ear, and there is a heart in his mouth. He holds a knife in his hand, appearing both threatening and comforting. Something about it is familiar, but I'm too weak, too close to the darkness. Shaking my head, I try to figure out why it's here, why it's important, and why my fingers can't seem to let it go.

The circus . . . The circus . . . I got it at the circus, didn't I?

Yes, I know I'm right, even as my body gives up.

Gripping the forgotten card in my grasp, I slump onto the hardwood, hearing the thump of my body hitting it, but I feel nothing. My blackening vision remains locked on the joker, the red color shining despite the years that have passed since I got it. My thumb brushes across its face, smearing my own blood over it.

It's the last thing I see, glowing with my blood, before the darkness takes me once more, but this time, I go somewhere warm and safe.

Someplace where I am free.

I will not die here.

THREE

T he call comes so brutally and swiftly, it nearly chokes me in my sleep. I've felt the call of the cards before—we all have—but never this strongly. Gasping for breath, I wrench myself from my small cot and cough, trying to clear the feeling of hopelessness and strangulation from my throat. Nothing I do dispels it. My chest is so tight I can't even take a full breath. Usually, a tingling sensation behind my eyes and a pull to follow a path come to me, but this time, I see her.

I see the one who calls.

I blink, and the scene before me flashes into another. I see an unfinished ceiling in an attic and blood splattered everywhere. The pain I feel is so strong, I double over, even as I try to extend the connection. Finally, I see a woman on the floorboards, unmoving. She's so small and still. For a moment, a boring two-story house flashes across her image.

Who the fuck is she, and why am I seeing her so clearly?

I want to call out, but I don't make a peep to alert the others around me in case the connection breaks. I feel as if I am being torn in two, with the woman in my vision and my cot at the circus.

Cirque Obscurum is a unique creature, and she never stops searching for freaks and outcasts. The cirque feeds on the pain and trauma that comes with being different. When we join the cirque, we swear a blood oath to her, promising to defend her and keep her going. As a child, I'd only known the magic of it, but as an adult, I recognize the danger.

What must be fed must always be fed.

The cards are an extension of that hunger, tied to our souls with the blood oath, so this feeling will have gone out to every one of us here. No doubt the others are gagging on the agony at this very moment, feeling confused and horrified by the deep anguish being pushed to us. Can they see her too? Can they taste her blood as I do?

I'm the ringmaster, so my oath is heavier than most, which means there's a chance I'm the only one who feels just how strong this call is. Whoever the woman is, she needs us now. Moreover, she belongs here.

I force myself out of my tent, stumbling under the strength of the call as I seek the other tents. Spade, Heart, and Club will have felt it, each of them as important as I am to the cirque, but as to their level of feeling, that's debatable.

When I stumble into Spade's tent, I realize I misjudged just how strong this is. I find him kneeling on the floor with tears running down his face as the emotions overwhelm him. I pull him to his feet and thrust a blade into his hand.

"Go get the others," I command, gasping around the pressure in my chest that only seems to double as I move. She's running out of time. "It's time to go hunting."

Spade supports himself against the tent poles before he stumbles out of the tent to gather Heart and Club. I watch him go, and when he's gone, I let some of my anguish out. A tear falls, and I hastily wipe it away so they won't see.

This card is different. Cirque Obscurum wants her badly.

This isn't something we can ignore.

We answer the call of the damned.

"We're coming, baby," I murmur, stepping out of the tent to meet the others. "It's time to bring her home."

EMBER

I wake to the sound of the front door slamming closed, the foundation rattling with the force of his lingering anger. I thank whatever deity for the reprieve, for the opportunity to rest before he comes home and continues his abuse. I listen for the sound of his car starting, the garish thing he insisted he needed as a statement of his success rumbling to life a second later. When the sound of the familiar engine fades, I try to move but I can't.

I can barely breathe.

There's no way to know just how many bones are broken right now. I know my ribs have suffered, and judging by how painful it is to breathe, that might be what ultimately kills me. It's not as if I can go to the doctor, not when the only one around for miles is the one who caused the pain.

There's something wrong with my leg too, but that pain is nowhere near as severe as my head. I gingerly press my fingers to my skull, feeling the bumps and bruises there. My face is swollen, my eyes refuse to open, my lips are split in multiple places, and there are cuts all over my face. I'm pretty sure my nose is broken. There's pain in my neck that worries me, but at least I stopped bleeding so severely. As I slept, I bled all over the attic floor. Now it's dry, making my dress stiff and uncomfortable. I try to reach for the numbness, if only to dull the pain, but it doesn't work. I'm cursed to feel every ache and bite of agony. Every time I try to sit up, my ribs scream at me and I collapse back to the wooden floor.

I still try. I won't die here. I refuse to die meekly. This attic won't be my coffin.

I try over and over, splitting wounds anew and making them bleed again. I don't know how much blood I have left to lose, but I don't care. I have to get out. I have to run. I have to escape.

My body is a traitor, though, and no matter how much I try to move, it's determined to stop me.

I collapse back to the wooden floor for the hundredth time, panting from my attempts and sweating with the exertion. I can't. Fuck, I can't.

As I lie here and stare up at the ceiling, the sun shines mockingly through the tiny window. I watch as dust motes dance through the rays, stirred by my movements. It almost looks like snow, like the bliss of a winter morning. I watch them dance across the light and yearn for something bigger. I gave my life to Roger, and he'll take all that I am if I stay. My body, my freedom, and my life hasn't been mine since my father died—not since I gave in and married to save my mother.

My existence has been a long line of disappointments.

As I clutch the joker card in my fingers, I realize I've been searching for the feeling the circus gave me all my life. The excitement and wonder have eluded me, and the strange child I was grew into a woman who bent to the whims of others when she should have fought.

Now, I'll pay for it with my life.

I don't cry. Instead, I recall that time of happiness, when I'd been carefree and my father had let me run through the tents. I return to the feeling of having my face painted, the wet brush moving across my skin as it smeared paint in a perfect design. I refused to remove the face paint for days. My mother was embarrassed by it at the grocery store when the other mothers stopped and stared. I remember the boy and the way his dark eyes caught mine and held. I remember the fortune teller, her words echoing in my mind.

Life will not be kind to you.

God, I thought she meant my exams at the time, not this horrible tragedy.

My fingers squeeze the card tighter, crinkling it, and my heart hurts for the child I once was. I was so full of wonder, so eager to chase the magic, but now here I lie, dying in an attic, my body broken and beaten. I will never be that innocent again. I will never dance through a circus, carefree and happy like I did as a child. She's gone, and soon, I'll be gone too.

How long before I bleed out? I don't know, but I hope it's sooner rather than later. I hope Roger doesn't return only to patch me up and force me to keep living. I can't do this anymore. I have to get out, either physically or by death. Either option is better than this.

My injuries are worse than I thought. I slip into darkness before I know what's happening, waking up later to find the rays coming from a different direction. How long have I lain here? What time is it? There are no clocks in the attic, and I don't wear a watch. I listen for sounds around me, relaxing when I only hear the creak of the floorboards as the house settles. My body feels heavy, and when I try to move this time, it still doesn't respond. My legs won't budge, and my arms may as well be boulders. They are unmovable. My entire body feels as if a great weight sits on top of it and holds me down. I can't even lift my head. All I can do is open my eyes and peer up at the dust motes still dancing like a beautiful ballet, somber and quiet to commemorate my death.

I enjoyed the ballet when my mother took me to it, though her dreams of me being a ballerina were dashed when I was refused entrance into the ballet school due to my gangly legs. Instead, she insisted on taking me to the performances. It always made me happy, the costumes intricate and pretty. I never understood how those were okay but the circus ones weren't. They were all performers.

The rumbling of a car engine rises outside, and I hold my breath, begging the universe to let it pass our driveway, but it slows, and I hear it pull in before cutting off.

Roger's home.

Oh, no. No, no, no.

I try to move again but it's pointless. I can barely breathe. I'm powerless to stop whatever happens next. If only I'd die. It's the one thing I can control now, and I refuse to be subjected to his whims until the bitter end.

I get to control this.

"Die," I rasp, willing myself to escape. "Please, just die."

That's rarely how the Grim Reaper works. He can't take me until my body gives out, and despite my pain and brokenness, it stubbornly hangs on. I'm going to suffer at Roger's hands again until he finishes with me.

Tears trickle from my eyes, finally able to drip free now that true fear is taking hold. I don't want this. I don't want him to find me.

The front door slams shut. I'd flinch if I could, but all I can do is close my eyes to the agony of what's coming. I hear him stomping around downstairs, the footfalls as angry as they've ever been. Today must have been a bad day at work, and he'll take it out on me. He'll make sure I know each grievance he had with his office or patients, and he'll hurt me for each one.

"Die," I rasp again as I hear him ascend the stairs with great big stomps. "Please."

"Ember," Roger calls, the sound echoing beneath me. I can feel his voice through the wooden floor. "I'm home."

"Die," I grunt, gritting my teeth as if that will help. "Just fucking die."

"Are you still alive up there?" he calls, amusement in his voice. "Sure would be a shame if our fun ended early."

He's right below me now. He's coming. All he has to do is climb the small attic staircase and open the door.

"Please," I croak, begging an entity that's not there. "Please."

Panic fills me as I hear him start coming up the small stairs. Although I can barely breathe, my chest begins to rise and fall rapidly, making my aching ribs shoot shards of pain into my heart.

"It doesn't matter if you died," Roger remarks behind the door. "I'm going to fuck you regardless."

My stomach roils, and I stare at the door in horror as he stops just outside it.

"Please," I beg one last time. "Please, let me die."

I'm not so lucky.

The doorknob turns, and tears spill over my lashes and down my swollen face, cutting through grime and blood on my skin. I can't move. I can't move. I can't . . . I'm not strong enough.

"Ember," he coos, "I'm going to have such fun with you."

I stare in horror as the door begins to open, the loud squeak of its hinges echoing around me.

EMBER

For a moment, my breathing stops, and everything inside me rebels at what I know will appear.

My ears are ringing, so maybe that's why I don't understand the noise for a moment—scuffling, like sounds of a struggle. There is the sliding of feet then something hitting a wall. I hear a muffled yell, more feet, and then nothing but silence. I manage to turn my head to fully face the door, awaiting what will appear there.

Did . . . Did Roger fall?

I can only hope, but I know fate isn't that kind, not to me.

The door slowly creaks open again, and the wood smacks against the wall of the attic so suddenly, I would flinch if I were able to. I peer through the darkness, my heart beating erratically like a trapped bird as I wait for his mocking face to appear framed in the doorway.

Only, what I see isn't Roger.

No, a head slowly appears in the opening, making my eyes widen at the sight. The face is covered by a creepy mask that makes my heart beat even more frantically. It's pure white but stained with blood and dirt as if it's an antique. The eyes are wide, black holes with cuts above and below. The cheeks are round, like apples, and bright red, leading to a macabre smile with red lips and big teeth. It has the word "Ha!" written across the forehead above thin arched brows.

It's horrifying, and as I watch, the masked face tilts to the side with that mocking grin. I should be screaming and trying to get away, but as I stare at the mask, I can't help but smile. I take in every detail, and something about it settles the fear inside me, morphing it into amusement and the feeling of . . . safety. It isn't something I'm used to experiencing.

The person behind the mask doesn't speak, but slowly, almost gently, a large hand appears and reaches inside the dim light of the attic. Their fingers are spread and held out to me in invitation. The skin is tan, like they spent hours in the sun, and the nails are covered in chipped paint, the skin marred with scars. They are so imperfect, unlike Roger or the life we must present. Maybe that's what calms me further as the pain seems to ebb away for a moment.

They wait with their hand silently held out to me, and something in me knows what it wants.

I must decide.

The hand represents a chance to escape from here, to escape the death that awaits me. It's my decision. I can stay and die or I can take the hand. I don't know if fate sent this person or if my pain called to them, but as I stare into the mask, I realize I don't care.

I won't die here.

Swallowing my blood, I manage to roll onto my side and then to my stomach. It takes every bit of strength I have in me. Gritting my teeth against the agony, I grip the wood and, with my eyes on the mask, I drag myself forward. My nails rip and break as I wedge them into the gaps between the floorboards. Each excruciating inch only makes me want to scream, the sound catching in my throat before it can escape, but I don't stop, leaving a gory display of blood in my wake. The dragging sound of my body is loud in the barren space, and they wait as I struggle, the hand still and patient.

My leg gets caught on something, and it stops my progress. With a whine, I slowly turn my head back to see the hurt one caught on a box. I kick it, once, twice. A whine leaves my throat at the pain that blooms from the movement, and when my leg is free, I spy the bright red drag marks along the floor, stretching out from the dried darker puddle I was lying in.

Turning back, I breathe a sigh of relief when I find the masked stranger still there, waiting patiently. They aren't helping, but they aren't leaving either. After all, nothing is ever that easy. They are telling me without words that if I want to live, I have to fight for it, and I will.

I keep pulling myself forward, using the strength in my arms despite my shaking muscles. I won't last much longer, but I won't give up.

I drag my body toward the light until I can't move any farther. When I'm nearly at their feet, the character kneels, bringing their hand closer to me as if they know I can't stand. With the last of the strength I have in my dying body, I slap my bloody hand into their waiting palm, the joker card held between my skin and theirs. I hadn't even realized it was still there, stuck to my palm with my blood.

Their smile only seems to grow, and I know this mysterious savior is proud of me.

I made my choice.

I chose to live.

What now?

For a moment, we just stare at each other, neither prepared to move. I don't have the strength, and whoever this is lets the silence stretch out between us.

I'm jerked forward so suddenly, a shriek escapes my lips, and I fall through the attic opening, down the stairs and plummet below, landing right in waiting arms. My eyes widen as I peer into another masked face, this one scarier than the last. It's a clown mask with a bright red nose and a red, grinning mouth, but its black eyes are lined with blue that cascades down its cheeks. On its forehead is a small spade symbol. Their strong arms hoist me higher until I'm held firmly within their grasp despite the murderous clown mask. I turn my head, laying it on their shoulder warily as the other jumps from the opening and turns to us with a nod, holding up the card so the red catches the light.

Some sort of silent communication seems to pass between them, and then the one holding me turns and heads down my hallway, making it seem small. It's then I realize how truly big the one holding me is. He's practically a giant, and he carries me downstairs effortlessly, straight into my living room.

There are two more massive figures here who are also wearing masks.

One has heart-shaped eyes and a kissing mouth with slashes across each cheek. The other is diamond shaped with red diamond cheeks. It has a creepy smile just like the others, and the person wearing it casually leans back against my fireplace.

The one with the hearts circles a chair in the middle of the room, and my eyes widen when I see Roger tied to it. His eyes are wide and terrified, and his mouth is stuffed with an apple with razors piercing the red skin of the fruit. His hands and legs are bound to one of the dining chairs with barbed wire, and it cuts through his clothes, drawing blood that drips to the rug below.

He won't like that. He doesn't like stains, I think idly as he struggles.

He tries to work his mouth and spit the apple out, his eyes landing on me. His struggles only seem to increase as he yells something at me. The words are muffled, so I can't make out what he's saying. The chair bangs with his efforts, his perfect suit askew and splattered with blood. It looks like there's a lump forming on his forehead, the raised portion casting a shadow as he moves about.

I suppose I should be scared, but I just relax into the masked man's arms as he holds me. I feel safe in his embrace, and either way, I'm not strong enough to move. My body is numb, most of the pain beginning to fade in favor of a blissful high that makes my head start to loll to the side. That's probably a bad sign, but as I stare at a terrified Roger, I can't seem to care.

I drink in his fear and memorize it. He fed on mine for so many years, so seeing my abuser, my tormentor so weak and scared makes me giddy. The feeling flutters in my chest, warming me.

The first masked man from the attic strolls past, swinging a red and black circus hammer in one hand. In the other, he holds up the joker card like a declaration for the others to see before handing it over to the diamond-masked man.

I'm guessing he's in charge then.

I can't tell what he looks like, but he's taller than Roger and wider too, though he is covered from head to toe in black. His hands are big, one perched on a black whip coiled at his hip. The other takes the card and holds it up to the light, inspecting it, and I see diamonds inked across his hands.

"You called," he says behind the mask.

His voice is dark and smooth, almost lyrical, like a song, and it echoes the beating of my heart, seemingly bringing it back to life.

"I did?" I ask, my hoarse voice barely loud enough to hear in the silence.

"You didn't?" he responds, tilting his head. The one with the hammer giggles at the gesture, the sound slightly manic. Roger looks between us, but I can't draw my eyes away from the diamond man.

"I-I wanted to live," I whisper, but he hears me.

"Is that all?" The silky question reaches inside of me to the dark place I hide. It rips apart my defenses, exposing my secrets and my darkest wishes.

"I-I wanted to live," I repeat, my eyes going to Roger. "And I wanted revenge."

Diamond man's fingers twist, and I watch in awe as the card suddenly disappears like a magic trick. "Then welcome to cirque." He straightens. "Shall we begin?"

"Begin?" I ask, confused as they move closer to Roger.

"To feed the call and seek your revenge," he tells me, the words wrapping around my soul. "Your eyes are bruised. Club, will you do the honor?"

The one with the hammer, the one from the attic, turns his attention to Roger before stepping closer. I watch, open-mouthed and alarmed but also a little bit happy, as the masked man slams his fist into Roger's face twice, aiming for each eye. Roger screams behind the apple, the force rocking the chair back. When Club moves away, I see Roger's eyes are already beginning to bruise.

"Your ribs. You're struggling to breathe," Diamond comments and then nods. This time, the one with the heart-shaped mask moves closer, plucking a knife from somewhere, and then he plunges it into Roger's side. I gasp, watching as he pulls the bloody blade free and twirls, almost dancing around the back of the chair before slamming it into his other side. He pulls it out, and when he does, Roger gasps, struggling to breathe, pain making his face pale as he screams behind the apple.

"Your neck is bruised. He choked you, did he not?" Diamond asks, though he doesn't seem to need confirmation.

His whip lashes out, and my eyes widen, watching the spiked black leather snap through the air and wrap around Roger's throat, cutting off his screams. The chair crashes against the hardwood, and then with an effortless flick of his wrist, the masked man yanks him across the floor until Roger stops at his feet.

Diamond crouches, tugging the apple from his mouth and throwing it toward the others. Club catches it, rubs it on his shirt, and lifts his mask to take a bite. I see blood in his mouth from where the razors cut him, the mask high enough to make out pouty lips and a clean-shaven face before he drops it again.

"What else, hmm?" Diamond calls.

"Her leg," the one holding me points out.

Diamond looks up, eyeing me as if to double check, and then he nods as he straightens. Without a word, he stomps his booted foot right down onto Roger's leg *twice*. I hear the bone snap as his scream rings out, loud now that he isn't muffled. It shouldn't give me satisfaction, but it does.

It all does.

Watching them reenact every vile, twisted thing my husband put me through only seems to make me happy. I guess I'm as broken as he said. Under it all, though, I do start to feel a little bad—not enough to stop this or to care when Club shoves the apple back into Roger's mouth, splitting his lips, but maybe enough to feel bad later.

He hurt me so many times, but part of me once loved this man. I guess that's hard to let go of, especially when he's being tortured before my very eyes.

Diamond straightens, looking at me. "I would offer for you to satisfy your revenge, but you're hurt. Shall I kill him quickly or slowly for you?"

I just stare, and when he speaks again, I swear I hear a grin in his voice. "We were called by you, for you. We're here for you. Your orders are ours to obey this evening. We're your wild dogs to command. This is your show. What you say goes."

I look back at a sobbing, bleeding Roger and know I can tell them to kill him and they will. I don't know why or how, but they will. They'll kill him for me if I ask, and part of me wants it, but the other part of me can't bring myself to take a life, even if it's the life of my bastard husband. He might have ruined his soul, but I still have mine.

I don't think I can take a life, and ordering them to do so would be like driving the knife in myself. Despite what he did to me, I have to be the better person. Besides, he will never hurt me again, not like this.

I'll give him the same chance I had—to live or to die from his wounds. Let's see how tough he really is.

"Don't kill him." I make my voice as strong as I can as I say the words. I move in the arms holding me with a wince, my eyes briefly fluttering shut when I can't draw in a breath. I can feel my blood dripping from me, staining his shirt, but he stands tall and strong. "Leave him there like he left me. He might die from his wounds or he might not, but it won't be on my soul or yours."

Club laughs. "She thinks we have souls."

I stare into the diamond mask, and he slowly inclines his head. "It's her choice." He looks back down at my husband. "You got lucky tonight. I wouldn't have been so kind. I would have ripped you apart limb from limb while you felt every bit of pain."

My heart skips, as I know he means it. They said I called them, that I command them. What does that mean? Maybe I should be more scared, but the weakness in my body makes my thoughts hard to follow. Everything is floating by now, and I know I'm still on death's door despite my four masked saviors.

"Let's go." Diamond steps over my husband's writhing body and moves toward me.

"Where?" I whisper.

"To the cirque, of course." He chuckles. "Where all brutal things go."

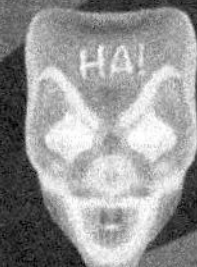

We don't hang around. The longer you stick around a crime scene, the higher your chances are of being caught, and we've already lingered here too long. The woman in my arms barely weighs anything at all, her body frail and injured. Despite the fact that a strong wind could blow her away, there is a cruel curl to her lips as she watches the sad excuse for a man writhe on the floor. Even though she spared him, she enjoys his pain, but who wouldn't when that person caused you so much agony and torment in the first place? I can't blame her for her smile, even if I think she should go further. I think she should rip his dick off and shove it down his throat. The injuries we can see are bad, but what about the ones we can't?

She's covered in so much blood, I wonder how she was able to be coherent for this. How had she been able to crawl to Club in the attic? We all heard the slow sound of shuffling and the grunts of pain that came from her mouth. Seeing the true extent of her injuries, I hate the bastard for making her crawl, even if it's a necessary part of the process. We have to make sure she wants it. Still, she should have died up there. We made it just in time. A few minutes later and whatever that bastard had been about to do to her would have killed her.

Even as we finish and gather our things, her eyes close and she slumps in my arms, out cold. Her injuries have finally become too insistent.

Club closes up the house while the rest of us head outside, our masks still firmly in place. We don't bother trying to hide her identity. No one would recognize her in her current state. Her face is stained red, and her body is broken and beaten. One of her legs is probably broken if the lump on the side of her calf is anything to go by, no doubt the bone sticking through. Her eyes are damn near swollen shut, and the rest of her face is just as bad. She breathes with a ragged rasp, her broken ribs digging into her sides. How badly is she injured, and how is she still holding on?

Though her eyes are closed now, I know they are a beautiful, cool gray color, unusual and bright against her dark hair. Without the injuries to her face, I know she'll be beautiful, but even with them, she's striking. She's also a fighter through and through. She may have thought she was going to die there, but she has the soul of a warrior, and she clearly has no idea how she called us.

"She doesn't seem to know about the card," I point out as we climb into the waiting black Dodge. It has a stolen license plate on the back that'll be changed out the next time we drive it. It's enough to remain obscure and unknown so someone doesn't come looking. That's the best we can hope for. By the time anyone thinks to look, the cirque will be gone and they'll be none the wiser. It's something we have done many times before.

"It was clutched in her hand," Heart says, peering at me through his mask. "She held it in her hand even as she crawled through the attic."

"Ah, yes. How you made her suffer," I sneer as I settle in the back seat with her in my arms. There isn't enough room for her to spread out, so I keep her nestled against me, her legs stretched out to touch Club on the other side.

I can feel Heart's frown rather than see it behind his mask as he turns from the front seat and scoffs. "She had to want it," he counters. "You know that."

"Yeah, I know that," I grumble, still not happy about it. With the severity of her injuries, I don't understand how she did it, let alone how Heart could let her.

Diamond is driving, his mask firmly in place to make sure no one can identify us. He glances in the rearview mirror every so often, as if to make sure she's still in my arms. He's the ringmaster for a reason, always making sure we're not being followed. Heart can't be trusted with anything except to do the unexpected and to make something bleed. Diamond keeps him in check, but I don't think Club and I could do the same. It's what makes Heart the perfect trapeze artist. He doesn't value his life, so he lets it hang in the balance high above the crowd without a net to catch him if he slips. He wouldn't have it any other way.

Club is the opposite. Ever careful and aware of the risks he takes, Club is a broody asshole none of us enjoy dealing with when he gets in one of his moods. The sword swallower would sooner gut us than let us make him uncomfortable, but luckily for him, we're a family. We take care of each other, just as we take care of our entire family back at the cirque.

As for me, I'm hardly anything to talk about. I'm good with animals, a talent that chased me from my home as a child and led me to Cirque Obscurum. My foster parents had been rich but not kind. They fostered purely for free labor, putting us kids to work in their mansion. Like most of the wealthy, they caged everything they didn't understand, including animals—monkeys, exotic birds, big cats. I'd been there for a year when chaos erupted. An escaped tiger faced me down in the kitchens, the beast starving and beaten. My foster parents thought it would make a darling pet and had forgotten that wild beasts don't belong in cages. I was twelve when I looked into the tiger's eyes and felt a kinship I'd never experienced with humans.

We were both frail and underfed, and in our similarities, we found a common enemy.

I climbed onto that tiger's back, and we escaped together, leaving a trail of blood in our wake. I named her Freedom. She waits for me back at the cirque like a beacon calling me home. She's my ever-present companion, along with these weirdos.

"She spared his life," Heart comments, shaking his head. "I would have killed the fucker."

"Why do you think she did that?" Club asks. His distrust is so thick, I can hear it in his question. He rarely leaves room for uncertainty, but we hardly know this woman. We only know that she called us and we came.

"Perhaps she wasn't ready to be as much of a monster as he was," I comment, shrugging. It's a noble thought that one could avoid being a monster. For many at the cirque, that's the only option we have left.

Club's eyes flash. "Then she is too soft for this," he says. "Look at her. She won't make it in the cirque. She may not even survive her injuries."

"No," Diamond interjects despite focusing on the road. He keeps his speed slow and steady so as not to attract the attention of law enforcement. If we get pulled over, that's it. We'll have to kill the cops, and then where would we be? "Look at her scars."

Frowning, I look down at her. Her clothing is ripped, but it mostly covers her. I don't focus on that now. Instead, I look at her skin where fresh and old blood coats it. Beneath the rusty color, I see raised marks that would normally be hidden by current fashions. When I find one, I find more, one after the other, like puzzle pieces clicking into place. Some of them are clearly cuts, the lines straight and even. Some of them are large burns that someone could mistake for touching a hot pan if not for the sheer number of them. There are small, puckered, circle scars clearly caused by the end of a lit cigarette and smaller ones that look like she was stabbed with a pen.

"Holy shit," I murmur, realizing just how many there are, all of them layered on top of each other until she's a patchwork of scars.

Diamond nods. "She's survived worse. I wouldn't doubt her."

Club sighs. "She may be finished mentally. What if she checks out?"

"Only time will tell," Diamond answers, his eyes on the road. "We'll stand with her until her choice is made."

We all become quiet then, each of us remembering our own choice and the moment we sold our soul to Cirque Obscurum. It was the moment we claimed our freedom and admitted we were monsters.

EIGHT

I'm so exhausted I can't even lift my head. I come to every now and then, escaping the darkness that waits to claim me, my eyes opening only to find scenes that don't make sense. The first time, I stare up at a masked face with a spade etched into the plastic. He looks down at me where I'm cradled in his arms. The seat beneath us jostles like we're in a car, and pain shoots through me, knocking me out again. The next time I wake up, it's to flashing bright lights and loud circus music. I get maybe three seconds to take things in before my body gives into the darkness again. I don't know where they've taken me, but I can hardly fight them. They saved me. They freed me. At this point, I trust them more than I trust myself.

The air around me is warm and thick with the scent of incense when I wake for the final time. I'm still weak, my body refusing to listen to my commands, but I'm coherent enough to realize I'm lying in a bed and that there's the unmistakable canvas of a tent above me rather than the plain ceiling in my bedroom. I shift, trying to raise my body, but before I can, a woman appears at my bedside, filling my vision as I nearly collapse from shock.

"You," I whisper, staring at her familiar face.

"Me," she replies with a smile as she starts to fuss around me. "Welcome home, little one."

She's older now, her face wrinkled and showing her age, but it's her. I know it is. She's the one I saw all those years ago, who seems to haunt my dreams even now. Her eyes are still the same milky white, but she sees everything as she watches me with a knowing look.

"I don't understand," I say, my voice still hoarse from everything I went through tonight—yesterday? I don't know how much time has passed.

She nods in understanding. "You will, but I won't be the one to explain it to you. The boys will be in soon, and they will tell you everything you need to know. In the meantime, how do you feel?"

I take stock of my body, realizing that my wounds are bandaged tightly. My leg is in a cast and propped up on pillows, and I'm clean, no longer covered in blood or wearing my ripped clothing. Instead, I'm in some sort of long slip.

"Like I was stomped on by an elephant," I answer, wincing with my honesty. "Who patched me up?"

"That would be Dr. Louie. He used to be a war medic," she says as she starts to straighten the blankets, making sure I'm covered. "Don't worry though. I cleaned and dressed you. I burned your clothing. I hope you don't mind."

I shake my head and immediately wince when it makes my skull ache. "Of course not. Will the doctor be in soon so I can thank him?"

"I'm sure he'll be by," she hedges. "But you should rest now. You don't have nearly enough healing sleep under your belt."

Frowning, I settle down in bed. "How long have I been out?"

"Four days," she replies.

I flinch. "Four days?" I repeat. "It's been four days since . . ."

I'd been about to say since I escaped or Roger met his match, but I clamp my lips shut. I don't know how much I should say here.

The woman laughs. "There are no secrets here, little one. We all know about the monster who did this to you." Her expression darkens. "We also know you could not kill him despite it." She tilts her head. "It's best if you embrace the darkness here, Ember. Any light you seek will only be found within yourself."

"What about—"

"Enough questions," she chastises. "Sleep, rest, and heal. You will find out more later."

As if she willed it so, my eyes slide shut, and I sleep once more.

When I open my eyes next, the old fortune teller is gone and in her place is a man. As my vision clears, I get a good look at him, and I shrink deeper into my pillows, afraid and also not, which is an odd feeling. My instant fear is due to the sheer size of him, not because he feels menacing. When I groggily look up at him, the corner of his pouty lips curls up.

"She wakes," he announces despite it only being the two of us in the tent. "How do you feel, habibti?"

"I . . ." I take stock of my body, shifting my arms and legs and realizing I can move more. "Better," I answer. "I feel better."

"Good. It's been over a week now. We were starting to get worried."

"A week?" I gasp, moving to sit up. "How has it been a week?"

He frowns and tilts his head to the side. "Do you not know how time works?"

"No. I do. I just . . . It doesn't feel as if it's been a week," I say feebly, grimacing. "Never mind. It doesn't matter. Where are we exactly?"

He grins, and it changes his face from stern to downright beautiful. Despite not recognizing him, he feels . . . familiar. When he reaches for a pair of wooden crutches off to the side, I get a good look at his arm and the spade tattoos there. A memory surfaces, one of that arm cradling me gently as they broke me free of my cage. He whispered words in a different language in my ear, words I didn't understand but knew were sweet. I blink and stare up at him.

"You were the one who carried me out," I whisper.

He pauses, his dark brown eyes flashing with pleasure. "You remember me?"

"How could I not? You saved me. You all did."

His expression softens. "Yes, habibti. We did."

Now that I can see his face, I realize just how handsome he is. He's tall, broad shouldered, and muscular in a way that speaks of hard work and heavy lifting. His face is square, thick, and strong, with a defined jaw and cheekbones. His skin is tan, better suited to someone who lives in a desert rather than the Midwest. There is a small, black spade tattoo beneath his eye, and I can see hints of others at the edge of his shirt, though I can't figure out what they are while covered. His black hair is short and slicked back in the style many men favor, but it's his eyes that capture me. They are bright in the way that whiskey is, an amber color that almost looks unnatural. This man is also beautiful in a way a cobra would be. Despite his smile, I feel like he could strike at any moment.

He holds the crutches out toward me and then sets them against the bed. "Come. I'll show you where we are and explain everything. Dr. Louie said you shouldn't be walking on that leg yet, so we got you these. I'll help you up."

"What do I call you?" I ask as I shift. "I'm Ember."

He nods as he moves to help me. "I go by Spade here."

It takes barely any effort for him to help me out of bed. As strong as he is, he practically scoops me up and drops me on one leg before shoving the crutches up under my arms. He shows me how to use them before he gestures for me to follow him out of the tent. It takes some getting used to, but after a few unsteady hops, I manage to get outside.

My jaw drops as soon as I do.

It's nighttime, but it's in no way dark. Bright lights surround me —string lights between tents, spotlights sweeping through the sky, and flashing lights farther in.

"The circus," I rasp as I spy the red and white striped big top over the smaller tents. "I'm at the circus."

"Not just any circus," Spade answers with a mischievous smile. "This is Cirque Obscurum."

My mind fills with memories of me as a little girl, running through these tents and finding my way to the fortune teller. She'd given me the card I held when I thought I'd die. They said I called them. The fortune teller mentioned that the cirque would come if I needed it, but that shouldn't be possible, right?

Yet here I am. Now, though, I am no longer that naive little girl dreaming of fanciful things and different worlds I read about in books. I'm all grown up, and I no longer believe in fairy tales. There has to be a catch. No one does such things for free. No one expects nothing in return for help.

"Why exactly am I here?" I ask, my voice hard.

I glance up at Spade as he stands beside me. His own smile is gone, replaced by deep contemplation.

"You called us, habibti," he replies, his eyes flashing like a wild animal's. "Your call was so strong, it nearly choked us."

"I don't understand," I murmur. "I don't understand any of this."

"You will," he answers, looking over my head. "Diamond will explain everything. He's coming this way now."

I spin clumsily on my crutches, following his gaze, and meet eyes as familiar to me as this place is. I used to dream of those eyes as a child, of the boy I saw briefly at the circus. He's no longer a boy though. His eyes are hard and dangerous and so dark, they reflect all the yellow lights around us. I thought Spade's were dark, but I was wrong. This man's are as dark as the depths of hell. They belong to someone who danced in the darkness his entire life and reveled in it.

My god, he's beautiful.

With a jawline and cheekbones that could only be sculpted by a master artist and those black pools in his eyes, he could easily be mistaken for a masterpiece in a museum. His hair is just as dark, part of it tousled like it had been styled at one point but he ran his hands through it too many times. His brows are thick and strong, and there's a wrinkle between them as if he wears the weight of the world on his shoulders. Gold glitters on his ears, piercings that reflect the lights above. His features are tied together by full lips that would be too feminine on other men, but somehow make him more masculine. A small, black diamond tattoo sits beneath his right eye, his moniker inked on skin. Beautiful doesn't even begin to describe him.

"Ember," he says by way of greeting in a voice thick with honey. "I heard you were awake."

I blink up at him. "You remember me?"

He frowns and glances at Spade as if to ask if I'm still ill. "Of course I remember you. We brought you here a week ago. We've all checked on you while you recovered."

My heart falls. He doesn't remember me. Not as a child. I suppose I look nothing like my old self, like the child who was able to dance between the circus tents with a carefree freedom I never had as an adult. Still, some small part of me hoped I made as much of an impact on him as he made on me, but that's silly. I was one of thousands he's probably seen, and I'm not nearly that special.

I straighten my back and face him, taking in his sharp jawline and strong nose. "Spade tells me you can explain why I'm here." I gesture between us, barely balancing on the crutches. Spade steadies me when I start to go down, but neither comment on it. "Go on then," I encourage. "Explain."

Diamond glances from me to Spade and back again, his dark eyes absorbing the lights into their depths. Amusement flickers on his lips before he shrugs. "Very well. You have a choice to make."

"A choice?" I repeat.

He nods and takes a step closer, invading my space. "To leave this place and never return, never speak of it again, or . . ."

"Or what?" I prompt when he doesn't continue.

His head tilts to the side, and he reaches up to cup my chin. I let him, not wanting to fight this man, and I'm glad I don't when the rough texture of his fingers touches my chin and tilts it up, warming me. He holds me there, his eyes piercing mine.

"Or you can stay here and swear your soul to Cirque Obscurum," he finishes. "You will belong to her, and she will belong to you, and you will never know what it feels like to be caged again."

My heart beats loudly in my ears. "Never?" I ask, hope in my chest.

"Never," he repeats and then grins. "Unless it's part of your act, that is."

Spade leans in. "You don't have to decide now. You can—"

"I'm staying," I interrupt, glancing at him but ultimately focusing on Diamond. It's an instantaneous reaction, something deep inside me answering without even letting me think. "I choose to stay."

Diamond grins and presses his forehead against mine. His scent of smoke and coconut surrounds me, and I nearly swallow my tongue as he hums.

"The only proper choice, darkling," he purrs. "I'll see you at three a.m. for the ceremony."

He leaves me there standing with Spade, breathless and aching despite my injuries. When he's gone, his words sink in.

"Wait. Ceremony?"

NINE

EMBER

The crutches slow me down, and despite wanting to explore the circus, I'm still healing. After watching me struggle, Spade scoops me into his arms again and carries me back to my tent. It's something he seems to do without thought. He lays me down on the bed before righting the blankets around me and tucking me in. "Try to rest. We'll come for you when it's time."

As he goes to step back, I catch his arm so he looks at me once more. "What ceremony?"

"You chose to stay, habibti. You must make that promise now," he answers darkly, the amber in his eyes turning molten.

"To you?" I murmur.

"No." The sly grin he gives me sends my heart racing. "To the heart of this place, to the cirque." There's a roar, like that of a large, wild animal, and it's so loud, it seems to rattle my bones. My heart pounds in my rib cage, but Spade simply smiles. His eyes seem to shift as he glances at the tent entrance. "Until then." He leaves, disappearing quickly, and then there's another sound from the animal, but it's closer and happier—a chuff.

It's the circus, I remind myself, but as I lie in bed, I can't help wondering why I agreed so quickly and what that means for my future.

Having a choice is strange. Before, I knew I would die in that house, and part of me had even accepted I would be Roger's punching bag until the day the darkness took me, but they gave me a choice tonight. I could have started fresh, I could have gone anywhere, yet even as I think that, the idea only fills me with fear. Here, in the one place where most people find thrills and strangeness, I feel at peace, at home like I did when I was a child. The feeling of safety fills my entire being, and it's something so foreign to me, it's difficult to accept. I don't know if it's the familiar smell of popcorn and cotton candy, the circus music, or simply the men who brought me here, but I feel safe.

Maybe that's why I decided to stay so quickly, though I can't discount the feeling that something within my soul answered before I could even consider the offer. Either way, I made my choice, and now I'm here. I don't know what that means, but I'll find out tonight at the ceremony. The mere mention of that causes something dark to unfurl inside me, something almost akin to excitement. How strange to feel so alive after being numb for so long. It's as if some sleeping animal within me wakes.

Pushing that thought away as I relax back in the bed, I look around with nothing else to do.

The tent is pretty spacious, with a small bed covered in colorful, mismatched blankets and pillows. At the base is an old wooden trunk, shut and locked. The floor has a huge, circular rug of many colors with grass growing around the edges of it. Posts hold the tent aloft above us, which is bright red. Lanterns and candles are spread around the rest of the room, perched on boxes and crates, illuminating the area in a cozy manner.

I hear laughter and screams of joy. I can smell circus food and almost feel the excitement and happiness of the visitors. It makes me smile despite the pain still lingering in my body, and I settle back to listen to the familiar sounds.

I must doze off eventually because when I wake, it's to a solid hand shaking my side. My eyes jerk open, clashing with bright orbs in the dark tent. "It's time," the sultry voice tells me as my eyes widen, roving across the man leaning over me.

It's not Spade or Diamond.

My eyes land on a small black club tattoo under his left eye, and I instantly know that's his name. They all seem to have taken the suit cards as their monikers for some reason. For a moment, I just stare, caught up in his beauty, the kind of which I've never seen before. His hair is black and shiny, even in the dim light, parted slightly to the side, and trimmed to just above his ears with each sideburn shaped into a triangle. His eyebrows are just as dark and thick as his hair, slashing straight across deep brown eyes that seem to swallow me whole. He has longer eyelashes than I have ever seen on any man, his nose is straight and long, and his jaw is chiseled and covered in a slight shadow of stubble, with more above his full lips. He's taller than me and lithe, but I can see muscles pulling at his oversized white shirt, which is tucked into loose palazzo pants.

He's beautiful, like the type of man you see in the papers.

I must be staring because he tilts his head. "Did you hear me?"

"Time?" I force myself to sit up, my cheeks heating at being caught staring at him. "For the ceremony?" I ask, my brain slowly coming back to life.

He nods silently, offering me his hand with long, clean fingers. I lay mine in his before I can stop myself. Something about him puts me instantly at ease. His other arm slides around me, and he helps me to my feet. I maneuver the crutches until I can hop at his side to the entrance of the tent. Once there, he stops, forcing me to halt beside him. "Do not be afraid, Ember. Nothing will hurt you here. You're not alone anymore." He steps from the tent before I can speak.

I follow him silently, his words filling my head as I hop through the grassy circus which is now quiet. It's strange to see it so dead after the noise of the night. The lights are still on, but the place is empty. Popcorn and nuts are scattered across the ground, along with tickets and forgotten toys left abandoned in the rush to return home. Tents stand in no particular fashion or reason, with wooden huts and stalls lining the path we cross before the big top, but we don't go inside. Instead, we head deeper into the circus, away from the showy public side and into the heart of this place.

Away from the lights and joy, we plunge into the darkness, and despite everything that happened to me within shadows, I go willingly. I follow Club deeper and deeper until the only light we see is that of the full moon.

When we round the final tent, I see them.

Three masked men stand in a row—Diamond, Spade, and Heart. As I freeze, Club moves to their side, pulling his own mask down until they all face me. Before them is a circular wooden table. Even from here, I can see carvings etched into the wood that seem to glow with an eerie blue light from within, something that shouldn't be possible. Candles litter the ground around the edges of the clearing, the flames flickering across the masks and trees, creating an ominous atmosphere as I swallow and tread closer. My crutches catch on the grass, but I don't stop until I'm before the round table. Something about it calls to me.

In the middle of the table, there's a dip, like a bowl has been cut into it, but it's empty right now, as if waiting to be filled.

I glance from it to them as they watch me, and then Diamond speaks, his voice confident and silky. "You made your choice today, Ember. You called us with the card, and now you have chosen to stay with us, with Cirque Obscurum. The safety, companionship, and power you'll find here come with a price. There must be balance. There must be payment."

"Payment?" I whisper, worry filling me. I have no money. I have nothing to my name. What other potential payment could I offer?

Part of me knew this wasn't a normal circus. I mean, they told me the joker card called them to me, and then they offered to kill my husband for me. There's something darker at play here, something else, but I won't change my mind or make the choice to leave.

I want to stay, but what's the cost?

"Cirque is more than a haven for the beaten and the damned. It's solace. It's home. It's a promise and an oath. It's everything, and it's our lives. Once you sell your soul to cirque, you will belong to it. You can never leave because your life will be tied to its life. Where it goes, we go. Its wants and desires will become your own. There are things in the dark, Ember, you can't even begin to understand, but you will." Diamond steps forward. "We have all given our souls to cirque. We uphold its wishes and desires. We answer the calls of the lost and forsaken, and we protect those who have no one else. Cirque is here. Cirque is everywhere. We freaks play the cards and we are the cards." He stops before the table across from me. "You're to be one of us. If you wish to stay, you must swear an oath to Cirque Obscurum and hand over your soul. You must become a nightmare that preys on other nightmares. Ember, will you do so? Will you give your soul to this place?"

The world seems to hold its breath around me as if it's waiting. Something inside me throbs with recognition, like I've finally found the place I was always meant to be.

"My soul will belong to the cirque forever?" I ask, my voice quiet, as if knowing this place has ears.

Diamond nods. "Until death."

I glance at the men standing behind him, and something within me relaxes. I wanted freedom so badly, but a bird with clipped wings can't fly far when captivity is all it's known. Maybe I was always meant for a cage, but now I get to choose what kind.

"My soul is yours." The words flow from me without hesitation, and the earth seems to breathe a sigh of relief.

"Not mine, ours," Diamond murmurs as he kneels, gesturing for me to copy him. I struggle with the crutches, so Spade and Club circle me, each taking an arm and helping me to my knees. It hurts my injured leg, but I swallow the pain—I have had worse—and I kneel at the other side of the table. Heart stands behind Diamond, his head tilted as he watches me. His mocking grin makes my heart race.

"Repeat after me. I give my soul willingly. Tonight, I swear an oath to Cirque Obscurum."

I repeat it quickly, and he nods approvingly.

"The cirque will become my home, my sanctuary, its performers my family and hunting companions. I swear my soul to the cirque. I swear on the cards to answer the call."

The words flow freely, and Diamond nods once more.

"I, Ember, swear it upon my forsaken soul. I swear to be one with Cirque Obscurum until the day the grave calls me home."

When I repeat it, he pulls a small dagger from somewhere and holds it out to me. His fingers grip the blade as he offers me the handle. I take it, my hand shaking slightly.

"Blood within, I give it willingly. I cut myself open for you." He nods at the blade, and I repeat the words before I slash the dagger across my palm, drawn by a power beyond us. My hiss fills the air at the sharp pain, and I hold my hand above the bowl, watching my blood hit the basin. Diamond's hand covers mine, forcing a fist and increasing the flow. The pain makes me lightheaded, but I stay strong as it fills the bowl, not crying out.

"This night and every night to come, I am yours. I swear this oath, and I offer you my sacrifice. Take me."

I repeat the words, and my eyes drop to the table.

The blood seems to be sucked into the wood, flowing from the bowl and out into the carvings, turning them red. It disappears until the bowl is empty, leaving a card where my blood was only a moment before. "Blood of ours, it is done," Diamond declares as I press my hand to my chest, my eyes on the card.

"Take it," he murmurs.

Reaching out slowly, I pick it up. It's the same thick black card as the joker that called them to me, but as I flip it over, I find it blank.

"Your future is yours, as is your name. Here, you are reborn to the cirque." Spade and Club help me stand, and I meet their eyes. "It's done. You're one of us now."

I don't feel any different, but I trust what they are saying, even if I don't fully understand it. "You'll need to pick a name, and when you do, the card will change."

"Why?" I ask.

"You're one of us now," Heart answers. "You're a nightmare."

I sway slightly but grip the card tighter.

I'm one of them.

I have a home, one that will protect me.

I gave my soul for that. The thought should terrify me, but if anything, I feel more at peace than I ever have. "Help her to her new home. You need to rest. We'll speak tomorrow," Diamond says. "For now, let your home shelter you." He turns away and walks into the darkness like a phantom, disappearing as I watch him go.

Glancing down at the blank card, I can't help but wonder what will fill it.

What will I be? Who will I be?

For the first time in years, excitement fills my soul.

TEN

EMBER

Club and Spade help me to a different tent, this one sitting farther back, nestled within the heart of the circus and surrounded by four others. I'm quiet, as are they, and for a moment, I just stare at the black tent. It's plain but large and in the shape of a heptagon. They release my arms, and I stumble, watching as they walk toward it.

"Your new home," one of them murmurs.

They part the material that forms the door, and I step within, glancing back at them as they drop it behind me, leaving me all alone. I turn forward, looking around at my new living space. It's emptier than the other tent I was in, as if waiting for me to fill it with my own things. There's a large double bed pushed against the back wall, framed by the black material of the tent, with mismatched pillows and blankets. The floor here is harder, although still covered by a bright carpet, but there seems to be flooring underneath. There's a wardrobe with a mirror on it and a huge, candle-filled light hanging from the ceiling, but not much else except a two-person table sitting in the middle of the tent with two chairs.

There's a black box on it, and I hop closer on my crutches, collapsing into a chair.

My head is spinning, and my emotions are muddled. A week ago, I was fighting for my life in an attic, and now, here I am, my soul given to a circus and four masked men claiming we are family. I can't help but wonder, despite my conviction, what I have gotten myself into.

Reaching across the scarred wood, I touch the box, my card clutched in my other hand. Taking a deep breath, I lift the lid. I made my choice, so now all I can do is accept it and keep moving forward. There's no point in looking backwards.

Ember is dead. They are right. I need a new name.

I'm not the same woman who begged for death in that attic. Here, I am reborn as something new, something unknown. Here, I can be whatever I want to be.

Within the box is a perfectly stacked pile of cards, and with hesitant fingers, I tip it, letting them spill across the table. My eyes catch on the joker for a moment. It's similar to the one I had before, glittering red. There are all the other suits as well, and when I flip them over, the backs have the traditional red and black diamonds, but there are words written there.

Tell me your nightmares.

I trace the raised wording on a random card before flipping it over. My heart skips a beat at the queen facing me. My fingers run over her cool, collected face, her mocking smile making one bloom on my lips. The power I feel within the card seems to echo a desire inside my heart. I want to be that strong. I want to be worthy of a name like that.

Then, I realize I can be.

Queen. I like it. They asked me to choose a name, and I have.

Diamond, Spade, Club, Heart, and Queen.

It seems they were right. Our fates are tied to the cards. We answer to them, and now, so do I.

Despite all the rest I received over the last week, I collapse into the bed and sleep more deeply than I have for years. The blank card remains clutched in my grip, as if I can't bear to part with it. When I wake, my head is filled with cotton. The day, the time, they escape me, and I struggle from the bed and onto my crutches. I glance down at the card in my hand and find it's no longer blank.

It's filled with the queen, and I can't help but smile. It seems the cirque approved of my choice.

Just then, my tent flaps part, and my head jerks up to see a man framed there. "You slept all day," he remarks. "You must have needed it, or at least the doctor said so. He checked on you while you were out. It's good you are up. Come, the performance is about to begin and I'm late. Very late. Diamond won't be happy, but the ladies always love my entrance." He grins, but I just keep staring.

This must be Heart, though I think a different name would suit him better. Maybe maniac.

His face is pale, and that's why the ink stands out so starkly against it. There's a heart under his left eye with a blood droplet falling from it. There's another tattoo under his other eye, a small, upside-down black cross. "Lover" is written in script above his left eyebrow, following the arch, and his bloodred lips have a spike piercing the lower one. I haven't seen many men with lip piercings. His eyes are bright blue, standing out vividly against his dark eyebrows and hair, which seem to shift colors as he moves. It's short and spiked on top at the moment, the flat sides exposing his ears, which have more piercings running down them. I glance back at his high, almost overly sharp face, and I spot the mole on his slightly crooked nose. He's tall and wearing nothing but some leather pants laced up the sides, flashing skin. His torso is bare, showcasing impressive muscles with deep abs and a V that makes me blush and look away quickly. More moles and freckles cover his arms and shoulders with additional tattoos scattered randomly about. There are too many to see and count.

I keep staring until his words sink in.

"Wait, performance?" I blurt.

"This is the cirque, after all," he teases as he backs into the darkness, leaving me staring after him.

I struggle out of my tent, heading where I think he must have gone. I can hear the cheers and chants from here, and I follow them, struggling through the tents to the big top. I can't believe I slept all day, but my body must have truly needed it. This is to be my home, though, so I need to pull my weight, and more than that, I'm curious.

It's been so many years since I was here, yet the same excitement fills me as I push into the big top and the magic it holds within.

ELEVEN

EMBER

The outside of the circus tent has red and white stripes, but the inside is uninterrupted black. As I step through the entrance and into the crowd, I can't help but take in the full audience. People fill the stands, vying for the best seat with many of them standing since it's so packed. Children and adults alike clap and laugh at the clowns currently frolicking around the arena, bashing each other over the head and pretending to play tricks on each other. There are three different clowns, and their masks are a little less creepy than the ones the guys wear, but not by much. Still, the audience seems to be eating it up.

It feels more like a nightmare circus than anything else, but like the crowd, I can't look away.

"Come this way," someone says to my right.

When I glance over, I find Club dressed in an outfit far different than anything I've seen him in before. Tonight, he's shirtless, his muscles on full display. Though he's smaller than the others, it's not by much. I drag my gaze up his torso and find him watching me with a patient look. My cheeks heat as I hurry toward him, and he leads me to a seat in the very front. Club sits me down with a stay gesture before disappearing again, leaving me to watch the show.

The lights dim and then go out suddenly, as if they had been waiting for my arrival. I hear people around me gasp in surprise. Their excitement is palpable, filling the air with tension that has my heart racing. The atmosphere at Cirque Obscurum is like nothing I have ever felt. It's as if the darkness calls to you, whispering your most illicit desires, and you can act on them here. I clench my fingers against my thighs to stop myself from reaching into the darkness, and instead, I sit back, eager to watch the show after so long. I hope it's just as good as I remember.

A single spotlight illuminates the stage, and I watch as Diamond appears from the shadows, stepping into the bright light where he very clearly belongs. Tonight, he's dressed like any respectable ringmaster. He's wearing a bright red brocade coat, the tails of it brushing the backs of his thighs, and his pants are black and look like leather, the same as his boots. On his head is a black top hat, which is trimmed with red and gold. My eyes linger on the diamond card stuck in the band. He allows the crowd to observe him for a moment, a knowing smirk tilting his lips at the screams and claps, and when it fades, he speaks.

"Ladies and gentlemen," he begins as the crowd quiets down, hanging on his every word. "Heathens and monsters. Tonight, you will see acts of bravery and foolishness. You'll watch as we dance with danger and invite you to join. Cirque Obscurum is no ordinary circus." He smiles, but it's sinister and seems to reach into my chest and grip my heart. "This is where monsters come to play." He strolls over to the crowd, choosing a young woman who sits three people over from me. The spotlight follows him as he moves. The woman is enraptured as he leans down and tips her chin up. "Tell me your nightmares," he says into the mic, his voice so sultry even I lean forward as he plays his role. He's sensual, mysterious, and menacing. I clench my legs together as he waits for her answer. His entire focus is on her as she blinks up at him in shock before seeming to wake from the spell he's weaving around her.

She grimaces and glances at someone on her right, a friend I assume. There's a whole group of them together. "Spiders," she answers.

Diamond nods and releases her. "Spiders!" he announces for everyone to hear. The lights shift, and shadows begin to crawl along the big top—thousands of spiders, the scuttling noise making my skin crawl. The woman screams, along with a few others in the crowd, and Diamond laughs.

The sound is so carefree and sinister, goose bumps erupt on my skin.

"Spiders are not monsters," he says, reaching his hand up. As if by magic, a tarantula suddenly appears in his hand. "They are great companions." He smiles down at the woman. "And they eat bugs." She shrinks away when he holds his hand out toward her, and the tarantula reaches out with furry legs. Then, with a movement of his hand, it's gone. Everyone gasps. The woman claps as the spider shadows disappear, her heart probably beating hard in her chest, but it is all an act. It's okay now.

Diamond glances at me suddenly, a slight arch of his brow the indication of his acknowledgement before he turns back to the center of the arena, but that one look leaves me breathless. "Are you ready to be on the edge of your seats?" Cheers erupt around me. "I can't hear you!" It turns into a roar, and he grins. "Very well. Then let the show begin." He bows, still wearing that wicked smile. "And welcome to Cirque Obscurum."

The lights plunge us into darkness once again, and when they come on, Club stands in the center as intense music begins to play. He stands next to a display of swords, his eyes hard as he looks around at the audience.

"What I'm about to do is very dangerous," he declares. "Sword swallowing is not for the faint of heart."

I lean forward as he pulls a sword from the display. Surely it can't be sharp, not if he's going to swallow it. Of course, as if everyone has the same thought, Club grins. "You all think this sword is fake, do you not?" There are some affirmations from the crowd, a few jests and jeers. "Shall I prove its sharpness?"

Someone rolls a table out laden with small fruits and vegetables —apples, oranges, and even cabbage. He picks up an apple and tosses it in the air. He moves so quickly, I barely notice him doing so, but I do see the two halves of the apple clatter to the tabletop just as everyone else does. I gasp right along with them. He does the same with an orange and finally with the cabbage, proving without a doubt that the sword is not only real but incredibly sharp.

"One wrong move and I could shred my insides," he says, turning back to the crowd. "I can't make any mistakes."

His eyes meet mine in the crowd as he lifts the sword to his lips and licks the edge of it. His gaze doesn't move from mine as he does so, and my heart clenches. It shouldn't be as sexy as it is, but I can't help the excitement that floods my veins as he gets to the tip and positions the sword above him. He tips his head back, exposing the full column of his throat. The music rises before he slowly slides the sword into his mouth and down. The crowd gasps and oohs and aahs as it sinks to the hilt, and then he bends awkwardly forward into a bow, his eyes meeting mine again with the sword sticking from his mouth. When he straightens and carefully pulls it from his throat, the crowd erupts with cheers before the lights go black.

"Our sword master, ladies and gentlemen. Don't let his pretty exterior fool you, he'll cut you if you let him." A chuckle fills the air along with Diamond's voice as he carries on. "Some might call beasts and monsters the same thing, but they would be very, very wrong."

The lights come on once more, and a tiger sits in the center of the arena, free of chains or cage. Panic erupts around me as people scramble back. The tiger just watches us all curiously. Spade suddenly appears from the darkness, dressed in fitted pants and nothing else. Even his feet are bare.

"This is Freedom," he says as he lays a hand on her head. "She doesn't like cages, so pardon me if we perform this act without one." The crowd settles, but many still push backwards in an attempt to put distance between them. "Tigers are a beautiful species. They are capable of great harm, but in the end, they want what we all want." He lets his words hang for a moment before he nods. "To be free."

The tiger stands and circles Spade, her eyes on him as he moves his arms.

"The trick to beasts is you must respect them," Spade says as Freedom comes up and nudges her head against his hip. "If you don't respect them, they won't respect you." Freedom stands on her hind legs, putting her paws on Spade's shoulders. His muscles bunch under her weight, and the crowd claps. "Can you believe these beautiful creatures are headed for extinction because of humans?" he asks, his eyes hardening beneath the light. "Tell me, who is the monster? The creature trying to survive or the human who kills the creature for sport?"

Freedom leaps from his shoulders and sprints toward the crowd on the other side. She stops just before them as they scramble backward and roars so loudly that most of the crowd covers their ears. Spade points in the other direction, right at me. He looks down his arm at me, meeting my eyes, wearing a smile on his face. Freedom sprints toward me, the crowd around me scrambling back, but I don't move. I meet the tiger's eyes as she comes to a stop right before me and roars. I don't know if this is a test or not, but I take it as one. Freedom chuffs in my face, and instinct has me raising my hand.

Someone behind me screams, "No!"

Another panics and tells his wife they are leaving, but I pay them no mind. I slowly raise my hand and place it against Freedom's head despite the baring of her teeth. The moment my hand touches her fur, she pushes her head against me like a cat and chuffs again.

"Respect," Spade says as he comes to stand beside Freedom. "It's the most important thing in the jungle." He lays his hand against Freedom's back, and she turns away from me to follow Spade. "But tigers aren't the only beasts here, just as I'm not the only monster."

More lights come on, and all kinds of animals appear from the edges —dogs, horses, a goat, a macaw in vibrant colors, and lots of small animals. An elephant strides through the tent flaps, its large feet moving carefully around the smaller animals. A camel trots in last, its annoyed expression telling me he doesn't want to be here. I watch a show of amazing, impossible tricks that I never could have imagined animals were capable of. One dog walks on a tightrope, perfectly balanced, and the elephant stands on its hind legs with Spade perched on its front leg. The macaw performs aerial tricks and even flies through a flaming hoop. By the end of the act, I'm clapping and shouting in excitement with everyone else.

"Remember, always respect animals," Spade says into the microphone, but his expression turns dark, "or they'll eat you the first chance they get."

Spade bows and runs out of the arena, all the animals following after him, his threat lingering in the air. It feels intentional, and somehow, I almost believe the animals know exactly what he's saying as they make their final rounds and exit through the same tent flap Spade did.

Diamond appears again, his top hat a little crooked.

"Have you seen any monsters yet?" The crowd erupts with their answer. "Yes? Well, you haven't even seen the worst of us," he muses before slowly looking up.

A spotlight appears, showcasing Heart in all his glory above us. He wears tight pants again and nothing else as he balances on a thin ladder. I'd always been enamored with the trapeze artists as a child. As an adult, I can't help but get to my feet with the rest of the crowd.

"We don't believe in cages here at Cirque Obscurum, and we also don't believe in nets," Diamond says, his eyes on Heart. "What's more exciting than the risk of falling?"

My heart drops as Heart launches himself from the small platform and swings from one side to the other. When he releases it and twists in the air before grabbing another bar, I scream with everyone else. He moves beautifully, like a butterfly, gliding easily from bar to bar until more trapeze artists join him, and they put on a real show. I watch him, captivated, as he performs. At some point, his fingers miss one of the bars, and I scream with everyone else as he falls before catching himself on another post. He turns and grins at the crowd, laughing as if he weren't close to dying. I realize it's all part of the act when the other performers continue as usual. Heart catches my eye and winks at me as he climbs higher again, continuing his act.

The show is a beautiful, thrilling display of circus performances. Every single audience member is entertained throughout the evening. When it all comes to an end, I sigh sadly like everyone else. I could watch the performance over and over again and be just as amazed every time.

Diamond comes out one final time, and all the performers stand by his side. Spade has the macaw on his shoulder, the bird sitting peacefully despite the roar of the crowd. Heart is happily wiping sweat from his chest, a grin on his face as he waves to the crowd. Club stands stoically, his hands folded primly behind his back.

"That's the end for now," Diamond announces. "Cirque Obscurum thanks you for your attendance. When you start to miss us and the thrill of the cirque, remember, your nightmares are sacred, and you'll find us waiting in them." Diamond throws his arms wide to the roar of the crowd, and the lights go out. When lights turn on for the crowd to exit, they are gone, leaving behind nothing but the mystery.

I remain in my seat, watching as the crowd disappears through the tent flaps. Once everyone is gone, they come back out.

Heart grins. "What did you think, Queen?"

"Magnificent. Beautiful," I gush, grinning. "Just as magical as when I was a little girl. You had me going there for a minute."

He winks. "All part of the act. However, you petting Freedom wasn't. Such a brave little queen."

Spade stares at me. "That was awfully dangerous of you. She could have taken your hand."

"I've spent a good portion of my life being afraid and careful," I say as I meet his eyes. "I think it's time I start to live a little. Don't you?"

Diamond snorts. "I agree. Tomorrow, you'll start looking for your place here." He helps me to my feet with my crutches. "For now, you should go back and rest."

"Shouldn't I help clean up?" I don't want them to think I can't pull my weight here.

"In time," he replies. "First, you heal, but your eagerness to take part is appreciated, darkling." He nods to Spade. "Help her get back. I have to take care of a few things."

That night, my dreams are full of circus acts and being part of them, of Heart sweeping down and lifting me into the air, Spade balancing me on one of his horses, and Club licking knives before they fly toward me. Eventually, I don't dream at all, and it's the best sleep I've had in years.

TWELVE

EMBER

I'm limited on what I can do while I'm on crutches. Dr. Louie says it'll be a few weeks before I can try walking without them, so I resolve myself to healing in the hopes I can walk faster. I can't do anything heavy for now, so I resort to helping in other areas.

I'm really bad at rigging and tying knots, and after struggling to get the knots tight enough for a few days, the master rigger takes pity on me and sends me to find another task. I'm incapable of helping clean the animal pens on crutches. I try, though, despite Spade telling me I can't, only because I want to at least attempt it. I get about a foot swept in an hour before he aggressively demands I leave it until I'm better.

That's how I find myself in the kitchens. While I'm forced to take breaks from standing because of my leg, I excel here. For years, I cooked perfect meals for Roger and the neighbors and friends he wanted to entertain. I've made meals for a lot of people and a few, so I'm good at it. The food comes out amazing, and the kitchen staff happily accepts me each day as I go in and help. I'm there for three days before I'm found.

Heart comes striding inside the kitchen tent, his eyes sweeping over all of us before finding me as I balance on my crutches and knead dough. I'm so focused on my task, I don't immediately notice, not until he reaches over my shoulder and pokes one of the dough balls.

"I was wondering where you were, Queen, and here you are, slaving away in the kitchen," he muses, watching as I work.

"I needed to find a way to contribute," I reply. "I can cook, and they welcome my help. Unfortunately, rigging wasn't my strong suit."

"Ah, yes. Joey mentioned you tried it. Don't worry, not everyone is strong enough for rigging." He shrugs. "Joey said he was impressed with your attempts."

"You're lying," I say, looking over at him. "I was terrible at it."

"Yes, but you were decent for someone who has never done it," he retorts with a grin. "Don't take it to heart. Spade is terrible at rigging too, only because he hates anything constricting. Even a tight knot can send him into . . . Well, I'll let that be something you find out on your own."

When he falls into silence, I glance over my shoulder. "Was there something you needed?"

He tilts his head and watches me for a few minutes. "They say you're good at cooking."

"I am," I admit. I'm not bragging, just stating the truth. I had to be good or else. "I spent years cooking every meal and preparing it again when it wasn't perfect the first time, hosting parties and get-togethers and guests Roger would bring home from work. This is what I know, so yes, I'm a pretty good cook now."

He's silent again, watching me. "Do you want to be?"

I pause, my eyes on my hands. They are coated in flour right now, and I have dough beneath my fingernails. The crutches dig into my underarms as I balance on them and try not to fall.

"Do I want to be good at cooking?" I clarify.

"Yes."

I stop what I'm doing and turn to look at Heart. He's a beautiful man, even if something sinister flickers in his eyes. "I think cooking is a good skill," I say slowly, considering my words.

"But do you enjoy it?" he presses. He grabs my hand and presses it against his cheek. It leaves a white handprint behind when he lets go, his eyes glittering in amusement.

"Why did you do that?" I murmur as he leans closer.

"I'd like to be marked by you, Queen. Even if it's only temporary." He leans back with a grin. "Now answer the question. Do you enjoy cooking?"

Biting my lip, I look down at the dough. "No," I admit softly. "No, I don't."

"Then don't do it," he says with a shrug. "Here, you do what you enjoy, so stop cooking."

"But—"

"No buts," he says. "Unless it's your butt, then that's okay, but you don't have to only do this. Try things and find what you enjoy. If it's not this, that's okay. We won't suffer for it."

My eyes linger on the flour handprint on his jawline. "And what do you enjoy?" I ask curiously.

He leans in with a grin. "Performing," he says. "Putting people on the edge of their seats." He leans closer until his breath fans across my cheeks. "And killing," he whispers. "I really enjoy killing."

Something stirs low in my belly, and I lose my breath, but before I can answer, he leans back with a grin.

"Anyways, Queen, I have things to do. I'll find you later and we can discuss other ways you can mark me. Maybe I'll even let you give me a tattoo."

"But I'm not a tattoo artist," I reply, frowning.

"I know." He laughs. "Isn't it great? See you soon!"

I'm left staring after him, flour on my face and my hands, wondering why on earth this whole interaction left me breathless and hungry for more.

THIRTEEN

What I like, what I enjoy.

The words circle around my head as I leave the kitchen for the day. After my encounter with Heart, I don't feel the same energy or passion to be there. I worried what the others would say, but they waved me away with knowing looks. It seems everyone here knows their place, where they belong, and what they enjoy. I'm just a spare part. Even at the circus, I feel like an outcast.

Maybe that's why I wander through its beauty, taking everything in once more. I want to belong to this place. I made an oath, but what happens if I'm useless to them? Will they leave me behind? I know my old worries are rearing their ugly heads, but it sticks, and I know I need to find a purpose.

I need to find a passion, a place, and if it brings me joy like Heart said, then all the better. It has been a very long time since anything did, though, so I don't know if I would even recognize the feeling now.

The bright colors of the circus blend into one as I struggle through the tents on my crutches. Everyone is busy preparing for the show tonight or resting, and no one pays me any attention, as if I am invisible. They have all accepted that I am here, but none have dared to get close to me. It makes me curious just how many of us arrive randomly since they are so accustomed to it.

It also makes me curious about their stories, even Diamond, Heart, Club and Spade—not that they will tell me. Despite them swearing me in or saving me, they have left me to my own devices except for checking on me quietly every now and then. Sometimes they appear when my nightmares are particularly bad, as if they call to them, which is an even scarier thought.

I'm lost in my worries when I stumble over a leftover popcorn tub. Righting myself, I lean over and pick it up, hobbling over to a bin so none of the animals that roam the grounds during the day eat it. That's another thing that shocked me. They truly meant it. There are no cages here.

As I turn from the trash can, my eyes land on a familiar tent. I haven't seen her since my first days here, and something inside me whispers for me to go in. It's that dark voice that often whispered for me to pick up the knife and end Roger at the dinner table. It isn't one I should listen to, but I find myself moving closer, as if I'm drawn by forces beyond my control. Before I even realize it, I've pushed through the flap, and I see her sitting there, waiting. A deck of cards lies on the table before her, and her eyes are on mine like she was expecting me.

She smiles. "I've been waiting for you, Queen."

FOURTEEN

EMBER

"What do you mean?" I ask, even as I head over and sit in the chair opposite her, just like when I was a child. Not much has changed in here despite how much I have. She's older, the years only making her more beautiful and mysterious, and I watch her hand hover over the cards before flipping them all to reveal the queens of each suit lined up.

"They told me you would come," she replies.

"The cards?" I question. I should scoff, but I have seen things here in my short time that make me believe her. This is no regular circus. Things happen at Cirque Obscurum that are unnatural and impossible.

Despite the strangeness and intense herbal smell, I feel at ease here. My worries disappear, and my muscles relax. I sit forward, eager to hear what she will tell me.

"I knew you would find your way to me eventually. You did back then, and you have now. I can teach you, Ember." I jerk my head up from the cards, and she waves her hands. They flip over once more. "I can teach you to read cards. I can teach you to be like me if you wish." She waits, her hand hovering over the cards as if waiting for me to pick my own future. There's no pressure as she waits curiously to see what I will do.

I could walk away and find something else to do, but my heart thrums in here. My eagerness and curiosity get the better of me. Something tells me that in order for me to know this cirque better and the men within it, I must first understand it, and that begins here.

"I'd like that."

The smile she bestows upon me makes me sit up taller, and when she waves her hands, the cards flip once more. Lined up in order are diamond, spade, club, heart, and queen. Does the order mean something? I don't know, but she flips them once more and shuffles them.

"Then let us begin. There's no time better than the present. There are many things you must understand to read the cards, to read the future of those who come to you. Here, you must suspend your ideals of your world and reality. Here, everything is not as it seems. Things you couldn't even imagine are real. This is where magic lives. Within the cards are the past, present, and future. Everything is linked in this world, Ember. Everything has a tie leading somewhere. People fear the dark because they know the truth we only accept here—that magic is real and alive."

I meet her eyes, my heart racing. "And cirque—"

"Is also alive." She nods. Suddenly, she throws the cards up. I sit back with a gasp at the abruptness and then again as they hover in the air for long seconds before they fall once more. "Here, Queen, we are not the masters. We simply answer the call as you have. We all have. We are its conduit. Pure magic flows through us. We do its bidding. The sooner you realize you can't control it, the sooner you will understand it." The cards arrange themselves on the table, lying face down in a random pattern as she taps them. "The past and the future are all linked, and I, and now you, are the key to keeping it all together, but to understand the future, you must first understand the past. Pick a card." She waits patiently, and with a shaking hand, I reach across the table, tapping a card at random.

When I retract my hand, she flips the card to show me a spade. "It's interesting you would pick this."

"Why?" I ask, frowning. She speaks in riddles, but part of me seems to understand them and why they are important.

"It is interesting that you, who was held captive in your marriage, would pick the card of a man who was held captive as well. You have wondered why there are no cages here, correct? It is his doing. He was held in a cage most of his life, tied to the wants and needs of people posing as parents. He was the second of our suits to be called to the circus, but his strengths were born with him, not grown here. Animals have always answered his call, and the cirque saw that and called him home where he could be free, as well as his animal." Before I can ask questions, she flips the cards and waits with an arched brow. I tap another at random, desperate for the information she is giving me on the men who have consumed my thoughts. They are as mysterious as the cards before me.

This time, it flips over to reveal a red heart, and she smiles. "Heart, despite his name, is often called heartless. It's ironic that he chose that name, though I think that's probably why he did so. He is all about confronting his fears head-on. He was a slave when the cirque found him, forced to sleep within the trees of his master's traveling shops. He was left to nature, and many think that's what drove him mad, or the many beatings he endured in the name of the heart." I must look confused because she smiles. "Only love can bore such madness, Queen, and Heart loved deeper than most, until it was taken."

She flips it once more, and I tap another. This time the black club flips over, and she rubs her thumb over it. "Club was born as an entertainer. We aren't the only circus, of course. He was born into the life, but unlike us, he had no family. He learned to respect the sharp edge of the blade, making it his own after it was used against him. His beauty was his greatest weapon and also his darkest sin. He was wanted by all, and they used that. He was not chained like you,

Ember, but you know all too well how easily one can be trapped even without restraints."

I swallow as the card flips, and this time, she flips another—diamond. "Our ringmaster, but you know that. You saw him here when you were a child. Unlike the others, he was born into the service of cirque." She flips the card back over. "All of them were destined to join cirque, but they still chose the oath, chose to bind themselves to this fate. Their pasts and futures collide. It's woven together. Everything is born as it should be, but choices can change everything. That is one thing magic has no control over—free will. Here, we learn to read it and offer the truth without bias. Here, we are the historians, the readers, and the keepers. We are the soul of cirque. Without us, there is no home or family." She levels her pale white eyes on me, her expression solemn. "We answer the cards, Ember, but you will control them."

FIFTEEN

I learn her name is Hilda and that she's been with the cirque for three decades, traveling from town to town and reading the cards for those brave enough to enter her tent.

The day after she showed me her cards, everyone is in a whirlwind of activity, packing up the cirque and preparing to move to the next stop. I haven't asked how they know where to go. There seems to be a nonexistent map, as if they simply follow a feeling and stop whenever it's right. I don't even know how they know when it's time to leave, since we've been at this location for a couple of weeks now. I honestly wouldn't put it past the cirque to instruct when and where to go. It has a mind of its own.

The old cars and trucks are all loaded up with people and supplies, the cirque tents, and stalls. One large livestock trailer is loaded with the elephant and horses, the other animals all placed into cars with the people. Even Freedom hops in the back seat of an Oldsmobile that Spade drives. No one else gets in that car with him, so that's where I find myself for the duration of the move.

"Where are we going?" I ask as I slide into the front of the car and arrange my crutches. Dr. Louie says I'll be on them for a while longer, but as soon as the bone is better, I can walk on a boot instead of the crutches. Within three months, I'll hopefully be back to normal. At least my ribs seem to have healed faster than my leg.

"I don't know," Spade answers honestly, checking the mirrors at all times. Not only does he check on Freedom where she sleeps in the back seat, but he also checks to make sure the trailers behind him are doing okay. We make up a long line of vehicles, and though we could be going faster if we just drove and met everyone, we move as a single unit.

A family.

"Then how do we know we're going in the right direction?" I ask, frowning.

He shrugs. "We just do. We'll know it when we see it, but it usually isn't far. We travel as needed between towns."

I'm not sure what his definition of far is, but it does end up taking five hours to get to our next location with our slow-moving convoy. At some point, Diamond stops and pulls us into a large, empty field. A sign welcomed us to New Lockland on the way in. It seems to be a quaint little town, and the moment all the trailers arrive, work begins.

Still on crutches, I'm not nearly as much help as I'd like to be, so I mostly stay out of the way. Every now and then, I'm able to help, but after stumbling and falling onto the grass a few times, Spade instructs me to keep Freedom company. That's how I end up sitting in the grass on the outskirts of the setup, Freedom lying behind me and allowing me to lean against her as we watch the smoothness with which Cirque Obscurum is re-erected. It's beautiful, like a choreographed dance, every person knowing their place. Diamond runs around and helps where he's required, making sure everyone has what they need. Heart is the one who climbs the beams and attaches ropes and lights without any support. Spade and Club both work on putting up tents and unpacking everything we previously packed away. I watch each of them as they work, salivating when they remove their shirts as the sun rises higher in the sky.

"I could get used to this," I tell the tiger at my back.

She makes a small growl of agreement and nuzzles my elbow until I pet her. For a tiger, she's incredibly domestic. How strange for everyone to be so afraid of her. She's no different than a house cat.

The cirque is raised by the time the sun goes down, and a few of the crew members run into town to hang flyers everywhere. To the small town of New Lockland, it'll be as if we simply appeared from thin air. Come to the cirque and enjoy a thrill. Dive into the mystery, and before anyone can ask any questions, we'll be gone again. I like the enigma of it all. How easy it is to make it a secret. How easy it is to fool people. No real magic is even required.

I find my way to my tent once everything is done and lie down on my bed, my underarms hurting because of the crutches. I'm getting stronger while using them, but I'm going to have to wrap the handles with something softer soon. The bruises they are starting to leave behind are troublesome.

It's late, but I can't sleep. No one else seems to have that trouble as I hear them all retreat to their tents and not come back out. Across the way, I even hear Dr. Louie snoring. He's so loud, he might as well be sawing wood, but at least he's far enough away that it doesn't penetrate too deeply into my tent.

No, what I end up hearing is the shuffling of the tents beside me. First Diamond, then Club, and then Spade and Heart. They quietly get up from their beds and begin whispering outside my tent, words I can't hear.

Curious, I move as silently as I can to my tent flap and peer out, only to find them walking away. They wear all black to blend in with the darkness. They also have on those terrible, horrifying masks they wore on the night they found me. They are quiet as they go, clearly intending not to wake anyone.

My curiosity has me following them, but I am far less graceful on my crutches than they are on foot. They move toward a Dodge and begin climbing in, until Heart sees me coming over the hill and grins.

"It appears we have a stalker, boys," he comments, watching me carefully pick my way over the grass. None of them try to help me, just watching, and it reminds me of the night they came for me.

"Where are you going?" I ask, coming to a stop before them.

"Don't you feel it?" Diamond asks, glancing over at me as he opens the driver's door.

Now that he mentions it, there's a buzzing sensation in my chest, like I drank too much alcohol and didn't notice. The moment I focus on it is the moment it grows until it turns into an itch. I have to clench my fingers on my crutches to stop from scratching myself.

Nodding silently in understanding, I meet Diamond's eyes. "You're answering a call."

He nods once and climbs into the car, clearly intending to leave me here without saying anything more.

"Can I come?" I ask, taking another hopping step forward. "I can help."

"You're on crutches, Queen," Heart points out. "There isn't much you can—"

"Get in," Diamond instructs. "Back seat."

I do as I'm told, shuffling until I can get into the back seat with my crutches and relaxing against the backrest. He hands me a mask as I settle in, and I take it gingerly. He already had it in here. Had he known I would come looking?

"Put it on," he says, meeting my eyes in the rearview mirror. "Don't take it off until we tell you to."

I glance down at the heart-shaped mask with a small red Q under the left eye. Both eyes are crying black and red, leaving a trail of ink. The cheeks are big and round and dusted with blush, and the smirking lips are painted red. It's perfect and seems to be a blend of all their masks.

I slide it on without question, liking the feel of the plastic on my face and the power that seems to settle over me as I wear it.

No one says a word as we start the car and leave the cirque behind. The farther away we get, the stronger the call becomes until I'm practically vibrating with it.

Heart pulls out a knife and begins twirling it through his fingers. He glances over at me and grins, eagerness in his eyes.

We follow the call of the cards, and they tell us where we need to go.

My body hums in excitement as we answer it together.

CHAPTER

SIXTEEN

EMBER

It becomes apparent why no one knows where they are going or where the cirque will set up. Diamond doesn't use maps or directions to find where he's going, simply follows the call, the one vibrating within our chests. Cirque Obscurum decides where the cirque sets up and what town it will be in. If there's a call in that town, she sends us there as well, which is what's happening now.

Diamond simply drives, his eyes on the road. Every now and then, he takes a turn, left or right depending on that feeling. No one interrupts his concentration. We all sit quietly in the car and watch the scenery pass through the windshield.

The town of New Lockland isn't large, but it isn't small either. This town is big enough to sport sizable subdivisions around it in large, circular patterns, but it's not the bustling metropolis of a city. It's within those subdivisions that we find ourselves, a nice middle-class neighborhood that feels too much like the place I came from. I know better than most that the perfectly manicured lawns and white picket fences can hide monstrosities. Just because the house is painted white doesn't mean whoever lives there is innocent.

Somehow, I'm not surprised when we pull up to a well-maintained white house. The shutters are open on the windows, more decorative than useful. The small porch has the same white metal posts as the rest of the street, each house a cookie-cutter copy in a different color. Some of them are pale green, some pastel blue, but this is the only white one. Like our masks, it hides something inside. It mocks us as we all climb from the Dodge.

"Should I wait out here?" I whisper, staring up at the dark windows. There's no movement inside, not at this late hour. The sky is clear, so the moonlight washes everything with a blue tint, showing that not even the wind stirs the flowering bushes before us.

I realize I probably shouldn't be here, not while I'm still on crutches. I don't know exactly what all this entails or if every call is as traumatic as mine. Perhaps we're going to find this person and bring them back without any trouble. No one has truly explained how this all works. I only know how my calling went and I barely understand that.

Diamond turns and looks me up and down, as if reminding himself that I'm still on crutches. I'm a liability. I know that, but it still hurts when he nods.

"For now. We'll come get you when we're ready."

I lean back against the car and watch as they forgo the front door in favor of the back gate. They move quietly, so as not to attract attention from the neighbors, but I'm not sure if they need to. This neighborhood feels as dead as it looks. Though nosy neighbors are always a thing in the suburbs, this place is more likely to ignore atrocities than look too closely at them.

As if the thought causes it, the call in my chest grows stronger, and I double over beneath the weight of it, gasping for breath. Fuck, it wasn't this bad at first. My crutches are the only things keeping me upright, that and the car I lean against. It ebbs away long enough for me to catch my breath before I straighten and begin following the path the others took. Whatever the call is, it wants me with them. It wants me to see, and I am helpless to ignore it.

The grass is so perfectly manicured, I don't even trip over it as I hobble through the open gate. The backyard is empty, no toys to reveal a child might live here or furniture to indicate anyone uses it at all. It's just as perfect as the front yard, and just as much of a mask. If your home looks perfect, no one questions what's inside. No one asks you about your nightmares.

The back door is sliding glass, and it gives me the perfect view of the inside. I hop onto the cobblestone patio, coming closer when I see movement inside. There's a lamp on, the small light source casting a yellow haze over everything near it. There's a couch and a book lying atop the table beside the lamp. It looks like a crime novel, one of those mystery, solve the puzzle books. The sliding glass door is open, stale air coming from inside. When my chest aches with the call, I step over the threshold, being careful not to make any sound.

I don't see any signs of the guys, but a few steps into the house, I hear a shuffle and a grunt of pain. I follow the sound to an open door at the top of the stairs—a basement. This house has a basement. I hadn't even realized. There weren't any openings outside to indicate there might be one.

The lights are on at the bottom of the stairs that lead to it, so with my newfound strength, I begin to descend them. Another grunt of pain sounds, followed by some thumping. I move slowly, deliberately, as I get closer to the landing. I don't look until I'm there. I refuse to. I'd rather be faced with the whole image than only a part of it, but when I reach the landing and turn, I wish I hadn't come down the stairs at all.

Diamond, Club, Spade, and Heart circle a man who is on his hands and knees on the floor. He's panting in pain, his hand clutching his stomach. He looks normal enough, perfectly middle-aged and respectable, except . . . this basement is clearly sealed off from the outside. The concrete walls are smooth and thick, and there aren't any windows to let in light. It's sparse down here, only a thin twin mattress shoved against the wall covered with dirty blankets breaking up the gray. Photographs hang on the opposite wall, each of them depicting a different person, a different woman, in horrible positions and settings.

That's when I see her.

A woman no older than twenty is huddled in the corner, her eyes bloodshot and her face dirty. She's too skinny, the kind of thin that comes from neglect and starvation. There's a manacle around her ankle that's attached to the wall, making sure she can't go anywhere. Her skin is rubbed raw where the metal touches her, as if she's tried and failed many times to free herself. She watches the guys circle the man on the floor but doesn't move, too tired to do anything but watch.

There is nothing in her eyes. Only emptiness, like she has given up, but as I look closer, I see a single spark within. No, not given up, not yet, but she's close to it just like I had been.

No one seems to have noticed my arrival despite me knowing I must have made noise.

"How many victims are on that wall?" Diamond asks the man on the floor. "How many have you hurt?"

The man laughs despite being at the mercy of these men. He lifts up on his knees and looks Diamond right in the mask. "Forty-three," he says proudly. "Forty-four if you count the one over there."

Diamond nods to Heart. "You heard him. Forty-four cuts. One for each victim."

I'm helpless to look away, my eyes riveted to Heart as he steps forward and begins to slice with a small scalpel rather than the large hunting knife he carried during my call. How many knives does he have on him? How many tools does he use?

"One, two, three, four, you should have locked your back door." Heart giggles as he counts. "Five, six, seven, eight, suffer a cut for every hate."

The man grunts but doesn't cry out, gritting his teeth against the small cuts on his back, shoulders, arms, and stomach.

"Forty-one, forty-two, forty-three, forty-four, your blood is coating the concrete floor," Heart finishes and steps back with a grin.

The man scowls at them, bleeding from all his cuts, but his eyes are still clear and brutal. He's hard in his pants, as if this is exactly what he wants.

"Is that all you've got?" he says, his eyes on Diamond.

I can't see Diamond smile behind his mask, but I feel the aura in the room darken. Club straightens and looks toward the woman chained to the wall, making sure she's okay. She still watches, no protests or screams for help coming from her. The only change I see is a small smile curling the corners of her lips as she sits with her chin on her knees like she's watching a movie.

Spade flips out a knife. "I say we take away his weapon."

Diamond glances at Spade and nods. "I agree."

The man's confidence disappears as Heart steps forward again and begins to unbuckle his pants. When he tries to fight him off, Club comes forward to help, keeping his arms folded behind his back as Heart tugs his pants down around his knees, leaving his wrinkled cock standing tall before us. Spade wastes no time as the man begins to scream, really fighting now. Without boasting or teasing, Spade brings his knife down across that dick, cutting it off.

The gore causes me to put my hand to my mouth. Something in me is repulsed by the scene. It's disgusting and horrible, but I can't look away. Another part of me, some deeper, darker part I have yet to examine, revels in the sight of the man screaming in pain, of his cock being tossed in the corner like dirty laundry. Spade wipes his hands on the man's pristine shirt, leaving behind a red stain.

Club releases the man, who collapses to the ground, sobbing.

Diamond turns toward the woman in the corner. "Would you like him to die or live?"

I notice for the first time she has the joker card beneath her hip. It's clean, unlike mine, but the red foil is unmistakable. How she managed to keep it on her, I don't know, but her fingers touch the joker's face, her bright blue eyes focused on Diamond.

"Die," she croaks, her voice rough. The bruises around her neck tell me she's been choked repeatedly. Her vocal cords may be damaged, but she says the word loud enough for them to hear.

Diamond nods. "Good choice. Serial rapists don't deserve second chances, even when they are dickless."

My eyes widen as Diamond steps forward and draws a sword I never noticed he had. It comes from a sheath at his back, beneath his clothing, and the sound it makes as it slides free is loud in the concrete room.

"May you suffer the same nightmares you caused," Club growls just as Diamond swings the blade, slicing clean through his neck.

I gasp and fall backward against the wall as his head hits the ground with a thump and blood squirts from the arteries. His eyes are open, wide in shock, and his mouth is opening and closing slightly from lingering nerve movement.

At my sound, everyone looks over at me, finally noticing that I've been standing here, but I can't stop looking at the moving mouth—at the horror and grotesqueness of it.

I have to get out of here. I can't stomach this.

Turning with the intention to climb the stairs, I feel a hand close around my good ankle, and I look over my shoulder and down to find Heart's mask looking up at me.

"Where are you going, Queen?" he asks, his eyes sparkling behind the mask. "The fun isn't over yet."

My stomach roils, my eyes latching onto the moving head. "I can't."

"You can," Diamond says, his eyes hard, "and you will. You are one of us. We obey the call. Now you will too."

Without any other choice, I slowly descend the last few steps.

SEVENTEEN

The call only seems to explode, expanding in my chest as my feet hit the concrete floor of the basement. I almost crumple from the force. My eyes begin to water as I try to fight it, and I do not understand what it wants. The man is dead.

Chest heaving, I raise my eyes as Diamond stops before me. His hand tilts my chin up so I face him fully.

"You are one of us. You made that choice, Queen. Deep down, you knew what we were when you called for us," he murmurs seductively.

"I was dying!" I protest, despite his words working deep into my soul.

"You were weak," he snaps as I shrink. "You still are. Do you want to be weak for the rest of your life, or do you want to be strong? Do you want to live as a victim forever or as a villain? It's your choice, but you must make it." He steps back. "The call must be answered."

The others repeat it as I glance between them, the call only increasing until I can't draw in a full breath. The pounding power demands to be answered, to be heard.

The cirque demands I accept.

It beats in time with my racing heart as I look around at them and then to the body. He was evil, just like my husband. He hurt people. Did he deserve to die? Who are we to decide? Then I look at the man's prisoner, meeting her eyes, and I know she deserved to decide, not us.

The victims deserve to decide.

That is cirque's power. It gives choices back to the powerless. It gives them a chance at revenge, at redemption. Maybe that's messed up, but only those who have walked in darkness can understand that because even when they are brought back into the light, the shadows still cling to you.

We will never be normal people after what we have endured.

We have been scarred by our history. Cirque knows that. It understands that there are shades of gray. We are the answer to the evil within this world.

Suddenly, I understand. I know what they want.

I relax into it, and the pain subsides as the call carries me across the room until I stand before the woman. She looks up at me through thick lashes, and in her eyes, I see familiar ghosts, ones that haunt me. Looking into her bright blues is like looking in a mirror. She reminds me so much of myself. The hopelessness, pain, and terror stains the soul, but she isn't broken, just like I'm not.

Maybe cirque wants to welcome me by helping me understand.

"I was given a choice, and now you have one." The words flow from me, brought by something deeper. The cirque speaks through me. It collects souls as payment, but only willing ones, then it turns us into its weapons.

"A choice?" she asks, staring at me in surprise.

"We answered your call." I nod at the card. "I know that all too well. You can come with us to Cirque Obscurum and find a new home with us. You will serve the cards as we do. Or you can be free to start again. It's your choice." I lay it out as factually as I can. I want her to decide what's best for her, and part of me is curious what she will pick.

I chose the cirque so easily. Will she be the same?

As she debates, I see her face clearly, and a small if slightly shaky smile curls her lips. "I want to go home. I want a second chance at my life if that's okay."

It surprises me, and I'm quiet as I watch her. Will the cirque really let her go? Can she return to a normal life?

Am I the odd one for choosing to stay? For accepting cirque and the dark, clawed hand it offered?

Did I make a mistake?

Diamond steps up when I don't speak. "Of course. Allow us to free you." They unchain her and offer her clothes before Spade silently hands over the man's wallet. "His money is yours. It's the least he can do. Take anything you wish."

"We hope you have a better life, one filled with happiness, but know if you ever need us, you have our card." Diamond nods at the joker she still clutches. "We will always answer the call." He glances around, and as one, they turn and head back upstairs.

I linger there, watching her as she stares at their retreating forms before glancing at me. There's hope in her eyes and determination on her face as she stands up taller. "Thank you. Thank you so much. I thought I would die down here, but because of you, I get to go home. Thank you."

I simply nod, and she hurries past me. She hesitates by the body of the man who hurt her, and with a wide grin, she kicks his head, watching it splatter against the wall before she spits on his body and steps over him. "Rot in hell. I'm going to live, you asshole." With that, she hurries upstairs, leaving me alone with my thoughts before there's a honk from outside.

Time to go back to cirque.

As I head back to the guys, my worries follow me.

The call has disappeared, but my heart is in an entirely new vise. Can I do this?

Can I become a nightmare?

A villain?

EIGHTEEN

The drive back is silent. No one looks at me, and I shrink into my seat. My heart pulls me one way, my soul another. I'm trapped, struggling under the mask the whole way back until we pull up before the cirque. The engine turns off, and we're plunged into silence.

Despite the car being parked, none of them get out until Diamond looks at me in the rearview mirror. "I'm giving you one last chance, Ember. One last out despite the fact that you swore an oath. If you leave now, we won't chase you. We will let you go. It's your choice to make, but if you step back into cirque, you've chosen it and us. You've been shown this life knowing what it entails." With those words hanging in the air between us, he gets out of the car, and the others follow, heading into cirque like four phantoms. They leave me in the car, my heart racing as I climb out and hesitate.

They are giving me another chance, another out, but why?

I glance up at cirque and see them waiting at its perimeter, hidden between the tents, watching. What will happen if I leave? I swore an oath. As I turn to glance down the road that will take me away from here, I can't force myself to move.

There could be another life out there for me. I could be happy again. Maybe remarry and get a job. I could be normal, but deep down, I know I would never settle. I'd never fully trust it.

How could I go back to a world without the magic of Cirque Obscurum?

I glance back at the tent and the four men waiting there, curious as to what I will do.

As I look between my two choices, my thoughts circle back to the lady from earlier. She thanked us. We killed. We're murderers, yet she thanked us. When they came for me, I was so relieved I would have given my soul for the safety and redemption I found in their company. I can't go back on that now just because I'm having second thoughts, my morality in question. I've seen the worst this world has to offer. Do I truly wish to go back and pretend I haven't. Can I?

Or do I become a monster, a nightmare like them?

Do I take back my power that was stolen, or do I fade into this world?

No.

I don't want to be a victim anymore. I lived my entire life for the whims and wants of others. I want to live for me now, even if that darkness scares me and makes me feel like a bad person. I turn back to cirque, my decision made.

I want to be the queen I was named after.

I want to save those who need us like they saved me.

I want to make them all pay for hurting weaker people.

I know this time, my choice is final. I'll hand my soul over and become what the cirque wants. As I take a stumbling step toward the bright lights, those four masks morph into welcoming smiles, all of their hands rising to welcome me home.

They wait as I head their way, and once I'm back inside the circus, I take Diamond's outstretched hand. He twines his fingers with mine and leads me through the tents, the others falling into step behind us. Looking up at him, I can't help but smile, and as his masked face turns and looks down at me, I know he's smiling too.

He's proud of me, which shouldn't warm me but it does.

I didn't even notice the cut on Diamond's arm until the light filters across the wound. My eyes widen, and I push up my mask. "You're hurt."

He glances down as we stop before my tent. "He attacked when we entered. It'll just need to be cleaned and stitched." Keeping his hand in mine, I tug him inside after me, and he grunts but relents. I push him down to sit on my bed.

"I'm good at stitching wounds. Doctor's wife, remember? Let me help." I hurry around the tent until I find the kit Dr. Louie left the other day, stating that I might need it. I understand why now.

Sitting on the bed next to him, I open the kit and look up. "Shirt off." He hesitates, and I can't help but smile. "I've seen a naked chest before, Diamond. You won't scandalize me," I say with a grin.

He chuckles and removes his mask before pushing his hair back with a sigh. He untucks his shirt as he stands and unbuttons it, laying it on my bed before sitting down. He holds his wounded arm close to me. My eyes drop to his chest unbidden, tracing the lines of muscles. Something close to desire starts within me, which isn't right.

"I thought I wouldn't scandalize you, Ember," he taunts, and I feel my cheeks heat as I look away, focusing on the kit until I have myself under control. Ignoring his smile, I clean the wound and prod the edges.

"It needs stitches," I murmur. Without meeting his eyes, I thread the needle and make quick work of closing the wound. It's not too deep, but it's long. After I'm satisfied, I add a bandage and sit back, fiddling with the kit.

His hand lashes out, his finger tipping my chin up, forcing me to meet his gaze. His head is bent toward me, so close our breaths mingle. "Do you always shy away from what you truly want, Ember? I'm curious."

"I wasn't allowed to want anything," I reply automatically, cajoled by his voice and the dark look in his eyes.

"You are now. So what do you want, Ember? In this moment?" he asks, forcing me to look inside myself.

"I want to know if your lips are as soft as they look," I blurt before my eyes widen at my confession. I have never been so brazen or fool-hardy before. I try to pull away, but he captures my chin, the slight pinch forcing me to freeze.

"Then take what you want," he orders.

Barely breathing, I meet his dark eyes and see hunger there as he watches me, daring me to act on my wants and not run away like I always have.

Before, I would have made an excuse and turned away, but tonight I made a choice. There is a slight tilt to his lips, as if he's betting himself that I won't do it—that I'm still weak like he called me earlier.

Between one breath and the next, I move. My hands land on his chest as I press my lips to his. His lips part in shock as I kiss him hard. He groans, and his hands grip my hair, holding me in place as he takes over and kisses me. His tongue slips into my mouth and tangles with mine, urging me to take whatever I want.

Even him.

NINETEEN

Diamond tastes like cirque—dark, decadent, and a little bit magical. As he takes control of the kiss and his hand tightens in my hair, I give myself over to him completely, wanting to know what it feels like to be consumed by him. Sex and intimacy have always been associated with pain and disappointment in my life before now, but something tells me it won't be like that with Diamond. It'll be something monumental, life-changing, and the urge to taste that is so strong, I try to move closer. I don't care about anything except eliminating the space between us. Diamond is currently kissing the life out of me. Perhaps that's what this is. Perhaps Diamond is a reaper and this is his way of sucking out my soul. If that were true, would I even care?

No. I think I'd happily give it to him.

Diamond's tongue sweeps along my teeth and dances with mine as he deepens the kiss. I moan against his lips, desperate for more. My fingers clench his muscles, feeling the strength there. I want him. I've never wanted someone as much as I want the man holding me. The desire racing through my blood is so strong, I choke on it, as if he has awakened my every darkest fantasy and is using them against me all with a kiss.

Just as I'm about to push him down onto my bed and go further, my tent flaps fly open. I jerk back, but Diamond's hands still hold my hair, preventing me from moving too far. He breaks the kiss, but he doesn't look away from my eyes, forcing me to see the darkness there as I pant. Part of me is embarrassed, but the other part tells me to continue and let whoever just walked in watch.

"Well, had I known what fun was happening in here, I would have come sooner," Heart teases from the entrance.

"What is it?" Diamond asks, still not looking away.

"Oh, it's Hilda. She needs Ember," Heart replies, shrugging.

"Can it wait?" I ask, glancing at Heart from the corner of my eyes.

"I wish it could." Heart sighs. "I'd love to watch the two of you fuck."

My cheeks flush at his words, and this time, when I try to look over at him, Diamond lets me. "What?" I rasp.

Heart grins. "Don't worry, Queen. I'd fuck you too."

My thighs clench together. It's vulgar and improper, but I'm thinking about it now, about the two of them and the others joining in too. I must turn bright red when my thoughts head in that direction because Heart whistles.

"Would you look at that?" he says. "I think our queen likes the sound of that."

"I . . . What does Hilda need?" I croak, trying to speak despite the raging desire simmering low in my belly. It was there before from kissing Diamond, but now I'm seeing all sorts of imagery that makes it worse. Later, I know I'll touch myself to the thought of it, whether it's a real offer or not, but for now, if Hilda needs me, I should go.

"She saw something in the cards," Heart says with a shrug. "She seemed really upset."

I sit up, my eyes widening. "She seemed upset?"

Hilda is one of the calmest people I know. I've never seen her do anything other than speak with a cool and collected tone. If she saw something in the cards that bothered her, then it must be bad.

Heart nods and presses his fingers against the tent flap, tilting his head like an animal while something dark lurks in his gaze. "Yes. Have you ever thought about how easy it would be to strangle someone with a circus tent?"

I blink. Perhaps now isn't the time to ask what he means by that. I glance at Diamond. "I should go see what she saw."

Diamond tilts his head. "You don't have to wait for my permission, Ember. You're free here."

I didn't realize I was doing just that, waiting to make sure he was okay with it. We'd been busy, after all, so I assumed . . . but that's the old Ember talking. The new Ember doesn't have an abusive husband who controls her. The new Ember doesn't need to ask for permission or apologize for things she can't control.

"Of course," I murmur. Before I think better of it, I press another chaste kiss to Diamond's lips, making his eyes widen in surprise, then I stand and head for the tent flap.

"One for me, Queen?" Heart teases with a grin and a wiggle of his eyebrows. It's a dare. He doesn't think I'll do it.

New Ember isn't afraid. New Ember doesn't care what people think of her.

I lean toward him and press the same chaste kiss to his lips, shocking him into silence. I don't think I've ever seen Heart so surprised before. His expression almost makes him look innocent, but the wicked smile that pulls at his lips right after shatters that illusion.

"Well played, Queen," he purrs as if it's a game. "I'll remember there are no rules in this game we play."

That sounds dangerous, but instead of dwelling on it, I wink at him and say, "I'll be back later," before leaving.

I rush toward Hilda's tent, expecting her to be chaotically yelling about something she saw in the cards. Instead, I find her sitting on the floor in the middle, her fingers sunk into the plush rug beneath her as if she needs to ground herself. Her pale white eyes are closed, but as I step inside, they open and something flashes in her gaze that I can't place. It's difficult to read Hilda's emotions on a good day, let alone when she consciously hides them.

"Heart says you saw something in the cards," I begin, going over to take a seat in front of her. I cross my legs and wait, knowing she'll tell me in her own time.

She hums a tune I don't recognize under her breath, but it sounds old and foreign. It feels like deserts and palm trees, an oasis in the middle of the sand. Every part of her vibrates with energy, and I watch as the cards come down from the table one by one, fluttering until they land face up between us.

"Your kindness will be your downfall, Ember," she says, her voice echoing. It's as if more than one person speaks through her, and the sound sends chills up my arms. "Happiness is not guaranteed, and the cirque must be protected at all costs. *They* must be protected."

"Who?" I ask, leaning closer, but she doesn't answer.

The cards catch on fire so suddenly, I jerk back, my eyes wide at the sight. The flames turn blue and then green as the cards shrivel and burn.

"He's coming." Hilda moans as her eyes roll into the back of her head. "He's coming."

"Who's coming?" I ask, afraid. "Hilda, who's coming?"

She blinks, and the flames suddenly go out. This time, when she meets my eyes, there's only the kindness I see every day. She looks confused about why she's sitting before me.

"I . . . What are we doing on the floor?" she asks.

"You said he was coming," I repeat. "Hilda, who did you mean?"

She frowns. "I'm not sure I know what you mean, Ember." Her eyes catch on the burned remnants of the cards, now unrecognizable after the flames. "What happened to my cards?"

I have no answers for her. I have none for myself. "You told me to come in and said that my kindness will be my downfall. You saw it in the cards. Then you said he's coming."

Her eyes widen, and she studies the cards again. "Which cards were they?"

I blink. Had I even looked at them? I was too distraught over what happened. Pressing my hand to my head, I try to remember but I'm not sure. I'm still learning, so I don't know how to read the cards yet. Foolish. I should have looked.

"I . . . I don't know," I admit. "I don't know."

Hilda stands. "I'll search for answers. For now, go rest." She shoos me away, and I stand, my eyes on the remnants of the cards. Somehow, as I look at them, the ashes seem to form the word "nightmare," but as I look closer, the wind from the tent flaps scatters them until they form nothing at all.

I must have imagined it. Hilda will figure it out.

Everything will be okay.

I lie to myself the whole way back to my tent, until I'm convinced I blew it out of proportion. It was nothing. Nothing at all.

I forget all about it when I enter my tent and find Diamond and Heart gone.

My disappointment outweighs my fear.

TWENTY

EMBER

My exhaustion comes out of nowhere. One moment, I'm fine, and the next, I can hardly keep myself upright. I know the night was eventful, and hobbling around on crutches doesn't help, but at the very least, I thought I could last a little longer. When I glance at the clock and see it's just after four in the morning, I realize I've hardly slept at all. That's the detail that ultimately claims me. When I lie down in my bed, I'm out before my head even hits the pillow.

My dreams flicker with abstract shapes at first, dancing between some forms I recognize and nothing I do, but they soon solidify into a scene I know all too well—my old house and life. The pristine white kitchen was always a nightmare to keep clean. Even without cooking, it would appear dirty, so I spent plenty of time scrubbing the white countertops and floor in the hopes Roger wouldn't come home and have an excuse to hit me. I stand in that kitchen now, the oven timer counting down as if a meal is about to be ready.

The door slams open behind me, and I jump, whirling to find Roger in the doorway. His face is contorted with anger as usual, but this time, there's something . . . off about it. There's something in his eyes I don't recognize.

"Why didn't you greet me at the door?" he demands as he throws his keys and wallet on the counter. "A good wife greets her husband."

I glance at the oven. The food inside looks burnt, the chicken I'd been roasting long since dried out. Dinner is ruined. The timer begins to beep, signaling for me to take it out. "I needed to remove the chicken," I offer as an excuse, despite knowing it's unsalvageable. "I was going to come say hello—"

I remember this memory well. It was a few weeks after my mom died. I'd still been struggling with grief, still trying to function and clearly failing.

Roger gets a whiff of the chicken as I open the oven door and his face puckers. "And you burned dinner," he growls.

Without warning, he grabs the back of the neck as I lean down to the oven. He clutches me so hard, I cry out in pain and reach out to balance myself, finding the edge of the oven door. I scream as it burns me, and I pull my hands back, fighting against him. I'm weak compared to Roger, so I can hardly do anything.

"Let this be a lesson," Roger sneers in my ear. "You greet me when I come home, preferably on your knees." He pushes my face closer to the oven door.

"Stop! Please!" I cry, desperately trying to get away.

"And don't burn dinner," he snarls before shoving my face against the oven door. The smell of burning flesh fills my nostrils.

I startle awake, screaming and terrified, my hands going to the scar on my cheek from the first time Roger truly showed his monstrous side. I'd never seen him so angry. After that, I was burned, beaten, scarred, bludgeoned, and anything else you can imagine. It takes me a few long seconds to realize it was just a nightmare and Roger isn't here with me, but in those seconds, my tent flaps fly open to reveal Spade.

"What is it?" he asks. "What's wrong?"

I'm covered in a cold sweat, and I vibrate with fear despite the realization it was only a dream. I'm shaking so hard, my teeth chatter. "I'm sorry I woke you," I murmur. "It was just a bad dream."

He stares at me for a second before he comes into the tent and climbs up on my bed. "Scoot over," he commands.

I do as he says, expecting him to sit on the edge of the mattress. Instead, he lies down and pats the pillow for me to do the same. When I do, he tugs me tightly against his body, his warmth chasing away my fear and the chill. The comfort I find in his arms makes me want to weep, but I hold it back.

"When I first came to cirque, my memories haunted me," he murmurs. "Having someone close helps."

"Who helped you?" I whisper, settling against him.

"Heart," he answers. "We both suffered from nightmares, and we chased them away together. We'll do the same for you."

When he falls silent, I turn my head to look at him over my shoulder. "Spade?"

"Yes?"

"Thank you," I whisper.

The next time I fall asleep, Roger doesn't invade my dreams. Only Spade and his tiger do, each of them offering warmth and chasing away my nightmares.

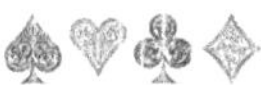

When I wake up again, Spade is gone. Instead, I find Club waiting for me outside, his arms crossed as he silently stares at the main tent.

"Hilda told me to tell you she still doesn't know which cards they were since none of hers are missing," he says in lieu of hello. "She just said to be careful."

I run my hand through my hair and wince. "Great. An ominous threat hanging over my head. Just what I need."

Club glances at me. "I can distract you," he offers, "if you'd like."

I hesitate. I still have a few more weeks on crutches, so I'm incapable of doing everything. Whatever Club wants to distract me with, I'm sure he'll take that into account.

"I could use a distraction," I admit. Both from Hilda's strange warning and the thoughts of Heart and Diamond plaguing my mind.

"I've been practicing a new act." He nods. "You can help me."

I raise my brows. "What? You're going to swallow something bigger than a sword? An umbrella?"

He laughs and gestures for me to follow him to the big top. "I deal in all blades, Queen. Not just sword swallowing."

Oh. I didn't realize that, even though I probably should have. He carved through the fruit and vegetables and wielded the sword as if he knew what he was doing. Of course he knows his way around more than that.

Various performers practice inside the main tent. Overhead, some of the trapeze artists and acrobats rehearse with a net beneath them.

"I thought Heart doesn't like nets," I comment, watching as one of the acrobats slips and falls.

"He doesn't," Club replies. "The net is for the others to use while practicing new stunts. Heart goes without, but he's a different animal. The others prefer to practice new moves with a net."

That makes sense. None of them are at the same level of crazy as Heart.

"So what's the trick?" I ask, but I didn't need to. In front of us is a large circle. There are little pegs on it and straps. It's painted with a gold star in the center, and red and white rings go out to the edge. "Wait, what's that for?"

"I asked Dr. Louie if you could participate and he said yes, as long as you don't put your weight on your bad leg," he explains, leading me over to the wheel. He takes my crutches and sets them off to the side before lifting me onto it. "Grab here and here," he instructs, slipping my wrists through the leather straps. "Legs go here. Don't put your weight on your booted one. The wheel should take some of the pressure off."

As he works to strap me down, the acrobats finish their practice and exit the tent, leaving only Club and me for now. He's standing incredibly close to me, his nimble fingers dancing along my skin as he checks the holds and fastens a leather strap around my waist.

"What exactly is this for?" I ask, my voice a little breathy because of his touch.

He glances up at me through his lashes, his eyes full of mischief. "Are you afraid of knives, Ember?"

I think about the question. I've been stabbed and cut. Knives have hurt me many times, but do I fear them? "No," I answer. "Not that I'm aware of."

He nods. "Good. Don't jerk around on the wheel. Hold still."

He moves to a table I didn't notice before, one laden with knives. "Diamond says I can add this to my act next week," he murmurs as he strokes the metal of the closest knife. "But I need to find someone willing to be on the wheel."

He picks it up and flicks it between his fingers.

"So you found me," I murmur.

"I could try to convince someone from the audience each night," he says with a shrug. "But for practice, I need a willing target." Without warning, he throws the knife at me. I flinch when it slams into the wood between my legs, the thump of it loud. "Relax," he says. "I won't hit you."

As if to mock me, he throws another. This time it lands beside my neck, so close I swear I feel the wind. I gasp, but I don't move, afraid that will be the reason he hits me. I understand now why he needs me to stay still.

He studies me, another knife in his fingers. "You're so pretty when you flush," he comments. "Bright like a star." The next knife lands above my head.

Desire pools low in my belly as he lifts the next one and flips it into the air. Club is dangerous in his element. Here, in this circus tent, he feels like a viper, coiled to strike. When he throws another, I don't flinch, trusting him, my eyes on his as he flings half the knives on the table.

"Not afraid at all," he comments, coming closer. "But that's not the whole act, little star." He grabs the edge of the wheel and moves it gently. I gasp as it turns, clenching onto the holds tighter, even if the waist belt is tight enough to hold me. "The second part of the act is me throwing knives at a spinning wheel. Does this excite you?" He slowly turns the wheel until I'm upside down, and he holds me there. My face is level with his groin, at the perfect height for—

"Yes," I rasp. Holy fuck, this excites me. If Club unzipped his pants right now, I'd suck him deep. I'm desperate for him, aching for the desire that could make me feel alive and reborn. I don't know what it is about this place or these men, but I can't seem to control myself—no, I don't want to control myself with them. When his hands slide along my leg, stroking down my thigh, I nearly whimper.

Old Ember would have accepted the torture, but new Ember is needy and commanding.

"Are we alone?" I croak, my fingers clenching tightly in the straps. My blood is rushing to my head in this position, but I don't care.

"Yes," he purrs. "We'll be alone for another fifteen minutes or so."

I tilt my head and look up his body to his eyes. In his gaze, I see the same desire I feel. "Then unzip your pants."

He pauses. I know he had the same thought I did. His length hardened slightly when I flipped on the wheel, but at my words, his pants tent.

Club is a different animal I've yet to figure out. He's stoic and carries himself with an air of nobility I can't place. When he speaks, his words are weighed heavily, chosen with precise care. When I tell him to unzip his pants, though, all that poise disappears and reveals the beast within.

"You don't know what you're asking," he warns. "You're still healing."

I know he doesn't mean physically—he's not pointing out my broken leg—he means emotionally, but I'm not afraid here. I've never felt safer than I do now, and it's because of the four of them. I belong to the cirque, to them, and I'm going to claim them just the same. I want them. All of them. The new person I am doesn't care about social constructs or silly rules outside of this tent. I only care about what I want.

Right now, I want to suck Club's cock deep into my throat.

I want to feel alive and powerful, and I know I can with him.

"Unzip your pants," I repeat, the sharp order filling the air between us.

He hesitates for one beat, two, before he lets his monster out to play. He reaches between us with a groan and unzips his pants, freeing his erection and letting it bob in front of my face. A bead of precum pools on the tip, and I yearn to taste it.

"Give it to me," I command. Even though I'm strapped to the wheel, I'll slip down if I let go, so I hold fast and open my mouth. Any hesitation he had before is now gone.

Club presses his dick against my lips, painting his precum along them, before he plunges inside. I gag at the suddenness of it, and he moans, his body going taut. He doesn't pull back, instead pushing deeper until my nose is pressed against his skin and tears spring to my eyes.

"I've imagined you just like this," he growls as he pulls out and thrusts back in, fucking my throat without mercy. "Strapped down, helpless against my onslaught." I feel the wood groan as he pulls out a dagger. "Shaking with pleasure as I trace a knife down your body." I feel the cold steel against my good leg. "But for now, I'm happy to fuck your perfect throat." He drops the knife with a clatter and begins to fuck me, his moans and the sounds of his cock gagging me echoing in my ears. Tears leak from the corners of my eyes as he ruthlessly fucks me, and I love it. I love every second of it. My pussy clenches, my own need covering my thighs as I wish I were naked so he could taste my own pleasure. I want him to fuck me just like he said. I want this brutal, dark edge.

I want them to remind me I am not ruined.

"Oh fuck." His balls slap against me as he forces his cock deep down my throat, fucking me hard and fast as he swells. "You're going to fucking steal my soul this way. I know it."

Despite his words, he doesn't stop. Saliva drips from my lips as I suck on him, and he deepthroats me until I feel him start to lose control.

"Next time, I'm going to strap you down and fuck your pussy until you scream," he tells me, "and then I'll let the others join in. You want to put on an act, baby girl, then you've got it."

When he slams deep inside, burying himself all the way down my throat with a bellow so my face is pressed tightly to his pelvic bone, I feel his cock jerk. Warmth fills my throat as he spills his seed there, marking me. I swallow it all, wasting nothing.

The sound of someone about to come through the circus tent has him pulling back and zipping his pants up. The clowns are coming in to practice, and I'm upside down with his cum dribbling from my lips, tears running from my eyes, and saliva around my mouth.

Club spins me upright, and my blood rushing back to my body makes me dizzy for a moment. As I gather my bearings, he reaches into his pocket and pulls out a handkerchief before gently wiping the saliva from my face. He leaves the cum. When he finishes cleaning me up, he leans in and kisses me deeply, sending me into another fit of desire.

"I bet you'd be dripping down your thighs right now if not for your clothing," he murmurs against my lips. "I can't wait to taste you, little star."

He steps back and spins me. "Now for the second part of the act," he says, walking over to the table and picking up a knife like nothing happened, but he's breathing heavily and his eyes linger on me, so he isn't as unaffected as he pretends he is. "Try not to give in to the dizziness."

I nod, wishing we had more time to play.

I focus on a spot at the top of the tent to stop myself from getting dizzy, and only then do I realize we weren't alone before. High up in the rafters, eating a bucket of popcorn, is Heart. He'd been practicing, and he never left. When our eyes meet, he winks, his grin so wide, it must hurt his cheeks.

If my panties weren't soaked before, they certainly are now.

TWENTY-ONE

Although Dr. Louis says my leg is healing, I'm still not well enough to help in any acts, not really. I'm off the crutches, but now I just have a boxy boot around my leg, so I'm forced to sit out tonight's show, watching from the sidelines as they amaze and terrify. The longer I'm here, the more the darkness within me rises.

I'm not the same Ember who came here all those nights ago. I feel stronger, more confident, and there is this wicked hunger inside me, demanding to be set free. It has a brutal edge to it, one born from death and pain. I thought my need for revenge died when I left that house behind, but I was wrong. It just lit the flames that I fan now instead of running from them.

I want these men, and I want this place, but it's more than that.

I want to answer the cirque. I want to be the blade in the darkness. I just have to give myself permission to, and I did that when I chose to return.

As if relishing and understanding my acceptance of what and who I am now, the cirque calls me. Unlike last time, it doesn't cripple me. Instead, it pulses inside me, like a heartbeat deep within, echoing through my body and soul. The constant thrum grows louder, asking to be heard. My eyes go to the guys as they perform, wondering if they feel it too, but they are oblivious.

It's just me. Why?

Turning away from the bright lights, I push from the pole I was leaning against and duck out of the tent. Outside in the empty darkness, the screams of the crowd seem far away, and that pulse only grows. I focus on it and start to move. Each step causes the heartbeat inside me to pound faster, and warmth spreads through me as if to assure me this is the right way.

I stumble across the worn grass, trying to focus on the call as it leads me away from the lights and crowds of the cirque and toward the fields behind us. The long grass blows in the breeze, the moon high above us but unable to pierce the darkness.

The call tugs me deeper into the grass, and I go willingly, open to it. The lights disappear, and when I glance back, I can't see the cirque nor hear the music, but I still walk. The grass brushes against me as I wander through it.

I don't know how long I walk for.

Suddenly, the long grass parts into a small clearing, where the stalks have all been ruthlessly stomped down. It's here I find the reason for the call. My heart clenches as two wide, terrified brown eyes clash with mine.

It's a boy, a child, half lying in the broken patch of grass as if his body can't go on, but judging by the drag marks behind him, it's clear he tried to.

Crouching, I spread my hands to show him I'm harmless as I watch him carefully. He's small, even for his age. He must be about ten or so, but he's so tiny that his bones stick out under his skin, and his whole face is gaunt like a skeleton. His eye sockets are hollow and bruised, there are cuts all across his pale, filthy skin, and his feet are bleeding. It's obvious he ran a long way.

This boy has been abused.

I don't see a card anywhere, which is strange, but the cirque called me here for a reason. Besides, I can't leave him here. I see resolve in his eyes, the belief I will abandon or hurt him like everyone else before. He's waiting for the blow, his body giving out and his soul ready to give up.

I know that feeling all too well.

"It's okay. I'm not going to hurt you." His lips part in disbelief, and when I move forward a little, he scrambles back, shivering in fear and cold, so I stop. "I'm Ember. What's your name?"

He swallows, his little throat bobbing as his eyes dart around, looking for a way out before landing back on me. He relaxes when he realizes he doesn't have the strength to escape, and his eyes settle back on me. I wait. I don't move, but I also don't give up. I can't leave him here, not when the wounds on his body have anger igniting within me. Who could hurt a kid like this?

"Noah," he croaks before swallowing again. "My name is Noah."

"It's nice to meet you, Noah. How did you get all the way out here?" I glance behind him for anyone who might be chasing him, but we are far from anything here.

He doesn't answer, and I nod.

"I'm from the circus." He seems to sit up taller, and I smile. "The one with the animals and clowns." I grin, and a soft smile tips up his lips. "Would you like to come with me? I can get you some food and help get you cleaned up."

"I've never been to a circus," he whispers.

"Hmm, it's a magical place," I promise, sitting when my leg aches, showing him I'm not going anywhere. "We have a tiger." His eyes widen, and I grin. "We have an elephant and so many amazing acts. You can even watch them if you want."

His eyes dart over his shoulder worriedly.

"Noah," I cajole, knowing I could lose him at any moment. He's like a scared animal. The cirque called me here for a reason, but this is more than that. This child has been abused, and I want to save him.

"You are better off leaving me," he finally responds, sounding far too grown up. "I only bring trouble."

"Don't you know?" My grin is almost wicked as I stand. He flinches but doesn't run. "We circus people crave trouble. Besides, everyone is welcome at the cirque."

I take a chance and slowly move closer, making my limp more pronounced to prove I am not a threat. When I stop before him, I crouch again so I'm not towering over him, and it's then I realize how truly small he is. He's just bones and pale skin.

I almost recoil in horror at the scars I see littering every inch of his back, which are revealed by the torn rags he wears. I don't know how he survived. Some are old, some are new and bleeding, and there are bruises in a kaleidoscope of blues and purples. He meets my eyes again, peering up at me through long lashes, making my heart clench. "I was bad," is all he says, his voice small.

Swallowing my horror, I reach my hand out, palm up. "I promise you, Noah. You're not bad. Let me help you."

"Why?" he asks, searching my gaze. Didn't I ask the same thing once? "Why would you help me?"

"The cirque is a safe place for everyone. We help as many people as we can. I was like you once. If you let me, Noah, I promise to keep you safe."

He looks from me to my hand before lifting a shaking limb and laying his tiny hand in mine. I smile encouragingly as I stand and help him to his feet. He wavers, shivering, and I know I need to get him to the doctor.

I tighten my hold on him, feeling the bones under his paper-thin skin. Smiling down at him, I try to fight back my anger so I don't scare him. "It's going to be okay."

It takes us a while to get back, but Noah refuses to let me carry him because he's worried about my leg. His concern makes me want to cry, but I hold back my tears so I don't scare him. Once inside the cirque, he seems both lost and awed. I know that feeling, know what it's like to be faced with something so grand and terrifying all at once. I escort him to my tent and wave down a rigger on the way, asking him to grab Dr. Louis for me.

"Sit, okay?" I point at my bed, and Noah hesitates. "What is it?" I ask.

"I'm dirty," he whispers, his eyes sad.

"I don't care about dirt, Noah. Please sit." I help him onto the bed and sit next to him as the tent flaps part. Noah hides slightly behind me as Dr. Louis enters, and I warn him with my eyes to move slowly.

He nods, getting the message. "And who do we have here?" he asks, setting his bag down before moving closer and crouching.

"This is Noah. Noah, this is Louie, the doctor who helped me." I nudge him gently as he peeks out.

"Hi," he croaks.

"It's nice to meet you, Noah. I'm going to look you over, okay? I can see blood, and I want to make sure nothing gets infected and make you feel better."

Noah looks up at me, and I nod. Noah copies the movement, and Louie smiles.

"Okay, so let's get this shirt off." I slide back and go to stand to give them privacy, but Noah's hand darts out and grabs mine.

"Stay, please," he begs, holding my hand tightly, eyeing Louie in fear. Louie turns away, but not before I see the tears in his eyes, and I know the feeling. It's difficult to be faced with such horrible mistreatment of a child.

"I'm not going anywhere," I promise. "Can he take a look at you? He fixed my leg, see? He's really good. I promise."

Noah nods, and we both sit stiffly as Louie looks him over, dressing his wounds before sitting back. Noah is silent the whole time, but it's obvious he doesn't like being touched, and he flinches if Louie moves too quickly. Still, he never once complains about the pain he must be in. His ribs are busted, his back is a mess, his feet are cut so deeply I don't know how he walked, and that's just his unhealed injuries. His whole body is scarred, and it's evident he's suffered years of abuse.

"You did very well, Noah. I want you to rest now, okay? When you wake, I want you to have little meals often. Your stomach shrank, so anything big will make you sick."

Noah nods. "I know I get sick if I eat."

Louie smiles, but it's tight as he glances at me and nods his head toward the tent opening.

I nod and stand. "I'll be right back, okay?"

Noah's eyes widen as he holds my hand with more strength than I thought possible. "Promise?"

"I promise," I whisper as I wrap my blanket around him. "I'll just be outside. Shout if you need anything, okay? I'll come running back."

He nods, holding the blanket tighter, and I follow Louie out. He rubs his face, looking exhausted. "The kid is malnourished and on death's door. His body . . . He has more unhealed broken bones and lashings than I've ever seen. The scarring on his back, though, I've seen it before."

"What do you mean?" I murmur, not wanting Noah to overhear. It's clear he's been through enough.

"A whip. He was whipped," Louie growls, angry just like me. "He needs rest, food, and love, lots of it. It will be a long time until he trusts anyone, but he seems to feel safe with you. Stay with him. Let him know it's safe."

"I will." I nod. "Thanks, Louie."

"Sometimes I wonder what the hell this world is coming to," he mutters as he wanders away.

Me too, I think as I step back into the tent and find Noah already asleep, curled into a tiny ball under the blanket. I head his way and sit heavily, rubbing his back as the cirque pulses inside me, demanding retribution.

"You don't have to tell me twice. This time, it's my hunt. This time, I'll become a nightmare." Leaning down, I place a soft kiss on Noah's cheek. "Tell me your nightmares, Noah. Let me face them for you."

"Stables Orphanage," he whispers, the words dragged from his nightmares where he's trapped.

"Good boy. Rest now. Let the cirque take care of you."

I watch as he settles in once more, and then I stand, letting my expression become cold as I turn and head out of the tent.

We have a hunt, and this time, I won't shy away from it.

TWENTY-TWO

Ember is waiting for us when the show finishes and the cirque shuts down for the night. She looks madder than I've ever seen her. "What's wrong?" I ask, checking her over. Did she get hurt? Did something happen during the show? I'll cut whoever hurt her.

"We're going on a hunt," she snaps, and we share a look.

"I didn't feel a call," Diamond hedges, speaking the words we're all thinking.

"I did while you were performing. I followed it."

I blink, confused as I circle her, taking in the grass stains on her pants and the fury vibrating off her in waves.

"There was this kid, Noah, out there all alone. He's been abused and was half dead when I found him. Dr. Louis looked him over, and he's resting now, but he's in really bad shape. It's going to take him weeks to heal from his wounds, and even longer from the trauma he's suffered. Poor kid," she growls, rubbing her forehead. "He said he's from an orphanage near here. The cirque wants us to hunt." Her eyes meet mine. "I want to hunt."

"Pretty, violent thing," I purr as I stop behind her, my mouth meeting her ear. "You want bloodshed."

"Yes," she admits without shame. "I want to hurt whoever hurt that poor boy. I want them to suffer."

"I didn't feel it at all. How weird," Spade murmurs.

"Where's his card?" Club asks.

"He doesn't have one," she replies, "but the cirque led me to him. It called, and I answered. It wants us to help."

"This has never happened before. Without a card?" Diamond glances between us. "I think we should think this through—"

"I'm going with or without you. Nobody," she snarls as she points in the direction of her tent, "deserves to be hurt like that. He's innocent. He's a fucking kid. Who knows what else they are doing there. He's skin and bones. Someone *whipped* him," she spits. "I'm asking you to come with me, but I can go alone. Either way, I'm going."

The others hesitate, but not me.

"You want to hunt?" I whisper against her skin, meeting Diamond's eyes. "Then let's hunt, pretty little killer."

It seems our queen has accepted who she is, and she looks fucking phenomenal. I don't know what seeing this kid did to her, but it sent her over the edge.

There's only so far you can push a person before they go insane. Everyone has a breaking point. I know all about that.

Her mask is firmly in place, and her hair is in pigtails as she stands at my side, looking up at the orphanage. Despite the boot on her leg, she kept up with us as we made our way here. It's not too far from the circus, just a few miles down the road, and we didn't want to drive and alert them. She didn't complain once despite the hindrance, her mind on our destination.

It stands on the top of a hill, an old gothic-style building in drab gray with huge iron fences and gates. "Stables Orphanage" is proudly displayed across the top of the iron, but it looks more like a prison than any home for children. There used to be flowering vines that climbed the walls, but they've long since died, causing everything to look even more eerie than it already does in the dim light.

It started to rain not too long ago, making our journey cold and miserable, yet Ember still burns hot with anger, and it makes me hard as hell. I want to feel that fury painted across my skin.

"If we go in there, then there's no coming out without blood on your hands," Diamond warns her. Even from here, we can taste the violence and death in the air. Whatever nightmares lie behind these gates, we'll face them, and it won't be pretty. It's been a long time since I've felt a place so evil—not since I was a child, facing my own nightmares.

She pushes her mask up despite the rules, looking us over before staring at the building. The storm clouds and rain will hide her identity, so no one corrects her, but it's a mistake that can't be replicated. We leave no trace, not even memories of our faces.

The rain smears her makeup, making her look like she's been crying even as she smiles wickedly. The red chalk staining the ends of her hair drips like blood. "I know what I'm here for. Let's hunt." There's no hesitation in her voice, no fear. She has one purpose and one purpose only: revenge for the little boy back in her tent.

If only I had an avenging angel like her when I was so young.

Gripping the back of her neck, I drag her closer, slamming my lips to hers in a brutal kiss until I taste blood. I pull back and grin at her as I tug her mask down, and then I adjust my own. "Let's."

Heading to the gate, I leap up and catch the edge of the iron, flipping over so I land on my feet on the other side. I see Spade and Club doing the same. Our girl simply shakes her head.

"Not a chance," she mutters as she heads our way and pushes the gate open. It wasn't even locked. Diamond follows her with a chuckle. "Show-offs," she adds as she reaches our side.

The storm covers our entrance and the noise of our footsteps, so there's no point in being quiet. We simply head right to the front door. Unlike the gate, it's locked, which is hardly surprising. Something tells me it's more to keep someone in, though, than it's meant to keep anyone out. Timing it with the next roll of thunder, I slam my boot into the wide, black double door. The handle snaps with a loud bang, and it blows inwards. The feeling of evil expands tenfold, nearly choking me.

Stepping inside with a happy hum, I look around the huge orphanage. The entryway is clearly for visitors, with flowers and chairs perfectly set out before two staircases leading up. It's an illusion, a pretty picture meant for well-off patrons looking to purchase a child. No doubt there are only special children they get to see if they come. There are always special children who are favorites. I was never one of those.

Water sluices from our bodies, hitting the perfectly polished wooden floor as we look at the walls. The pitter-patter of the rain hitting the windows covers our booted feet as we dismiss the illusion and head deeper into the labyrinth of the house. Diamond points upstairs, and I nod as he heads up the winding staircase with Spade in tow.

Club follows Ember and me down the corridor past the stairs. Back here, it changes completely, the illusion falling away. Behind a wooden door is a metal gate that's locked from the outside. We share a look before I kneel and quickly pick the heavy metal padlock and open the door. As soon as we step through, we're in a long, dark corridor. Snoring reaches my ears, and my eyes swing to the right to see a warden or a guard stretched out on a sofa. I jerk my head at Club, and he nods, heading in there to stand guard while I follow Ember down the hallway.

On each side are metal doors with sliding hatches, something we'd see in a prison, not an orphanage. She stops at one randomly and slides it open before leaning down to peer inside. She gasps, the sound harsh to my ears, before she hurries to the next and then the next, her anger growing with each reveal. Frowning, I peer through one, and my heart skips a beat at the ten or so kids clustered in the back of the tiny room. Their dirty, tear-stained faces turn toward me with terror, as they don't know if I'm there to harm them or not. The smell coming from the room makes my eyes water. There's nothing in there—no bed or toilet—only a dirty concrete floor.

The urge to retch is strong, not because of the smell but because of how thin, dirty, and beaten they are. Some of them have bruises, while others have bleeding wounds. They flinch at the light I let in, like they haven't seen it in too long.

White-hot fury fills me. I can barely stop myself from bursting.

Stepping back slowly so as not to scare them, I storm over to Ember, who's halfway down the corridor, her face stricken with both grief and disbelief. Being faced with evil is one thing, but being faced with evil directed at children is another. I understand. Children and animals are innocent. Anyone who preys upon them isn't worth the dirt on the bottom of my boot.

She turns to me, fury and pain in her gaze. "Kids," she rasps. "These cells are all filled with starving, abused kids."

"Hey! Who the hell are you?" comes a loud, jarring voice. We both turn to see a hulking man standing at the end of the corridor, keys hanging from his waist along with a baton and a whip. He has dark, cruel eyes. "Who the hell are you, and how did you get in here?" he repeats, uncertain when he catches sight of our masks.

Ember's eyes turn to me, just as dark as the man's. There will be no mercy from her this evening. "Kill him and make it hurt," she commands.

"With pleasure." I smirk. Turning to the man, I tilt my head as I watch him. "Will you scream, little piggy?" I call as I stalk toward him. He steps back, looking from Ember to me, confused and afraid. "Oink, oink." I giggle as I leap, hitting the wall on the left and flipping. I roll as soon as I hit the floor and come up behind him. He doesn't even have time to react.

Sliding close to his back, I grin as I blow on his ear. "Boo."

He jumps and whirls around, fumbling with his baton as I laugh.

I grab his hand before he can pull it. Even if was able to get it out, a baton is hardly the worst I've been hit with. Nothing hurts like a hot fire poker. Nothing. I sweep my leg out beneath his, and he tumbles to the floor. His face turns red as he struggles to get back up, but I pounce, crouching above him.

"Oink for me," I order.

"I'll kill you!" he roars, reaching for his whip. I laugh and slide a knife from my side, the sound lost in the rumble of thunder. I grab his meaty hand and hold it down before I plunge the blade in hard, pinning it to the floor as he bellows. His eyes bulge as he struggles below me, his blood pooling under his palm. "Red blood, red as stone, red blood on the bone," I sing as I pull another blade. "Where to next, piggy? Should we carve off some fat?"

"You're insane," he wheezes, tears springing into his eyes.

"You have no idea, little piggy." I giggle as I drag the blade across his fat belly and slice. He screams, but I keep going, spraying myself and the walls with blood. I feel it dripping down my mask as he fights, his hand tearing more with each struggle.

Lifting the blade, I inspect my handiwork before grinning up at Ember. I expect to see terror in her eyes, but if anything, she seems pleased. It seems our girl is embracing who she truly is. The insanity and darkness that lives within us now lives in her. The demons we let out to play dance like shadows on her shoulders.

"Little piggy, little piggy," I taunt as I drag the blade up and press it against his neck as he shakes his head, sobbing. "Bye-bye, piggy." I stab it down, slicing through his artery, wanting him to stop making sounds, stop hurting children, and die.

I watch the blood pool below him. Pressing my hand into the warm liquid, I drag it down my mask and then stand, turning to the wall and writing, "Tell me your nightmares."

I just finish the last letter when I hear footsteps.

I look up with a snarl as another guard lumbers into the corridor, drawn by the noise the thunder couldn't cover. This one is faster, however, and he yanks out his whip, letting it soar through the air. I turn cold as it hits Ember, catching her by surprise. She smashes into the wall, a scream of pain echoing behind her mask, and I'm on my feet before I'm conscious of it. I'm not fast enough, and it flies through the air again, but it doesn't hit its mark. This time, her hand snaps out and wraps around the end of the whip. Seemingly as shocked as I am, she holds on as it cuts into her hand with a strength I never expected. Her blood hits the floor like a declaration, and her eyes turn to me as if she's ensuring I'm okay. Then, with a wicked grin, she winds the end around her hand and tugs, pulling the guard closer.

He snarls, fighting her, and she skids across the floor, but she holds the end firmly. When I reach her side, she grabs me. I help her hoist the end of the whip over my shoulder and then plunge to the floor in a swift movement he can't prepare for. He goes flying, hitting the floor before his body is dragged toward us. Releasing the whip, she steps around me, grabbing a blade from my side as she goes. Before he can get to his feet, she throws it. It embeds in his chest— not deep enough to kill but enough to slow him down. He climbs to his feet using the wall despite the wound. Snarling, he keeps his eyes locked on her, and that's all it takes to seal his fate. With a wink at her, I run at him and turn in the air, slamming my boot into the knife in his chest until it sinks to the hilt.

He falls to the floor, dying slowly as I look at my girl once more, my chest heaving.

We both turn when there's a scream and see the once sleeping guard come sailing from the room, hitting the opposite wall. The sound of his neck snapping is loud. Club wanders from the room, looking between us and the bodies.

"He woke up," is all he says, making me laugh, but then my eyes land on Ember again and the bloody cut on her arm.

I step closer to her, watching her eyes widen as I lean down and drag my tongue along it, tasting her blood. "Heart," she warns. My hands land on her hips, dragging her closer. I push our masks up and press my lips to hers, letting her taste her blood as I back her up, only for her to hit Club. His hands bracket mine as we hold her between us, and her moans fill the air. Bloodlust runs through me and into her as she tugs at my clothes to get closer, making me hard as hell.

Diamond's whistle cuts through the air, and we break apart to see him and Spade standing in the open gate, looking at the bodies with a grin. "I see you already had some fun. Come on. We found the warden and other guards. Let's finish this."

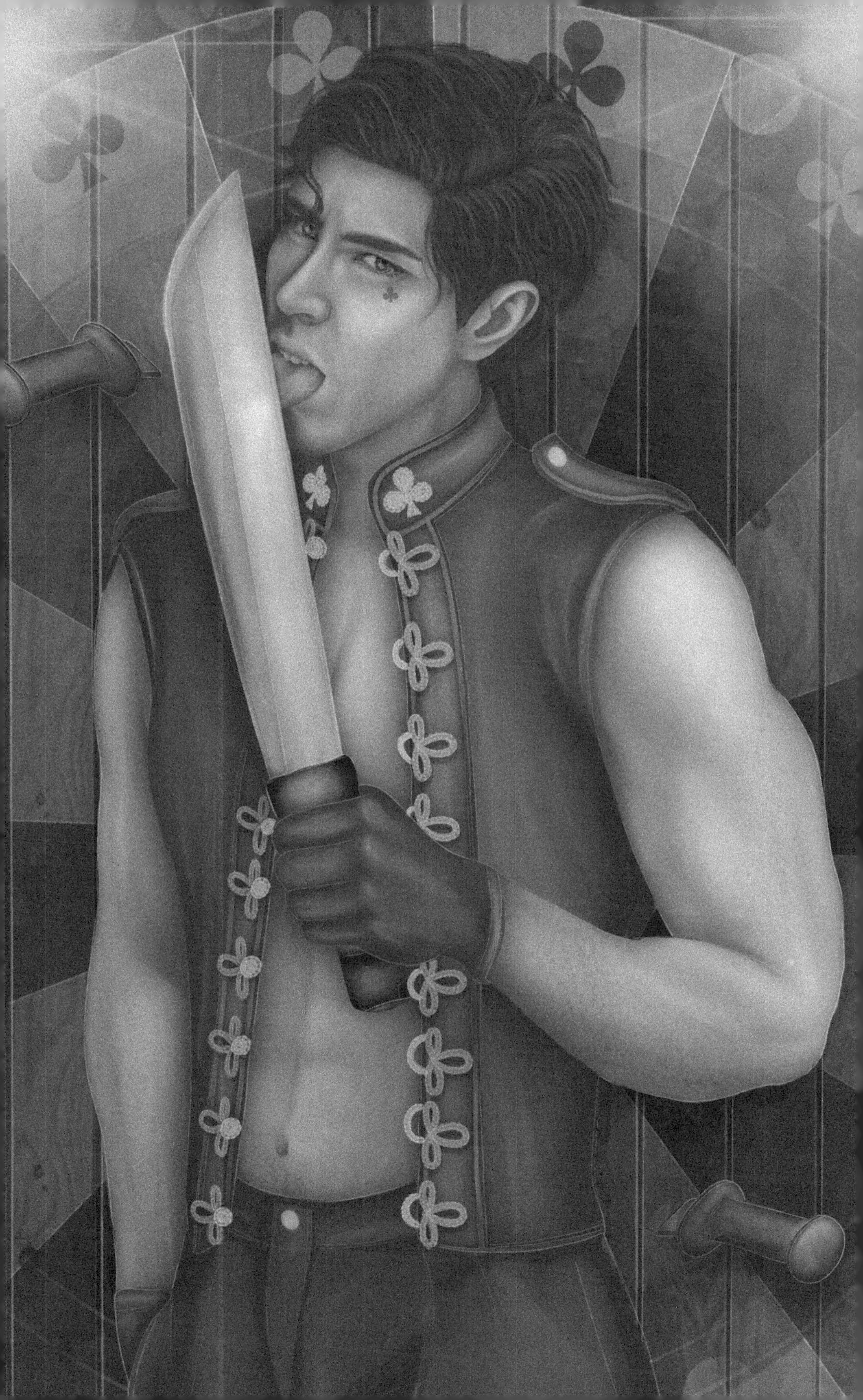

TWENTY-THREE

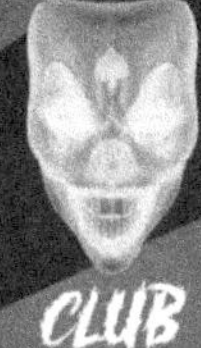

The blood on the walls creates a horrifying image. Perhaps we should have been cleaner about this so the kids don't see it when we free them, but part of me thinks they've seen far worse. They already know the evils of the world. A little blood from their monsters won't hurt them any further. It will probably make them feel better.

When Heart and Ember were busy with the guard, I peeked into the room closest to me and felt my heart drop. The boy from the cirque was in bad shape, but some of the kids here are even worse off. It's a wonder he escaped, especially with such prisonlike doors. There has to be at least ten kids shoved into every room, each so malnourished, their bones poke through their skin. They cower away from our approach, not understanding we're here to save them. No kid should ever have to see such evil. Those who do, well . . . I suppose they end up at the cirque, just as I did.

Unlike Heart and Spade, I didn't come to the cirque as a child. I was already an adult shaped by evil. My card came when I helped an old woman who was being mistreated on the street by a group of rowdy teens. I didn't know it then, didn't understand the meaning, but Hilda always had her ways of looping someone in. She saw something in me, saw the monster behind my eyes, and offered me the key to my cage—one of my own making.

Where I come from, there aren't opportunities for kids. You either get out or you become a part of the seedy underworld of drugs and crime. I didn't get out. I couldn't, not when my mother was trapped there. I did what I needed to protect her for as long as I could. She'd been owned by an asshole of a man, a pimp named Georgiano who sat at the very top of the pyramid in my city. You didn't fuck with him, and if you were owned by him, you could never be free unless you paid to be. Five hundred thousand dollars cash. That was how much it cost to free my mother. See, she was one of his favorites. I suppose I was lucky that he allowed her to raise me despite her job as a prostitute. I guess I should have been grateful when he acted like a bit of a father and taught me how to survive.

Instead, it only filled me with anger.

I saw the way my mother was treated, so as soon as I was old enough to understand, I started saving. At seven, I was doing odd jobs here and there. By twelve, I was running drugs. When I turned nineteen, I had my own drug ring, and I saved up enough to pay the freedom cost for my mother. I'd gone to Georgiano with a shopping bag full of cash and tossed it at his feet. He only looked down at the money with raised brows.

"For my mother," I declared, a cocky teenager who had no idea how unfair the world could be. "For her freedom."

Georgiano looked me in the eyes, gold rings on every finger. The bastard was fond of lions and had a gold one on a chain around his neck. The idiot thought lions were the alphas of the animal kingdom. He never once realized how appropriate it was that male lions don't do anything but sit at the top, lazy and fat, while lionesses do all the work. Still, he was large and had a whole system at his beck and call.

"I bet you saved a long time for this day," Georgiano said, calm as usual. He lit a cigar and rolled it between his teeth. "Very well, Heath. You've earned it." He gestured for someone to grab her like everything was well. I foolishly believed him. Gangs have their own code, and a deal is a deal, but Georgiano spent years holding my mother hostage, and despite her being his favorite, selfish men don't like letting go of their belongings.

I watched them drag my mother out, her eyes bloodshot from whatever drug they gave her. Most days, she was too blissed out to know I was there. Sometimes, she looked at me and cried, apologizing for what I must face. I never blamed her. I never once thought she could control it, but I could for both of us.

"You've grown up well, Heath," Georgiano said as he came down from his throne and caressed the side of my mother's face. She didn't jerk away because of the drugs in her system. "But there is one lesson you have yet to learn."

I'd been foolish. I stood taller, thinking he was about to impart some knowledge I could use on the streets. "What's that?" I asked confidently.

Georgiano looked me in the eyes. He looked me in the fucking eyes as he pulled a gun from nowhere. "Life isn't fair, and people like you don't get what you want."

I had no time to react. He pulled the trigger before I could shout. I watched my mother's body collapse to the floor, her eyes open and unseeing. My only consolation was that she didn't feel it. She had enough drugs in her system that she never even knew. I screamed and leapt toward Georgiano, but his guards caught me.

"Throw him out," he ordered as if it were another Tuesday. I suppose for him, it was. "Make sure he increases his percentage to me. If he can save up this money, then he has more to give."

They threw me out and thought that would be it. They thought I'd just accept that. I never even got to bury my mother. I never knew what they did with her body. I returned three days later with every gun and blade I could find and killed my way through his compound. They nearly killed me, but in the end, I stood in the midst of their bodies, looking down at Georgiano with the joker card clutched in my hand. I'd been swaying on my feet, losing too much blood, when

Diamond, Heart, and Spade came for me. I felt our connection then just as I feel it now. It's an awareness, a life link, but I never found my mother's body.

Now there's another: Ember. Her link is just as bright as ours.

"Club," Ember says. I was so lost in my memories, I didn't even realize I'd stopped walking and now stood at the base of the stairs. "Are you okay?"

I meet her eyes and see genuine concern there. If anyone would understand, it's her. She was an adult too, just like I was.

"This place reminds me of . . . bad memories," I admit.

I slept in a threadbare room, tossed aside while my mother was expected to work. When she was finished for the day, then she was allowed to care for me. I'd been as malnourished as these kids, a baby struggling to survive. She hadn't been able to breastfeed due to the drugs in her system, and I suppose she felt it would taint me in some way because of what she did before she came to see me. When I was older, she would sneak in bits of her own food to feed me. We both survived as best as we could.

Ember was a few stairs above me, but at my words, she comes back down and grips the sides of my face. Her hands are covered in blood, but it doesn't matter. It's not the worst thing I've suffered.

"Do you need a minute?" she asks, looking earnestly into my eyes. I can only see her bright, pretty eyes through her mask, eyes that never should have known the pain she has. I wish I could take away her nightmares, but if I could, she never would have found the cirque. Our nightmares are what make us who we are. They brought us together.

Nightmares are what created us, and nightmares are what feed us.

"No," I murmur before I pull her hand from my face and lift my mask just enough to press a kiss against her bloody knuckles. "No, let's get these kids out of here."

She nods. "Later, you can tell me your nightmares and I'll chase them away."

My heart squeezes. "As I will do to yours."

The queen. Our queen.

She takes my hand and leads me up the last of the stairs, and we enter yet another nightmare, but we can face this one together.

I'm not alone this time.

TWENTY-FOUR

Club's face is hidden behind his mask, but I can still see the darkness in his eyes. This place brings something inside him to the surface, and I wonder what brought him to the cirque. I only know hints from the cards. I haven't asked any of them about it, figuring they'll tell me when they are ready, but I see the ghosts that haunt Club, just as there are ghosts that hound the others. I suppose we're all haunted and that's how we arrived in Cirque Obscurum. I'd like to wipe away their darkness, but it's a part of them now, just as mine is.

The first time I saw them hunt, I flinched away from the blood. Now, in this building, I relish the feeling of sticky, drying blood on my hands and the fear in the guards' eyes who kneel before Diamond, Heart, and Spade as we reach the top of the stairs. These people are true monsters, the kind that shouldn't be allowed to live, let alone be around children. I don't know how many children there are yet or how young they are, but each of these men will pay for what they have done.

"Which one is the warden?" I ask, my voice thick with fury. "Which one calls the shots?"

Diamond looks at me before gesturing to a woman at the end of the line. The others must be guards, but it's clear this one is something else. She's tall and limber, her graying hair pulled back in a severe bun. Even as she kneels before us, she doesn't look afraid, her cool gray eyes hard and unwavering. She doesn't fear us, but she should.

"What's your name?" I ask, standing over her. When she keeps her lips pressed together, I pull the blade from my hip and hold it against her cheek. "I said, what's your name?"

She meets my eyes with the air of somebody used to being in control. It's the same look my husband had. "Fuck you."

Her voice is accented, telling me she's from somewhere outside the States. European maybe?

"Are you a mother, Fuck You?" I ask, pretending like her venom doesn't bother me. "Are any of these children yours?"

When she doesn't answer, I swipe the knife across her face, cutting her cheek. It's not deep, but it's enough to bleed and hurt. She grunts in pain, but when she meets my eyes again, she doesn't reach up to wipe the dripping blood away. I cut the other side for shits and giggles. A woman doing this to children is some other kind of evil. I expect this from men, but from a woman? I guess the maternal instincts in me can't fathom it.

"No," she growls. "None of them are mine."

I nod. "I thought so. What sort of mother could mistreat so many children?"

"She makes them call her Mother," one of the guards pipes up, clearly thinking he will survive if he cooperates with us.

I turn my head toward him. "Oh?"

He's younger than the others. "Please," he says when I meet his eyes. "This is my first night. I was going to go to the police in the morning."

"Shut up, Stephen," one of the others growls, but Club slams the hilt of his knife against his nose to shut him up.

I straighten and move over to the man. "Tonight is your first night?"

"Please," he begs. "I didn't know what this place was. I just needed the money. I have a kid. She's sick. Needs medicine. Please, this isn't my fault."

I squat down in front of him, studying his eyes. I see truth there, but I can never be too sure. He looks broken by what he's seen. "Do you have a picture of her in your wallet?"

He nods vigorously, so Spade reaches into his back pocket and pulls it out before flipping it open. He thumbs through the little plastic flaps before handing it to me. I look down at a picture of a bright, blonde-haired girl. She can't be older than seven, her toothy grin sporting gaps where she lost her teeth to the tooth fairy.

"What's her name?" I ask, flipping to find a picture of the same little girl, now bald and sitting in a hospital bed. She hugs her dad, both smiling for the person behind the camera.

"Mary," he rasps, his eyes watering. "Her name is Mary."

Nodding, I slide the wallet into his breast pocket and pat it. I stand and gesture to Club. He comes forward and cuts the ties holding the man's wrists together. He gapes in surprise as Club helps him to his feet.

"I suggest you tell no one what you saw here," I warn him, "and don't worry about calling the cops. We'll take care of it."

He nods and hesitates. "The keys for the cells are in the warden's pocket. She keeps them on her at all times." He takes off down the stairs. I wait until the door slams closed to focus on the others.

"I have kids too," another guard cajoles. "Jimmy and Katrina would be upset if I don't come home."

"Would they?" I ask, narrowing my eyes. "And how long have you worked here?" He clamps his lips shut, and I nod. "That's what I thought. Somehow, I think Jimmy and Katrina will be fine without their evil father."

Without me saying a word, Club swipes his blade across the

guard's neck. The sounds he makes echo around us as he collapses and bleeds out. We're silent as the noises die away.

"Who are you people?" the woman asks, her eyes still narrowed, completely unfazed by the sight of her guard dying. That tells me all that I need to know. She doesn't care about life, adults and children alike.

I move over to her and bop her nose with my bloody hand. She leans away with a look of disgust.

"Who are we?" I repeat, tilting my head. "I suppose we're your worst nightmare."

She snorts. "No. You're not."

I see ghosts in her eyes. I often hear that people who have been hurt will hurt others, but this woman is too far gone to save. We choose what we become. We either let the evil that hurt us destroy our soul and make us the very same thing or we do something about it. There's no helping someone like this, and even if we could, I wouldn't want to. The kids in those rooms deserve better. They deserve for their demons to die.

"Kill them," I say. Heart and Diamond take out the other two guards, leaving only the warden. "Are you afraid of death?"

The woman tips her chin up. "I have died many times over. Death doesn't frighten me."

I want this woman to suffer for what she's done, but she's as unmoving as a boulder. I want her to scream, I want her to cry, but something tells me she won't do any of those things. Something tells me she'll go to her death without complaint, probably the same way she faced life—cold and uncaring.

"Allow me," Diamond murmurs as he kneels beside her. He doesn't brandish a knife. All he does is look into her eyes. They stare at each other for what seems like forever before Diamond whispers, "Tell me your nightmares."

Her lips part, and I can tell she struggles with her answer, as if she doesn't want to speak the words. Ultimately, Diamond is his own beast, and the word slips from her lips in a barely audible whisper.

"Fire."

Heart giggles. "Being burned alive is the worst way to go, I hear." He tucks his knife away. "I'll go grab some gasoline."

He disappears downstairs as Diamond looks over at me. "There are no children up here." He reaches into the warden's pocket and pulls out a ring of keys. "You three go get them out. Heart and I will take care of this one."

I look at the woman again, at the way she stares unflinchingly at me. Anger fills me again. It's not enough. *It's not enough!*

Without thinking, I swing. My fist connects with her jaw, and she goes down with a gasp and a grunt of pain. "That's for Noah," I spit. I jerk her back up by her hair. "And this one is for the other children." I grab her arm and twist, breaking it just as Roger once did to me. This time, she lets out a satisfying cry of pain as I drop her arm and kick her down. "Evil fucking bitch."

No one stops me. No one keeps me from hurting her. Each of them nods in understanding before we separate. We pass Heart on the way downstairs, two large metal containers of gasoline in his hands. He whistles a happy circus tune and grins at us as we pass.

"I hope you brought the marshmallows," he says. "We're going to have one hell of a fire."

Watching him climb the stairs, I realize I love that man.

There are ten cells total. As we unlock each one, Spade encourages the children to follow him out of the house while Club counts them. Some of the rooms have ten children. Some have even more. A few are empty. They are all too skinny and frail. Spade has to carry a couple of them because they are too weak to move on their own.

"Fuck," I curse once we reach sixty kids. "Dr. Louis is going to be busy."

One of the rooms holds only a single kid, an older girl. Her eyes are hollow as we open the door, and she scrambles back.

"We're not going to hurt you," I tell her, holding my hands out. "We're getting you and your friends out of here. We'll take you somewhere safe."

"You promise?" she croaks. As she lifts her head, I get a good look at the bruises around her neck in the shape of a hand.

"I promise." I nod, fighting my anger so I don't scare her. "We're going to burn this hellhole down."

She nods and hesitates, tears forming in her eyes. "I can't walk. I . . . I need my wheelchair."

My heart twists. Fucking monsters!

I kneel and meet her eyes. "I don't know where that is right now, but we can carry you out. Would that be okay?" She hesitates when Spade steps around the corner and kneels with me. "This is Spade. He can help you." I notice the small, grungy stuffed animal clutched in her hands. This girl has to be fifteen at least, maybe older if she's been malnourished for too long. When she moves, I realize it's an animal I recognize. "Spade has a tiger."

Her eyes widen. "A real one?"

Spade nods. "A real one. Her name is Freedom. Would you like to meet her?"

"Yes," she murmurs, and then without any more hesitation, she reaches up for him to help her.

Spade lifts her without strain and carries her out, all while telling her about the other animals he trains and works with. We'll have to find her a wheelchair. I didn't ask why she needed it, but something tells me she came to this place in it, and they treated her like trash.

"That's all of them," Club says as he comes around the corner. "We checked the whole house just in case. They are all outside, and I've already called the cirque. They are bringing out one of the trucks so we can take them all back."

I nod and grab his hand. "Then let's burn this place down."

As we walk through the entryway, Diamond forces the warden to the base of the stairs. She's tied up, her eyes wide and panicked now in a way they weren't before. Heart giggles as he dumps the rest of his gasoline on top of her.

"Stop! You can't do this! Someone help me!" she screams, struggling to free herself, but there isn't much she can do while tied up with a broken arm.

Her cries make me smile, and when I step outside of the house, I see some of the children smiling at the sight too. This is for them.

Heart comes strolling out, but he leaves the front door open so we all get a good look at the warden as she screams and struggles. She's framed like a fucking masterpiece.

"Who would like to do the honors?" Diamond asks, pulling out a box of matches.

At first, no one volunteers, but after a few seconds of silence, a boy limps forward. He's probably sixteen, but my guesses are skewed due to their abuse. His eyes are hollow, and he's covered in dirt, but he stands tall despite his limp as he takes the matches from Diamond. He pauses before the entryway, watching the warden scream.

Another child walks up and puts her hand on his shoulder, and then another, followed by another. Eventually, all of the children who are able to walk stand with him, offering comfort as he strikes the match.

"For Juliet," he rasps, holding the match before him.

"For Juliet," the children repeat, and then other names are voiced, honoring them—Molly, Darah, Brendon, William, Gary, and Veronica. The list goes on and on.

He throws the match. We watch the house go up in flames, the blaze rushing toward the warden. Her screams grow more shrill, more pained, as the entire place begins to burn. We view it together, the evil being engulfed by the inferno. We're silent, listening to the crackling of the flames and the sudden, abrupt stop of the warden's screams just as the truck pulls up.

"Time to go," Diamond commands, turning to help the kids into the large trailer we usually use to transport animals. It's not ideal, but there are so many of them, we couldn't get them out quickly any other way.

The boy lingers as he watches the flames, but the others follow Diamond. I step up to rest my hand on his shoulder.

"Who's Juliet?" I ask him, staring at the destruction.

"My sister," he rasps before turning to look at me. There is something so broken and haunted in his gaze, it wrecks me. "She was my five-year-old sister."

My chest squeezes. "I'm sorry we weren't fast enough."

"You got here," he croaks. "That's what matters."

When he starts to cry, I wrap my arms around him, offering comfort as he lets it out. My own tears spill for him, for all of them, and for all they've lost. I hope we can help them and give them what they need.

As I assist him into the back of the trailer and climb up with them, I catch a glimpse of Heart running toward the fire with a bag of marshmallows in his hand. Some of the children giggle as he whoops and starts shoving them onto a stick.

"Who wants one?" he shouts. "Marshmallows for everyone!"

More smiles follow the giggles, and a part of me falls even more in love with the man, with all of them, as they gently help the children and take complete care to make them comfortable.

When they climb into the back of the trailer with us, Heart with his massive stick full of roasted marshmallows of various shades and Spade with the young girl in his arms, we settle in for the ride.

"Where are we going?" the boy closest to me asks, his cheeks still tear streaked. "Where are you taking us?"

"To the cirque," I tell him. "We'll help you get better, and then when you're ready, you can choose to stay or go. Either way, you'll be safe. We'll make sure of it."

He nods and then leans his head against my shoulder. "Thanks, ma'am," he says, but the way he says it, it almost sounds like "Mom." My hand flutters to my stomach. I'd almost been a mother once. How convenient that the cirque is giving me the opportunity to be one to these children.

No card, but a call all the same.

Diamond's eyes meet mine over the heads of the children clustered around us, each of them exhausted but relieved. Something passes between us, but I can't name it. He almost looks . . . angry, but something tells me it's not directed at me. Whatever demons Diamond carries are great.

I wonder how magnificent he is when his beast comes out to play.

I wonder how well it will play with mine.

TWENTY-FIVE

My girl gets the kids settled in, checking on them twice to make sure no one has any immediate needs. Dr. Louis helped them all as best as he could. Many need time to heal and lots of meals, and we'll offer them that here, giving them a sanctuary until they are ready to fly free if they want.

It seems it's not enough for my queen though. She's still angry, still wound up as she paces in her tent. We watch her, taking in the glorious picture she paints. We feel it too, the pain and fury from that place. Even the flames can't tame the horrors we saw there, but she was magnificent tonight. Watching her hurt that warden was a show all in itself, and she was its puppet master.

It probably wouldn't be appropriate to tell her I was hard while watching her cut into the woman or that I almost came when the flames turned into screams, but when her eyes meet mine, there is something wild in them I understand better than most—madness with no outlet.

It's why I do what I do. It's why I kill. Why I hunt. Why I hang above crowds and offer death-defying stunts.

Our girl needs an outlet.

I prowl her way. She's too busy pacing to realize how close I am until I step into her path, our bodies pressing together. She stumbles backward, but I capture her and pull her closer. "Queen," I purr, licking her mask before I reach her ear. "Do you want to play with me?"

She hesitates, frozen between what she knows is right and what she feels. It's a fine line most people walk, balancing between what they know they should do and what they want to do. Usually the latter loses, but not with me. It always wins.

Biting her ear, I grin when she gasps. "Play with me, Queen. Let out all that anger. Let it be free or it'll rot your insides. There's nobody left to kill tonight, so let's fuck instead."

She startles at my bold words, her eyes wide as I pull back. "Heart…"

"Don't want to play with me, Queen?" I hum, tilting her chin up with my finger as my other hand drags down her body. "Or don't want to admit you want to? Tonight, you can let go. You embraced the nightmare inside you, and you hurt the woman and liked it." Her eyes blow wide when she realizes I noticed. "You liked it, and it wasn't enough. You need more. I'll be your outlet for tonight."

"Heart," Diamond warns, concerned that I'm pushing her too far.

"No, she needs the shove," I snap as I move closer again, my other hand grabbing her ass. "Don't you? Or you'd hide away and let it destroy you, worried about how you *should* be rather than what you *want* to be. Didn't anybody tell you, Ember, that at the circus, you can be whatever you want? I want to be yours."

Her hand hits my chest, and I see flames burning in her gaze, but something holds her back—something keeps her locked away from me even though I'm pushing. Pulling her mask up, I stare into her bloodstained face and let her see the raw truth in my gaze.

"Take it out on me," I tell her honestly, licking her cheek. "I can handle it. Rip me to pieces if you need to, Queen. I'm here, and I'm yours."

"What if I hurt you?" she whispers in horror and hunger.

"I'd like it," I admit with a grin. "They won't let you kill me though." I nod my head toward the others who are watching, showing no signs of leaving anytime soon.

When her head turns back to me, I see the decision in her eyes. Reaching up, she pulls her mask down, her eyes darkening further. Gone is the sweet, innocent Ember who was worried about hurting me, and in her place is the beast that was born from nightmares.

"You want to play, Heart?" she purrs, her voice lower and filled with a hunger that makes mine grow. My dick swells in my pants as she presses against me, dragging her hand up my chest to grab my chin just like I did her. "Then let's play. Get on your knees for me."

She pushes me down, and I sink to my knees for her, my mask firmly in place as she pets my chin softly. "Diamond," she calls. "Whip."

There's a moment of hesitation, and then the whip lands at her feet. She bends down and picks it up, letting the coil slip through her hand. The sight makes my cock twitch, and a moan escapes my lips. My body braces, expecting pain, wanting everything she will give me.

"You want me to hurt you, don't you, Heart? Despite it all, you'd thank me for it." Her words caress my body like silk, leaving me panting, and she hasn't even touched me yet. This girl might have been weak once, a victim, but there is nothing left of her.

Not anymore.

This is our queen.

This is our nightmare.

"Yes," I answer. "I want anything you'll give me."

The whip lashes out, slashing across my chest. I hiss in pleasure as it tears through my shirt. The fabric gapes open, and she moves again, hitting it with the whip a second time, the tip lashing my chest. A stinging welt rises, and it has my hips tilting forward, seeking the pleasure she offers.

She snarls in annoyance at my lack of pained reaction and loops the whip around my neck while grabbing one of my daggers. "I want to see all of you. I want you to be weak for me. I want to use you."

The whip curls around my neck, tightening slowly with each word, and then the dagger slices down. We both watch my shirt flutter to the ground, leaving my chest bare for her eyes. She feasts on me, her gaze making my heart race. The touch of her eyes on my skin almost has me spilling in my pants.

"Queen—" I start to taunt her, but she tightens the whip, yanking until I'm silenced, my air cut off. Her head tilts as she watches me. I don't struggle. I can feel my face changing color as my lungs scream, but I let her, keeping my eyes on hers without flinching. I'd let her kill me and fuck my dead body if that was what she wanted, and I'd fucking do it happily.

If she wants my life, then it's hers.

If she wants my air, then she can take it.

If she wants me to carve out my heart, then I'll do it with a smile on my face.

Black edges my vision, but my smile doesn't waver.

"Ember," someone warns, but we ignore them as I grab the whip and pull it closer to her, tightening it even more. It hurts so fucking good I roll my hips.

She watches me, drinking in my reaction, and when I'm about to pass out, she releases it, letting the whip slacken. I draw in deep breaths, coughing slightly as my eyes water. My heart races and my lungs ache with the sudden pressure, but my first word makes her laugh darkly.

"More."

"More? Why would I give you what you want?" she retorts. "There is something I want from you. If you want me to turn this fury into fire, then stoke it." Stepping back, she perches on one of the crates in her tent and spreads her legs.

I moan shamelessly, wanting what she's insinuating. "Please," I whisper.

"Beg for me. Beg for it," she orders as she pushes her pants down and strips off her shirt, leaving her naked for my eyes. There are groans from the others, but I ignore them. She's mine tonight.

Mine. All mine.

I drink in every raised scar on her perfect skin and every soft curve before my eyes land on her pussy. It glistens for me, so pink and ripe, begging to be eaten as she parts her thighs wider.

"Fuck," Spade mutters.

"Please, Queen," I beg, dropping to my hands and knees as I bow for her. "Please let me touch you. Let me taste you. Let me burn in the fire we started."

She watches me for a moment, and then her legs spread farther apart.

"Crawl to me," she orders.

I do so gladly, not stopping until my hands slide up her legs to her bare hips, and I press my face to her pussy, inhaling.

She forces my head up. "Did I say you could touch?"

"Please," I implore. Using the dagger in her hand, she pushes my mask up until it sits on my head, and then she drags the sharp edge along my lips. I feel them split, and my hands tighten on her hips, drawing her closer as I pout for her. She watches blood drip down my chin before leaning down and licking it away.

"Make me come, Heart. Make me come, and I'll play with you again. I'll give you what we both know you need," she whispers, telling me this isn't all for her. It's for me too. She saw my madness and realized I need this as well.

I don't waste a moment, even with my bleeding lips. My hands slide under her ass and lift as I open her for my mouth. I seal my lips around her cunt, and I suck until she groans. Chuckling, I rub my lips along her throbbing clit and then down, licking around her hole until her hand grips my head. Her nails sink into my hair until sharp pain spears into my skull, and my hips hit the crate she's on, rubbing against it as she pushes me closer to her pussy. She's all I can taste, see, and smell, and I fucking love it.

I want more.

I want to fucking drown in her.

Thrusting my tongue into her, I drink down her taste, licking up every drop as she rolls hips her hips, grinding her cunt into my face. My lips sting in the best fucking way, and that pain mixed with the pleasure of tasting her has me humping the crate until it hurts.

I circle her clit until she cries out, pressing her hips closer, then I flatten my tongue and slide it down, circling her hole before dipping lower and slipping into her pretty ass. Her gasp tells me she likes it, and I silently promise to bury myself in this pretty hole later to hear that sound again.

Switching my hold on her ass to one hand, I slip my other between us and thrust two fingers inside her, filling her channel as she cries out. I curl them, rubbing fast as my tongue lashes her clit in a brutal, harsh rhythm until she drips all over my face. Adding another finger, I stretch her and press them deeper. It must hurt, yet she clenches around me, silently begging for more.

Wrapping my lips around her clit, I suck hard, and she practically comes away from the crate. I slip my thumb between her parted cheeks, pressing against her pretty asshole and slipping inside—a promise.

Rolling my eyes up her body, I marvel at the view this sinner is getting. Her mask is still in place still, and her pretty, pink-tipped breasts heave, matching the blush spreading across them.

She's close, and I want to see it. I want to burn it into my brain so when my nightmares come knocking, I can replace them with this. It's as close to heaven as I will ever get.

I coat my fingers in her pleasure instead of blood, and I coat my lips in a silent promise instead of taunts.

I'm hers.

I press my thumb deeper as I close my teeth over her clit, and with a scream, she comes. Her thighs clamp around my head until I can't breathe, and her channel clenches tightly on my fingers as she gushes around me, her legs jerking. I lick her through it, watching every single reaction of her body until she slumps, her pussy still fluttering around my fingers.

I reluctantly pull them free and sit back, waiting for my next instruction as her eyes open and lock on me. Leaning down closer, she sweeps her gaze greedily over my face, making me sit up taller.

"Say thank you, Heart. Thank me for letting you make me come," she orders, her blade pressed to my dripping chin.

"Thank you, my queen. Thank you for letting me make you come."

Grinning, she rips her mask up as she lowers to her knees before me, her lips crashing onto mine as her hands rove down my body and grip my dick. Humming into my mouth, she pulls away slightly. "If I wrap the whip around you here, will you come for me?"

Holy fucking shit.

I swear I see stars.

"God, please," I beg, thrusting into her hand.

She yanks the whip closer and wraps it around my cock, slowly tightening it. It hurts so fucking good, yet I can't stop myself from rocking into it, my lips seeking hers. Our tongues battle as she strokes me with the whip, making me gasp until I can't take it. I'm so wound up from tasting her that when she tightens it again, I bellow into her mouth and fall into her as I spill across her hand and the whip. She licks my face as I come.

"Good boy," she praises, and then she loosens the whip as I fall farther into her.

All the fury and pain are gone. All that's left is pleasure.

Pleasure she controls.

She pushes me to my knees and grips my chin, kissing me solidly. "Thank you for understanding," she whispers just for me. "For giving me an outlet." She kisses me again and gets to her feet, looking down at me as I kneel, panting for her.

"Anything for you," I say without hesitation.

Her smile makes it all worthwhile. She grabs the whip once more and heads past me, over to Diamond, then tosses it at his feet with a cocky smirk. He watches her with his eyebrow raised. "Next time, you're using it on me," she orders. With that, she grabs her toiletry bag and heads out of her tent.

All of us stare after her. Groaning, I roll onto my back, sprawling on the floor.

"I'm in love," I declare.

Maybe I should feel horrified about what I did with Heart last night, but I don't. He wanted it, I wanted it, and it didn't get out of hand thanks to the others' presence. I'll admit I blushed hard this morning when I saw them at breakfast, but they treated me like nothing was different.

They accept me as I am. In fact, they like it, especially Heart.

He wanted more, and maybe one day, I'll fall with him, letting him welcome me into the darkness. After all, last night was just a taste—one that left me awake all night remembering. Even today, my body is sensitive, flushed, and covered with goose bumps. These men have changed everything. They awoke something inside me.

Shaking off my thoughts, I check on the kids. Dr. Louis is with them, and they are resting and eating, which is good. I don't want them to feel trapped or scrutinized, so I leave them in peace. Then I head to Hilda. Her tent has quickly become my second home. As I step inside, the usual scents wrap around me welcomingly, relaxing all my tense muscles as I stride over to what has become my chair.

She's waiting like usual, always knowing when I'm coming.

She watches me, her eyes narrowing. "Something in you has changed."

I blink, paling slightly. Does she know what I did yesterday? That I took a life? That I fully embraced the cirque?

She gives me a slow, understanding smile. "That's good. You're nearly ready."

"Ready for what?" I ask softly.

"You'll see." She lays out the cards and nods at me. "Read them to me. Let's practice this morning."

I read the cards over and over. Each time, I get closer to the truth, and when I leave the tent, I begin to understand what she meant— I'm almost ready to take over for her.

"Where are we going?" I ask Club once more.

He spares me a grin as he drives, and I roll my eyes and settle back for the ride. He found me outside my tent and told me to come with him. I accepted because, well, what else do I have to do? Plus, I like spending time with him. I didn't expect him to steal Diamond's car or drive us away though. We pass the countryside and turn into a neighborhood, and I sit up taller as we head into town before parking on Main Street.

He gets out and heads around to my side, opening the door and offering me his hand, and it's only then I realize he's all dressed up. He's wearing a black waistcoat and a long shirt underneath with matching black slacks and shined shoes. He looks extremely handsome, and I feel very underdressed in my floral peasant dress.

I must be staring because his lips tip up. "Like what you see, Ember?"

I blush furiously and give him my hand. He helps me out and backs me into the door as it shuts.

"I'm glad," he says without waiting for my answer. "I dressed up for you."

He threads his fingers through mine and tugs me after him, and we walk along the sidewalk hand in hand. He smiles and nods his head at a few of the locals passing by, but they give us a wide berth. I feel eyes on us, and when I glance around, I notice nearly everyone has stopped what they are doing to watch us, marking us as outsiders. Club doesn't notice or doesn't care, whistling as we leisurely stroll past the quaint, little shops in the sunlight.

When we stop at the corner, a birch tree shading us, I tug him around to face me. "Is this a date?" I ask.

"And if it is?" he counters, a happy grin on his lips.

I can't fight my smile; his is just that infectious. Clearing my throat, I try to fight the giggle that wants to escape. "Then I'd ask where we are going."

Leaning in, he kisses my cheek. "Good girl. Come on. Today, we aren't freaks. We're just a couple on a date."

Holding my hand, he leads me through the little town. We window shop and sit in the park, enjoying the sunshine, talking, and just spending time together like all the other couples. When we get hungry, he escorts me to a diner on Main Street, but when we step inside, the whole place goes silent.

As the day passed, it became clear we'll never be anything but outcasts, and this only reminds us of that now. Every eye locks on us, the locals unwelcoming and distrustful.

"Mommy, are they the freaks?" a kid whispers.

The mother covers her kid's mouth and leans closer, keeping her eyes on us. "Yes. Don't talk to them."

Club sighs, noting all the unwelcoming stares and harsh whispers, and turns to me, his shoulders slumping. "I'm sorry, Ember. I really wanted to give you a normal day." He looks so crestfallen. I hate it. Unbothered by the stares, I cup his face and tilt it up, smiling at him.

"I don't need normal. I need you, just like this, nothing different. I'm happy when I'm with you. Screw them and their judgment. Let's go home and have fun instead. They don't deserve us. They don't deserve you." I raise my voice, looking around the diner. "They can stare, but we all know they are just jealous because our life is filled with fun and laughter because we're free."

His eyes widen, his mouth falling open before it shuts, and then the widest grin I have ever seen him wear lights up his face, reaching his eyes. "That's the best thing you've said all day."

I giggle as he reaches down, slipping one arm under my legs and the other across my back. He picks me up before turning and pushing the door open with his back. He laughs with me as he hurries back to the car and helps me in. Both of us ignore the whispers and stares. Let them hunger for what we have. Once he's in his seat, he reaches over and takes my hand, lifting it to kiss my knuckles.

"Let's be outcasts together, baby," he purrs.

"Together." I grin, happy and in love.

TWENTY-SEVEN

EMBER

I expect Club to drive back to the cirque. Instead, he pulls the car into a spot out of town that's clearly used by local teens for parking, if the dents in the gravel are anything to go by. There's no one here right now, but the tall hill gives us a nice view of the sunset and the grandeur of nature spread before it.

"Come on," Club says before kicking his door open.

I follow, climbing from the car and coming around to the front where he stands. Before I can ask what we're doing, he wraps his fingers around my hips and places me on the hood, then he climbs up after me. We sit so we're leaning against the windshield, our legs stretched out across the hood as we watch the sun slowly descend toward the horizon.

A blanket of peace falls over us until I breathe easier and deeper than I ever have.

"It's beautiful," I muse, my eyes locked on the way the sky slowly changes from blue to red to yellow, and then finally purple. The stars blink into existence shortly after, and the moon rises behind us. Sometimes I forget how truly exquisite our world is. I rest my head back against the windshield and absorb the cosmos. It's been so long since I've just been able to look up and enjoy them.

"Have you ever wished you were among them?" Club asks, his eyes on the night sky. "The stars, I mean."

"Yes," I admit with a small smile. "There were a few times when Roger locked me outside and made me sleep in the backyard." When Club turns his head toward me, I sigh. "I'm safe now, so it doesn't matter, but when I was out there, shivering, I often looked up at the stars and wished I could just . . . fly away. I wished I could be up there, safe and far away."

"What was his reason for locking you out?" he asks, his fingers clenching his knee in anger on my behalf.

"I don't remember really," I reply. "I think once was because I missed a spot while dusting, but to be honest, it could have been anything. Maybe I didn't cook dinner right. Maybe I didn't cook what he wanted. Maybe I spoke too long to the cashier at the grocery store. Maybe I didn't look nice enough that day. If I wasn't fast enough to greet him when he came home from work, I'd get some kind of punishment." I glance over at him, my lips turning up in a bitter smile as my eyes trace over his handsome face. "Truthfully, being locked out at night wasn't so bad, not compared to . . . well, you know."

His face contorts with anger. "You should have let us kill him."

I sigh once more, wishing the memory of my husband wouldn't ruin this moment like so many others. He feels far away right now, and that's how I want it. I don't want to live in the past forever. "It doesn't matter now. I'm safe. Besides, I'm here with you. This is all I need."

When I reach for his hand, he threads his fingers through mine without hesitation. The warmth of his calloused palm makes my heart race. It's such a gentle, innocent touch, yet I feel it down to my soul.

"You don't even know who I am," he murmurs, watching me closely.

"I know everything I need to know," I counter, "but you're welcome to tell me more."

He smiles. His face is normally stoic, but when he smiles, he's beautiful. His angular face demands to be touched, so I give into the urge and cup his sharp jawline before pressing my forehead to his.

"You're welcome to try to scare me, sword swallower," I whisper, "but I'm not afraid of you."

He chuckles, and the sound spears right through me. "Who says I want you to be afraid of me?" he asks, threading his hand into my hair and holding me against him as if he's worried I'll disappear. "I'd rather you fear losing me."

"I already do," I whisper. "All of you . . . the cirque. You're my home now, and I don't want to lose you." The threat from the cards flashes through my mind again, a looming sense of doom I still don't understand. Neither Hilda nor I have been able to find the answer, and I don't understand it. Sometimes, the cards can be so forthcoming, but other times, they are vague and mysterious.

"Good," he murmurs. "Then let me claim you. I don't want to talk about the past tonight. I'd much rather focus on our future, and mine is with you."

Club presses his lips to mine in a gentle kiss that surprises me. Our last encounter was fast and rough when we'd been trying to beat the clock before someone else walked in on us. Now, the kiss is encouraging and exploratory, as if he's searching for answers on my lips. It's so gentle, it threatens to break my heart, and I almost can't handle someone being so delicate with me, like I'm worth the effort.

I press my hand against his chest and slip it beneath his button-down shirt to stroke his muscles. The kiss deepens, and his other hand trails down my back to grip my ass and pull me closer to him, grinding me against his hard length. I moan into his mouth, and he swallows the sound. That's what breaks the dam inside me.

I throw all caution to the wind, despite being out in the middle of nowhere where anyone could drive by and see us at any moment. I want him. I want him right here. I want him right now. I want him to shove the darkness he keeps behind his wall deep inside me. I want him to destroy and remake me. I want to feel his knives on my skin, his tongue between my thighs, and his dick inside me.

"Club," I murmur into his mouth, and he pauses, sensing my need.

He grins against my lips. "Tell me what you want."

"You," I reply. "All of you."

His fingers release my hair and wrap around my throat, splaying across it before he squeezes gently. "How do you want me?"

"Deeply, darkly . . ." I rasp. "Dangerously."

He leans forward and nips my chin. "As you wish, Queen."

He flips us and shoves me down on the hood of the car, his body coming over mine. I hit the metal a little harder than I expected, but I hardly care, not when he reaches into his pocket and flips open a pocketknife. It's small compared to the ones he uses in his show, but it's wicked sharp, so sharp I know it could slice through skin like a scalpel.

"I like knives," he purrs, the metal catching on the moonlight.

"No shit." I wiggle beneath him, begging with my hips.

"Would you like it if I used it on you?" he asks, his eyes focusing on mine. "Would you like to bleed for me?"

I nod without a hint of shame. Even now, the thought makes my channel clench, and his fingers tighten around my throat.

"The others won't like the marks I leave on you," he admits. "They'll want to add their own."

He lowers the knife and presses it gently against my collarbone. There's a tiny sting before he leans down and traces whatever mark he left on me with his tongue. I jerk beneath him and groan. When the knife trails down to the top of my dress and cuts the material without effort, I practically purr, my thighs rubbing together. He cuts a long line down until my dress hangs open and I'm bare.

"You're so beautiful when you're like this," he muses, leaning up to get a better look at me.

"Like what?" I ask breathlessly, needing more.

His eyes meet mine. "Full of darkness." His eyes are black pools, his own darkness dancing in his gaze, begging to be let out. "I liked it when your mouth was wrapped around my cock, Ember. This time, I won't leave you wanting."

He slides down the hood of the car until he can stand, then he grabs my thighs and pulls me to the edge of the hood, my ass hanging off the shiny metal. I watch as he kneels before me, but I tense when he holds the knife between my thighs. I've had knives near my pussy before, and it wasn't a fun time. I'm covered in scars, and I'm no different down there, but he doesn't seem to notice as he leans down and presses the flat of the blade against my clit. He doesn't cut, but the cold steel shoots through me and I gasp. I don't move though, afraid he'll hurt me.

"Tame your fear, Queen," he murmurs. "You have nothing to fear here. Not from me, never from me."

I try, but my past threatens to come up through my throat. My heart kicks wildly in my chest, and my body is so tense, my shoulders hurt.

"My real name is Heath," he says suddenly, and I look down my body at him, meeting his eyes. "I don't have a last name, not that I know of. My mother wasn't given one, so neither was I. I was raised around prostitutes and criminals, and by the time I was seven, I was running drugs." He unbuttons his shirt and shrugs it off. "This scar right here is from a bullet when I was nine," he says, pointing to a starburst scar. There's a tattoo of an ouroboros now that wraps around it, as if it's displaying the scar rather than trying to hide it. "This one is from when Freedom got me when I wandered too close and she didn't like it." He points to a long, thin scar on his bicep. It's small for a tiger scratch, but clearly not meant to be life-threatening.

He points to a scar on my inner thigh, a particularly large one. It's ragged and poorly healed, one that'll never go away. I swallow and meet his eyes. "Roger thought I was flirting with the neighbor because I thanked him for the casserole his wife sent over when she had too much. He sliced me open with a serrated bread knife."

He nods, and although the corners of his eyes tighten, he doesn't get angry. He points to a series of five small round scars, all puckered and ugly on top of my left thigh. There are three more on my right.

"Cigarette burns," I whisper. "Each for a different reason. I don't remember all of them."

His fingers trail up to my stomach, to the lines there. I turn my face away, not wanting to talk about them, but his strong fingers grip my chin and force me to look into his eyes. He traces the scars again.

"I . . . I was pregnant," I choke out. "Roger didn't want kids."

This time, his features contort with anger so intense, it washes over me. Despite the fury simmering in his eyes, he leans down and presses a kiss to every slash, to every scar there before moving to my thighs and doing the same, tracing each and every one. His eyes meet mine.

"You are not her," he rasps. "Not anymore. You are not afraid. You do not fear the darkness. You are the darkness. Just as I am, just as Spade, Diamond, and Heart are." His fingers tighten on my knees. "You're not alone."

"I'm not alone," I repeat, my eyes on his, afraid to look away and see the ghosts surrounding us.

He nods. "Never again."

The moment lingers between us, hanging heavily in the air, and then my mind clears. The fear dissipates, and another emotion takes its place—desire.

"Pick up your knife," I say. He does so without hesitation. I grab his hand and guide it to my collarbone where he already cut. "Here," I encourage. "Carve a club."

He jolts in surprise, his eyes widening with both desire and shock. "Are you sure?"

"Yes," I murmur. "Do it."

He watches my face for a few seconds before he comes over me and presses the tip of the knife to my skin. It stings for a moment, but then it fades to a dull ache that makes my pussy throb. He moves with a skilled hand until he leans back and admires his handiwork.

"All done," he murmurs, folding up his knife.

"Good," I whisper. "Now fuck me." When I see his expression, I add, "I said I wanted all of you." I lean up and wrap my arms around him and whisper, "We're the freaks, remember?"

I reach between us and unzip his slacks before reaching inside and cupping his cock. He's as hard as steel, and when my hand wraps around his length, it jumps. He groans, and then his hand encircles my throat again.

"As you wish," he growls, repeating his words from earlier.

The gentle exploration disappears. Gone is the sweet man who wanted to take me on a normal date, and in his place is a demon who likes to play with knives.

He turns me and presses the tops of my thighs against the front grill of the car before shoving my chest down on the hood. His fingers splay on the side of my skull as I rest my cheek against the cool metal, holding me there as he uses his other hand to grab a fistful of my ass and squeeze. His dick dances at my opening, dripping with excitement just as I do.

"Say you want me," he commands, rubbing the head of his cock along my folds.

"I want you," I tell him, desperate for him as I push back for more.

"Say you need me," he growls.

"I need you." I shake my ass.

"Good little star," he purrs just before he slams inside me.

I cry out in surprise and pleasure as his pelvis hits my ass. He doesn't give me time to adjust. Instead, he pulls out and slams back in, fucking me hard and rough. My thighs press painfully against the grill, but I don't care. I feel the cold steel of his blade against my spine a moment later, leaving tiny red lines along my skin. I cry out with each stroke, with each stinging cut he adds every so often when he presses the knife in just a little more.

When his hand grabs my hair and jerks me back so my spine arches painfully, he nips my ear and the knife appears at my breast.

"Tell me you choose me," he demands.

"I choose you."

"Tell me you love me," he snarls, the blade tracing my nipple.

My throat closes up, and I try to turn and meet his eyes. He doesn't let me, forcing me to look at the road where headlights appear.

"Tell me you love me," he orders again. "Say it."

I open my mouth, close it, and then figure what the hell. I do love the four of them.

"I love you," I rasp, my hands gripping the metal hood as the headlights grow closer.

"Good girl," he purrs. "Now tell me that you crave this darkness, that this is everything you've ever wanted."

He fucks me harder with brutal thrusts. Headlights wash over the gravel ground, rushing toward us. Soon, they'll get an eyeful of Club fucking me against the hood, and we aren't stopping. If they stop, they'll die. I almost want them to.

The headlights wash over us, blinding me for a second, and the car slows, watching, before whoever is driving revs the engine and takes off, leaving us in darkness again.

Club chuckles in my ear. "I almost wanted an audience for this. Now be a good girl and tell me."

"This is everything I've ever wanted." My eyes roll back in my head as he traces his blade around my breast and leaves small lines there. "God!"

"Good little star," he purrs. "Now shatter for me."

He fucks me so hard, I cry out with every thrust, then I shatter just as he ordered, my orgasm slamming into me until I see the stars he claims I am, my voice rising into the air around us on a keening cry. I'm still quivering and crying out when he groans in my ear and jerks inside me. He pulls me from the hood and pushes me onto my knees, opening my mouth with a painful grip. He forces his dick down my throat, and I come again, screaming around his length before I gag and grip his thighs in an effort to catch my breath. He doesn't let me pull back, his warmth spurting down my throat. His moans fill the air around us just as mine did a moment before. I can't breathe, my eyes rolling back as I struggle for air, only for him to pull back at the last moment. I gulp in great lungfuls of air, my chest burning, as he pulls me to my feet. My legs threaten to collapse, but he supports me so I don't fall. He slams his lips against mine, tasting himself on my lips.

When he leans back and meets my eyes, I chuckle. It starts off as something small and then grows to full laughter. He joins in, both of us panting and trying to catch our breaths throughout our laughter. He holds me in his arms and hugs me close, me in my split dress and him in his slacks.

"Let's go home," he says once we're able to stop.

I nod, and when he picks up his white shirt and wraps it around me, carefully fastening each button, my heart seizes painfully.

I do love him. I love them all.

I also accept every bit of darkness that comes with that.

TWENTY-EIGHT

EMBER

A week passes without incident. The cirque puts on its shows, and I watch from the sidelines, helping when I'm able. When Dr. Louis comes to check on me again, I happily hold my boot out for him.

"Please tell me it's time," I beg, smiling.

Dr. Louis has been busy, and it shows on his face. He's been taking care of all the children, making sure they are gaining weight in a healthy way and mending those who came with wounds. They are often found running through the circus tents, happy and smiling —not all of them, but many. They will never forget their time at that orphanage, but at least we can help them make good memories. I spend time with them every day, telling stories of dragons and princesses who don't need to be saved and princes who are brave and caring. They listen closely, absorbing the stories, and I know they believe it now. They may be fairy tales, but they saw the guys and me rescue them. There's hope, and we're a part of that.

"I'd say it's about time for it to come off." Dr. Louis nods as he taps the boot. "You'll need to work on regaining muscle mass, but I think you should be okay."

He carefully unstraps the boot and pulls it off, then he flexes my foot and checks everything. "Any pain?" he asks.

"A dull ache sometimes, especially on cold nights," I answer.

He nods. "Unfortunately, I can't help that. You'll likely deal with that forever now, but at least it's healed and you can walk." He gestures for me to get up. "Let's see."

I stand and gingerly put my weight on my leg. There's no sharp pain or sudden cramp, so I take one step and then another. Grinning, I turn back to Dr. Louis and throw my arms around him.

"Thank you," I say, wanting him to know how much it means to me. Dr. Louis took good care of me while I was injured, and now I can walk again. I'm finally free of the boot!

"No need to thank me." He flushes. "It's part of the job."

"Don't be so humble," I tease. "You're amazing. Look how well you're taking care of the kids."

"Anyone would do the same," he says, his face reddening further.

"No," I protest, shaking my head. "You and I both know they wouldn't."

Those words linger between us before he clears his throat. "Right. If you have any more pain, let me know. Take it easy on that leg for a while though. I wouldn't want you to injure it again. No jumping off tall things or doing any cross-country running," he teases before patting my head and walking out the door, leaving me to stare after him with a smile.

I flex my calf again and laugh at the feeling of it. "Finally," I murmur before heading out of my tent.

Hilda insists we meet every night. I enjoy our sessions, and the closer I get to reading the cards as well as she does, the longer she insists we practice. That's why I find myself in her tent past midnight, my eyes starting to glaze over as I stare at the stack of cards before me.

"Once more," Hilda encourages, "and then we can finish for the night."

I nod dutifully and sigh, my gaze on the stack. I focus on what I want the cards to show me. I reach for the static in the air and the feeling buzzing beneath my skin. I close my eyes and dig deeper, fading into the darkness in my soul, then I place my hand on top of the stack.

"Show me," I whisper. I pull my hand away and open my eyes, watching as the stack vibrates with energy. For a moment, it does nothing, and then three cards slide from the middle of the stack and spring into the air.

I blink, especially when one of them is the joker card, the same one I once clutched in my bleeding hand.

"How did that get in there?" I say, and then I focus on the other cards. Awareness slams into me the same moment it does Hilda. I stumble back from my stool and look at her with wide eyes. "Hilda—"

"I see," she rasps. "Go! Warn the others!"

Just as I throw the tent flaps open, the first screams fill the air. My head jerks in their direction, and I stumble toward the sound, my fingers clenching tightly. Flames begin to climb a tent at the farthest edges of the cirque before leaping to the next. More screams split the night, but this time from pain instead of fear.

Horror fills me as I rush deeper into the cirque.

"Wake up!" I scream as loudly as I possibly can, my voice cracking in terror. "Wake up! Fire! There's a fire!"

I take off running in the direction of the flames, but the other sounds reach me a second later. Whoops and hollers of excitement.

"Die, freaks!" someone shouts before laughter follows.

White-hot fury slams into me so brutally, I nearly stumble beneath it.

"We're under attack!" I yell, switching my warning. "We're under attack!"

Diamond rushes through the tents in front of me so suddenly, I startle. His mask is on his face, and he holds a machete in his hand. He sees me and tosses me my mask and a large wrench used for rigging.

"How many?" he asks.

"I don't know," I answer as I slide my mask on and lift the wrench. "But the fire's spreading fast."

We rush after the screams and shouts of excitement. The night lights up with the inferno as the flames dance along the tents, spreading like a disease. We pass by one with people screaming inside, desperately trying to get out and finding themselves trapped. Others throw water on the blaze, trying to stop the flames from spreading, but it's hungry. It consumes and destroys everything in its path, and my fury grows. My only relief is that the children are on the other side of the cirque, so someone will have time to warn them.

A man appears before me, his eyes bright with destruction as he carries a gasoline can. I recognize him—not because I know him, but because he was in the diner, staring at Club and me when we walked in. Another man appears behind him, also easily recognizable.

"The townspeople," I growl to Diamond, telling him all we need to know.

The assholes from the town have decided we're not welcome here.

"Look at these freaks," he calls to his buddy, laughing, and then he spits at my feet. "You should burn with the tents."

I smile behind my mask, even though he can't see it. "Oh, I'll burn," I coo, "but not until I go to hell. Right now, it's your turn."

His eyes widen as I rush him. I guess he didn't expect me to do something about it. He certainly didn't expect Diamond to go after his friend. I slam the wrench into the side of his head, knocking him out cold before he knows what hit him. Diamond hacks the other man in half, silencing his screams of horror almost immediately. Blood splatters over his bare chest, speckling his mask, and when he turns to me, he makes such a pretty sight.

"Come on," he growls. "Let's hunt."

With the flames surrounding us, we prowl through the grounds, stalking those who would dare attack the cirque. She's angry, her fury as hot as my own, so we feed her with the blood of those who wronged her.

Someone gets the flames under control, keeping it from spreading, but at least a quarter of the cirque burns. We find fifteen men, all from town, each carrying a weapon and a can of gasoline. None of them are prepared for us to fight back, apparently thinking freaks are weak, but they have no idea of the hornet's nest they kicked.

When we reach the edge of the cirque, we find the last of them running into the night, fear in their eyes as both Diamond and I appear from the flames, our clothes and bodies coated in blood. What a sight we must make.

I memorize each of their faces as they look over their shoulders, marking them for later.

No one burns down our cirque and gets away with it.

No one.

TWENTY-NINE

The cirque is a mess. Fear streaks the pale faces searching for me in the crowd, looking for answers. Everyone hesitates, unsure. It's my duty as ringmaster to look after them and keep them safe. I failed. I feel that weight heavily when a small hand slips into mine. Looking down, I peer into Ember's blood-speckled face, her mask pushed back to expose it.

"Okay, we need people to make sure that every fire is out. Someone needs to check on the kids too. Save what parts of the tents you can. Gather our . . . Gather our dead," she chokes out. "Diamond and I will double-check the cirque in case any more townspeople are hiding. Let's go!" She claps her hands, and people burst into movement, looking determined now that they have a purpose.

"Thank you," I murmur, grateful for her at this moment. Usually, I'm in control and know what to do, but this was unexpected. Even now, the smell of charred flesh burns my nose and screams ring in my ears. Some of my people died tonight, and I couldn't do anything for them. I couldn't save them.

"Of course. We're family," she replies before tugging my hand to get me moving. "We need to make sure no one is hiding."

I fall into step with her as we search every corner of the cirque. We find Club protecting the kids, making sure those who are still whimpering in fear know they are safe. He huddles with them in the center, instructing any who are okay to check on those who may not be. Heart is dangling above tents, trying to rectify some of the damage and seeing if they can be saved. We'll have to replace what we lost, and he does his best to mend what can be temporarily fixed. Spade is helping carry our dead, his face stricken, with Freedom trailing along behind him, chuffing in sadness. Even the tiger senses what a huge loss this was. All are somber and angry.

I feel it too.

How dare they attack our home? Our people?

They'll pay for it.

When we find one of the assailants, alive and hiding behind a tent, a strength I didn't know I possess fills me. I lift him with one hand as he groans and presses his palm against a wound on his side. When Heart appears behind me, I throw the man toward him. My voice comes out flat and furious. "Tie him up in the big top. I'll check for others." I glance at the pale, scared man. "Then we're going to have a little talk."

I know my smile is sinister, and the audible gulp he lets out only confirms that. Heart giggles as he leads him away, Ember stoic at my side. I follow her gaze to see one of our clowns, Monty, face down in the grass a few feet away. His arm is stretched toward a tent, as if warning whoever may be inside, and there is a knife in his back.

A small head pops out from inside the tent. "Is it safe now? The clown said I would be safe hiding here." The boy's eyes fall on Monty and begin to water, as if he only just realized what happened.

Ember looks at me, stricken, then drops to her knees. "It's safe now," she says, holding her arms open, and despite the blood on her, the child rushes into her embrace. She lifts him into the air and turns, wandering to the closest circus staff member. "Can you take him to be with the others?"

"Of course."

She hands the child over, and when she looks back at me, there is bloodlust in her eyes that I feel in my very soul.

Our queen is angry, very angry, and she wants revenge.

By the time we clear the cirque, we find three of their men alive, all with various injuries. We tie them up in the big top and stand before them, our masks in place. Blood covers most of us from chasing and killing their people, and we let them see it so they will understand that they won't be making it out of here alive.

Heart chuckles as he leaps up onto one of the rigging poles and dances across it, a knife in hand as he begins to sing. "Duck, duck, goose!" He points at one who recoils as far as the bindings will allow him. "Won't you come to roost? I want to play, play with you today!" He leaps at them, and they shout in fear. "Boo." He chuckles as he skips backwards, sliding around Ember. "I wish I saw you kill them. What a sight."

"Heart," she warns and points at her feet. "Sit. You can play with them when we're done."

"Promise?" he asks, sulking.

"I promise." She pats his head, and he sinks to his knees at her side like a dog. It seems our queen has tamed our beast, or at least made it so he only answers to her. She strokes his hair as he continues to play with the knife, drawing in the sand as I step forward.

I cross my arms, eyeing the three men as Spade stands to one side, Club on the other.

"Speak or I will let Queen and Heart play with you. Trust me, you don't want that. Both are feeling very emotional right now," I warn. They aren't the only ones either. Club snarls, smashing his fist into one's face as he wiggles, trying to get away. Spade kicks another with a barked order to speak. We're all angry and on edge.

"You're surrounded and alone," I tell them, my voice low and deadly. "You're in the cirque now. No one can save you, and you'll beg for death before we're through with you. *Speak*. Last warning."

The one in the middle glances at Ember. I don't know what he sees in her face, but his eyes widen and dart back to me. "We hate you," he spits. Despite his fear, his hatred wins out. "You can kill us. That won't change anything."

"Oh, we aren't going to kill you. Not at first," Ember taunts. "First, we'll play with you."

He glances at her again, his nostrils flaring in disgust, but his fear is strong. Ultimately, that wins out. "Some guy—"

His friend elbows him. "Shut up," he hisses.

I pluck a knife from my side and throw it. I might not be as good as Club, but I can keep up. It embeds right in his chest. He gurgles and gasps, looking down in horror as he begins to die. "It's rude to interrupt someone when they are speaking," I warn as I glance back at the man in the middle. Both him and his friend struggle in earnest now. "Carry on."

Ember skips forward and crouches before him, pressing an axe to his chin. "He means now, otherwise . . ." She drags it down, slightly cutting his throat, and he recoils, trying to escape her.

"I don't know, okay? Some guy who was passing through was speaking to us about you guys. He told us where to find you and how easy it would be to stop you since the police won't care what happens to you. You're not like us. You're freaks. It seemed like a good idea!" He jerks again. "Get her the fuck away from me!"

Ember sits back, tilting her head. "What man?"

"I don't know, a stranger," he hisses, and then he spits at her despite his fear.

We freeze. She slowly lifts her hand and drags it down her mask where he spit. "You'll regret that," she warns, gripping the axe and jerking it back. His agonized scream rents the air as she drives it down into his leg with all her strength and keeps chopping, hacking it off from his knee. His friend screams, fighting to get away as blood splatters him. I watch, considering his words, while Heart claps happily and cheers at my side. None of us make a move to stop her as she turns her eyes to his other leg and starts to chop.

"He's right," I remark over his screams. "The police don't care. We're outsiders, freaks. They won't lift a finger to help us. We either need to kill them or punish them somehow. Either way, we're on our own."

"They came here, to the cirque," Heart reminds me. "They came to the place with no rules, no laws, and walked in of their own accord." His grin is vicious. "I say we give them what they want— freaks."

Ember, now panting and covered in blood, glances back at me. "They will die. They came here for death, so they'll get it." Grabbing the man's jaw, she forces his mouth open as he wakes from pain-induced unconsciousness. He begins to struggle again, despite his severe blood loss. "Don't move or this will go wrong."

He stills, eyes wide as she grabs his tongue. He panics, grunting in fear as she pinches it between her fingers.

She grins and slices it off with her axe before tossing it at his friend. "Spit at me now, you bastard."

His scream is a unique sound without his tongue, and then he passes out again, slumping to the floor. She stands and steps back, bloody axe in hand. His blood pools in the sand, and I know it won't be long until he's dead.

"She's right. Kill him." I nod at the other one. "Then we'll burn all the bodies. We'll get rid of every trace we were ever here. It's time to move on."

Turning away, I head out to give the order. The man's bellows fill the air behind me as my family descends on him and takes out their anger for the deaths and destruction they caused.

I can't help but smile. It's like a symphony to my darkness.

THIRTY

EMBER

We pack up in record time, wanting to be gone before the sun rises. We can't change the scorched earth, and we can't take our dead with us. We bury them under a nearby tree, adding markers and praying for their safe passage to the next life, and then we're on the road.

Our hearts are heavy, and we're exhausted from a long night of cleaning up and dressing wounds, but we know we need to keep going. We take turns driving, and this time, we travel farther than before, almost six hours until Diamond is finally happy.

There is no rest for the wicked, however, and once we find a perfect field by a river, we begin the process of setting up. It's unusually quiet and sad today despite set up normally being a happy affair. Even the kids feel it. They help as much as they can, and seeing them try to cheer everyone up puts a smile on my face, but I can't forget what happened.

The cirque felt like a safe place for us survivors, but is it really? I guess only time will tell.

We fall into a routine. It's been a week since the incident that made us flee, and nothing else has happened. We're still grieving the losses, and it's clear the cirque feels it keenly, but life can't stop, not even for death.

That's why when the call comes that night, I'm not surprised, though I do notice it's coming more frequently now. The guys mentioned it only happened every few months a couple of years ago, then almost every month, but now it's every week.

There's just so much suffering in the world, evil taking over and preying on the weak. We're all that stands in its way, and the cirque knows that. It also gives us something to focus on, to take back our power, so as always, we answer.

This time, the call takes us farther outside of the small town we're near. We drive past the big houses to an old church and cemetery on the hill, overlooking it all. The stone sign proudly declares it was built over a hundred years ago.

As I glance at the graves, I feel misery.

The call takes us through the graves and the ancient headstones, toward the newer ones at the back. We pass the chapel and walk toward a grove of trees and a small crypt. There's Greek or maybe Latin writing on the stone plaque above the small gray and white building. The door is locked by a chain that seems newly used, since there's no dust or cobwebs despite the rest of the area being covered.

I nod at it, the call pulsing deep in my soul, letting me know we're close.

"Spade," Diamond orders.

Without a word, Spade heads over, grabs the huge bronze lock, and yanks down, snapping it. My eyes widen at the strength it must have taken to perform such a feat, and yes, a little desire courses through me. He winks at me like he knows my thoughts as he grabs the huge door. His arms strain as he opens it. Club helps while Diamond, Heart, and I wait, watching for what will be on the other side.

Whoever it is has to be alive, right?

So then why are they here?

We all cover our mouths at the stench that fills the air as the door finally opens. My eyes strain in the darkness until Heart turns on his lighter and throws it inside. There's a weak groan, and we share a look. I step in after Diamond, horrified by the sight waiting for us.

There's a teenage boy, no older than sixteen, curled up at the very back in smelly, thin clothing, shivering from the cold. He blinks against the sudden light.

In his hands, he holds a bent joker card.

His mouth is split, and most of his face is covered in mottled purple and yellow bruises, so days old at least. One of his arms hangs at an odd angle, and he's obviously tried to secure it to his chest. All of his exposed skin is covered in burns and cuts.

His throat works as he tries to speak, but nothing coming out at first. He forces himself to sit upright, leaning heavily back against the stone wall. "Who are you?" he asks, his voice raw from disuse and pain, as if he's spent a great amount of time screaming.

How long has he been here?

Days if I had to guess from the stench and state of him.

"You called us," Diamond says softly, nodding at the card. "Tell us what happened."

He blinks, glancing down at the card and back at us, confusion in his gaze. I understand the feeling of confusion and desperate hope that comes with knowing you're about to be saved.

"My . . . The people I thought were my friends left me here to die. They were always mean, bullying me, but I was just happy to have them. I never thought they would go this far." He coughs, and we wait. "We came here to drink and have fun . . . well, that's what they told me, but when we got here, they all ganged up on me. They started beating me. I thought they were going to kill me, then they burned me and—" His face fills with shame, his hand dropping to his pants. I realize they are ripped, and my heart aches for the young boy and the innocence he lost. "They took turns with me. I couldn't stop them. I thought that would be it, but then they threw me in here, laughing the entire time. They said I'd die here and no one would care." His face lifts, tears slowly tracking down his cheeks. "They were right. No one will care. I'm one out of ten siblings. My family is dirt poor. They won't even notice I'm gone, or they'll think I ran away. Nobody cares."

"We do," I tell him softly. "We care."

"We can help you get better and find you a better life, or you can come with us. You can also have the revenge you seek and make them pay for what they did to you. The cost will be the rest of your life. It will be ours. You will join us, Cirque Obscurum. It's your choice," Diamond explains. "Either way, you're safe now."

They left him in here to starve, alone in the darkness, with nothing but the dead for company.

It's the darkest form of torture and a horrendous death.

"I don't know if you're even real, or if this is a hallucination, or if I'm dead, but I want revenge. I choose revenge. I want them to suffer for what they did to me. I want them to pay," he growls, and despite his injuries, he manages to sit a little taller.

"So be it." Diamond holds out his hand, giving him the opportunity like he did with me. He has to want it, after all.

We can't save them if they don't want to be saved.

The boy climbs to his feet with a painful groan and lays his hand in Diamond's, his eyes hardening.

"Take my life," he says. "Take everything, just let me see them suffer first."

I glance at the others, knowing we'll all be covered in the blood of this boy's enemies before sunrise, and I'm looking forward to it.

THIRTY-ONE

"What's your name?" I ask the boy as we help him to his feet. He's in rough shape, weak from lack of food and his beating. He'll take time to recover, but at least we found him before it was too late. He keeps the joker card clutched in his hand as we help him out of the mausoleum. I don't think any of us want to force him to hand it over. Not yet. We have plenty of time for that.

"Melvin," he answers, his throat rough. "It's Melvin."

"It's nice to meet you, Melvin," I reply, helping him make his way across the uneven ground. Many of the graves are in disrepair here, either because they are old or because the caretakers no longer care about this part. The mausoleum is well-kept, though, as if someone tends to it often. Of course the rich get better service even in death. They forget those who can't afford such a grand statement of wealth.

"How many of them are there?" Club asks, his mind already on the task at hand. He's likely planning out every detail, wanting to make sure we don't miss an opportunity. Melvin decided he wants revenge, so we'll give it to him, even if we have to carry him to each destination.

"Three," he answers softly. "Two boys and a girl."

"Do they live close by?" Diamond asks.

Melvin nods. "Yes. About five minutes up the road. We all lived in the same part of town."

"We'll drive," Spade says, gesturing to the car. He knows as well as we do that this boy won't be able to walk far. His strength is already starting to fail. Likely, he has some broken bones we can't see or at least some fractures, but he's being a trooper with the pain. Revenge is a great motivator.

We all pile in Diamond's black Dodge and follow Melvin's directions to a subdivision. I'm surprised Melvin came from the suburbs, but I'm not surprised the others do. Sometimes, kids like these can be the meanest, especially if they are their daddy's little princess or mommy's little man.

We pull up outside a quaint white house that matches all the others. They are all perfectly manicured and built exactly the same, like the builder could only come up with one design and figured a hundred more would be great. It's horrible. I prefer the bright splashes of color of the cirque, but this is exactly the kind of place Roger would have liked. That thought only makes me hate it more.

"Who does this house belong to?" I ask, looking up at the dark windows.

"George. He's the leader," Melvin says. "The others listen to every word he says."

Spade pauses. "And how old is George?"

I understand his question. None of us want to kill a kid, but Melvin asked for revenge, and we have to give it to him. Still, it feels a little wrong.

"Eighteen," Melvin says. "The three of them are all eighteen. I'm the youngest. I won't turn eighteen until next year."

"Oh," I muse. Well, that fixes that. They are old enough to know better. Besides, they tried to kill Melvin and clearly had every intention of doing so. "Well, let's get George taken care of then. Which window is his?"

Melvin leads us around back and points to a window with a light on inside. The curtains cover it, but we can see through a gap that George is within. He's sleeping like a baby, sprawled across a bedspread with cowboys drawn on it despite the fact he nearly killed a kid. He probably thinks Melvin is already dead.

Bastard.

Heart reaches up and gently pries the window open. George doesn't stir, but then again, I don't expect him to.

"We can't do it here," Diamond says. "We'll take him out to the woods with the others."

There would be too many potential witnesses if we did it here. His parents are probably snoring away, unaware of the little monster they raised. Unless they are monsters too. Monsters often make more monsters.

Heart gestures for Spade to come inside with him. I watch as they sneak through the window and stalk around, searching. Heart picks up a nude magazine open on the bedside table and wiggles his eyebrows at me. I roll mine and gesture for him to hurry up. His giggle is so soft, it doesn't wake the kid. No, what wakes him up is Spade pressing a cloth against his mouth. It takes three seconds of struggling before he passes out. Heart lifts him and roughly tosses him out the window, uncaring how he lands. He'll probably have bruises from it, but that's the least of his worries.

We repeat the process at Alan's house and again at Veronica's. None of them get the chance to scream, and none of them struggle for long. We shove them all in the trunk of the car and drive back out to the graveyard. How poetic that they'll find themselves in the same spot they left Melvin in. Melvin seems tickled pink by the idea, smiling despite his injuries and inability to hold himself up. He's currently slumped on a gravestone, watching as Heart ties the three kids up in the mausoleum with their backs together.

Diamond kicks their feet to wake them up. When that doesn't work, Club tosses a bucket of water on them, and they come to, sputtering.

I sit beside Melvin, watching. Melvin is leaning against me, needing support, but this position still gives him the ability to look cool, something I know a kid his age would be worried about.

"Welcome to the game, little shits," Heart declares as they look around and start panicking. Veronica starts to scream, so Heart slams his baseball bat into the ground right beside her leg. "I suggest you stop that, girlie, or I'll have to take your tongue."

She immediately shuts up, whimpering and trying to press back against the other two boys. Weak. She's only part of the group as eye candy. George tips up his chin and looks around before finding Melvin sitting against me. His eyes narrow in anger.

"What the fuck is going on, dweeb?" he snarls. "What are you doing?"

"How are you still alive?" Alan asks, staring at him. "You should be dead."

"Oh, you tried," Melvin croaks. "Almost succeeded too, but my friends arrived." He gestures to us, and I smile behind my mask.

"Friends?" George spits. "Don't be stupid, Melvin. We're your friends."

"Is that how you treat all your friends?" Diamond asks, kneeling. "Nearly beating them to death and locking them in a crypt?"

George's face twists, but it's a mask just as ours are. "That's what he told you? He's lying. The dweeb is always lying."

"Shut up," Melvin spits. "You can't pretend your way out of this one, George. Daddy isn't here to save you this time."

George's mask slips away. "You should have died."

"Why?" Melvin asks. "Because you don't like me?"

"Because you don't deserve to live," he spits. "Not a dweeb like you, wasting space and time. You've always been a freak. We took pity on you because of who your parents are, but I'm tired of you tagging along like a lost puppy."

"A freak, huh?" I ask, tilting my head. "It's a good thing we're freaks too, isn't it, Club?"

Club glances at me, and I can tell he's smiling behind his mask. "That's right, baby. We're all freaks."

"So I guess it's a good thing Melvin called us," I purr. I glance over at him. "You think you can stand?"

"For this, absolutely," he says, but when he goes to stand, he grunts in pain, and I have to help him.

"Fast or slow?" Diamond asks Melvin.

Veronica begins to whimper again, fighting against her ties. Alan is struggling too, fear in his eyes. Only George sits still, his chin tipped up, unafraid of death.

Monsters make other monsters.

"Who's your daddy?" I ask him, but he keeps his lips tightly shut.

"The mayor," Melvin offers helpfully. "He's an asshole."

I nod. "Of course he is." I hold out my knife. "The fast way."

Heart holds his bat out. "The slow way." He giggles.

Melvin reaches for the bat but hesitates. "I don't know if I have the strength for the slow way," he admits before grabbing my knife instead.

Smart. Melvin is a force they are not prepared for, and that was their mistake. They should have considered him an ally, but at least these monsters weren't able to corrupt him.

"How did they get you into the mausoleum?" Spade asks Melvin.

Melvin weighs the knife in his hand. "Veronica asked me to meet them to hang out. I always liked her and thought she finally liked me back. I thought we were going to be making out by the end of it. Instead, it was all a ruse. George and Alan jumped me the second I got in here." His eyes meet hers. "She laughed the entire time."

Any questions regarding Veronica's involvement disappear in my mind. She's worse, letting them kill someone for her entertainment. The abuser might be a monster, but the person who watches and does nothing is so much worse.

"Alan first," Melvin says. "He kicked me first. I'll give him the same honor."

As I help Melvin closer, Alan starts to grunt and try to free himself.

"Stop, Melvin! Stop! Please! We made a mistake! We won't do it again!" he begs.

"No," Melvin says, leaning down. "You won't." He plunges the knife right into Alan's chest without a moment of hesitation. Usually, when faced with the reality, everyone, even those desperate for revenge, hesitates. Not Melvin, though, and my estimation of his strength goes up. Alan gurgles and slumps over, but it's Veronica's screams that suddenly pierce the air.

Heart grabs her jaw and squeezes painfully, cutting her off. "Now what did I say, girlie?" He pulls out a knife, and she voices a muffled scream, tears running from her eyes.

"Don't," Melvin instructs, and Heart immediately puts his knife away. "I have something better for her. She's claustrophobic." He points to the half-opened stone coffin behind us.

I grin, impressed as hell by him. "Now that's a nice idea. I like that."

Melvin meets George's eyes. "Do you regret it even a little?"

George's lips curl. "No. I'd do it again."

Melvin nods. "I thought so." He sets the knife down and stands up. "I changed my mind," he says before reaching for Heart's bat.

Heart giggles and tosses it to him. Melvin doesn't waste time, clearly thinking he won't have the strength to swing more than a few times. He bashes the bat against George's head, and the asshole goes down. He swings again and again, splattering blood over us, the walls, and the floor.

Veronica starts to scream again, so Heart jerks her up and tosses her into the open coffin.

"A little assistance?" Heart asks before Spade and Club come over to help him push it closed. Diamond stands next to me, both of us watching as Melvin destroys his bully's skull until I'm certain no one will recognize him.

Veronica's scream cuts off suddenly when the stone lid closes. Only a faint whisper of it can be heard, and it makes me smile.

Melvin sways, and I reach out for him, stopping him from toppling over.

"The card?" Diamond says, holding out his hand.

Melvin reaches into his pocket and presses it into Diamond's hand, still panting from the effort of swinging the bat. Despite his weakness, his eyes are alight with a fire I know will serve him well.

"To the cirque?" Diamond asks. "Or a new life?"

Melvin wipes his face and meets our eyes. "The cirque," he rasps. "I never fit in anywhere else."

I grin. "Then welcome home, Melvin. Welcome home."

THIRTY-TWO

I watch the exchange closely, taking it all in from my spot behind a grave.

I watch *her*.

She wears a mask just as the others do, the smiling grimace ugly and distasteful. It hides the beautiful face I spent years perfecting. I want to rip it away and punish her for such a statement. How dare she gallivant across the country with these monsters? How dare she play with them?

She's supposed to be mine to play with.

The boy passes something to the man, and when he holds it up, I catch the glimmer of a red joker in the moonlight. Another card, another pattern. The card is important somehow.

Ember turns as if she feels my eyes on her, but I sink lower so she can't see me. It's not time yet, but soon she'll pay for what she did. Soon, she'll scream my name, and she'll be back home where she belongs.

THIRTY-THREE

I let the guys settle Melvin in after seeing the doctor. The kid has been through a lot, and despite his strength and bloodlust tonight, as soon as Dr. Louis touched him, he started to sob. Not wanting him to feel embarrassed, we gave him the space he needed, but I know full well he has a long journey of healing ahead of him. And the memories? They never go away. You just have to try to replace them with something better. Maybe that's why I find myself lifting my head when my tent flaps open, my mask clutched in my hands.

My own memories fill my head, brought on by Melvin's confession.

They stole his innocence, and I remember what that feels like.

I remember the pain and humiliation.

I want to replace it. I want something good to hold onto, and when I see the four men who saved me, I know I want it to be them.

For others, they are their ending, their damnation, but for me, they are my salvation, my angels, and my hope for a better future.

They would never hurt me unless I asked. They would never

leave me. Even now, they watch me, knowing something is wrong, ready to fight my invisible foe for me.

"Ember, what's wrong?" Diamond asks, stepping farther into my tent, his brows drawing together in worry.

"I need to paint over the past," I murmur. "I need to replace the bad with the good."

"Okay . . ." Spade tilts his head, unsure what I need from them.

"I need you. I need you all to do that. Make me forget every time he touched me, every time he took my body. I need—no, I *want* you to replace the pain with pleasure. I want to be alive and not his."

Club's smile is slow and sexy as he watches me. "I think we can do that, don't you guys?"

Heart grins and steps closer, leaping onto my bed, and then he wraps himself around me from behind, resting his chin on my shoulder. "You want all of us, Queen? Can you handle that?"

"Yes," I whisper as I run my eyes over them before I clear my throat. "I want all of you."

"Your wants are ours to fulfill," Diamond purrs, sliding his mask up onto his head so I can see his face. "But you must be sure. I don't want your regrets to rise with the dawn. You can't take back what we do here in the dark, Ember. You can't give yourself to us and then run the next day."

"I'm not running, not anymore. I want this. I want you." I meet every single one of their eyes before I reach back and tangle my fingers in Heart's hair, tugging him down and pressing his mouth to my neck. "If you want me."

"More than anything," Club says without restraint.

"More than life," Spade adds, moving closer.

I glance at Diamond, waiting for his answer. The smirk he aims my way as his eyes drag down my body makes flames lick at my insides, and desire pools low in my body. He watches me like he wants to eat me alive and has been holding himself back, and then his gaze meets mine. My breath whooshes from me at the pure hunger I see there. "You're all I want," he says. "I'll happily share you,

Ember, if it means I get a taste of what I've hungered for since the day I met you."

There's something about his confession that has me shivering and leaning back into Heart as if he will protect me from Diamond—which is insane, asking the beast to protect me from the devil.

I refuse to let embarrassment take hold. Instead, I move on instinct. Turning, I grab Heart's chin and yank him down, kissing him.

He moans into my mouth, his hands hauling me onto his lap and pressing me against his straining erection as he bites my lip until I taste blood. A hand grabs my hair, yanking my head back. I open my eyes as I pant, meeting Diamond's hard gaze.

"You've already had Heart, and we both know if you two play, you won't be able to enjoy the rest of us." It's the truth, but the hard touch has me ignoring his word, grinding into Heart who snarls. "Tell him no. He only listens to you now."

I look back at Heart and lick my lips. "Be good, you can have me last." His nostrils flare, his hands gripping me as if he won't let me go, so I harden my voice. "Or not at all."

His lips tilt into a pout, but he releases me, and I gasp as Diamond lifts me from him with one hand and then throws me. I slam against a body, my hands smacking into a firm chest, and my head jerks up just in time to see Club's smirking face before he drags me to my toes and crushes his lips to mine. His hands slide down my body to grip my hips and press me against him, letting me feel every hard inch of his physique.

Losing myself in the kiss, I grip his shirt tighter, rubbing against him as another body presses against my back. Their hands slide up my chest, across my neck, and to my chin before turning me around as another pair of lips meet mine. My eyes flutter open to see Spade, and I whimper as he sucks on my tongue.

I expect Club to back away, but his hands slide down my thighs, and I gasp into Spade's mouth as he lifts me, holding me between them, my ass pressed against Spade's hard length while Club's mouth slides down my throat, kissing and licking until I moan between them, desperate for more.

Spade's hands move up, lifting my shirt as he goes, and Club and I break apart for him to toss it away, leaving my torso bare for their greedy hands and mouths. Spade's lips trail down my spine while his hands slip between us, cupping my breasts and tweaking my nipples as Club tugs my pants down, but our position makes it hard.

Snarling, he drops me and falls to his knees, taking my pants with him and tossing them over his shoulder. His hands slide up my legs as he gets to his feet, dragging his mouth up my thigh, over my hip, and up my chest as he goes. Spade turns my head again, kissing me as Club's mouth seals over one of my breasts, his teeth tugging at my nipple until I gasp and moan into Spade's mouth.

"So pretty," Spade mumbles. "You taste so good, Queen. Open your pretty thighs so I can taste you there too."

Club turns me and lifts me once more, gripping my knees and pressing them to my chest. My eyes widen at the position. I am completely exposed and vulnerable. My eyes meet Spade's as he reaches behind him and removes his shirt, leaving his bronze chest bare for my hungry gaze. He doesn't give me a lot of time to ogle him, however, because he drops to his knees, grips my ass, and tugs me closer until his face is pressed against my pussy.

My cheeks heat as he inhales, but his hungry moan has me shivering, and then his tongue touches me, licking down my cunt and back up. My heart pounds in anticipation and desire. I look at Diamond and Heart, who are watching. Heart paces like a trapped animal, while Diamond smirks as he leans back into my bed, enjoying the show.

Club chuckles darkly in my ear. "Look at him on his knees for you. Look what you do to us, Queen. He's going to worship you until you scream, and then I'm going to fill that pretty mouth with my cock while he takes your greedy cunt. That's what you want, isn't it?"

My head falls back, hitting Club's shoulder as my eyes sweep over his handsome face. I reach up and push his black hair back, holding onto it as Spade's tongue drags along my cunt. "Yes. I want that. I want you all inside me. I want to feel you so deep it hurts."

"Fuck," Spade growls, his voice vibrating against my flesh. His tongue swipes over my clit as his eyes meet mine. "I want to see you like that, split between us, dripping with our cum."

As I watch, his tongue drags along my pussy and dips inside me, his gaze holding me prisoner as he fucks me with it. My eyes shut before Diamond's order rings out.

"Eyes open, Ember. Watch what we do to you. Watch who is touching you, fucking you."

Whimpering, I open my eyes. Spade rewards me by sliding two fingers into my channel alongside his tongue, stretching me as he fucks me. I can barely move in the position I'm in, trapped for their greedy touches, and something about that only makes me hotter. I cry out, desperate to rub against him and force him deeper, harder, anything, but I can't.

Club's mouth slides along my throat, trapping my pulse between his teeth as Spade's mouth seals around my clit and sucks while he thrusts a third finger inside me, and I'm lost.

Pleasure explodes through me like a tidal wave of flames, burning me alive as I scream for them just like they said I would. It's so strong, I swear I see stars behind my closed eyelids, and when I open them, I'm panting, but they don't give me time to recover. Club drops me to my shaky feet, and I crumple to my knees facing Spade. His lips glisten with my cream, but I don't care. I pull him closer and kiss him, until I have to rip away to breathe.

I meet Club's eyes as he smirks. His pants are gone, leaving him naked as he strokes his long, hard length. "Open your mouth, Ember. I'm going to fill it, and I won't stop until you choke on my cum like a good girl."

Spade turns me, pressing me down until I'm on my knees, my ass aimed at him, and I lift my head so I can meet Club's dark eyes. He steps forward, pressing his hard, dripping cock to my lips. I open them wide for him, but he rubs his tip over them instead, painting them with his desire as Spade's hands widen my thighs, and I feel him press against my pussy from behind.

"Look at you," Club murmurs. "Perfection."

Swallowing, I open my mouth wider, sticking my tongue out. He obliges, stroking himself as he rubs it along my tongue before he reaches down and grips my jaw, forcing it wider before he feeds me his cock. He's so deep, I start to choke, but he doesn't pull back. He pushes deeper until his balls slap into my chin, and I struggle, tears springing into my eyes as I breathe rapidly through my nose.

"She's taking all of me," Club says. "Fuck, she was made for us. If I get inside that tight cunt, I won't last long with the way she's sucking me."

Spade's breath blows over my back, making me shudder, and I press backward, wanting him. His cock drags along my pussy, bumping my clit until I rock into him, and when I go to pull from Club's cock to demand he fuck me, he fills me in one brutal thrust.

I scream around Club, who surges deeper before pulling back and thrusting into my mouth, fucking it. They find a rhythm quickly, using me between them, but their entire focus is on my pleasure. Their hands stroke every inch of me they can reach, and Spade tilts my hips so my knees are almost off the floor and his cock hits that spot inside me with each thrust. I reach out blindly, digging my nails into Club's thighs until he bellows. His cock jerks in my mouth as he hammers into my throat, making it hurt.

Burning pleasure spreads through me, making me beg for more. I suck Club deeper as I clench around Spade, causing him to growl behind me.

I look up to see Club watching me, his jaw clenching as he grinds his teeth. His hand slides down his chest before gliding back up, and the sight is so fucking sexy, I clench down on Spade who smacks my ass.

Diamond appears beside us, and my eyes widen as he grips my hair, pressing me deeper onto Club who moans loudly. The sound is sexy, tightening something in my belly until I'm racing toward another release.

"That's a good girl," Diamond praises, angling my head for me and pushing me down. "You're doing so well. You were made for us, weren't you?"

I nod my head as much as I can. I'm so fucking close.

"Then show us. Come for them. Let them feel you," he orders, and something about that causes me to fall over the edge.

Clenching down on Spade's cock, I come. I suck Club desperately until he bellows, his cock swelling and jerking in my mouth as he shoves it as deep as he can, and I feel his come slide down my throat. Spade groans, his fingers digging into my hips as he fights my tight cunt, trying to get deeper until he spills inside my pussy.

"Good girl," Diamond praises, stroking my hair as Club releases me and I swallow, my mouth and jaw aching. Spade leans down and kisses my spine before slowly pulling from my channel. I would fall forward face first, but hands keep me upright, and my eyes meet Diamond's.

"We're not done yet," he warns. "You're going to take both me and Heart, remember?" I swallow hard, my thighs slick with my and Spade's cum, yet my clit throbs at his words, wanting just that. "I'll take that as a yes." His smirk makes me lick my lips. "How do you want me, Queen? For one night, you can have me however you want. You can be in control."

I know that's a rare offer. Diamond craves control, he likes to be in charge, so the thought is heady.

"On your back," I tell him, my voice hoarse. "I want to ride you while Heart fucks my ass."

It's something I tried once—not by choice, and it hurt—but the idea of having Diamond in my cunt and Heart in my ass? Yeah, I want that, and I trust them too. They will ensure I enjoy it.

Diamond steps back and strips out of his clothes, leaving him naked and oh so fucking gorgeous. It almost hurts to look at him. He's a work of art, and knowing he belongs to me for the night has my thighs rubbing together. When he lowers to his knees like a sinner and then falls to his back, I lose all sense of control.

I crawl to him, sliding up his body. He groans and drops his head back, veins bulging in his throat as he restrains himself, giving me what I want—control over him.

I grind my cunt against his hard, thick dick while I lick his throat, biting and sucking until he shakes below me.

"Ember." He finally breaks, his voice a plea, and something about our stern, strong ringmaster begging me to ride him makes me crazy. I bite down until I taste blood, and he groans, his hand coming up to grip the back of my hair and urge me on. "Mark me. Scar me. I don't care. Just don't stop."

A dark chuckle behind me has the hair on the back of my neck rising, and then hands slide down my back. "Hmm, keep biting him. Take it out on him because this'll hurt a bit."

Heart's voice is dark and crazed, and without warning, his cock slams into my pussy. I bite down hard out of reflex, and Diamond moans below me, jerking. Heart pummels into my wet cunt, making it hurt before suddenly pulling out, leaving me empty and unsure. I move back from Diamond, feeling his blood on my lips, and glance over my shoulder to see Heart there.

He grins crazily when he sees me watching him, his hands rubbing my ass and pulling my cheeks apart as he pushes me down. "Scream for me," he says as I feel his wet cock press against my hole. My eyes widen, and my mouth opens to ask him to be gentle, but then he drives into me, working through my tight muscles as I scream.

Diamond turns me, his lips meeting mine, our kiss tasting of blood and desire. I bite down, taking it out on him as Heart forces himself deeper until he's fully seated in my ass. It hurts yet it feels good, especially when his fingers rub across my clit and pinch it, making me moan into Diamond's mouth.

Breaking the kiss, I peer down at Diamond as he grips my hips. "Heart, feed me to our girl."

My heart skips a beat, and a moment later, I feel Diamond's hard cock pressing against my pussy, Heart's hand directing it. I lean back, forcing myself onto his length, stretching around him. I'm so full with Heart inside me as well, but as I rock, I slip lower until I'm fully seated on him.

Both of them are inside me. I moan and bite Diamond's neck again as he groans.

Heart starts to move, filling my ass and pushing me deeper onto Diamond's cock. I can do nothing but push back, riding Diamond and taking Heart. Pleasure spasms through me, slightly painful but so fucking good that my eyes slide shut as I lose myself in the hard, fast pace we set. Our bodies slap together, Heart's cock branding my ass while Diamond's claims my cunt.

I rake my nails down Diamond's chest before I realize what I've done, curling them to stop. I go to pull away, but he grabs them and presses them into his skin, cutting himself with them. "I'll proudly wear your marks, Queen."

Biting my lip, I rake my nails down his chest, watching blood well, and the sight makes me clench on him. "You like seeing me bleed for you?" he growls, lifting my hips and dropping me faster as they work me on their dicks. "Like the sight of it?"

I nod rapidly, and Heart yanks my head back, meeting my eyes upside down. "Then make us all bleed. Let us cover you in it." He drives into my ass as he speaks, and then I scream as he bites into my neck so hard I feel my blood run down my chest, dripping onto Diamond below. The sharp agony should have horrified me, but I gush around them, screaming in ecstasy.

Diamond arches up, digging his teeth into the other side of my neck, and the feeling of them both inside me, their teeth in my skin . . . I shatter.

Screaming, I drag them into oblivion with me.

Diamond's groan echoes into my throat while Heart snarls, fighting my ass before bellowing his pleasure as I feel his cum pump deep inside me.

They keep me there, trapped between them, their cocks filling me with their seed as I nearly pass out from the pleasure. Slumping between them, I let them rain kisses along my skin.

"You did so well, Queen," Diamond praises. "So very well."

Carefully, he lifts me from them, and I slump, rolling to my back. Every inch of my body aches and shakes but in the best way. Heart appears above me, grinning, and I whimper as he reaches between my thighs. Heart rubs his fingers through his cum, and as I pant below him, he paints a heart on my heaving chest with his release.

I can't help but shake my head, even as he falls to the floor next to me, Diamond on my other side. Club and Spade crawl over, collapsing into a pile of sweaty bodies on the multicolored floor. I stare at the ceiling and can't help but laugh.

Soon, the others join in, and when my laughter fades, I smile brightly.

My body isn't theirs despite me giving it to them. It's mine. I own it. I control it.

I use it.

They are mine, not the other way around.

THIRTY-FOUR

Peering down at Ember, I can't help but smile. I can taste the dawn in the air, but it's still early, so I should let her sleep, especially after the way we fucked. She's exhausted, and when she sighs and snuggles deeper into my side of her bed, I can't help wanting to wake her to taste that noise, but I don't. I let her sleep, but I know I won't be anytime soon. Slipping from her side, I leave the others wrapped around her.

I dress and head out to check on the cirque, something ingrained into me since I was a child.

Unlike the others, I've been here since I was young. I barely remember anything before the cirque. I grew up around striped tents and performing. It became my safe place and my happiness, and they became my family. Hilda often said I was brought here to lead the cirque, and I'm starting to believe she's right. My destiny was never my own, but I would choose this place time and time again.

These people are my family.

Wandering through the tents, I find myself standing in the main path to the big top, looking from one silent tent to another. This place transforms at night, but my favorite time is always now, when it's quiet and everyone's safe and sleeping.

It lets me know I'm doing something right. Even knowing Ember is resting brings me joy. I've felt this weight since I was a child, but being with her last night lessened it, allowing me to breathe. With her, I'm not the ringmaster. I'm just me.

A soft voice reaches me. "Diamond?" I glance back to see a sleepy Ember in nothing but one of our long shirts, her hair mussed, yet she looks so beautiful, I'm lost for words. She heads my way, rubbing her eyes as she stops at my side. "Are you okay?"

"I didn't mean to wake you," I murmur. "I just like to check on everyone before I start my day."

"Do you ever rest?" she teases.

"Not really," I reply. "There's always so much to do, and I don't want to let anyone down."

"Sounds like you." She nods, looking over the cirque. "But I don't think it will fall apart if you allow yourself to sleep. Maybe you're just so used to being in control, you don't know how to do anything but."

I swallow hard at her perceptive, innocent words, and then she glances at me, her eyes gray in the early morning light as she seems to memorize my face.

"What?" I ask, feeling too raw, exposed, and vulnerable.

She turns to face me fully. "You know, I think I saw you as a child."

My eyes widen. "What?"

"You've been here since you were young, right? I saw a boy. I didn't place it entirely until now, but he reminds me of you. I think he was you."

I smile. "I guess we've been connected longer than the others then." My smile fades as I stare into her beautiful face. "My real name is Atticus."

It feels important that she knows that when no one else does, giving her a part of me no one else has or ever will.

"It's nice to meet you, Atticus." Her smile is bright, and she takes my hand. "Now let's go back to bed. Everything else can wait for the sun to rise. Until then, you're mine, not the cirque's."

Swallowing my protests, I allow her to lead me back to her bed.

I let her take more of that weight from my shoulders, and when she glances back at me, smiling, I see the little girl who came all those years ago. I remember her now. How could I have forgotten? She watched me with fascination then. She still does.

I wonder if I still look at her the same—with hope.

THIRTY-FIVE

EMBER

A few nights later, things in the cirque are running as they should. Despite the attack and lost lives, we've managed to repair what we can and replaced what we couldn't. There's still a permeating sadness due to losing friends and family, but not even that can dispel the excitement for the show tonight.

The cirque is full of families and curious townspeople who are eager to see the show and the freaks they were warned about. They always look down upon us, but they flock to come see us perform in waves. I think most people yearn for what we have, and because they can't have it themselves, they call us freaks, but if they had the opportunity, they'd drop everything in a second and join us. Cirque Obscurum isn't for everyone, and joining this circus isn't like joining others, but they don't know that. They are still curious. They still split their hearts open every night and briefly forget that we're supposed to be the outcasts.

Tonight is no different. The stands hold more children than normal, only because the kids have been allowed to watch. I spy Melvin among them, his expression just as excited as everyone else's as the stands fill. Tonight, I'm just as eager to see the show. Heart promised there was something I needed to watch, so here I am, excited to see what new act one of them has come up with. They never stop adding acts to their show, always practicing. Just the other week, Club brought out his spinning wheel and put someone up there from the crowd after I denied acting in it for him. There was no way I could handle that in public, I had however had to rub my thighs together as he threw the knives and she screamed, the scene reminding me of when I'd been on the wheel. The woman hadn't looked anything less than aroused when he helped her off, but he only directed her back into the crowd with a knowing look my way. Later that night, he strapped me to the wheel and performed the same act, though it had some adjustments.

Perhaps Club has added new knives to his act, or maybe Heart has choreographed another dangerous, high-flying act. Spade could have taught Freedom a magnificent new trick. Regardless, I'm eager to see it, sitting on the edge of my seat. When Diamond comes out to begin the show, I vibrate with the same excitement as the crowd, my fingers clenched in the loose skirt around my thighs.

"Welcome, ladies and gentlemen," Diamond coos, "freaks and rebels, sinners and saints, to Cirque Obscurum. Tonight, we have a very special show for you, one that will have you shifting in your seats—either in discomfort or desire, it's your choice."

There's a murmur that shoots through the crowd as he smiles, the look saccharine and sinister, but then he meets my eyes, and I know I'm in for a real show. Diamond has something up his sleeve, and it's for me and me alone. I straighten, my fingers clenching my skirt harder. What secret have they been keeping, and how did they manage to keep it?

The show continues. Club goes through his sword swallowing act and then picks someone from the crowd to be on the wheel. It's no less arousing this time, but this isn't new. This isn't what's meant for me.

Spade comes out with his animals and puts on such an incredible show, I clap with everyone else. His interactions with Freedom are always my favorite. There's respect between them, a connection that I've never seen anyone have with a wild animal. They might as well be family. The crowd is equally as impressed as I am, oohing and aahing at every trick.

When Heart comes out with the other trapeze artists, I think this must be it, but although Heart does a few new moves I haven't seen before, it doesn't seem to be the surprise. It isn't until they start pushing out a great stage that I lean forward. I've never seen the contraption before. It's huge and round around the bottom with large metal petals coming out like a flower. When Diamond steps out without his ringmaster jacket on, my eyebrows shoot up.

What is this?

"Are you enjoying the darkness?" Diamond asks into the microphone.

The crowd erupts in cheers and whistles. A few women scream in shrill excitement that hurts my ears. My eyes remain on Diamond.

"Good," he purrs. "Because we're about to dive deeper into your sins. I'm going to need someone from the crowd."

The crowd immediately erupts in shouts of "Pick me!" and "Over here!" as he hands the microphone to Club and starts to unbutton his shirt. He shrugs it down his shoulders and tosses it off the stage, leaving him in his leather pants and boots. His eyes sweep over the crowd, searching for someone to use in this new act, but when his gaze finds me, I know it was all for show. This trick is meant for me. Still, I don't immediately stand up. This is entertainment, so I stay in my seat until he steps down from the stage and starts stalking along the audience. The women scream louder when he comes close, reaching for him, but when he shakes his head, they sit back down in their seats with a pout. He reaches me and offers me his hand, and I look up into his eyes.

"Join me," he purrs, his long fingers gesturing toward my hand.

I reach up and slide my hand into his. He yanks me from my seat before I can stand and then starts pulling me toward the strange stage.

"What is this?" I whisper, but Diamond doesn't answer. Instead, he looks back at me and grins without giving me a hint. He drags me into the center of the stage with an order of, "Stay," then he turns back to the crowd.

Club brings the microphone up, but Diamond doesn't take it. He only leans forward to speak.

"The devil is a heathen and a dangerous threat to our souls, so it's no wonder that we call people who can perform extraordinary feats daredevils, right?" he says as Spade brings a dirt bike onto the curved stage. I stare at it in surprise. "My lovely assistant here will make things even more exciting, isn't that right, Ember?"

I nod, afraid my voice won't work in front of so many people.

He walks around me before he tips my chin up and forces me to meet his eyes, his expression serious.

"Don't move from this spot, Ember," he warns. "If you do, we'll both die."

My eyes widen, but I can't ask questions, not in front of the crowd. Instead, I make sure my feet are planted precisely where the marks are, and I watch as Club steps away from the stage.

"The devil's in the cirque tonight," Club coos into the microphone with that suave voice he uses. "You're getting a real treat. The ringmaster rarely strips his coat off and bares it all. Get on your feet and show him just how much you appreciate his sacrifice."

As if they have no choice, the crowd stands and starts to cheer, whistles and shouts filling the air, but Diamond only has eyes for me as he moves over to the dirt bike and climbs on. With a teasing grin, he kick-starts the bike, and it roars to life. He revs it, warming the engine, and I stiffen. No one explained what was going to happen. My only instructions are not to move so I won't, no matter what.

My eyes stay on him as he starts to slowly drive around me. This doesn't seem too bad, but just as I think it, the stage starts to move, lifting and closing. It's not a stage, it's a cage—a sphere. My eyes widen as he comes close when the bottom of the sphere comes together. A few others come forward to snap the petals into place, strengthening them as the top of the sphere closes around us. All the while, Diamond drives oh so slowly around me, giving the crew time to complete their tasks. The moment it's all locked into place, Diamond guns his engine and takes off, roaring fast circles around me. If I move, it'll throw his act off. He could crash into me, so I stand stiffly and watch as his speed starts to accelerate and he begins to climb the sides of the cage. The smell of gasoline fills the air around us as he burns the throttle, his eyes bright with excitement. Every time he comes around, our eyes meet, and I'm reminded that this is dangerous. Though Diamond makes it feel like we're having fun, this act is perilous enough that no one else performs it. I've never even heard of it before now.

He spins fast around me, his speed increasing as he circles me, driving sideways inside the sphere around me. The movement makes my hair dance around my shoulders and lift, and my skirt swirls around my legs, threatening to rise with the right burst of air. It isn't until he has his speed up and reaches out to me, however, that I lose the ability to breathe.

Diamond releases one of the handlebars and lifts his arm, his fingers touching my waist, dancing beneath the edge of my shirt and stroking my skin. He's moving fast, so it's an odd sensation. The urge to move is strong, but I remain still, desperate to keep my composure and not ruin his act. Distantly, I hear Club speaking to the crowd and their cheers as they watch, but in this cage, I'm only aware of the man currently stroking me and driving me insane. All I can truly hear is the roar of his motorcycle as he touches me. His fingers trail up and circle my rib cage, then my breasts, driving me insane with each stroke. When he drops back to my hips and then releases me, I'm finally able to take a breath, but he only moves from driving straight to a looping figure eight around me, coming extremely close to grazing me with his tire. The closer he gets, the more I tip my chin up, determined to remain steady. When he revs the engine and goes along the top, his hand reaches out and strokes a strand of my hair, driving me insane.

The dirt bike slows, and he comes to a stop before me, his grin wide and his eyes so dark, they absorb all the lights around us. I expect his praise. What I don't expect is for his hand to cradle the back of my neck before he pulls me in for a kiss. It curls my toes and stokes my arousal even higher. I'm so wet that I worry I'm dripping down my thighs. I throw my arms around his shoulders as the cage starts to lower. He continues to kiss me, his hand squeezing the back of my neck hard. The crowd roars with excitement as he drags me forward. He breaks the kiss long enough to lift me onto the dirt bike in front of him, facing him so I'm riding backward, then the moment the cage is lowered, he takes off down the ramp with me on the front of his bike, my body humming with pleasure.

Club works the crowd as we disappear. Once we're through the tent flaps, he stops and kisses me feverishly. His fingers wrap around my neck and squeeze, tilting me back against the motorcycle. When his other hand sweeps under my skirt and feels my wetness, his eyes flash.

"You were such a good girl," he purrs, stroking me.

"I know. I think I deserve a reward."

His grin is wicked. "Perhaps, but they expect their ringmaster back in there."

Diamond is covered in a fine sheen of sweat. I am too. The heat of the dirt bike filled the metal cage, but I don't care about anything except his hand between my thighs and his lips on my skin.

"Let them wait," I say, gyrating against his hand.

He chuckles. "It's you who will wait, Queen." He strokes me one last time and pulls away. "Makes it all the sweeter."

I mewl in protest, but his fingers on my neck remind me who's in control right now.

"Behave," he growls. "You're not ready for me yet."

"Says who?" I growl back, annoyed and aroused.

"Says me," he hisses before he captures my lips in a brutal kiss. He nips my bottom lip, making me bleed, and I moan into his mouth, desperate for more. "Now be a good girl and go sit back in the crowd."

"You really are a devil," I snarl as he helps me off the bike before dismounting himself.

His eyes meet mine, the black irises so dark, they seem to suck in all the light. "Did you forget, Queen?" he teases. "Just because it sometimes feels like heaven doesn't mean you're not very much in hell." He kisses me one last time as Club appears with his shirt and coat. "We're all devils here, even you, but especially me."

He winks and rushes into the ring to talk to the crowd again. I scowl after him, needy and desperate, and when Club smirks at me, my scowl deepens.

"One of you better fuck me as soon as the show's over," I warn him, "or else someone's going to bleed."

Club's grin widens. "I'll pass the message along."

THIRTY-SIX

By the time the show ends, there's a transition period of taking things down and putting the animals to bed, so I'm left needy. Although I'm still aroused, I remember where I am and what our duties are. I know things can wait, but it still irks me. To take my mind off it, I join in and help clean up, thinking the quicker things are finished, the quicker I can get what I want, but by the time the lights are lowered and the last guest is sent on their way, I'm no longer so on edge. Arousal is a muted hum in the back of my mind. Instead, I focus on the lights around me.

The string lights are still on to guide us to our tents. Soon, even those will be turned down and only a few lights will remain. Tomorrow, the show will go on again, and then the next day, until we move on and repeat the same process. We may be in this area a little longer, though, because it sits in the middle of three different towns. Each night, the show brings in a variety of people, but rarely repeat customers. They come to see the show once, and the temptation of it scares them. Once is enough for them, but I'll never get enough of it.

"I thought I'd find you out here," a voice says behind me.

I don't turn around to look. I already knew who it was before he spoke. Diamond walks with a certain flare the others don't have, as if every step is a performance.

"Have you come to tease me?" I ask, but the words lack the venom they might have had earlier. Exhaustion dances at the edges of my mind now, and although I'd love to fuck Diamond into oblivion, he made himself clear. Whatever beast he thinks he is, he doesn't believe I'm ready for it all alone.

Whatever.

"Perhaps," he muses before taking a seat next to me. We're sitting on the edge of a wooden stage used for various acts. It's stored outside when we're not using it, and it creates a perfect place to watch as the lights start going out across the cirque.

"Great," I say, glancing over at him with a raised brow. "Well, let's see it. What do you have for me?"

His smile is gentle, far gentler than I've ever seen it before. It gives him a boyish appearance that would melt most women. For me, however, it reminds me that he hasn't been innocent in a long time, and that it probably happened violently.

"You're irritated with me," he observes.

"Of course I am," I reply, rolling my eyes. "You worked me up in front of a crowd and then left me wanting. What woman wouldn't be a little agitated after that?" I tilt my head. "I'm not mad though. Your responsibility is to the cirque first."

"You're a part of that responsibility," he remarks before reaching out to take my hand. "I can't leave you needy."

"I'm fine." I huff, crossing my arms. "Don't worry about it."

His dark chuckle should be threatening, but instead, it shoots straight to my core and I'm reminded just how much I want him.

He's silent for a few moments, as if waiting for something, and when another light goes off amongst the tents, his fingers stroke my palm. "I grew up in the cirque, you know," he says, drawing my attention. "My father raised me here. He was a daredevil himself, and he was good at it. When I was little, I wanted to be just like him."

"Are you?" I ask.

"Yes and no," he admits. "I was a daredevil before I became the ringmaster, and I was better than my father was. He didn't like that, even if he wasn't able to perform anymore, but that's where our similarities end. He was weak and often afraid. He hadn't really wanted a child, and I think he spent more time with me during performances than he ever did outside of them. When my mother died, and he was forced to make the decision to take me in or send me away to an orphanage, and he took me only because Hilda told him I was meant to be here." He meets my eyes. "He wasn't the best man, but he was my father."

I study him for a moment, drinking him in, before I nod. "My father is the reason I was able to come to the cirque as a child, the reason I saw you. My mother didn't like it, thought it was improper, but my father indulged me often. He was a good man, but when he died, we were easy prey for Roger." I sigh. "That's to say the men in our lives shape us, yes, but they aren't all that we are. I can tell you think you have more of him in you than you do." I lean forward and cup his jaw. "You said we're all devils, and that's fine, but that doesn't make us bad. Not really. It just makes us misunderstood."

He blinks in surprise. He's not wearing his ringmaster coat anymore, only his shirt and pants.

"You know, sometimes I forget what you suffered before you came here," he murmurs. "You wear your anger so well."

I shrug. "I can't change what happened. I can only live for now." I smile. "I should remind you that you promised to tease me, and I have yet to feel teased since you joined me."

"Oh?" he says, grinning. "Are you still dripping from my touch earlier?"

"Of course I am," I grumble. "You know that. Everyone else was too busy to help me. I'm one second away from touching myself."

"So do it," he says, his eyes hungry.

I still. "What?"

He leans closer. "Reach between your pretty thighs and stroke your clit for me," he commands. "If you're so needy, I want to see it."

I glance around, hesitating despite the lights going out. Most have gone to bed, but there is still a chance others will linger about or come walking up. There's no cover here.

"What if someone sees?"

"Let them," he growls.

"The children—"

"Are in bed," he interrupts, "and far on the other side of the cirque."

He lifts my hand and brings it over my lap. "Touch yourself for me, Ember. Show me how needy you are for me."

"You could just fuck me," I point out.

He grins. "Not yet."

I pout my bottom lip. "Devilish man."

"Beautiful queen," he purrs, his eyes stealing my soul once more. "Touch yourself."

I throw all caution to the wind. This is a game we're playing, and part of me feels as if this is also a test. I want to please him. I want him to praise me. I want him in every way possible.

I trail my hand up my thigh and under my skirt, pushing it aside to reach my core. I'm not wearing underwear, as he well knows, so the moment I find my slickness, I moan and tip my head back.

"Good girl," he purrs, reaching up to caress a single finger along my throat, my collarbone, and between my breasts. "How wet are you?"

"Drenched," I answer, circling my clit with my fingers. "For you."

"Oh, I know," he murmurs. "I wanted to fuck you right there in that cage. I wanted to fuck you on the motorcycle. I want to fuck you right now, but I want you to gush from thinking about what I'll do to you when I get you all to myself."

Thinking about just that, I stroke faster. I press two fingers inside myself, moaning at the stretch, and my hips start to move forward and back. It doesn't take long before I'm panting. I've been desperate for release all night, and Diamond only made it so much worse.

"That's it," he purrs. His hand cups my breast and tweaks my nipple through my shirt. "When I get ahold of you, you'll scream my name. I'll wipe every memory in your mind away and replace it with my image. I'll haunt your dreams."

"Yes." I stroke faster. "Yes, I want that."

"I'll mark your skin, carve my own symbol next to Club's. I'm going to take you to the brink of darkness and push you off the ledge," he whispers in my ear, and my pussy pulses around my fingers. "Dance in the darkness with me, Ember. Dance with the devil."

I pant his name beneath my breath, and he moans before his lips find my neck.

"I want you."

"Then take me," I rasp, so close to exploding.

"No," he growls, the sound dangerous. "Not yet."

I mewl in protest but grind harder against my hand. "Then watch what you make me do."

The release rises like a tidal wave and washes over me violently. My legs shake as my pussy spasms, and I throw my head back. His hand slaps over my mouth to capture my moan as I come around my fingers. It's not enough though. I want more. Oh god, I want so much more.

"That's enough for tonight," he purrs against my throat. "But first . . ."

He reaches between my legs and grips my wrist, dragging my hand up to his mouth. "I want to taste what was meant for me."

He licks my fingers before sucking them inside his mouth. I gasp as he cleans them, taking every last drop, and hums with pleasure.

"Diamond," I beg, desperate for him.

"Not yet," he murmurs, his own arousal stretching his pants. "Not yet."

"For fuck's sake, why not?" I growl, annoyed, aroused, and desperate.

There's fire in his eyes, a raging beast locked up tight behind a cage. He holds the key in his hand, ready to burst out, but he's purposely holding himself back.

"Because I'll destroy you," he snarls. "Because I'll remake you and fuck you until you shatter. Because I won't stop when you beg me to. Because I will take all of you." He grabs my chin roughly. "I will *consume* you, Ember, and you aren't ready for that. You only had a taste of me last time. I let you take control. When I fuck you this time, I will ruin you."

Club appears out of the darkness behind him like a vengeful wraith, his eyes dancing with fire.

"Now be a good girl and let Club fuck you," Diamond orders. "I'll tend to myself."

"I could help—"

"No," he snarls. "I'll tend to the beast. Go." At my hesitation, he flashes his teeth. "Go, Ember."

I stand when Club takes my hand and starts to pull me away. I don't release Diamond's until I'm too far away to hold on, our fingers sliding apart. It pains me to watch him sit there, his eyes riveted to me.

"Diamond," I rasp, worried for him.

The devil who sits on the stage.

The beast who barely restrains himself.

The man who sits in darkness.

THIRTY-SEVEN

I haven't seen Diamond since last night, and I'm concerned. Even after spending an amazing night in Club's arms, my thoughts go back to our surly ringmaster and the devil I saw in his eyes. For some fucking reason, I want to be the one who releases his beast.

I find myself in the big top midday when everyone else is resting for tonight's show, searching for our illusive leader to no avail, but then a whistle cuts through the air. My head jerks up, my eyes widening when I see Heart. He grins at me, hanging upside down from his trapeze wire. One knee is bent over it, and the other leg is near his head. There's no net or safety precautions below him as per usual.

"Queen," he purrs, "welcome to my web of fun. Want to play?"

I should say no, I should find Diamond, but something about the dare in his voice and the taunt in his eyes makes me think he expects me to and that it would alter something between us. Flirting and being with Heart is like walking . . . well, a tightrope. One wrong move and I'll fall, and he won't be there to catch me.

You have to be brave enough to love a monster like him and strong enough to prove it.

The thrill and danger is exciting, pushing me to be better than I was, and maybe I need that right now. I'm feeling a little raw after last night, so maybe I need to remind both of us that I'm no fragile flower.

I'm a queen.

"Queen, do you dare?" His whisper wraps around me, and I can't help but smile.

I turn away without giving him my answer, and I feel his disappointment wash over me, but when I reach the bottom rung of the ladder and kick off my shoes, his inhale fills the air. I don't look at him as I grip the metal rungs. The ladder goes straight up, more of a pole with handles, and it stretches to the very top of the tent where the platforms are attached.

Taking a deep breath, I pull myself up and start to climb, not looking down or back. I don't let myself think, just feel. My hands grip the metal rungs one after the other. I can feel his anticipation, can hear him on the wire, so I turn to see him. He's on his feet, his head tilted as he watches me, and when I meet his gaze, he flips forward, landing on his hands, his feet in the air as he starts to walk toward the platform across the thin wire. My mouth drops at the stunt, and I reach up to the next rung without looking. My hand misses, and I gasp, slipping, my arm hanging down as I lose grip with my feet. He hears and rights himself, watching but not helping.

Gritting my teeth, I yank my arm up and grip the next rung, and he nods in approval, running effortlessly across the rest of the wire and then sitting across from me in front of the platform.

Using all my strength, I quickly ascend the rest of the ladder, and when I pull myself up onto the wooden platform, I meet his eyes, not looking down. Fear makes my heart pound, along with anticipation. My whole body shakes from adrenaline and terror, but when he lifts his hand, holding it out to me, I step closer, heading his way, our gazes locked together. My toes hit the wire, my hand stretched to reach his, and he slides backwards. His hand is still held out to me, his lips tilted up in a smirk.

"Well, Queen?" His seductive whisper makes me swallow. "Will you go backward or forward or freeze out of terror? I can taste it. Can't you?"

Refusing to be weak, I slide my foot onto the wire, taking a deep breath as I slide the other on after. I wobble, my eyes widening as my stomach plummets, but I spread my arms wide like I saw the others doing. It helps keep me upright, and even though I sway from side to side, I don't fall.

His grin only grows, and he slides back again, making it look easy, his hand still held out to me. He rides the air like a bird, effortlessly, and I can't help but slide closer.

"Good girl," he praises. "Look at you. Our bodies weren't built to be trapped on the ground, Ember." He slides back the entire time he speaks. I follow, focusing on his words like a lifeline, even as terror makes my legs shake. One wrong move and I'll fall to my death. "We're meant to soar, to feel the highs of this world. We're not meant to be safe at all times. That isn't living. That's just another form of death. Don't you think?"

"I've felt death," I murmur, moving closer still. "I don't want to feel it again for a very long time."

He stills then, waiting. "So then prove you're alive. Show everyone right now you're free."

I keep going until my hand hits his, and he grins wider. "Look at where you are, Queen. Look at how far you've come." I glance back, my eyes widening when I realize I've traveled over half of the tiny wire hanging in the air, and we stand hand in hand in the middle.

I know I shouldn't, I know it's stupid, but my head turns, and I look at the ground below. The distance from here to there sinks in. The way I'm taunting death sends me off balance. Fear freezes me, and I start to fall.

He releases my hand, letting me.

In slow motion, my feet slip from the wire and I free-fall, my scream erupting from my throat as my heart and stomach plummet.

I catch the wire with one hand at the last second. My entire body screams as my weight hangs on that one limb. My other floats below me as my feet kick, my screams filling the air.

He crouches above my hand, peering down at me.

"Help me," I beg.

"Help yourself, Queen," he orders darkly. "I'm not your savior. You are your own ruler. Take it. Save yourself."

"I can't," I rasp. I turn my gaze back to the ground below and my certain death.

"You can and you will. You're strong enough, Ember. It's time you realize that. Come to me, Queen. Come to me in all your glory. Look death in the eye once more and tell it you aren't his, that your soul is yours and yours alone. Your life is yours to lead." I drag my gaze back to his, tears squeezing from my eyes as my heart pumps triple time, my fingers starting to slip.

I'm going to fall.

I was such a fool.

"Do it, Ember," he roars. "Save yourself or fall. If you can't be strong enough to grasp your life, then you haven't changed from the woman we met all those nights ago and you might be better in death's embrace." He straightens, moving back over the wire, making it clear he'll watch no matter what happens.

He won't save me.

It's up to me.

He's right. It's time I fight for this life. They saved me all those nights ago and have protected me ever since. If I can't save myself now, then am I truly any stronger than I was?

Yes, I know I am.

That Ember is dead, and this new one is a fucking queen. She won't die here, not like this.

I yank my other arm up and grip the wire, gritting my teeth as I try to lift myself, but my muscles burn, and I drop back down. The wire bounces, almost causing me to let go, but I hold on tighter. Sweat trickles down my temples, and I bite my tongue until I taste blood before I swing. My bottom half moves like a pendulum. I can't rely on my upper-body strength alone, so this is the only way. I swing until I come up and over the wire, wrapping my leg around it, gripping it as it continues to bounce.

It's not pretty or elegant at all, but I'm on it, and when it finally slows, I sit up, panting. Blood drips from my lips, and my heart is pounding, but I grin. Heart watches me with pride and hunger in his gaze.

"There you are, my beautiful queen." He drops to his chest, sliding along the wire until he's before me. "I knew you could do it." He sits up, copying my pose. "Now, let's play." He flips to his feet. I'm not capable of that, but I climb to mine a lot less gracefully, holding my arms out for balance. He flips to the other platform, holding his arms out as he waits for me once more.

Taking a deep breath, I run across the wire, laughter tumbling from me at the floating sensation. It feels like I'm flying, and when I run into his arms, he twirls me before slamming me against the wooden platform, grinning down at me.

"Now it's time to really play, Queen." He forces my head to the side, and I gasp when he bites down on my throat. I slap his shoulders, but as the pain melts inside me, I curl my fingers into them, pulling him closer, my thighs falling open as he lies above me. His tongue soothes away the sting as he licks up my neck and across my cheek to my lips, tasting my blood. "You bleed so prettily for us. Watching you fly like that made me harder than ever." He grinds into me, letting me feel it through the thin, skintight pants he wears for practice. "You would have looked so gorgeous floating down to the ground."

It's fucked up, he's talking about my death, but I slide my hands down his sculpted back to his ass, gripping the firm cheeks and tugging him closer. I grind into him as my clit throbs, desire coursing through me with my pounding heart. All my adrenaline and fear transform into hunger.

"Just as pretty as you look under me. Shall I make you fly again, Queen?" he whispers into my lips, his hands hitting the wood on either side of me.

"Yes," I beg, rolling my hips, needing him inside me more than I need my next breath. I can feel his racing heart matching my own as he rubs his solid chest against mine, and then he lifts up, ripping my shirt and pants off, leaving me bare.

His greedy eyes rove over my body. "You look so good on my wire, ready to tumble for me." His eyes look crazed as he reaches down and pinches my nipples until I cry out, digging my nails into his ass to pull him closer.

"Heart," I implore before I realize what he wants.

He wants me to take control of my life, of my desires and my body. He doesn't want Ember; he wants his queen. He wants this bright, alive performer, not a scared woman chained to the floor. He wants to soar with me.

Gripping the stretchy material of his pants, I shove them down and wrap my legs around his waist. My mouth falls open on a moan as he bites my neck again, making it hurt.

"Make me fly," I order, raking my nails down his back until it bows as he snarls. "Make me fly for you, Heart. Show me how it feels."

His hands slide down to grip my hips, and in one smooth movement, he buries himself inside me. His eyes pin me in place as he forces himself deep inside my slick channel. The pleasure and pain make me sing my delight to the rafters as he fucks me.

He pulls from my pussy and slams back in. The force pushes my body higher up the platform, toward the edge, and my eyes widen as he smirks and does it again and again, until I'm hanging from the edge. I start to panic, but I grip his shoulders and stare into his eyes, then I let go.

I relax into him, showing him my trust and devotion.

I might die, but it would be worth it.

He pushes me farther, until my ass reaches the edge of the platform.

My head hangs down, blood rushing to it as my upper body practically levitates in the air. My hands remain on him, trusting him to keep me safe.

"Heart." My back arches as I lift my hips to meet his wicked thrusts, and my nails dig into his shoulders, making blood pool and drip from him onto me. Neither of us care as we fuck harder, our bodies slapping together as he pounds me into the wood.

"You're mine, Queen, my little soaring bird," he states.

"Yours," I respond, closing my eyes as ecstasy pounds through me with each stroke of his cock.

Flipping me, he slams back into my body, gripping my hips as he pushes me farther off the platform until I'm looking at the ground. I jerk my head up and look at the air around us. "Arms out," he orders. "Fly for me."

I do as I'm told, spreading my arms so I feel like I'm flying. He keeps me from falling forward, the spark of danger, of falling, making me cry out and clench around him.

His hands bruise my hips, his blood smears on my skin, and when he pushes me forward until I almost fall, I come with a scream. His roar of satisfaction echoes through the tent as he fills me with his release, keeping him on the edge of falling as ecstasy rolls through us, our bodies locked together.

I slump, and he holds me, his lips brushing my ear in a gentle kiss as his voice wraps around me. "You fly so prettily, Queen. My wire will be here whenever you need to be reminded of who you are and what you're capable of."

Tugging me back into his arms and away from the wire, he curls around me as I pant and smile, closing my eyes in relief and happiness.

My heart still soars like he told me it would.

THIRTY-EIGHT

I keep my feet firmly on the ground for the rest of the day, helping prepare for tonight before I find myself at Hilda's tent. I haven't had a lot of time to practice lately, and I've been feeling a little lost without it. I didn't realize how much I've come to rely on the cards and how they settle me, so I head inside, letting the familiar scent of incense wrap around me as I take a seat opposite her at the table.

"You've been busy." She smirks without opening her eyes.

I feel my cheeks heat, but I grin. "Sorry I'm late—"

"You're allowed to enjoy your life." Her eyes open, and she leans over and takes my hand. "Life is much more than obligations, Ember. It's about new experiences and finding happiness in little moments. You might have joined us out of darkness, but you're allowed to walk in the light as well."

"Thank you," I murmur, squeezing her hand before tilting my head. A question pops out. "Did you ever have a family or a partner?"

She smiles, turning my hand over and rubbing her thumb across the lines in my palm, no doubt reading them, but she answers my question anyway.

"I did once. We were happy for many years. She worked as a rigger. She was five years younger than me, and we didn't meet until I was in my forties. She took the job by chance. We were never meant to meet, but she was my very best mystery. For a woman who sees everything through cards, I never saw her coming. It should have terrified me, but she was the best thing that ever happened to me. We spent years together with our family here, happy and in love. She died many years ago now due to illness. I wish I could say it was something I didn't see coming, but I did. I saw it, and it killed me. There was nothing I could do, and upon her deathbed, she smiled at me. She lived every day like it was her last, and it was one of the reasons I fell in love with her in the first place." She smiles sadly, her gaze distant.

"Even though she's gone, I don't regret it. The happiness we shared lives on with me now, and the memory of our love will keep me going until we meet again. My soul belonged to the cirque, it always will, but my heart was hers and will be in the afterlife. You're the owner of your heart, Ember. Don't give this place everything. Keep some for yourself and find your stolen moments, your love."

I cover her hand with both of mine. "It sounds like you were lucky to have each other, and I have no doubt she's waiting for you on the other side. I'm glad you found love. You deserve it."

"As do you," she murmurs, her eyes softening as we stare at one another.

We are two sides of the same coin, two women destined to know the future through the cards but lost in their own.

She's right. I walk my own path, and I write my own destiny. I sold my soul to the cirque, but my heart is mine to give, and I already have.

I fell in love with the men from this circus, and no matter what happens, I know this is where I will be until the day I die—not because I'm bound to, but because I want to.

"Enough." She grins, pulling away. "The past is just that. Let us focus on the future, shall we?"

I nod, letting her focus on that. She spreads the deck before me, and we practice since I'll be taking over readings from now on and I want to make sure I'm ready. Next, she lays out the other deck—the black one tied to cirque.

"What do you see, Ember? Look into our future." Her voice is far away as I stare at the embossed, black foil deck, something inside of it calling to me.

I reach out blindly, closing my eyes, and shuffle the cards before I flip them over. My heart hammers as I stare at where all the face cards should be.

There's nothing but the card of death.

My eyes jerk up, meeting Hilda's. Her mouth is parted, her eyes wide in fear as she glances from the card to me. "Quickly, Ember. Tell me what you feel," she demands.

I try to sit back, but she yanks me forward onto the deck. "Do not break the connection," she hisses.

Nodding despite my fear, I slide my hand over the deck, focusing once more. "They are screaming at me," I tell her. It grows louder the more I focus on it, and I have to cover my ears. "A warning! It's a warning!" I yell. "It's coming. Death is coming."

I black out, the screaming taking me and my soul.

When I come to, I'm lying on Hilda's chairs. She forces me to sit up and take a drink, and I meet her eyes. "Does that mean what I think it means?"

She nods nervously. She's scared.

"Death is coming for the cirque."

We spend the next hour trying to find out what and how, but it's useless, and I end up wandering aimlessly through the tents. My soul aches, and I'm scared.

I felt fear in the cards . . . the touch of the grave. They weren't wrong.

Maybe because of that lingering touch, I find myself at the big top, slipping inside and watching the performance filled with life.

Happiness saturates the air, and I wish I could smile and clap with them, but my soul is dark.

I watch the show, but my heart is troubled, my mind on the cards, and the cirque seems to pulse around me, as if to agree with me.

Something is coming, something bad.

I just wish I knew from where or how.

My eyes land on my guys as they bow. Will I be strong enough to protect them, or will this be our final show?

THIRTY-NINE

The reading eats away at me, my mind trying to figure out what it could mean. This place was supposed to be our happiness, our freedom, and now something looms over us.

But what?

No matter how many times I seek answers from the cards, they remain silent and steadfast. Death is coming, but that's all they'll tell me. Hilda reminds me that they don't always do our bidding, that they sometimes withhold information so we can make our own choices, but we need answers. *I need answers*. Not knowing is half the horror.

My anxiety prevents me from sleeping, so after hours of tossing and turning, I give up and leave my tent. The town we're in has a lush forest around it, but in the field we're set up in, there are large oak trees. They are probably hundreds of years old, and their branches are so large, they dip down to the ground and back up, leaving nice seats the children have enjoyed during the day. Tonight, I find myself there, my fingers trailing over bark that has seen generations of people come and go. What must they have seen? I find comfort in that now. Time continues on no matter what. Even when I'm gone, this tree will stand as long as nothing comes along to chop it down. That kind of strength is beautiful, and I pull from that now, hoisting myself up on the dipping branch and straddling it. I absorb the strength beneath my fingers, needing it. If I'm stronger, perhaps the cards will give me more information.

Whose death? That's the biggest question. Which one of us will die? Or will we all perish?

I don't know how long I sit here, my legs dangling from the tree, my eyes focused on the leaves above my head. I can see stars through the lush foliage. The wind rustles the branches, and if I squint my eyes just right, the stars look like they are twinkling violently. It's such a pretty sight, I don't realize I'm not alone until a tiger leaps up on the branch beside me.

I jolt in surprise, my arms windmilling as I start to topple over backward. Before I can slide too far, however, strong arms wrap around me from behind and steady me again.

"Sorry about that." Spade laughs. "I told her not to startle you. She doesn't always listen."

I blow out a puff of air and pat Freedom when she bumps her head against my shoulder. If someone would have told me that I'd have the opportunity to pet a wild animal like a house cat a few years ago, I would have called them crazy. The bond Spade and Freedom have is enviable, but she seems to enjoy my company as well. I take every opportunity to give her attention, but only when she asks for it. I've seen Freedom lash out at someone when they threaded their fingers into her fur and she didn't give them permission to touch her. I have no desire to heal from claw marks.

"You couldn't sleep?" I ask, glancing over at him as he hooks a leg over the branch beside me and takes a seat. He's dressed in loose linen pants tonight, as if his sleep were interrupted.

"One of the horses was pregnant," he replies. "She decided to give birth tonight, so I was helping there."

I straighten. I hadn't even known one of the horses was pregnant. "The baby?"

"Healthy and fine, just like its mother," he says with a smile. "Our family grows."

His words remind me that it may shrink again soon, and my shoulders slump. He strokes my back, offering comfort.

"What's wrong, habibti?" he murmurs. "I checked your tent when I was returning to bed and found it empty. What's troubling you?"

I sigh, unsure how to explain. I don't want to worry them, especially when I don't have any real answers myself.

"I read something in the cards," I murmur. Freedom chooses that moment to pull away from my touch and disappear up in the branches of the large oak tree, off to explore.

"Something bad?" Spade asks, tilting his head.

I nod. "Something bad, but I have no other information so I don't know what it really means or who the cards are talking about. All I know is something is coming."

Spade studies me, his beautiful, light brown eyes reflecting the stars and the few lights left on at the cirque. He's always beautiful, especially in his performance outfit, but dressed down like this, he's even more stunning. It feels like he could sweep me away into the desert at any moment. I'd let him. I'd let all of them sweep me away to wherever they wanted to go, even hell.

He reaches up and cups my chin before stroking my jaw. "You know," he murmurs, "when I finally made it to the cirque, it took a long time for me to stop looking over my shoulder for danger."

"This isn't that," I argue. "The cards—"

"Are not set in stone," he interrupts. "Hilda tells me that it's only a possibility."

"This is different," I rasp. "Even Hilda was afraid."

He tilts his head. "I see, and this fear of the unknown keeps you awake." When I nod my head, he sighs. "I understand."

He also dropped a little hint of his past, so I can't help but lean into his touch. "What did you look over your shoulder for?"

The branches rattle above us as Freedom treks along them, her soft chuffs echoing in the air around us. He smiles up in her direction, pleased that she's enjoying herself.

"My foster parents," he admits. "My situation wasn't quite like the orphanage of the kids we saved, but it was close." Anger filters through me, but before I can open my mouth to rant, he presses his finger to my lips. "Shh, habibti. I've been safe for over a decade now. This is just my history."

"Sorry," I say sheepishly.

"Don't be," he murmurs. "I enjoy your protective nature. Still, I'd like you to know where I come from." He leans back against the branch and tugs me after him so we're lying together on top of it. "I was born in the middle east, but I found my way into the foster system here when I was seven. My parents died from some disease that I can't remember and there were nice, rich couples looking for charity projects. I became one of them."

I nestle closer to him for comfort, my fingers stroking his bare chest. Something tells me this isn't a nice story, and I'm prepared for it.

"The couple who fostered me was indeed rich. I was so excited, thinking that these well-off people wanted me, that they could grow to love me, but from the moment I arrived at their mansion on the East Coast, I realized that wasn't the case at all. They didn't want children," he murmurs, his eyes riveted to the stars. "They wanted workers."

"How terrible," I rasp, imagining a tiny Spade desperate to be loved, only to find cruelty instead.

"It was, but at least we were somewhat fed. We certainly didn't eat the same things as they did."

"How many of you were there?" I ask, catching his use of "we."

"Five," he answers. "Two girls and three boys. They put me to work in the gardens mostly, but sometimes, during parties, I was forced to walk around with a tray of drinks and cater to their rich friends. Not a single one of them questioned a bunch of kids working around them. I have memories of being five and offering little slices of cheese to grown, drunk men, but at least I wasn't on the streets. At least I wasn't dying of the same diseases running rampant through my country. They reminded me of that often."

"So what happened?" I ask. "How did you find your way here?"

He takes a deep, rattling breath. "They fed me, but not much, not enough to run far. It was a strategy. If we didn't eat too much, we wouldn't have the strength to run away. Apparently, they learned their lesson before I arrived there. They had a history of using that tactic, and the state continued to allow them to foster, but my escape . . . That's simple. Freedom."

"Freedom?" I ask, frowning up at the tiger in the top of the tree.

"Yes. She was also their captive, arriving a few years after I did. They kept her in a cage in the back garden. She was a source of entertainment, just as I was. She was underfed, but not so much that she wasn't still terrifying. I saw a part of me in her, a caged animal at the mercy of others. She must have seen the same in me. When I started talking to her while I worked around her cage, she'd sit and listen. At some point, I grew foolish enough to pet her. Imagine my surprise when she let me." His soft laughter tells me this was a bit of happiness from his past, that Freedom became that.

"There was a party, another extravagant thing to celebrate something. I couldn't tell you what it was, but the house was full, and we were dressed in our work outfits and given trays. Some drunken asshole knocked into mine as I was walking past and spilled all my drinks. The silence in that ballroom was deafening as everyone turned to look at me. I'd been hit before, but never quite like I was by the man who ran into me. At the silence, he turned and backhanded me."

He shifts against the branch, readjusting me so we're more comfortable. "I remember tasting blood in my mouth as I sprawled across the floor. I remember looking up at him with blood dripping down my lips. I also remember my foster parents watching, drunk and unconcerned, as one of their guests moved to hit me again. When his boot hit my ribs, I screamed and scrambled away. He was drunk and really clumsy. I assume the only reason I avoided being beaten into a pulp was because of that."

"They all sound like assholes," I comment.

"They were, but it's okay. There are always bad people in the world. What they did to me wasn't nearly as bad as what they did to the girls they fostered. I was too young for their games at the time. They preferred their boys to be older."

I gasp and move to sit up, but he holds me against him, his embrace strong and reassuring.

"Don't worry for me, habibti. I escaped, and I got the others out too."

"How?" I ask.

I can feel his smile rather than see it. "When that man tried to come after me again, I ran out of the house and found myself in the back garden. Freedom was sitting up in her cage, her intelligent eyes watching me. She chuffed at the blood on my lips and the way I held my ribs. I walked up to her cage and touched my fingers to her forehead, and she let me, pressing against my palm, asking for help, just as I was asking her." He laughs. "I was a skinny, weak, little boy, but Freedom? She's a queen just like you. She always has been, and she didn't deserve her cage, just as I didn't deserve mine. It was a silly instinct to pull the pin on her lock and open it. She could have killed me, but she didn't. Instead, she climbed down slowly and looked at me as if to say, 'Well, come on, skinny boy. Let's escape together.' She refused to move until I climbed onto her back and pressed my face into her fur."

"So you got out?" I murmur, and on the back of a tiger no less.

"We cut our way out," Spade corrects. "We left through the ballroom, taking down anyone in our way. Some of them laughed when they died, so drunk they didn't realize what was happening. A few of them screamed and tried to run, but my foster parents weren't in the crowd of those who died. They sensed trouble and immediately locked themselves in their safe room, so although we escaped, for a long time, I thought they'd come after me."

"You named her Freedom," I remark, "didn't you?"

He nods. "I did. I tried to set her free after we were safe, but she refused to go. She's been with me ever since. She knew the boy named Roman, and now she knows the man name Spade. I'm both."

I lift up and look down at him, reaching up to cup his jaw. "You freed each other. She needed you just as you needed her."

His eyes sparkle. "Yes, and neither one of us will ever be placed in a cage again, just as you won't be." He strokes my jaw. "My queen. My Ember."

I lean down and kiss him, seeing him for who he is. Spade is always the gentlest of my men, the most sensitive. I assumed it came from being so close to animals and seeing their unconditional love, but it's more than that. It takes great strength to suffer such injustices, to be mistreated and refuse to ever treat anyone the same. It takes strength to remain as gentle as he has, especially with all the badness he sees every time the cirque calls him. It makes me want to protect him despite knowing he doesn't need it. He's a force all on his own. Just because he's sweet doesn't mean he isn't capable of doing terrible things to save those he cares about.

Spade's lips are plump and full, a feature that should be feminine on his face, especially with his long lashes, but it only adds to his masculinity. As I nestle against him, he smells like vanilla and incense, like he was in Hilda's tent recently. I know the two enjoy meditating together. Perhaps he was there at some point today.

When he kisses me, it feels like home, just as it does when I kiss the others. He's gentle and slow, delivering an all-consuming kiss that starts on my lips and ends in my soul. When his hands slide down my back, I moan into his mouth, suddenly desperate for more, needing to taste the freedom he exudes. I'm still not sure if this is all a dream, these men whom I so easily gave my heart to, but I know what I feel is as real as the tree beneath us. What we feel for each other is as old as this wooden giant, as if we were always meant to find each other.

"I need you," I murmur against his lips. "Please."

"You don't have to beg me, habibti," he purrs. "You always have me."

I thank the stars that I'm wearing a nightdress instead of pants this evening. I reach between us and stroke his hard length through his linen pants, moaning at the hardness there. He's so ready for me and as desperate for me as I am for him. I tug the waistband of his pants down, freeing his length, but there's no room or easy way to remove his pants completely, so I leave them where they are, with only his cock exposed.

I pull my nightdress up around my hips and rise to straddle him. Wrapping my fingers around him, I stroke and draw a moan from his lips. His large hands span my waist and hold my nightdress up for me so I can rub the tip of his cock through the wetness between my thighs. I'm leaking for him, desperate to take him, so I quickly direct him to my opening and begin to ease down his length. We both groan as I rock my hips and work down until I'm fully seated. My legs dangle in the air, both of us nestled on this massive branch of this ancient tree, a tiger rummaging through the leaves above us somewhere. Neither of us seems to care about the strangeness of it. Here, there's no oddness. We are just us.

I can't use my legs for leverage, so I end up rolling my hips back and forth, shooting pleasure through my pussy when my clit rubs against his pelvis.

"Yes," he purrs, his hands clenching my hips and helping me move. "Ride me, habibti."

I rock against him, creating a slow buildup of pleasure. There's no rush, no hurried, desperate roughness. It's gentle, passionate, easy, and beautiful, just as Spade is. My tiger tamer. My kind killer. Because he's so gentle with me, I'm the same with him.

Our climaxes build together, as if we choreographed it that way. We rock against each other, the gentle wave making both of us sweat within a few minutes. We moan together, our fingers caressing each other's bodies, and his lips kiss along my neck before he gently tugs my nightdress over my shoulder so he can nibble me there. It's so soft, tears spring into the corners of my eyes.

I've never felt so thoroughly cherished as I do with Spade.

"Come for me, habibti," he purrs against the shell of my ear. "Take me with you."

"Yes," I cry, knowing I could never leave Spade behind no matter the situation. I'd take him with me. I'd take them all with me. Even into death . . .

We shatter together, our cries as soft and gentle as our lovemaking. He whispers words in his native language I don't understand, but they still feel like sweet nothings in my ear. When his hands wrap around me and hold me, I do the same to him, holding on so tightly, I'd be afraid of hurting him if he wasn't so large and muscular.

"I love you," I croak, my tears still falling every so often. Home. This is home.

"And I love you, habibti," he replies.

"Until death?" I ask, my heart throbbing painfully.

"Even after that," he murmurs before kissing my forehead.

Sleep suddenly finds me in Spade's arms, exhaustion finally winning out against fear. I don't realize I've fallen asleep until the world suddenly moves and shifts, and I crack my eyes open and realize Spade is carrying me back to my tent.

Freedom walks beside him, her head brushing against my dangling arm every now and then, offering comfort and kinship.

Another queen who escaped her cage.

We're all just beasts looking for love, I suppose.

FORTY

EMBER

A few days later, the cards still haven't given me any answers. Frustration has me trying to open myself up more to the powers behind them, to the cirque itself, as I watch the children play and grow into themselves. Freedom looks good on them, even Melvin, who looks far healthier than when we found him. They have all put weight back on, their eyes brighter, but some of them are still quiet, their souls damaged beyond what a few weeks or even months of care can cure. It'll take years for some of their trauma to fade. It'll never go away completely, but eventually, it could lessen. My hope is that we can continue to offer them a healing environment to find themselves in.

Since I'm so open to the energy around me, to the cirque, she warns me of their arrival before I see the car come around the bend in the road. I straighten and whistle, warning everyone else. The kids immediately stop what they are doing and look in my direction.

"Get out of sight," I tell them, "just in case there's trouble."

The older kids gather everyone and move them into the tents. I know they'll keep them safe until we find out what the police want.

It's never good when the cops show up, especially after the

attack. Part of me worried they would retaliate at our audacity to survive and thrive, but instead law enforcement is on our doorstep. It looks like something happened to bring them our way.

Diamond appears at my side first, the others right after.

"What's going on?" Spade asks, his eyes on the single cop car pulling off the road.

"I don't know," I reply, "but something doesn't feel right."

The gloom that's been hanging over me since the cards spoke of death darkens as two cops climb from the car and adjust their belts. One of them has a large mustache he clearly takes pride in. The other looks young, fresh, like a rookie. Neither one of them glances at the tents with kindness as they take it all in, their lips curling up in disgust.

"What can we help you with, officers?" Diamond asks, his voice taking on the same tenor he uses for shows. He's clearly trying to avoid any trouble before it begins. We can't afford any more death after the last attack, even if it hangs over our heads like a promise.

"We have no business with you, circus freaks," the older cop says, his eyes hidden behind aviator glasses. He looks over our group before his gaze settles on me. "Our business is with Ember Campbell."

I tip my chin up. "I don't go by that name anymore."

"Funny," the rookie says, "because you're still married, as far as we know."

The older cop doesn't correct him, but he straightens, his gaze on me behind his glasses. He doesn't spare any of the others a glance, as if he doesn't care. Other members of our family appear from the tents, curious about what's going on.

"What do you want with Ember?" Diamond asks.

"It's none of your business, freak," the rookie sneers.

Diamond smiles, and the rookie stiffens at the look. It's not a nice smile. "Everyone in this cirque is my business," he says, his tone threatening. "Now, tell us your reasons for encroaching on our camp."

The rookie's lips curl, and he opens his mouth to respond, but the older cop holds his hand up to stop him, and he snaps his mouth closed immediately.

"You've been reported as a missing person, Mrs. Campbell." I grit my teeth at the use of the surname, but I hold my response until he finishes. "Your husband, Dr. Campbell, reported that you'd been kidnapped by these . . . people. We're here to bring you home."

My blood goes cold, and I take a step back. "My husband?"

"Come with us and we'll take you home," the officer says with a nod. "Then we can put this all to rest."

The gloom over my head darkens further. "No," I tell them.

"Now, Mrs. Campbell—"

"Don't call me that!" I snarl, taking another step back. "I want nothing to do with that man! You've delivered your message. Now leave."

The rookie sneers. "Don't be stupid. No one chooses to stay with these freaks."

"I did," I hiss. "I do. No one kidnapped me. This is my home."

Club curls his fingers around my forearm, offering comfort, and the older cop takes note of the movement. When his hand twitches toward the gun on his hip, Diamond snarls.

"I suggest you don't make that mistake," Diamond warns. "We're not being aggressive, officer."

He pauses, clearly realizing just how outnumbered he is. "You're going to come with us, Mrs. Campbell."

"No," I repeat. "I'm not. He doesn't own me. I'm not property. He filed a false report. You should be investigating him and his malpractice."

The cop's eyes flash, and I realize he knows what my husband is up to but he's also been paid off.

"Home isn't here," he says carefully. "You either come with us now or we'll make you. Stockholm syndrome is a real killer."

"Come on, girlie," the rookie cajoles, and because he's an idiot, unlike his partner, he takes a step forward and draws his gun. "Get in the car."

Everyone surrounds me, my family, my cirque. Each of them offers me strength, protecting me. I tilt my chin up, bolstered by their support. The rookie freezes, his eyes widening even as his partner hisses at him to stand down.

"Listen to your master," I tell him, and he tenses. Oh, he really doesn't like that. "I suggest *you* get in your car and leave. I won't be going anywhere with you, and you can tell my *husband* I don't belong to him. That hold expired the night he tried to kill me."

"Alright," the older one says. "Okay. We're leaving." The rookie whips his head toward him, but the older cop sneers, "Get in the car."

The kid clearly doesn't like it, but he listens because he doesn't have any choice. He holsters his weapon and turns to climb into the car. The older one hesitates for a moment.

"We're leaving," he declares, his eyes on me. "But we'll be back."

"I'd warn you against that," I retort, my expression hard.

He pulls his glasses away and reveals eyes too blue for someone so slimy. "Your husband sends his love."

My stomach roils as he climbs into his car and turns the engine on.

By the time he disappears around the bend, I lose the breakfast in my stomach, my body trembling and covered in a cold sweat.

My men don't leave my side, but the gloom over my head gets worse.

FORTY-ONE

It doesn't take us long after the cops depart to decide what to do. We're leaving, and now. They know where we are, and it was a clear threat. They'll be back and probably with backup. I know it won't end well. Men like that with guns have been killing people like us for far too long. They also have the power and means to get away with it.

We're just freaks, after all.

I won't let my family be hurt, nor will I be dragged back to Roger.

Diamond gave the command, but my plea made him do so. We could stay and fight, but something in me knows that won't end well. The cards are still hanging over my head, the warning of death . . .

Is this it?

Maybe if we are fast enough, we can escape it.

My hands fist the costume Club gifted me, and I look beyond its bright silks to the cards. I can feel them pulse, still feel their intention.

Death, death, death.

It repeats in my mind like a mantra, and my fear only grows. Closing my eyes, I thrust the silks away and cover my ears. "Please, stop," I beg the cirque. It doesn't relent, only grows stronger.

Even if we run, he'll come after me no matter where I go. I thought he would let me go, but I was wrong. Has he been planning this all along? He's a doctor. He has money. He can get away with just about anything. There's no telling what he'll do as payback for not only me leaving him, but also for what my guys did to him. They embarrassed him, they scarred him, and worst of all, I stood up to him.

The cirque's presence tightens around me until I gasp. Is it him? Is he the death that's coming?

It's a possibility, and the idea that the man who tormented me for a large portion of my life is the reason I might lose my happiness, my new home, fills me with a terror and type of fury I have never felt before. It darkens my soul, calling to the cirque.

I should have killed him. I should have ended it when I had the chance.

I realize now what Hilda meant about kindness being my weakness. I let a man who hurt me, raped me, beat me, and tried to kill me go. I thought it made me better than him, but it only made me a weak fool.

It didn't make me stronger; it made me stupider. I should have known only death would stop a man like him, and now it might be too late.

Is there a place in this world where we can run to escape this promise lingering in the air?

Worse yet, will they run with me?

I don't know, and that scares me. We are strong and powerful, but there is something infinitely more dangerous about a man who has nothing else left to lose while I, on the other hand, have everything.

No, I can't let it end like this.

We'll go. We'll escape him and this warning. We have to.
I won't lose my home again.
He won't take another thing from me!

267

FORTY-TWO

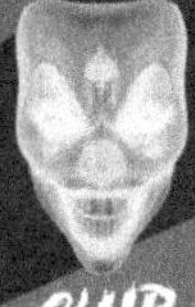

We travel for two days, but Ember doesn't seem any more settled. It worries us. I know all too well the fear she's experiencing, so we hold her at night in her tent. We offer her the comfort and strength she needs when she's feeling weak. No matter what she's thinking right now, he can't have her, and neither can the police.

She's ours. She's our queen, our heart, our everything.

Nothing will take her from us, and I will hold her close until she believes that.

I stay awake all night, watching her face and realizing she doesn't escape her worries even while sleeping. When dawn rises, she gasps awake as if a brutal nightmare demands she rise. My heart twists into knots at the pain in her eyes as she looks at me. She cups my cheek, and I lean into her warmth. Her eyes sweep across my face as if memorizing it, as if she's worried it will be the last time she sees it.

I lean in and kiss her softly, wishing I could take these concerns from her eyes, stop her nightmares, and change her past, but I can't.

Like all of us, she's stuck with the horrors that brought her here. I won't let them claim her again, just as my own have been dampened. I pour that into my kiss.

I will keep her safe no matter what.

I will keep our family safe.

I feel her tears against my skin, and each one is like a brick in my heart. I carry them with me, a reminder of what we are fighting for.

A pulse yanks us apart and wakes the others, our eyes widening.

"A call," I murmur, and she nods, swallowing hard. "Are you okay to do this?"

"I have no choice. None of us do," she reminds me. "We answer the call no matter what. It's our duty."

"I choose my heart over duty," I tell her. "If you can't, then I will stay here with you. I will choose you."

I expect the cirque to strike me down, but I don't care. I fear losing her more than anything else.

Her smile brightens her entire face before she leans in to kiss me softly. "I love you for that," she whispers. The words make my heart skip a beat, and hope and love pound through me so hard, I'm surprised she can't feel it. "But I can handle it. I'm stronger than any of you know. I have to be for what's coming."

I fear that she's right.

I never know what to expect when we get a call, especially so early in the morning. It can't mean anything good. Most sins are committed in the dark, when people feel brave. Something about that oppressive cloak makes human monsters courageous enough to commit heinous sins, but right now, the sun shines brightly down on us. It's a cozy day, a happy one, and we hesitate at the entrance to a wildflower field where the call drags us.

It feels strange.

The others clearly agree with my wariness, but we spread out, trying our best not to disturb or crush the flowers as we prowl through their midst, searching for the source of the throbbing echo in our souls. The call gets stronger as we search until we see a man sitting in the middle of the field with flowers crushed around him. I whistle to let the others know he's here.

Tilting my head, I prowl around him and crouch, my eyebrows rising under my mask at the sight. He's not hurt. In fact, there isn't a single mark on him. His skin is tan and perfect, his hair glossy and styled. Even his clothes are pressed and unwrinkled, but his expression is dead.

Next to him, surrounded by flowers, is a revolver with a joker card beside it. It's the most pristine card I've ever seen on a call.

He doesn't seem scared nor shocked to see us. He simply blinks and glances down at the gun, and I realize why we're here. He isn't in danger. He *is* the danger—to himself.

He's going to kill himself, and with some instinct deep inside his soul, he called us, even if he didn't realize what he was doing.

"You called us," I murmur, not letting Diamond speak. Something in his eyes reaches into my soul and calls to my own pain. I know what it feels like to think there is no way out. My family, the cirque saved me, and now, Ember saves me every day.

Sometimes all it takes is one helping hand, one word, one act of kindness to change the trajectory of someone's life. Despite the numbness in his eyes, he called to us, which lets me know he isn't as far gone as he wants us to believe.

Somewhere deep inside, he wants to live. He just doesn't know how.

"Is this really how you want to end your life? Here, alone in a field?" I ask carefully.

His laugh is bitter, and it raises goose bumps on my arms as his fingers stroke the gun with familiarity. "I didn't think anyone would care or that anyone would come." His eyes rise to mine, and I swallow.

Sometimes it isn't the monsters that live outside us that are the most dangerous—sometimes it's the ones that live within us.

"You called us," I repeat. "We will always come. Do you have a family? Anybody?"

This one is different. There is nothing we can slay for him. He has to be strong enough to do it himself.

"Not anymore," he croaks. "There was a woman once, a fiancée, but after the war, I couldn't be what she needed." He looks back at the flowers. "How could I be? I hurt her every night, fighting off my dreams, my attackers that don't exist anymore. A car backfired and I scrambled for cover, still hearing the screams. I can see, smell, and feel blood on my hands. I don't deserve to live, not when so many of my friends died in my arms." He shows his palms like the blood is still there, and for him, I bet it is. "So many died, and I lived." He looks up at me. "Why? Why me?"

"I don't know. Sometimes there's no reason. It just is what it is. You're alive, and they aren't. It isn't because of some great plan or because a God deemed it so, and it also isn't because you were better. You got lucky. So many fought and died to live. Are you truly going to give that up?" I murmur.

He swallows and grabs the gun, but he hesitates.

"We can't force you to live. You have to make that choice, but you called to us. Deep down, you wanted someone to offer you a helping hand. It might seem bleak and helpless now, but take a breath, and then another. Let the moment pass. Today will end. Dawn will come once more with new opportunities. It's never too late to start over. Don't die here and end that. Death is final. It's easy. Living is harder. Your friends . . . Would they want this, or would they want you to live?"

"They are gone," he snaps.

"And you are their legacy. Their memories live on with you. I can't take away what you have endured, and the cirque knows we can't fight these demons for you, but I think someone strong enough to fight for their country and their friends is strong enough to fight for his life . . . for his future. Don't let their sacrifices be in vain." I hold out my hand. "It's your choice—live or die here. I won't make it for you."

He glances between me and the gun, ghosts passing through his eyes. "I don't deserve to live," he says. "It should have been me, not them, but I'm here. You're right. They'd hate me for doing this." He picks up the gun, and I tense as he lifts it, but he simply hands it over and stands instead of pointing it at himself.

Nodding at me, he turns and walks through the flower field, but a weight seems to have lifted from his shoulders. At the edge of the field, he looks back at us watching him, a new light in his eyes. "Well? Are we going?"

I'm not saying it'll be easy. He'll still be haunted by his past, but he made a choice today.

He chose life, and now he has to fight for it.

FORTY-THREE

On the ride back to the cirque, we learn the soldier's name is Greg Stonewall. He's in his late thirties and obviously wrestling with his demons, but he's taking a chance with us. He chose to live, and I respect the hell out of him for it. Here, the only information we know about war is what the newspapers tell us, but that all pales in comparison to the reality of it. Roger, as a doctor, should have been drafted and sent to help, but he paid someone off to go in his place. I hated him for that, not because he got out of going, but because I wanted him to go and possibly never come back. It would have been a reprieve. If that makes me a terrible person, then so be it.

This man, however, doesn't deserve the demons plaguing him. I can see it in his eyes. He's a good person, or at least he tries to be.

When the soldiers returned from war, they were celebrated as heroes. It wasn't their fault that they were sent overseas, but it was their fault that they won. I can't remember how many lives were lost, but it was a lot. Roger never let me read the paper for too long, so I couldn't get a thorough image of it in my mind, but I know it was bad. We all know it was bad. Those of us who didn't have to go were left with the information that someone else was fighting for us, and for what? The terrible people that many of us are? I never understood it, but I hadn't experienced freedom the same way others had.

Now, here is this man, a survivor of that war, but can one really call it surviving? The government brought these men home with their phantoms and demons and expected them to go back to normal life. They didn't help them in any way, and it wouldn't surprise me if Greg wasn't the first to stare down the barrel of a gun.

What I wonder, though, is how he got a joker card.

I'm sitting in the back with Greg and Club, while Spade, Diamond, and Heart sit in the front. I'm no stranger to the process of the joker card, as Hilda gave me my own so long ago, but this man doesn't look like the kind to come to a circus, especially since he'd been to war.

We already introduced ourselves and went through the motions, but we fell into silence after. When I glance over at him, Greg looks back at me with bright eyes, something in them speaking of hope.

"So have you ever been to Cirque Obscurum before?" I ask, having already lifted my mask. There's no longer any need to hide my identity with him.

He shakes his head. "No. Never."

I hum under my breath, curious. "Where did you get the card?"

"The card?" he asks.

"Yes, the joker card." I pull out the pristine card and hold it up. "This one. It's how you called us."

He glances at the card and away. "Can I keep it?"

I hesitate and look up at Diamond in the mirror.

"It's usually meant for us to take it," Diamond says, "but it's not mandatory."

Greg nods gratefully and takes it from me with a shaking hand. "You want to know where I got it?" When I nod, he sighs. "I didn't actually know it would call . . . people. I thought . . . Well, I thought I'd see my buddy again. We fought together overseas. His name was Edmond Ford. We just called him Ed."

"Edmond Ford?" Diamond repeats, something in his tone catching our attention.

"You knew him?" I ask.

Diamond nods. "He was a teenager at the cirque when I was a kid, but I didn't have much interaction with him. He left a few years after he came of age." His eyes meet mine in the mirror. "I guess we know where he went."

Greg nods. "Ed was a great man, always helping out and making sure we were safe and accounted for. We became close, and one night after we'd had a bit too much to drink, he handed me that card and told me not to lose it. He said it would come in handy when I needed it, and all I had to do was hold it and help would come. I always thought he meant like . . . theoretically, not actual help." He tucks the card into his breast pocket and pats it. "Anyways, he died the next morning. Bomb dropped on us. I was lucky enough to be out at the wall. Ed? Not so much."

His words are pained, as if the memory itself carries a heavy weight. I don't doubt it does. He speaks of Ed in a particular way, as if they were brothers. Losing someone like that sticks with you.

I pat his knee. "Even in death, Ed is taking care of you," I tell him. "And now it's our turn to do the same."

When we arrive at the cirque, there's a welcome party waiting for us. Since the kids arrived, it's been like this. They wake and realize we're gone, then they wait until we return safely, both to make sure we're okay and to help whoever comes with us. Sometimes, it's no one. Lately, it's been other children. Tonight, it's a veteran who needs a purpose.

Greg's eyes light up when the kids come rushing forward, gushing excitedly about how they are happy he's there and asking if he brought any sweets. He glances at me, confused, and I smile.

"They all have their own nightmares, Greg. They are here to heal." I tilt my head. "They could use someone to look after them, kind of like Ed used to do for you."

His face contorts with emotion, and in the low light of the circus bulbs, I see his eyes glisten.

"I can do that," he rasps. "Something so innocent shouldn't have demons."

"But they do," I murmur. "We all do." I rest my hand on his shoulder. "But together, we can overcome them."

Greg nods. "I'll protect them with my life."

"I know you will," I answer with a smile. I see hope in his eyes, a newfound purpose giving him something to reach for. This is what he needed. This is the home he sought. Now he's here, where he belongs.

It's not often our call ends without bloodshed, but for tonight, I'm thankful it did. I'm thankful I am here to see Greg laugh with a crowd of children begging to check his many pockets for candy.

I'm also grateful that he gave Club his gun without hesitation.

FORTY-FOUR

Sleep came easily that night. I spent it wrapped around Heart, but when I awake the next morning, I'm alone in my tent. I stretch and pull on some loose clothing, the need to be comfortable strong today. I put my hair up on the top of my head in a bun and step out into the sunshine. It's strange to think there's a sense of doom hanging over us and that Roger could mess this all up, but for today, we're in a different town, far from the cops who found us, and the sun is shining.

I go in search of the others but find their tents empty. No doubt they are off completing their tasks for the day. Today, I don't have anything to do, as we're already set up and everyone has their tasks. Later, I'll find Hilda and we'll ask the cards for clarification on the looming threat, but for now, there's nothing to do but enjoy myself.

I don't find any of the men in the food tent, nor in any of the surrounding ones. When I ask Dr. Louie if he's seen them, he informs me that Diamond and Heart went to hang up posters around town for the show but that he thought he saw Club and Spade in the circus tent, so that's where I head. I wonder if they are practicing a new act. I love when they try something new. It seems as if they are never happy with the same old performances. They are always learning and pushing themselves harder. When I enter the circus tent, however, it's empty save for long ribbons hanging from the rafters.

I frown, looking up at the new streamers in confusion. I touch them and find they are soft but sturdy, the bright red fabric clearly meant for something other than decoration. The ribbons are wide when I pull them open but easily scrunch together. As I look at them, the other ribbon suddenly jerks away and wraps around me, capturing me. When I see Club's teasing face through the ribbons around me, I relax. For a moment, I reached for the knife at my hip.

"What are you doing?" I laugh, trying to free myself and failing. "Is this your attempt to capture me?"

"It isn't an attempt if I'm successful," he teases, leaning in for a kiss. "Good morning."

"Good morning," I reply. "Is this for something new?"

He nods. "Spade had the wonderful idea of trying an aerial silk act. I'm not so sure myself. Being in the air is usually Heart's thing."

"Heart would love this," Spade says as he appears behind Club. He, too, leans in to kiss me. "But he's not the only one who can fly."

"I prefer to have my feet on the ground," Club reasons. "I don't think this is for me."

"Nonsense." Spade tsks. He reaches for the silk I'm not wrapped up in and tugs. "I saw this act at another circus we passed before you came along, Ember, and I've been searching for the silks ever since. I finally found them, so now you get to witness our attempts."

Club rolls his eyes. "How exciting."

Spade taps his shoulder, running his eyes over him in a lingering way that heats my skin. "You're limber enough, so this should be easy for you, sword swallower. Don't discount yourself just yet." He eyes me. "I'd wager Queen would also be great at it."

I perk up. "I can try." Then I remember Dr. Louie's warning. "As long as I don't drop too hard on my leg. Dr. Louie says I need to be careful."

Spade nods. "Then you will wait. When he clears you, we'll

string you up in silks." When my eyes darken with his words, he clears his throat. "Of course, we could always suspend you without danger of injury."

Club brightens. "I like that idea better."

"I don't want to get in the way of your practice," I murmur. "I can leave if it'll help."

"No," Spade says, shaking his head. "You're staying. Practice first. Fun later."

The next hour is spent with me watching them attempt different holds in the silks. Spade is probably the best teacher for this. He's patient and soft-spoken. When Club gets annoyed with a particular hold not working, Spade is there to reassure and realign him. Both of them learn together as a unit, and I know eventually, they'll be able to bring this act to the show, the tiger tamer and the sword swallower, dancing in silks. When Club says he needs a break, they stop, and Spade looks over at me. Both of them are covered in a fine sheen of sweat. It highlights their muscles as they stand in their skintight pants, looking at me.

"Ember," Spade begins, and the way he says my name makes me sit up straighter. "Come here."

Spade is always the sweet one, and his command comes in his soft, tender voice, but there's something firm in his words, as if it leaves no room for argument. I stand immediately and walk over to him, desperate to know what he has planned for me.

"Were you paying attention?" he asks.

I nod. "It's all in your hold and the way you wrap the silks."

"Good girl," he murmurs. It's the same voice he uses on Freedom. It's the difference between leading with love and anger. Spade gives his love to those he cares for freely.

"You can't go too high," he says, "or Dr. Louie will have my head, but we can show you."

Club reaches up for the silk and wraps it around my waist before tying it at my back. "Or we can simply have you," he whispers in my ear. He tightens the knot before I can answer, and my heart rate kicks up a notch. I tug at it, but it holds strong, keeping me bound between them. Club kicks my feet out from beneath me, and I swing up with a screech until I'm upside down. Club holds me still, so that my head hangs level with Spade's pelvis. He strokes my legs before he grabs my pants and tugs them up and off, leaving me bare, then he slowly spreads my legs. My hands shoot out to latch onto Spade's thighs in an attempt to steady myself.

"Look at you, already glistening for us," Spade purrs. "We haven't even touched you yet."

I gasp as one of them swipes a finger through my wetness, testing me. "Watching you is sexy," I admit. This position makes all the blood rush to my head, but I manage to steady myself and form a coherent thought. "Of course I'm wet."

Club groans at my admission. "You're practically dripping, baby. I can't wait to bury myself inside you, but first . . ." He kneels so he can see my face. "I want to see you suck Spade's cock like this." He reaches up and pulls Spade's pants down, revealing his hard length.

For a moment, my breath freezes in my chest. Spade grasps himself and tries to step back, but Club grabs his hips with a chuckle and tugs him forward. As I watch, wide-eyed, Club's hands slide up Spade's body, making him shudder and release a tormented sigh.

"Look how hard he is for you, so ready for you to swallow him." Club's hands slide lower, and as I watch, he circles Spade's length, making him jerk in his fist.

"Club," Spade warns, his voice breathless, but he doesn't sound angry—no, he sounds desperate.

I glance up at Spade to his wide eyes burning brightly, looking between Club and me like he can't make up his mind. Dropping my gaze once more, I watch Club stroke Spade's length, pumping him until he whimpers.

"I don't want him to come anywhere but in that pretty mouth. Next time, though, I might just let him." Spade and I groan at that idea as Club grabs my head and directs me forward, pressing my lips to the tip where a bead of precum appears. "Open wide, little star."

I do so without question, parting my lips. Spade isn't rough, but Club grabs a fistful of my hair and swings me forward so I gag on Spade's cock. The momentum moves me back again before I can truly choke, but Spade takes over and follows me, gently thrusting down my throat, his soft groans filling the air alongside the sounds coming from me.

"That's it," Club purrs. "You take him so well."

My pussy clenches at his praise, and I'm desperate for more, but suspended as I am, I'm at their mercy. When Club stands and disappears, I try to anticipate where he'll touch me. Spade suddenly bottoms out in my throat, pressing inside as Club tilts me, my spine bowing as Spade keeps my head pressed back. I'm parallel with the ground now, floating in the air between them, but Spade doesn't stop. The way my back is bowed is almost painful, but I forget that the moment I feel someone's mouth on my core. I cry out around Spade's cock, my body starting to shake.

Spade strokes my neck as he presses inside, his hands exploring my throat moving around him. "So beautiful. You're so perfect, it should be a crime."

Club swirls his tongue around my clit, his fingers probing my entrance, and I explode so fast, I nearly convulse with my surprise. My legs shake as they drape over his shoulders, weak from such a quick release. He hums against me, sending sharp tingles through my core, and stands.

"You taste just as good as you look," he purrs before I feel him settle between my thighs. "I need you so badly. Come on my cock next, Queen. Mark me with your release."

He thrusts inside me. I'm so wet, he meets no resistance as he bottoms out and immediately pulls out to slam in again. I cry out when Spade pulls back, but it's cut off when he slides into my throat. They match their rhythms, Spade pressing in when Club pulls out of my pussy, Club pushing in when Spade pulls out. They fuck me with wild abandon in the middle of the circus tent, suspended from a silk. I convulse between them, my body no longer my own, my cum dripping to the floor below. Fingers stroke my entire body as they fuck me. My hands can do nothing but hold on. I have no control at all, and I love it.

Spade groans, his hand clamping around my throat as his pumping grows erratic.

"Not yet," Club growls. "A few more seconds."

"I can't," Spade rasps. "I'm going to come."

Club furiously thrusts inside me, hard and fast, his body beginning to tighten. I shatter between them, my body convulsing over and over again as they race to their own orgasms.

"Now," Club growls just as he slams inside me and holds, his cock jumping in my core, forcing me into another release. I can't cry out because Spade does the same to my throat, filling it until it spills out around my lips and drips down my cheeks. When they finish, they pull out, leaving me suspended between them until they gently unwrap me and lower me to the ground.

"That's our queen," Club coos as they embrace me, his mouth sliding over the mess on my face—Spade's mess. "So perfect and ours."

They drop tiny, featherlight kisses over my face, down my neck, and along my shoulders, and I can't help the goose bumps that erupt along my arms. I let them hold me, let them love me, and when I wrap my arms around them and sigh, they nestle closer.

"I think I like aerial silks," I croak, my voice raw.

Their soft chuckles make my heart swell, and I pull them tighter against me.

My tiger tamer and my sword swallower.

FORTY-FIVE

"Remember, best behavior," I warn them.

Greg's eyebrow arches, and Melvin sighs at me since I've already repeated this a million times this morning. The truth is, we have no choice but to go into town. We need supplies for all the new members we've been taking in, and Melvin and Greg volunteered to go. I think Greg only did it for Melvin, since he's grown protective of the kid, and Melvin wants to help so desperately. He's still healing, but he's doing a lot better, and as he has healed, his personality has begun to shine. He, along with Greg, have been looking after the other kids, but it's clear he wants to do more. It's almost like he's worried that if he isn't useful enough, we'll leave him behind. We won't, we've told him that, but I know it's a hard instinct to lose.

Greg, he, and I drive into town. The guys are busy, and I know they won't be happy, but when Melvin approached me with the idea, worried about some of the kids' missing items, I couldn't say no. I don't see any harm in going to a shop in broad daylight. The town is small and quiet. They haven't seemed bothered by our arrival, and I know we are far away from the cops and Roger, but I'm not dumb. I keep my eyes peeled, and at the first sight of danger, we're out of here.

"We could have asked some of the hands," Greg reminds me as we climb from Diamond's car. He's right, we could have, but I guess Melvin isn't the only one feeling the need to prove themself useful.

"We're here now." I smile at him, wrapping my jacket tighter around me. As we step onto the sidewalk before the store, we automatically put Melvin between us, and we smile at each other when we realize what we did. Greg opens the door and holds it for us, and we duck inside as a tiny bell rings.

It's a small store, clearly family run, with bright white walls with posters and sales. There are only five aisles, but it's enough for what we need. A bored, young man is reading the paper behind the register at the back. He doesn't even look up as we enter, only shouts, "Hello."

It's perfect.

Grabbing a few baskets, I hand one to each of them. "Get everything we need, and we'll meet at the checkout. Don't worry about expense. Let's ensure they never want for anything."

I watch them hurry down different aisles, and I choose the hygiene section. There are a few young girls, so I make sure to fill the basket with anything we might need before dropping it at the register and grabbing another. I'd rather make fewer trips into town, especially right now, so it's important we stock up when we can.

"Do you have any more of this?" I hold up the bottle I need, and the bored kid blinks at me before glancing at it.

"Uh, in the back, I think. Let me check." He looks me over once more, his cheeks heating, before he ducks into the back of the shop. I browse the aisle, crouching to grab some pads from the bottom shelf, when the bell over the door rings. I spare it a look but don't see anyone, so I turn back to the pads and grab a bunch more of different sizes for the future. A shuffle of feet echoes in the aisle.

"Ember." My name is tight with worry and fear—Melvin.

I jerk my head up, frowning, before terror fills me and I freeze.

Standing at the end of the aisle is Melvin, the basket gone from his hand, his face pale, and there is a hand on his shoulder in a clear threat. It's the one person in this world I never wanted to see again—Roger, my husband.

He smiles at me. "Hello, wife. I've missed you."

I straighten, leaving the basket on the floor as I face the man who still haunts my dreams. The daylight illuminates him, making him look like an angel, but I know the devil that hides under that charming smile and perfect clothing. For a moment, I'm back to hiding in the dark, hoping he won't hurt me.

I'm not her anymore.

Stepping closer, I drop my eyes to Melvin. "It's okay," I tell him, forcing a smile before I meet Roger's eyes again. "Let him go."

"No, I don't think I will." Roger's hand constricts on his shoulder, and Melvin's eyes tighten, but he doesn't let out any sound indicating it hurts, even though we both know it does. My hands clench into fists at my sides.

"What do you want?" I demand.

"What do I want?" His laugh startles me. It's sudden and wrong. "I want my wife to come home, of course."

"Never happening. Let him go and leave, Roger. Just leave us alone. I spared you once. I won't do it again," I warn.

"Are you threatening me, Ember?" he purrs, tugging Melvin tighter against his body, his hand tightening once more on his shoulder. Melvin lets out a gasp of pain, one that goes straight to my heart like a spike. "You've grown brave in your time away from me. Not to worry. I can break that again. If you come home now, I'll let them live. I only want you. If not . . ." His hand tightens even more, his threat obvious. "Well, we both know I know exactly how to make it hurt and end a life. You're mine, Ember. Now come home."

He holds out his other hand. Gritting my teeth, I glance at Melvin, trying to assure him it's okay as I step closer, needing to get him away from Roger before he hurts him further.

I glance briefly at Greg, who is sneaking up on them, no doubt hearing the commotion, and I shake my head slightly. We can't risk him hurting Melvin.

"Now, Ember. I'm losing my patience. This is your last warning," Roger snaps.

"I will never go with you," I spit as I step closer, reaching out and gripping Melvin's arm. "This is your last warning. If I see *you* again, I won't spare you. I'll kill you myself."

A noise behind me has Roger glancing away for a second.

"Hey! What the hell are you doing?" the teenager calls as he emerges from the back. It's the distraction we need. I grab Melvin and push him through the door behind him and Roger, shopping forgotten. Greg runs after us, and we dive into the car and take off without any delay, desperate to get away.

My heart beats strongly in my throat as I realize how close we were to being in trouble. When I glance in the mirror, I see Roger standing in the middle of the road, his hand lifted in a wave and a mocking smile on his lips.

The message is clear—he'll see me soon—but I meant what I said.

The next time I see my husband, I'll kill him. He won't hurt my family.

He won't take my home from me.

FORTY-SIX

It only takes one look at Ember's face for me to realize something is very wrong. I drop from the silks I'd been playing on, my bare feet hitting the big top floor as the others follow my gaze. All of us instantly forget the setup we were working with.

"Ember?" Spade asks nervously.

She's pale as she glances between us and swallows hard. "Roger is close," she announces. Those three words are filled with terror, and a fire ignites within me I can't contain, my madness flaring as I see her fear.

I never want her to be afraid, not like this, and I prowl toward her, needing her to understand she's safe. My eyes run across her body, checking for any injuries, but she seems unharmed.

"He threatened her," Greg says at her side. Melvin is tucked under his arm, but Greg looks at Ember, checking her over.

"Take Melvin and watch him," Diamond snaps.

Greg nods, shooting Ember another worried look before he wraps his arm around the kid and guides him from the tent, leaving us alone with our girl.

"What happened?" Club asks as I circle Ember, pulling her into my arms and placing my head on her shoulder. She lets out a shuddering breath and leans back into me, her hand covering mine on her stomach.

"We ran into town to get supplies. He showed up while we were shopping. He threatened Melvin in an attempt to get me to go with him. I managed to get out, but he's here. We have to leave. He'll come—"

I slide my hand across her face and cover her lips as I press my mouth to her ear. "Breathe deeply for me," I command. Sliding my other hand up, I press it against her chest so she's tight against me. "Breathe with me. In." I take a breath and release it. "Out."

She slowly starts to relax, leaning back into me.

"No more going into town alone. We do everything together," Diamond orders. "But we aren't leaving." He shares a look with us. "Let him come. He'll have a fight on his hands. We can't run forever, Ember. We'll make our stand. This is our home, our people. You are our queen. He can't have you. Understand?"

She nods, kissing my hand, so I let go of her mouth, kissing her neck as she relaxes further. "He *will* come," she warns us.

"Let him," Club replies. "I've been wanting to go a second round with him."

My dark chuckle makes her shudder. "I've been saving toys for when he arrives," I admit.

We calm her as best as we can, but we can still feel her concern, and I don't blame her. If he's here, then it's for one thing only—her.

"He'll never get you," I promise in her ear. "I'll kill him before he even touches a hair on your head."

She nods, but I know only time will prove my words. Diamond is right. We aren't running anymore. This will only end when we face him, so let him come. That doesn't mean I'll let our girl be terrified and living on edge though. He stole her life for years. He doesn't get to now.

I want her to be happy again. I crave her laughter and unweighted smile.

I direct a look at Diamond, who nods and glances at Spade and Club. "Tighten security. Put out the warning. If he comes here, I want him alive. He's ours to deal with."

Holding my girl tighter, I tug her after me.

"Wait, I should help. Where are we going?" she asks as I lift her and throw her over my shoulder. She yelps but lets me, and when I set her on her feet at the back of the tent, she watches as I swiftly set up what I have in mind.

"Here." I hand her some of the paints we use for posters and point at the wooden board. "Throw it. Take some of your anger out. Scream, snarl, do what you need to."

She looks confused and hesitant, so I grin.

"Just trust me. Try it."

Shrugging, she tests the weight of a small pot of paint and then swings her arm back and throws. It hits the wood, splattering bright red across the surface, and she grins before choosing another and throwing that too. This time, she giggles as it splatters, and without sparing me another look, she grabs another and another. She launches them at the wood, and they make a satisfying splatter.

Grabbing my own, I throw it and watch the different colored paints mix on the board as she starts to smile, even if she doesn't realize it. She tosses one after another until she stands back, panting hard, her fear gone.

I don't like her terror unless it's aimed at me.

She spares me a quick look before heading over to the board to check it out. "What a mess," she murmurs as I step behind her.

"No, this is a mess." Dunking my hands into the paint, I swipe it across her cheeks before she can stop me. She yelps as she whirls, bright blue handprints on her face. Her eyes are wide, and she points at me.

"Heart, don't you dare—"

I step closer, twining our hands until hers are covered too. She groans at the feeling as I grin at her, tilting my head.

"I like it when you're messy," I whisper hungrily, dropping my eyes to her lips. "I like it when you're angry. I also like it when you're crazy, but I don't like it when you're scared. Do you understand?"

She nods, swallowing as I watch the movement with a groan. I search her eyes, seeing the spark of desperation in her gaze as her lips part in desire. She looks at me like she wants to devour me, and I can't take it.

"Fuck it," I snap.

Pressing her against the board, I press my lips to hers. My paint-covered hands slide across her arms, up to her cheeks, and tilt her face, smearing paint on her skin as we kiss hungrily. Her hands slide up my back, taking my shirt with her, her nails digging into my skin as I moan into the kiss.

I lose myself in her, our greedy hands sliding over each other, staining our skin, but neither of us care as we fight to be as close as possible.

Most call me insane, and they'd be right, but for her, I'd let go of my last shreds of sanity to see her smile again.

I'd crawl through fire for her.

I'd cut every inch of me with glass just to keep her safe.

I never thought I was capable of loving another person, not after everything I lost, but Ember possesses my soul, my heart, and my body. I won't live without her, and the thought of almost losing her today makes our kiss turn brutal, until she whimpers as she tugs me closer. Neither of us want to break apart, even as our lungs scream at us.

Pulling back, she meets my eyes. "What if this didn't work? What if this didn't cheer me up?" she asks roughly.

"Then I would have set up some shit for you to smash with hammers."

Her smile grows, but with it, the sun dawns again. "I love you," she murmurs.

"Good, then you understand a fragment of just how much I adore you," I reply as I nip her lip. "I'm going to frame this art we made, and instead of smashing shit, I'm going to smash you." Throwing her over my shoulder, I set off toward her tent while she laughs and smacks my ass.

Her laughter rings through the cirque, bringing joy only our queen can create, lighting up our homes and lives.

FORTY-SEVEN

EMBER

The stack of cards sits before me. I've read them a hundred times, and they still give me the same answer, so I read them again and again, but it never changes. I'm consumed by it, trying to draw a different conclusion, but it's the same every single time.

Death. Fear. Something bad is coming.

I know it has to do with Roger. He made that very clear, but past the warning, I get nothing else from the cards. They remain steadfast and silent when I need them most. I need a different answer.

The cirque has become my home. I'm happy here in this place meant for freaks and outcasts. I've found where I belong. Some part of me knew that as a child. I was always obsessed with the circus, and when my father brought me to Cirque Obscurum when I was young, it felt right even then. I wish all the events between then and now didn't occur, but I know it was necessary for me to become who I am. It was part of my journey, however sad it may be.

I can't let Roger swoop in and take it away from me. I can't let him take away my happiness again.

I reach forward and spread the deck out, hovering my hands over the cards once more, seeking clarification.

Hilda appears through the ten flaps. She left a while ago to fetch dinner, but I claimed I needed a few more minutes.

It's been an hour.

Her eyes soften upon seeing me, but there's strain at the corners too. We've both read the cards, but I've been obsessive about it. Still, it doesn't change my need for a different answer.

"Ember," she says, drawing my attention as I stare at the same card I've drawn a million times—death. When I look up at her with furrowed brows, she blows out a breath. "Child, we can't force fate to our whim. We can only read it."

"But I need . . . more. I need something else," I croak, pulling another card—fear. My shoulders droop. "This is my home."

"It's home for all of us," Hilda reminds me. "Don't think that I don't care just because I don't draw the same answer repeatedly. I don't wish death on anyone in this family, but it does occur."

"But this time, it'll be my fault," I grit out. "I brought him here. I'm the reason he's coming."

Hilda pauses at my words, at the pain behind them, before she comes over and takes a seat beside me. When I go to shuffle the deck again, she covers my hand with hers, stopping me. I glance up at her, at the wisdom in her eyes.

"It is no more your fault than it is mine," she says, shaking her head. "If we were all measured by other people's darkness, then we would be in trouble indeed, no?" She pulls me into a hug. "Death may come, but we'll face it when it does, Ember. You won't be alone in that. You won't face him alone."

I don't realize I'm crying until I sniffle and hug her back, feeling teardrops plop on her shoulder. The sobs rack my body so quickly, I can't breathe, wrapping its tendrils around me. I let my fear spill out —fear that it'll be someone I care about, that it'll be one of my men.

"Don't let it consume you," she rasps, holding me tightly. "He has no claim on you, and when he comes, we'll remind him of that."

Even as Hilda comforts me, I realize that the new woman I am isn't okay with her answer. Old Ember would have accepted it, but new Ember doesn't want to wait. She wants to act.

But how?

FORTY-EIGHT

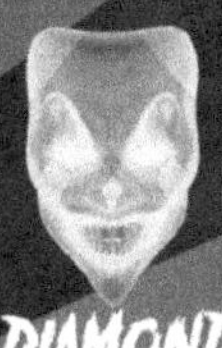

I watch as Ember sits in Dr. Louie's tent, her pant leg rolled up as he prods her calf. It's been months since she came in with broken bones, so beaten that it took a week just for her to be able to sit up in bed. Her husband did a number on her then, but he won't get a chance to repeat his actions.

We should have killed him when we had the chance.

None of us will say it, though, not to Ember. She already recognizes the mistake for what it was. She was trying to be a good person, but sometimes, you can't be when the demons come knocking. Sometimes, you have to battle darkness with darkness.

"It looks good," Dr. Louie says as he turns her leg and bends her knee, testing it. "Everything is healing well."

Ember sits forward with a grin. "Does this mean I'm fully cleared now?"

Dr. Louie taps her knee. "I suggest continuing your stretches and gaining your strength back, but otherwise, I don't see why not. You've been doing well with putting muscle back on."

Ember beams under Dr. Louie's praise, and I don't blame her. We all like to see Dr. Louie proud. He's practically a father to us. The last time I was hurt, I was so overcome with emotion as he cared for me, I cried—not that I'll ever tell anyone that. It just means that Dr. Louie is a special part of the cirque. He looks after every single person who comes through these tents, every member of our family. He tends to cuts and scrapes, illnesses, broken bones, and sour stomachs. He sees the worst of us, and I know it wears on him, so when he sees us healing, it heals a part of him too.

"How does it feel?" he asks Ember. He's careful when he touches her, always asking permission first. He knows our girl as well as we do.

"Better than ever," she says with a smile, flexing her knee for good measure. "I'll be doing gymnastics in no time."

Dr. Louie laughs and pats her knee before standing. "Well then, I'd say you're all healed, my girl."

Her smile falters a little. "Not yet," she murmurs, looking down. "I can't be yet."

Dr. Louie seems to understand what she means—that she may be healed physically, but she still has internal things to mend. With Roger still skulking around, I don't blame her. It's like her trauma is literally haunting her, a problem we'll soon take care of.

"It'll come," Louie murmurs before he reaches for her shoulder and gives it a squeeze, ever a source of comfort in the cirque. "You're family. This is where you belong, Ember." When she looks up at him in question, he adds, "We take care of our family."

She nods and stands. "Thank you, doc, for everything."

In her eyes, I see the knowledge that she belongs here, that this is her home, and she'll fight tooth and nail to keep it safe.

I wouldn't have our queen any other way.

FORTY-NINE

EMBER

I'm restless. Hilda won't let me near the cards again, and despite being cleared, the guys won't let me perform right now. I feel annoyed, and I walk around the cirque in search of a purpose, anything to keep my mind from being consumed by my constant worry and fear. Even now, the hair on the back of my neck rises as if I'm being watched, leaving goose bumps across my skin. I speed up my steps and glance over my shoulder, reminding myself I'm safe here. Night may be falling, but my family is here.

A shadow darts between tents, following me, and my eyes widen. Heart pumping with adrenaline, I quicken my steps, moving between two more tents to make sure what I saw was real, but then I see the shadow again.

I search the area, refusing to hide. I'll lead him into a trap instead. My eyes land on the equipment tent, and I rush over, ducking inside and dousing the lantern as I pick up a hammer and wait with bated breath. I put my back against the curtain near the entrance, my feet on a box so no one can't see me under it. My eyes widen as I try to make out every detail in the dark, my hands shaking slightly as I hold the hammer aloft, ready to attack.

From one breath to the next, I try to slow my racing heart and loud breathing, and then the ten flaps move, bowing inward and admitting someone. With a yell, I dive at them, swinging the hammer, only for it to be caught midair by a strong hand, holding my arm high above me while the other grips my throat. It cuts off my yell and squeezes. It takes a moment for my eyes to adjust, but when they do, I swear they bug out of my head.

"Diamond?" I whisper, staring into his familiar eyes.

"I caught you, Queen. The hunt is over. Now what shall I do with you?" He backs me into the tent as my fear morphs to confusion and then lust at the darkness I see in his gaze. "I was going to let you go, but then you ran. Don't you know you should never run from predators, Ember? It makes us want to chase. It makes us hungry, and in the dark, all alone, you are too tempting to pass up."

The backs of my knees hit the equipment table, and it jitters from the force, knocking items to the floor, but neither of us spare them a look. I'm trapped in his dark, hungry gaze, my body controlled by his. My heart races in anticipation, and my thighs clench together in want. All this time, he has never crossed the line, but he will tonight.

He's done holding back, and I can't fucking wait.

Gripping tighter, he forces my fingers to spasm, and I drop the hammer into his waiting hand. He slides his long fingers languidly across it, watching me before pressing the hard edge of it against my cheek and dragging it down my throat, pausing over my pounding heart. "You were going to use this on me?"

I nod. Something about his silky, dark voice steals my own. The air fills with promise and violence, yet I can't seem to look away, barely able to blink, and my eyes burn from staring at him.

He tuts and lowers it before he circles my hardening nipples through my blouse with the hammer. "Maybe I should use it on you then. Fair is fair, don't you think, Ember?" he purrs as he drags it down, flipping it in his grip and pressing it against my crotch. Fear slides through me, but I don't back down.

"I've been behaving all this time, being good and not touching you, but I want what's mine. Do you understand?" My eyes widen, and he grips my chin so hard I whimper. "Words, Ember. Consent right now or walk away, because if you say yes, I won't stop no matter how much you beg. You must understand that."

"I—" I swallow hard, glancing down at his lips.

"Say yes or tell me to get out," he orders, his voice harsh. "If you say yes, you're mine, all of you, and I will do whatever I want with you. Last warning."

Dragging my eyes back up to his, I lick my lips with anticipation. "Yes. Yes, I'm yours."

I expected him to kiss me, but instead, he rips off my blouse, the cool air brushing my exposed chest and causing my nipples to tighten. He watches my chest heave with my heavy breathing until he finally leans down and captures a nipple between his teeth. His eyes meet mine as he slowly clamps down, observing my every reaction. Pain and pleasure mix until it becomes too much, and I cry out. He stops and waits for me to still, and with purposeful movements, he bites deeper, pushing me to the brink before he lets go. The blood rushes back to my nipple and makes it tingle as he turns his head and does the same to the other one. My moans fill the air, my eyes sliding shut as I shudder against him.

Gripping my wrists, he jerks my arms up and then behind me so my chest arches out and my eyes snap open. The ache in my shoulders mixes with the pleasure in my body and has me gasping.

"You keep your eyes on me the entire time. Don't shut them or I will force them open," he warns. "You will know who is fucking you, Ember. You will watch every depraved thing I'll do to you and know that you wanted this."

Keeping my hands pinned, he grabs some rope from the table and winds it around my wrists. It burns as I try to tug free to no avail, and then his hand slides across my chest, tweaking my sore nipples while his other one pulls the hammer away.

His smirk is brutal as he flips it in his hand. Confusion swirls with my lust as I wonder what he's going to do.

Holding the thick wooden handle of the hammer, he forces it between my thighs, and then his feet step on either side of mine, closing my legs so tightly that I grind into that handle to the point of pain. The thick, square head sticks out and presses against his cock as he leans down and bites my throat.

My cry fills the air, and I try to pull away, but I'm trapped between him and the table, my pussy rubbing against the wood. It hurts but also feels so good, especially when it presses against my clit, making me whimper.

He pulls his teeth away and licks before moving down and biting again. He repeats this over and over, marking every inch of my neck. His hands find my hips and yank them back and forth, forcing me to grind against the wood.

When his voice comes, it's muffled against my skin. "You're going to come like this, Ember," he says. "I'm going to make you. You're close already, no matter how much you don't want to accept it. I taste it on your skin and see the tremble in your limbs. Keep fighting though. I like it. The harder you fight, the harder you will fall."

Groaning, I roll my hips. It hurts so fucking good as I grind my clit into the wood through my pants. I rock into the pain, consumed by it, and when I splinter apart, I scream into the darkness.

His chuckle fills the air alongside my cry as he lifts his head, his smile crooked as he watches me pant and shake. When the pleasure finally abates, I slump with a whine, my pussy throbbing and aching from the pressure. His hand slides down my front as he steps back and extracts it from between my bruised thighs.

Throwing it over his shoulder, he runs his eyes hungrily down my body. "I'm just getting started, my love."

Before I have a chance to wonder what he means, he rolls me, his hand coming down on my back and pushing me over the table until I'm bent across it. My hands are tied at the base of my spine as he grips my pants and tugs them off. I can feel my wetness spread over my thighs and pussy, and when he kicks my legs open wide, I know he can see it.

His fingers slide through my mess, and a moment later, I hear him sucking them clean, the slurping noise making me shudder. "You taste divine, and look at you, all puffy and pink. Ripe for the taking."

Turning my head, I strain to see in the dark.

"And take I will," he continues. I hear shuffling, and then the thick head of his cock prods my entrance before he slams inside me. The force makes me scream, pain spasming through me as he buries himself as deep as he can. I'm wet, but it still hurts, and when he pulls out and thrusts back in, my eyes squeeze shut as my body tries to adjust to him. Just as I start to, he pulls from my channel. His hands grip my hips and then part my ass, and his wet cock presses against my hole there.

"Di—" I start to protest, but he pushes inside with a snarl, forcing his cock past my stinging muscles. The pain nearly makes me black out for a moment. I try to escape, to move away, but he holds me there as he roughly slams deeper into my ass with each thrust.

"Please, no, stop!" I beg, kicking back, tears squeezing from my eyes. It hurts so much, but like he promised, he doesn't stop.

He doesn't care.

I said yes to the beast, and he won't be chained again.

He offered me a way out, but I rejected it. Now I have to survive this.

It should scare me after everything I have been through in my past, but deep down, I know Diamond would never hurt me. Not really, not like Roger. He'll push my limits and make me feel things I have never felt, but he will never break my body. He'll use it and worship it, and the fucked-up part of me loves that.

I get wetter as I beg him to stop, the word "no" turning to "yes." The idea of him taking me against my will makes me so slick it's embarrassing.

He fucks my ass hard and fast, the force slamming me into the table until it creaks and groans, my nipples dragging across the abrasive wood as I'm yanked back and forth.

"Look at you, split open for me. This tight little ass is all mine. You're crying, but your pussy is dripping for me. You like it, don't you, Ember? Like me claiming this pretty ass, fucking you hard and fast like an animal? Even when you say no, you beg me for more."

Whimpering, I bite down on my lip until I taste blood. He tilts my hips and forces himself so deep into my ass, I know I will hurt for days, and then something hard presses against my pussy entrance. My eyes widen, and my body freezes, but he doesn't care. He rubs it over my pussy, the hard edge hitting my clit.

"I want you filled to the brim. I want every inch of you claimed," he purrs as the hard edge presses against my entrance again and he pushes it inside me. My eyes widen as I try to glance back, but I can't see him. He forces it deeper, the stretch between that and his cock taking me to the edge of too much and yet not enough. This time, he slowly pulls it from me and works it back in, loosening me up as his hips rock, his cock swelling inside my ass.

"That's it. Take it deeper. Let me watch you come apart like this. Let me do every dark and depraved thing to you," he growls, and when he pushes the thing all the way inside me, I feel something thick at my entrance.

The hammer.

He's fucking me with the hammer.

I revolt a little, but when he starts to move, I lose myself in the pain and pleasure, and all morality and protests disappear.

His thrusts are brutal, bordering on too much. It hurts but it also feels so damn good, forcing me higher even as I cry out, words falling from my lips that only seem to spur him on.

"Please, no, yes, stop, more."

I can't make up my mind, but it doesn't matter. I'm not in control here, and he won't stop until he gets what he wants.

Leaning over me, he bites my neck once more, and my scream rips through the air as it sends me over the edge, making me come.

My pussy clenches on the handle, my ass on his cock, and with a groan against my skin, he pumps into me before swelling inside me and finally spilling, filling my ass with hot ropes of cum.

Shaking and still riding the high, I writhe below him, my eyes crossing from the pleasure until it finally ebbs away and I slump.

His teeth pull from my neck, and he kisses the bite better. "You're perfect," he praises. He lies on my back for a moment, so I can feel his pounding heart, before he straightens and pulls from my ass. I wince, and when he starts to pull on the handle, I cry out.

"Shh, almost over, my love. You did so well," he murmurs as he pulls it free, and when I'm empty again, I gasp.

After undoing my hands, he turns me and lets the table hold me up since my legs are jelly. I must be a mess, with bruised lips, tears dripping down my face, and marks all over my neck, but he looks at me like I'm the most beautiful, precious thing he has ever seen.

He leans down and kisses me softly. "Perfect," he says before leaning back.

I'm unable to speak. I just stare.

Lifting the hammer between us, he arches his brow as I eye the dripping, glistening wood. "Clean up your mess, Ember," he orders, sliding one hand into my hair, the other pressing the wood to my lips.

I open my mouth, and he slides it in. I lick and suck on the wood as he watches. I do as I'm told, cleaning off my cum, and when he pulls it from my mouth, he grins proudly at me.

He pets my hair as I pant. "Good girl," he praises, tossing the hammer away as he leans down and scoops me into his arms, which I'm thankful for since I still can't feel mine. "Now, let's get you to bed."

Snuggling against him, I drape my arms around his shoulders, my tear-stained face pressing against his chest even as a smile curves my lips.

I survived Diamond's darkness.

I survived the devil of the cirque, and I fucking loved it.

I'm asleep when the call comes.

Diamond jerks awake next to me, his hands and legs thrown over mine. We share a look, and he kisses my forehead softly. "Get ready. We'll meet outside in five."

I nod and scramble from bed as the cirque urges me to move faster, the pounding of the call making me gasp as I hurry over to my chest and grab an outfit at random. I have many now. They just keep appearing thanks to the guys. They call it my hunting gear. After all, I should look the part, just like they do.

I hold the outfit up, and my eyebrows rise. It's not something I would have worn before, but that's the point. Gathering my courage, I slip on the leather pants and skintight black bustier before shoving my hair up into a messy bun.

I don't have much time, but I smear on some clown makeup, creating Vs above and below my eyes and then my lips. Turning to the mirror, I check myself out, nodding in approval, then I grab my mask and slide it into place on my face before I head out to meet them and answer the call.

It's growing stronger.

The call pounds so hard in my chest, I have to wrap my arms around myself to hold it, like I might splinter apart at any moment.

I have a really bad feeling, but the call must always be answered.

Diamond pulls over on a rocky, deserted country road and glances back at us. "Time to hunt."

Nodding, I slide from the car, watching as they put their masks in place, and we share one more look before turning to the narrow dirt road and heading the way the call demands.

We don't have to walk for long. Around the next bend, covered by trees, is an abandoned building. It's shaded and clearly forgotten. Glass from the windows crunches under our feet as we walk to the open door and peer at the darkness inside.

"I don't like this," I admit.

"The cirque is never wrong," Diamond murmurs, but even he seems more reserved as he steps inside. The call hammers in our chests now, so we must be close. We follow our leader in, letting our eyes adjust to the light as we move deeper into the huge, empty room.

No, it isn't empty, I realize as we come to a stop.

In the middle of the abandoned concrete building is a body. It's turned away from us with a puddle of blood lying under the figure, which makes us halt. It's clear from how still they are that they are dead.

My eyebrows tug together in a frown as I search the area. If they didn't make the call, then who did?

Clapping fills the air, startling me, my eyes widening as Roger steps from the shadows. He wears a sinister grin on his face, one that makes me shift with unease. Each clap of his hands is deafening, echoing around the large, cavernous room as shock and fear course through my body.

Chuckling, he stops and holds up a card between two fingers, letting it catch the light.

A joker.

He called us here.

"Hello, wife," he purrs. "I've been waiting for you."

FIFTY-ONE

My blood runs cold at his words and the gleam I see blazing in his cruel eyes. For a moment, a shudder of fear passes through me as I stare at my husband. Roger is completely at ease despite the fact we outnumber him. That's what makes me realize he must be planning something. Roger would never be so sure of himself otherwise.

"It's a trap," I whisper, my voice shaking a little. I'm proud that it doesn't tremble more, that I'm able to fight against my fear. I'm not alone here. I'm not facing my monster by myself.

Diamond stands tall at my side, his eyes as dark as his soul as they focus on the man before us. "How clever of you," Diamond purrs. "Did you take his card before or after he died?"

Roger sneers at Diamond, distaste dripping from his expression as his wicked eyes run down Diamond's body. "Does it matter, freak? You weren't so hard to track down. You ran like you thought you had a chance of escaping me." He looks at me. "As if she could ever get away from me."

"I don't belong to you," I declare. This time, there's no shake in my voice as I raise my chin in defiance, letting him see the truth in my eyes.

Roger meets my gaze. "Yes," he says, a smirk pulling at his lips, "you do."

He snaps his fingers, and more movement comes from the darkness around us. People I've never seen before step out of the shadows, advancing toward us. Each of them is armed with various weapons—baseball bats, lead pipe, a machete. They all stare at us with hatred, as if we did something wrong to these strangers.

They don't hate us because of what we do.

They hate us because of what we are.

Not a single one of them could ever understand that there aren't any freaks in this world. There are only humans. Those of us who are willing to admit there's darkness and learn to live with it are stronger, and they don't like that.

Now, we stand before them in our masks, and I know they'll murder us if given the opportunity. We kill to protect and save, but they'll kill us out of jealousy and desperation.

Which of us are the real monsters?

Spade tenses at my side, but there's no other outward sign that my men are uncomfortable. They look around at the dozen men surrounding us, sizing them up. They have the numbers, but there's one thing they've forgotten in this trap.

We've accepted the darkness.

We are the darkness.

We are their nightmares.

Diamond grins. "It's a nice attempt, Roger," he says. "I'll give you that."

Roger scowls at Diamond's use of his name. "This is where you die, freak."

Diamond's grin widens. "No," he says, shaking his head. "But it could be where you do."

He moves without warning. Between one blink and the next, Diamond lunges toward the nearest stranger. He grabs the man before he can so much as raise his machete and snaps his neck with a resounding crack before the man drops to the floor, lifeless.

Everything is silent for a moment as Diamond meets Roger's widening eyes, and then all hell breaks loose.

Heart leaps to the right, a knife I never saw him pull in his hand. Diamond picks up the lost machete and starts hacking at those who surround him. Spade uncoils his whip and lashes out, wrapping it around an attacker's neck and yanking him over to his waiting blade. Club pulls out his own knife, but he stays beside me instead of leaping forward. I hoist my bat up, prepared to smash in any motherfucker's skull who gets too close. What I expect to be a quick fight is anything but. When one of the men rush forward, something flashes at his hip, something on his belt. When I swing and get slammed backward by his shoulders, I realize what it is—a police badge.

Roger brought fucking off duty cops with him.

"Motherfucker," I snarl as I swing my bat at the man. It connects with his forearm, and he shouts in pain. That explains why they aren't going down easily. They have fucking training.

Club strikes one of the men who tries to lunge toward me, slicing him across the chest. The man goes down with a howl, but we're making progress. All the while, Roger stands before us, illuminated by the moonlight streaming in through the damaged roof like he's a fucking angel. He probably chose that spot for that reason. He smirks as he watches with his hands in his pockets, unconcerned that once we dispose of his goons we'll come after him. This time, I won't show him mercy. I've learned my lesson.

Heart has one of the pipes now, and he swings it with insane strength while dancing out of the way of their weapons. He connects with one of the men's jaws, and the snap tells me he broke it. He giggles the entire time, as if this is the most fun he's had in years.

"Be careful where you dare to tread. The ground is littered with the dead. Ones insane and ones devout, I'll knock you all the fuck out," he sings as he swings the pipe, giggling every time he connects with one of them.

Spade's whip cracks behind me, and I can hear Diamond growl at someone, but their numbers are dwindling. We're winning. I meet Roger's eyes and bare my teeth.

"What do you look so smug about?" I hiss. "You're about to die."

Roger laughs. His eyes actually fucking crinkle. "Am I, wife?" he asks, tilting his head to the side. "Or am I just getting started?"

As if he fucking choreographed it, more men appear from the shadows—twice as many as before. They hold weapons—no guns, thankfully, but these people came here to inflict pain. Their choice of weapons reflects that. I see shovels, pickaxes, knives, pitchforks, and large wrenches, whatever they could get their hands on. Their eyes are on us, full of menace, and my heart drops.

"Club," I rasp softly.

"I see them," he answers, and for the first time, I hear a thread of worry in his voice.

Diamond glances over his shoulder, and his eyes narrow. I can tell he's assessing the situation, trying to figure out the best course of action, but I know what it is before he does.

We need to go.

Diamond realizes it right after I do. "Together," he commands, backing up to us while keeping the men at bay.

Spade does the same behind me, his back coming to meet my own as we regroup in the middle, our weapons held up. On my right, Heart is still dancing after the men, getting too close and enjoying himself despite the clear disadvantage we find ourselves in.

"Heart," Diamond hisses, pure command lacing his tone.

We're getting out of here one way and one way only—together.

"What were you saying, wife?" Roger goads, grinning at me. "How you're ready to come home?"

"I *am* home," I spit, "and it isn't with you, you limp-dick bastard."

Club reaches back and touches my hip in reassurance, and Roger's eyes follow the movement. Fire ignites in his gaze as he recognizes the familiarity between us.

Roger's face contorts with fury, and he finally pulls his hands from his pockets, taking a menacing step forward. "Did you spread your legs for this freak, Ember?" he snarls. "Did you roll around in the filth with him?"

I raise my chin, but I don't answer his question. Instead, I say, "I don't *belong* to you."

"Did you fuck him?" he shouts, taking another menacing step forward. "Did you spread your legs for this freak like a whore?"

Heart laughs at him and finally moves away from the men, joining our group. He hitches the pipe over his shoulder and flashes a cocky grin.

"Silly Roger." He laughs. "She fucks all of us! Our queen does as she wishes!"

Roger's face morphs into the monster he normally keeps inside. He stops moving and focuses on Heart, who laughs at his expression. The men around us stop and look to him for direction.

"Fucking freaks," Roger spits and reaches for the small of his back.

My heart stops.

I underestimated him yet again. There are no guns around us, but I never thought to look for them either, so when he pulls a handgun and points it at Heart, terror claws its way up my throat.

"Heart!" I cry, but Roger pulls the trigger before anyone can move.

The bang echoes around the room, ricocheting inside the concrete walls and making it seem even louder than it is. Heart stops dancing around, his laughter cutting off as he looks down at his stomach. Red blooms across his dark shirt, making it darker.

"Oh," he says, looking at it before peering up at Roger. "That wasn't very nice."

I scream and lunge toward Heart, trying to stop him from collapsing to the ground. Spade grabs his other side, helping me as Club and Diamond swing at the men to keep them back. We push toward the exit. Everyone shouts around us, and when the men come closer and try to get us, Spade lets go of Heart and snaps his whip out, leaving me to struggle to hold him up. His strength is obvious as he manages to remain on his feet despite the gunshot wound. His arm is tight around my shoulders as I drag him along.

"Hold on, Heart," I rasp, dragging him while the others watch our backs. "Hold on for me."

"I am. Death can't take me from you, Queen. Don't worry," he murmurs, but his voice is a little less lively than it usually is.

"Go!" Diamond snarls, swiping the machete across one of the men.

Roger points the gun at us without pulling the trigger. He grins when I look over my shoulder and blows me a kiss.

"This isn't over, Ember," he coos. "You can't run forever."

He's right, I think as we barely make it to the car. Once we're inside, the men beat against the Dodge, trying to bust out the windows, but Diamond throws it in gear and presses the gas pedal. We mow down a few of them on the way out, but I don't even pay attention.

My eyes are on the man with his head in my lap, my hand clamped over his wound.

"Hang on for me, Heart," I croak, tears welling in my eyes. "Don't you fucking die on me."

"I would . . . never," he whispers, closing his eyes, his body going limp.

"Heart!" I cry, trying to shake him awake. "Diamond! Go faster!"

The engine revs as Diamond pushes the Dodge as fast as it will go, but I don't know if it's enough.

Fuck! I don't know if it's enough!

FIFTY-TWO

I pace outside the tent, knowing I can't be in there even though I want to be. Dr. Louie has already kicked me out twice, saying he needed to focus and couldn't handle the fear filling the air. I don't blame him.

"He's going to be okay," Spade tells me as I walk back and forth, practically wearing a hole in the ground with my path. Club sits on a crate beside the tent flap, flicking a knife through his fingers. It's his way of not panicking, just as pacing is my coping mechanism.

"We don't know that," I growl, feeling angry, desperate, and afraid.

Heart lost so much blood. Dr. Louie said we were lucky the bullet didn't hit any major organs, but he's still in there, having to dig it out and stitch him up. There's also no guarantee that he'll be okay after losing so much blood, especially since it took way too long to get back. I considered demanding we go to a real hospital, but I knew as well as the others that they wouldn't help us there. Plus, I didn't trust them to save Heart, not like I do Dr. Louie.

Heart won't be doing trapeze for at least a month while he waits to heal, and he'll be so pissed about that when he wakes up.

Freedom stands beside Spade, her tail twitching back and forth from the tension in the air. She looks at the tent flaps as if waiting, and she seems just as angry as I am. Heart is one of her favorite people. He always gives her the best scratches.

Diamond is inside with Heart, and I saw worry flash in his eyes just before doc kicked me out. The gunshot is bad. We nearly lost him, but I trust Dr. Louie to bring him back.

In the meantime, I can't stay here.

I can't do nothing.

Fury eats away at my gut, threatening to spill out at any moment. I can practically taste the acidic pain on my tongue. It demands retribution and revenge. Roger was already marked for death, but now I'm going to make it fucking hurt. I'm going to flay strips from his flesh. I'm going to pluck his fingernails off one by one. I'm going to carve him up into teeny tiny pieces and force them down his throat. He'll know pain worse than anything he's ever done to me because he tried to take Heart from me.

He tried to take what belongs to me.

"I can't be here," I rasp, stopping my pacing.

Both Club and Spade look up at me.

"Why?" Club asks, his gaze too intense.

"I'm going to Hilda's tent," I say, turning away. "I need to . . . I need to read the cards."

The reminder of the warning that death is coming weighs heavily on my shoulders. If Heart dies . . .

I can't even think about it right now. I need to consult the cards and see if I can learn anything else.

"Just be careful," Spade says, reminding me that I'm in the most danger.

Roger won't like that we escaped, but this is some sort of game to him now. He wants me alive, and he won't stop coming until I'm within his grasp. That isn't going to happen, but I also won't let him hurt what's mine.

I move through the cirque with purpose, my strides long and

rushed. When I push into Hilda's tent, I'm surprised to find her there. She's standing, her arms crossed over her chest.

"I was wondering how long it would take you to show up," she says. Her eyes flash as she gestures to the table. The cards sit upon it as they always do, but something feels different this time. With my fury burning in my throat and my hatred of Roger in my heart, the cards feel . . . stronger. The pull I feel to them nearly suffocates me.

"Take a seat," Hilda says, and her voice echoes with many. "You're ready."

Ready for what?

I don't ask the question out loud. Instead, I walk around the table and take a seat. Before I can place my hand over the cards, they spring into the air and float before me, shaking with the energy in my core. They flip and move between the fronts and backs, flickering between the faces, then they begin to glow, becoming brighter.

I don't ask what's happening. I don't need to.

He hurt my family. We barely made it out of there, and Heart nearly died. Roger expects me to run again, but he doesn't know the Ember I am now. He doesn't realize who he fucked with.

But he will.

I tilt my chin up as the cards begin to vibrate and then circle faster and faster. I can barely follow their movements as they start to burrow beneath my skin, digging in, but the small points of pain ease once they make it inside. I am the cirque now. I was always meant to be the cirque, ever since I was given the joker card as a child, and now I'll never be alone again.

Hilda's weathered hands come to rest on my shoulders.

"You're ready," she says again, and it feels like a blessing from the one who carried the cards before me. "Ember, queen of the cirque, hunter of darkness."

"Yes," I hiss, strength flooding my body with the cards. My back bows with power and darkness. The queen of hearts flips out and hovers before me—the final card. With a final flicker, it slams into my chest and slides inside. This one burns the most with a pain I know is meant to be a reminder of everything we're going to face. I stand and roll my shoulders, my body buzzing with energy, and my fury expands even further.

I won't run ever again. I won't hide. I won't be afraid.

Now, it's time to hunt.

FIFTY-THREE

"Go," Hilda urges as she steps back. "It's time for you to meet your destiny."

Understanding floods me, along with my anger, and with a sharp incline of my head, I turn and leave her tent. I avoid everyone as I hurry back to my own. My steps are determined as power floods through me, the cirque pulsing deep in my bones.

It had been patiently waiting for me to claim it.

I sold my soul, but in return, it gave me its power.

Ducking into my tent, I move through the low lamp light to my box of outfits, ripping it open and staring deep inside before grabbing a fistful at random.

My eyes catch on the mirror, and I freeze. My own eyes glow in an unnatural way, and my lips are tilted in a cruel smile.

I'm coated in Heart's blood, but I leave it as a reminder. I do change my clothes, though, since mine are torn and soaked. If I'm going to face down Roger, then it will be on my terms. He will expect me to run and hide.

Not anymore.

If he wants me, then he'll get me, but before the sun rises, he'll realize the woman he is hunting is also hunting him, and she isn't scared anymore. No, she's a fucking nightmare.

I could get the guys and ask them to come with me, but this is my fight, and I won't risk my family again.

I will end what I started by doing what I should have done months ago.

I dress quickly, donning some fishnets and black shorts before pulling on a corset, half black and half red, split down the middle with an ornate Q embroidered on the chest. Reaching behind me, I struggle to tug it tighter, and after swearing and sweating, I finally get it done and add a pair of my thick-soled black boots.

I grab as many blades as I can carry before turning back to the mirror.

Smeared in blood and weapons, I look like a creature of death.

I look like a hunter, and as I smile at my own reflection, I know that's exactly what I am.

I'm leaving cirque, heading toward Diamond's beat-up Dodge, when I feel something following me.

My hand slides down my side to grip a blade, and I whirl, only to still at the sight of the tiger. Freedom pads after me with her head down, clear intention in her eyes. Wherever I'm going, so is she.

This is her family, and one of us is hurt. She's loyal, she's a huntress, and she plans to come with me, but I'm not sure it's a good idea.

"No, Freedom. Go back," I order, my eyes narrowed. "This is my fight. I'll do this alone. Protect the others."

Her head lowers, and she flashes her fangs in warning. I press my lips together as we stare each other down, but I know I need to leave before they come looking for me.

This is my hunt, not theirs.

"Fine," I snap, grinding my teeth. Spade will be so mad if she gets hurt, but Freedom is a wild animal, and trying to control her is impossible. "Stay close and don't get hurt, okay?"

I open the door of the car, and she hops in, sitting in the passenger seat as I climb behind the wheel. I spare her another look and snort. "I can't believe I'm going to hunt down my husband with a tiger and cirque power flowing through me. How strange is my life?" Turning on the engine, I pull my mask down. "Let's do this."

She mewls in agreement, and I speed away from the cirque.

The need to spill blood fills me, and fury keeps me moving.

I know I'm not completely sane right now, but I don't care as glass crunches under my boots as I stalk through the darkness, hunting my victim.

I start in the obvious place—the ambush site. It's empty. Bodies still litter the floor, but Roger isn't here, and I don't find any signs of life, so I keep moving.

Cops. If I can find them, then I can find him. I don't know how I know that but I do, and I trust in the cirque's instincts as I turn and follow that power.

I leave the car behind, knowing they couldn't have gotten too far. Most of them were injured, and this place is a crime scene, so I know they won't leave the area.

I walk only a mile or so before I see a fire. Freedom and I silently stalk closer, crouching in the grass as I grin. Three of the cops sit there, one wiping blood off his hands and face as they huddle around the flames, scared of the dark. They should be. They don't have a clue what nightmares it holds.

Like me.

"I can't go home like this. Tell me why we're listening to this asshole and waiting here in case they come back while he goes home?" one of them sneers, clearly pissed off at the state of their little group.

I don't care about his injuries or these men, but his words tell me all I need to know. They know Roger well.

They are perfect.

Bloodlust pumps through me, along with adrenaline, as I stare at their backs. I don't need all three. I only need one—just to talk.

Eeny, meeny, miny, mo. My smirk turns evil as my finger lands on the one to the left.

"I guess you're the lucky one," I whisper as I nod at Freedom. "Wait here."

I sneak up on the three men, grabbing my unsuspecting victim, the one in the middle. I slam his face into the fire as he screams in shock and pain. The flames lick at my gloved hand, burning me, but I hold him there. The one on my left gets to his feet, rushing me, but I kick out. He hits the ground hard, and I release the man whose face burns as I duck under the other's swinging arm, only to come up with a blade, gutting him from navel to neck. He falls backward, gurgling and screaming, trying to decide if he should cover his neck or his intestines falling from his stomach.

Turning, I face the chosen one as he clambers to his feet, his eyes wide. His friend rolls around on the ground, screaming as he covers his face, while the other tries unsuccessfully to push his insides back into himself.

"What the fuck?" He draws a gun from the small of his back and points it at me. "I don't care if he wants you alive. You'll pay for that."

I whistle and step back. He frowns in confusion just before a blur shoots past me.

Freedom lunges forward, burying her teeth in the man's thigh. He screams, trying to kick her off. I grab his fallen gun with a laugh and point it at him. "I wouldn't do that if I were you."

He freezes, Freedom still gnawing on him.

"Here." I tap my leg. She releases him and pads over to me, licking her blood-covered fangs. "We need him alive for now."

"What the fuck?" he bellows, his face pale as he covers his mauled thigh. "Why the fuck do you have a tiger? What the fuck? I never should have gotten involved!" He crawls backwards until his back hits one of the crates they were sitting on. Blood coats the grass below him, looking like spilled oil in the firelight.

I let the gun hang loosely at my side as I cock my head, watching him.

"You're right. You shouldn't have gotten involved, but you did, and now you're going to die." Crouching down, I grin at him as he shudders, trying unsuccessfully to staunch the bleeding. "I'm a doctor's wife, you see. That wound, it's bad. You're going to bleed out in under three minutes. Now, I can either make your death faster or make it hurt a lot more. Your choice."

"Help me," he snaps.

He might not have a working leg, but he has the audacity of a man, that's for sure.

Freedom growls at my side, and he flinches.

Moving closer, I rub my fingers through his blood before dancing them up his leg, and when I meet his wide eyes, I dig them into the wound, pushing into the meat of his thigh as he screams in agony.

"I don't need your body, just your mouth, so tell me what I want. Where is he? Where is Roger?" I purr, lifting my fingers free and sucking on them, tasting his blood. "I can taste your fear."

He starts to cry with big, heaving sobs. "Oh god, please—"

"God can't help you now," I retort. "Only I can. You have three seconds or I'm going to let Freedom play with you again." She stands beside me, her mouth gaping in warning, and he shrinks back as I laugh.

"One."

"Please," he rasps, holding his hand out as if to fend me off.

"Two," I sing. "Three—"

"Okay, okay! Fuck, fuck him, fuck you. He's staying at the old farmhouse not far from here, the only building around, okay? Now get that thing away from me."

Patting his injury, I grin as he cries out. "Good boy. She's not the one you should fear though. It's me." Pulling one of my blades out, I grin as I turn it, letting it catch the light.

"Wait, please, I helped you—"

"You did, which is why I'll make it quick. Well, quicker." I plunge the knife into his throat as I stare into his terrified eyes, and then I pull it free. His blood squirts across me as I watch him die. It's not as fast as you'd expect, and when he finally slumps to the side, blood still pumping steadily from his neck, I wipe my blade on his pants and stand.

Whistling a merry tune, I tap my thigh, and Freedom falls into step beside me as we prowl away from the fire and the bodies.

I'm coming for you, dear husband. I hope you're ready.

FIFTY-FOUR

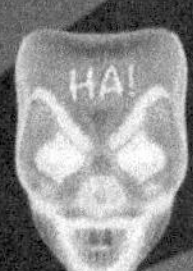

We stop the wagon we borrowed from the cirque right next to Diamond's Dodge. I climb out, searching the horizon for my girl and Freedom.

When she didn't come back from Hilda's, I went to find her and quickly realized the truth—she went after Roger. I would have done the same. We all would have.

He hurt one of us, and she's blaming herself.

She shouldn't be alone. She should know by now that we go where she goes.

"Stay here," Diamond orders Heart in the passenger seat. He's pale and holding his side, but he's up and moving, refusing to be left behind. Doc gave him some sort of drug concoction at his request that will keep him alive and moving while we find our girl, but he'll need to rest after. For now, we have to find our queen.

Kneeling, I inspect the pawprints alongside footsteps. "They went that way." I point off into the grass, and the others converge on me, even Heart. "Looks like we're on foot."

"Fun." Heart groans, but he sets off in the direction I indicated, not one to be held back when it comes to her. We all know he would do anything for her, and we also know better than to argue with him. We walk by his side silently. The wind rustles the long grass around us as we move away from the cars and the place where Roger ambushed us.

Luckily, we don't have to go too far, shadows moving around the fire we come across. Crouching to hide, we watch our girl, knowing we can't stop her.

Nor do we want to.

My mouth drops open in surprise and desire as she takes down all three men. There's a cruel, almost manic air about her as she tortures one, and it makes me hard. When Freedom helps her, I can't help but grin.

My two favorite girls spilling blood? There's nothing better.

Heart sighs dreamily. "She's torturing and killing for me. How romantic."

"You know what? I would say you're screwed, but you're right." I nod, watching as she kills the last man and then stands. With Freedom at her side, she takes off, moving deeper into the wilderness, leaving the bodies and blood behind. We wait until she won't turn and notice us before we head to the campsite, making sure they are truly dead.

"She knows where he is," I murmur as I watch her in the distance. "She's going after him."

"It's her hunt," Club says.

"He's right. It is." Diamond tosses one of the bodies into the fire and wipes his hands. "Burn the other two. Leave no trace that she was here. We'll follow her and only help her if she needs us to. If not, this is her night. We are simply here just in case."

Picking up one of the other bodies, I toss it into the fire as Club gets the last corpse. We watch them burn before our eyes turn to our girl.

"Let's go," I say, and we silently move after her, stalking her silhouette through the wilderness.

We walk for at least another hour, tracking her until she finally stops before a farmhouse, the lights blazing inside.

The house is very similar to the one we saw the first night we met our queen, and the irony doesn't escape me.

Thunder rumbles in the turbulent sky, as if brought on by her rage, and we watch as she slides her mask down and walks toward the house, seeking her revenge.

FIFTY-FIVE

EMBER

The white farmhouse comes into view, and I can't do anything but scowl. Why do the worst monsters always flock to the color white? Is it because they can never be as pure as the color? Is it an illusion to hide what true monsters they are? Either way, it doesn't surprise me that this farmhouse is the home of Roger's games. He always liked pristine houses. He was very particular about white, always demanding it was clean when I lived with him before, presenting the perfect man, marriage, and house. Now, the color only pisses me off. How dare he pretend? How dare he choose this as his last stand?

Freedom strides beside me, her tail swishing back and forth. She's on edge and ready, as angry as I am. Just as I can feel the pulse of the cirque in my veins, I can feel hers. We're both part of the same family and furious that one of us was hurt.

I'm reminded again of Heart's injuries, of the way he looked down at the wound. Fear flashed through me, but more than that, I felt anger. Roger has taken so much from me, nearly killed me, but I'll be damned if he takes anything else. Heart is recovering now. I have no doubt Dr. Louie will keep him safe, but before I can return to his bedside and offer my support, I need to slay our demon.

My demon.

The blade feels weightless in my hand as I stroll closer to the farmhouse. The cops' blood still splatters my body, so I know I must look crazy, but I don't care.

Let me look like a monster. Tonight, I'm going to be one.

I'll be the nightmare who will haunt my husband. I'll be the last thing he sees, and he will beg for forgiveness before I'm through.

The lights are on in the farmhouse, giving it a picturesque look that belongs on a Christmas card. The yellow light washes out the windows and streams across the perfectly manicured grass, its bright tendrils not reaching me in the shadows. It would be pretty if it wasn't hiding the evil bastard I'm here for. For a moment, I wonder what happened to the people who actually lived in this house. Part of me hopes they are just out of town on business. Otherwise, the people who were here before, be they innocent or not, are probably dead. Roger wouldn't have thought twice about killing them.

"What do you think, girl?" I ask Freedom as we approach, sliding my free hand through her fur in comfort. "Should we knock or just walk right in?" She makes a soft chuffing noise in answer that makes my evil smirk grow. "That sounds like a walk right in. Alright."

We round the house to the front door and step up onto the white wraparound porch, the wood creaking under my boots. I take a deep breath, easing my thoughts so I can focus. Roger is a dangerous monster, and if I'm not on my game, things could go south. Luckily for me, I'm not alone, not with Freedom beside me. Still, I remind myself that I'm no longer the Ember from so many months ago. I'm not the helpless woman who'd been beaten and nearly killed. I'm not the same woman desperately crying in the attic, waiting for death.

I'm something else now.

The cards beneath my skin shift, reminding me they are there and that power flows inside me. With a smile, I roll my shoulders and reach for the doorknob. I twist it slightly before kicking the door open. It goes flying with a bang, slamming against the wall and leaving a dent behind as I step into the warm hallway.

"Honey, I'm home!" I call, giggling at my words.

There is no answer.

I immediately realize the lights are coming from hundreds of candles, the tiny flames flickering along the hallway walls with wax melting onto the floor. It's as if Roger set up some sort of great, romantic gesture, even if it comes across as creepy, and it makes me scowl.

This could all be a trap, but I also know I'm not leaving here with Roger. He has no idea I've become a monster. I made a mistake in letting him live, and I won't make it again.

My boots creak on the floorboard as I step farther inside. Freedom, in contrast, makes no noise at all despite her weight. She moves behind me, stalking silently, just as I do. I peek around the corner of the first doorway and find the empty kitchen. There are more candles there but nothing else. Some of them are on top of the refrigerator, the wax dripping down the front of it, giving it an eerie look. Those ones are red.

I continue forward, easing deeper into the house and checking each doorway, only to find them empty. It isn't until I reach the living room that I find him.

Stepping into the room, I take in the sight of the man standing with his back turned to me. He's looking out the window, his hands in his pockets, appearing as casual as I've ever seen him. He's dressed in new clothing, and he cleaned himself up. His hair is perfectly styled, and his clothing is ironed. He looks every inch the man every woman dreams of.

But not me.

He was never my dream.

"I watched you come closer," he remarks as he stares out the window, his voice pensive but not afraid. Why would he be? To him, I will always be the cowering, broken girl he married. "You didn't even try to hide."

"Why do I need to?" I ask, my voice hard as I watch him. "I wanted you to know when I was coming for you."

He chuckles under his breath before finally turning to look at me. Just like always, his face is perfectly groomed. It's been months since his injuries, so he's all but healed now, but there's still a small bump in his nose that he wasn't able to fix. One of my men broke it, and he can't erase that. I bet that slight imperfection drives him mad.

His hands still linger in his pockets, but when his gaze shifts to Freedom, I tense. She can take care of herself, but I don't want his eyes on her at all. She stands behind me, her tail curling around my thigh as she offers support and protection.

Roger looks me up and down, taking in my outfit and the blood covering my skin. His expression tightens ever so slightly, the muscle jumping in his jaw the only sign of his displeasure. "Those circus freaks have changed you."

"Yes." I nod, tilting my head as my smile blooms. "They have."

He tsks. "Such a shame. You used to be the perfect housewife. No worries," he says as he pulls his hand from his pocket, revealing a knife, the sharp edge catching the glow of the candles as he meets my eyes. His gaze is filled with the evil and rot I know lives inside him. "I can make you like that again."

He lunges for me. I should have been prepared for it, but instead, I only have a few seconds to bring my arms up and grab his wrist as we both go tumbling to the ground. Freedom growls, clearly intending to jump in, but I hiss over at her.

"No! This is my fight!"

She immediately backs down, but not without an angry growl. She watches, waiting to see if I need her help as she paces away from us in agitation.

Roger may have gotten the jump on me, but that doesn't mean I'm helpless. I'm stronger than I used to be, and when he tries to shove the knife into my stomach, I'm able to hold him off. My hands grip the blade, it cutting into my palms, and my blood runs down my arms and across my body. This is the last time he will ever make me bleed. I grin up at him as I push the blade up and away from me, cutting myself deeper. His hands shake as he tries to resist, but the power in my veins helps me shove him. When I snarl obscenities and kick, he actually flies off me long enough for me to scramble to my feet.

Crouching, I reach for my blade once more as he scrambles to his feet, his chest heaving.

When I face him, I see something flash in his eyes I've never seen before—fear.

It's a hell of a drug.

"What's the matter, dear husband?" I ask, grinning as I lift my bleeding hand and lick a line across my palm as his face pales, and he hesitates. "Tiger got your tongue?"

With an unhinged laugh, I turn to lunge. I swipe my blade at him, but he dodges out of the way at the last second, missing being gutted by a millimeter. I don't let it frustrate me. I swipe out again and again, dodging his attacks and making sure every movement of mine counts. We dance back and forth across the floor, our breathing loud in the quiet farmhouse. It's my blade against his, my anger against his manipulation.

My back hits the wall when I leap to avoid a wild swing, and plaster rains down on me. I duck under his knife just in time for it to embed in the wall where I was standing. Sliding behind him, I slice his leg, making him snarl and turn to chase me once more. He goads me with each step, spitting his own insults. The word "whore" is thrown around a lot, but most of his insults fall on deaf ears. He swings his blade toward me, and I jump back just in time, but not before the edge catches on my corset and slices through it. A bloody cut appears on my pale skin, another wound to add to the list of injuries he has given me.

"I really fucking liked this corset," I hiss as I lunge toward him, laughing when I catch his bicep and tear through his clothing, his blood blooming from the cut.

He bares his teeth at me as he glances down at it, the sight of his blood infuriating him even more. "Bitch."

I wave my knife at him, the sight of him bleeding giving me way too much joy. "What are you going to do about it, asshole?"

He doesn't bother with words as he leaps toward me, and this time, the intention in his eyes is clear. He was playing before, but now he wants to kill me. Well, that makes two of us. We crash together, all snarling teeth and angry hisses. He lifts his arm, ready to bring his knife down across my face, and I lift my own to block it. The clang is loud, reverberating down my arm as I push, trying to lift him away. We are locked together like that, the blades starting to lower toward my face from his strength until, with a gasp, I push them to the side, flinging his blade away with the unexpected movement, but mine goes flying as well. Now, we only have our fists. That's fine. I can kill him with my bare hands.

"You deserve to rot in hell," I snarl as I swing my fist with my full weight behind it and the power of the cards flowing through me.

"You're going to rot there with me," he goads. "You're wearing blood once more, dear wife."

"I'm going to wear yours too," I hiss, narrowing my eyes on him as he dances under my wild swings. "I'm going to bathe in your blood when you're dead and fuck every single one of those circus freaks while I'm covered in it."

The power of the cirque flares in my veins as I move forward, but Freedom makes a sound, and I make the mistake of glancing over at her. Roger's fist swings and lands a blow across my jaw, snapping my head to the side. Pain flares where he hit me. My hand slowly lifts to prod at the bruising skin before I slowly turn my head back to meet his narrowed eyes. I bare my teeth at him like a wild animal would, knowing my eyes are glowing and wrong. Fury fills me for everything he has done to me, to my family, and what he continues to do. It fills my veins with a power that can't be contained.

"That's the last time you'll ever hit me, Roger," I growl. "I hope you remember the feeling when I rip you open."

He stares at me, a mocking grin on his face despite the flash of fear I see in his eyes. "Come on, baby. You know I'm going to do much more than that. I haven't forgotten the beautiful way you screamed when I fucked you as you were dying. I want that again. I might even fuck you after you're dead just so you know that every inch of you, even in death, belongs to me. It's time you remember who you are."

Fury taints me that's so thick, I can barely breathe through it. I'm tempted to throw myself at him again, but that isn't what I need. Instead, instinct has me raising my hand and holding it in front of me, palm up.

"You're right," I muse as I feel power flow through me. "It's time I remember who I truly am."

Roger stares at my hand in confusion, arching one eyebrow. "What?" he grunts. "What is this?"

Between one blink and the next, a deck of cards appears in my palm, perfectly stacked, and the power inside me uncurls like a dragon.

"They teach you magic tricks at that freak show?" Roger sneers. "Are you going to pull a rabbit out of a hat next?"

"Close," I say, my smile slow and bloodthirsty. "I'm going to pull your intestines out of your throat."

He lifts his arm, preparing to hit me again, but I don't move except for my slow smile.

The deck of cards begins to glow, and he pauses, confused. "Ember, what—"

"It's not Ember anymore," I declare, meeting his eyes. The cards rise into the air, spreading out before me, and he backs up. "Bow to your queen."

The cards shoot toward him, and he grunts as they slice his skin. One of them cuts his cheek, leaving a red line behind. He reaches up and touches it, his finger coming away red, and his lips split into a sneer.

"You're lucky it's a clean cut," he says.

"Oh?" I mock. Another card strikes him, this time slicing a jagged mark across his forehead. "Is this better?"

"You bitch!" he spits. "You're going to pay for that!"

He lunges, but the cards are faster. More than that, I can feel them start to glow beneath my skin. The cards that fly next are sharper, more painful. I reach for another knife at my hip and pull it out.

"You hurt what's mine," I say, licking the blade like I've seen Club do a hundred times, christening it with my blood. "If it had just been me, I'd have let things go, but because you hurt Heart, I'm going to carve out yours and give it to him."

The glow beneath my skin slides along the blade, and when I lash out and cut a line across his bicep, he howls in pain, stumbling back.

"Stop this!" he snarls. "I am your husband!"

"I'm your husband," I mock, laughing, and then cut his forearm. He falls backward, but I follow him. "How pitiful."

When he reaches toward me, I slice down. The knife cuts through skin, muscle, and bone, and the resounding thump as his hand falls to the floor is music to my ears. The yell that tears from his throat is a symphony.

"Oh no!" I say, laughing. I pick up his hand and wave it at him. "Need a hand, Roger?"

He cradles his arm against his stomach, his face twisted. Despite his anger and his attempts to seem more powerful, the fear in his eyes is undeniable.

It's the most beautiful sight I've ever seen.

He doesn't know when to quit though. He comes at me again, trying to kick me, and my cards slam into his thigh, embedding themselves there. They dig inside, and he starts to scream in earnest, the long, haunting sounds echoing. I shiver with delight. I understand his obsession with my pain now.

"Scream for me, Roger," I purr, "just like you used to tell me to do."

I cut again and again, slicing pieces away. A sliver here. An ear there. A finger when he points it at me. The sound of my knife cutting through skin is one I'll never forget. I take pieces off his body as if I'm preparing jerky. Each time, I toss the pieces over to Freedom, and she tears into them, much to Roger's horror. He tries to scramble away and cut me at the same time, but with each slice of my blade, he loses more strength. Blood covers the floor, making him slip and slide. At some point, he stops coming for me and focuses only on getting away.

"What's the matter, dear husband?" I coo. "I thought you were going to teach me a lesson?"

"You're a crazy bitch," he spits, but it lacks his usual venom when he moans in pain. Cards stick out of his skin all over his body, buried deeply. He's bleeding everywhere. Soon, he'll pass out from blood loss, but I want it to hurt badly first.

I flick my fingers, and a queen card appears between them. "That's not very nice," I tell him. "Didn't anyone ever tell you gentlemen don't call ladies a bitch?" I tilt my head. "Of course, you're not supposed to hit a lady either, but here we are."

I shoot the queen card at his face, grinning when it hits his eye and digs in. He screams, the sound shrill and desperate.

"You don't want to do this," he implores. "I'm your husband, Ember!"

I laugh. "You aren't my husband. You're just a bug that needs to be squashed."

Freedom paces around the room, eager to join in. As if realizing I've been keeping all the fun for myself, I straighten and look over at her. Our eyes meet, and she stalks forward, rubbing her face against my thigh.

Looking down at him, I say, "I used to be weak, but I'm not anymore. Now I save people from monsters like you. I hunt the demons down and make them pay." I squat. "And I really, really enjoy killing them. They deserve every bit of pain they get, just like you do."

He starts to sob, but I feel nothing except satisfaction. "Please, don't," he croaks. "Please."

"You had your chance to leave me alone," I say, watching him. "You could have lived if you just stayed away, but now, my mercy has run out. It was misplaced. You don't deserve it. You don't deserve my kindness. You certainly don't deserve life," I sneer before slamming my knife into his kneecap.

He screams, sheer terror in the sound.

I'm done now. I've done what I came here to do. The thing is, I meant what I said. Roger Campbell doesn't deserve to live. I won't let this monster walk free so he can harm someone else. I'm doing the world a service. I should get an award or something.

"Freedom," I say as I straighten. She looks up at me. "Your turn."

She roars and lunges forward. Roger screams as she buries her teeth in his stomach. The crunch is deafening as she pulls away. His skin stretches and tears, revealing his insides. He looks down at the wound with wide eyes. His cry is strangled, and as if Freedom finds it annoying, she lunges for his neck and chomps down. The sound cuts off, turning to a wet gurgle as she tears out his esophagus. He finally stops moving.

There's no coming back from that.

"Good girl," I tell her, smiling brightly at the mess that used to be my husband.

Clapping and whistling comes abruptly from behind me, and I turn, surprised to find Heart, Diamond, Club, and Spade there, their eyes alight with fire. They cheer me on as if I'm an actor putting on a show. I never even heard them enter. I wonder how long they've been there, how long they watched, but judging from their expressions, they saw pretty much everything.

Grinning, I take a bow, making them cheer louder.

I pick up my knife as Freedom munches on Roger's lifeless body and lean down.

"Excuse me, girl," I tell her. "I have a gift to give."

I press the blade into his chest cavity, carving into his ribcage until I can reach in and wrap my fingers around his heart. With violence that I taste in my bones, I yank it out. It's still warm in my hand as I turn and walk up to my men, stopping before Heart.

"A gift," I tell him as I hold out the bleeding organ. "A heart for Heart to make up for your injury."

He squeals and claps his hands to his cheeks. "Ah! You shouldn't have!" He takes the heart and holds it up like a trophy for the others to see. "My queen gave me her husband's heart!"

The others laugh and cheer, and I can't help but join in.

All the while, Freedom feasts behind us.

Offering them my bloody hands, I grin widely. "Let's go home."

It's done.

It's finally over.

I am free. *We* are free. There are no more ghosts to haunt us now. Only the hope for our future and the knowledge that we can face anything together.

FIFTY-SIX

Sunlight streams through the trees and lights up the circus tents, making the bright colors dance in a beautiful kaleidoscope. The tents are a mix of old and new, of patched and unblemished, but together, they make a quilt of perfection. The sun warms me from the inside out as the cards swim beneath my skin. I trust them completely—the cards, the cirque. I am hers as she is mine. We all belong here.

This is home, something I have always searched for and finally found.

It's been a few days since my confrontation with Roger. We haven't moved, choosing to remain here in a town where the cops seem to have disappeared and a gruesome scene that was attributed to wild dogs was revealed in a farmhouse miles from here. They saw the teeth marks and were convinced. I suppose folks out here would never suspect a tiger attack.

It's been peaceful since then. Every night, our tent is filled with audience members who come to shout and cheer for our acts. Heart is still on bedrest, much to his annoyance, but we've kept things going. He's itching to return, but until then, he shows the heart I gave him to everyone who will look. It's currently preserved in a jar in his tent, high on a shelf like a real trophy. In exchange for my gift, he carved a Q on his collarbone. They all have. On my own body, each of their suits is a scar, some older like Club's and some newer like Diamond's. I wear the marks with pride, just as they do.

Food tastes sweeter now, as if ridding the world of my monster allowed me to become who I was always meant to be. Hilda says it comes with the power of the cirque and that it's expected. I don't really know. What I do know is that I sit in her fortune teller tent at night and stare into the eyes of giggling girlfriends and nervous boyfriends, and it's become easier to read people's souls. I've only given out two joker cards, one to a little boy with ghosts in his eyes. His big brother hovered protectively outside. He's a good big brother, but not a strong one. I gave them each one. They looked at me with confusion but took the joker cards gratefully. I know we'll see them again soon.

I take a deep breath, enjoying the scent of summer mixing with the sunshine. In front of me, Greg runs around with the children, laughing with them as they tackle him and try to take him down. He takes pity on them and collapses, shouting in mock fear as they pile on top of him. Some of the older kids look on with smiles, most of their eyes bright and their phantoms fading.

Club is showing some how to throw knives, being patient with them as they throw them and they bounce off a tree. One of the little girls, Viola, sits with Freedom, her back against her as she knits a daisy crown. When she sets it on Freedom's head, I can't help but smile. Diamond is sitting with a young boy, showing him how to do a magic trick. Both Spade and Heart tell stories to another group. We've welcomed so many children here.

This is what happiness is, I realize.

Here, in the sunshine, in Cirque Obscurum, is happiness.

There will always be darkness in the world. Monsters will lurk in the shadows and nightmares will follow, but we'll be there to meet them. We'll be there to chase it away with the sunshine.

"My queen, your presence is requested with the children!" Heart declares. "Apparently, they think they should be knighted!"

Grinning, I make my way over to them, my heart full and mind clear.

I grab the umbrella Heart hands me and hold it aloft like a sword. "Alright! Who's ready to slay dragons?"

Their cheers go straight to my soul, and I know I am home.

Here, in Cirque Obscurum, where nightmares come to die.

EPILOGUE

Six months later . . .

"You called?" The dark whisper wraps around me, making me shiver as I glance over my shoulder with a grin to see Diamond framed in my tent doorway. Spade, Club and Heart are behind him.

"I did," I murmur as I turn to face them, my hair flowing over my shoulder as I stand, naked and waiting for them. Their greedy eyes trace every inch of my body, and I know they love each dip and scar. My thighs clench, and desire spirals through me.

Diamond steps closer, no doubt sensing my intention. I always need them, and tonight is no exception. We have all been busy the last few days, setting up in a new place, and I haven't gotten to play.

Tonight, I want to play with each of them. I want them to remind me where I belong.

"You once told me you wanted to live and get revenge. You have both now. Is that all you want?" he murmurs as he stops.

"No." I smirk as I prowl toward him. "I want you all forever."

Gripping my ringmaster's hair, I yank his head back as I kiss him, my eyes going to my other men who step inside, letting the flaps shut behind them. Desire and hunger glimmer in their eyes as they watch me. Licking Diamond's lips, I pull away slightly as I meet his gaze.

"Tonight, your queen wants all of you."

"What our queen wants, she gets," he murmurs, licking his lips as his hand slides across my hip. He tugs me closer, dipping me as his lips find mine again in an all-consuming kiss.

Groaning into his mouth, I slide my hands across his built shoulders, down his muscular arms, and up his abs, greedy to touch every inch of him. I break the kiss with a gasp and turn his head, kissing down his throat and chest before I bite his nipple. His hiss fills the air, and suddenly, I'm flying.

I bounce as I hit my bed, but I don't have time to complain because he's on me within a moment. He rolls us so my arms are behind me, pinned between our bodies, his chest to my back, and his mouth meets my ear as he hooks his leg around one of mine and forces it open.

"Behave. Let your men fuck and worship you, my queen, and then you can have your monster."

My heart slams in my chest as Club steps between my legs, his clothes gone, as he strokes his huge cock, running his eyes down my body. "What our queen wants, she gets. You know that."

"Club—" His name ends in a scream as he lifts my left leg, throwing it over his shoulder, and slams into me, forcing his huge, hard dick as deep inside of my slick channel as he can. My eyes cross as my back arches. Leaning down, he captures my nipple in his lips, sucking and twisting as he pulls from my clenching body and thrusts forward, setting a hard, fast rhythm. Some nights, I like it soft, while others, I want the devil, and tonight I want their darkness.

I want them.

"Look at what you do to him. Feel what you do to all of us. You drive us crazy," Diamond purrs in my ear, making me shiver and clench down on Club. He groans into my skin, lifting his head as he captures my other nipple. I rock my hips into his brutal thrusts, taking him deeper, the wet sound of our bodies coming together loudly in my tent.

He straightens suddenly, lifting my hips into the air with the force of him fucking me, and turns his head to kiss my leg. His other hand slides up my hip and across my cunt, where he rubs my clit until I cry out and clench around his cock. Snarling, he fucks me harder, faster, as his teeth bite into my leg.

Pain and pleasure mix, and I explode with a scream, taking him with me, his groan muffled against my skin as his hips stutter before slamming deeply into me, pumping me full of his hot cum.

Gasping, I slump back into Diamond, shaking as he kisses my jumping pulse. "Good girl, now take your beast tamer."

I open my eyes, and Club steps away from me before Spade takes his place.

"Spade," I beg. "Please."

"He tames wild animals, Queen. Now let him tame this wild, perfect pussy," Diamond coos.

"I had you this morning, my love," Spade murmurs as he forces my thighs wider, to the point of pain. "Yet I want you with an intensity that borders on painful, so hold on because you'll need to for what I have in store."

"I can take you, all of you. I was made for you." I tilt my head back, widening my legs. "Show me your worst, beast master."

Despite Spade's usual softness, he grabs my thighs, lifts me from the bed, and spears me onto his cock.

Spade is huge but slick with my and Club's cum, so he fits inside me, stuffing me full of his dick.

I almost choke at how full I feel, and when he starts to move, I see stars. My moans echo around my tent as Diamond's hand slides across my chest and covers my breast, squeezing and pinching my nipple. Pleasure shoots straight to my throbbing clit, building me up until I'm begging wordlessly for more.

"You're ours," Spade snarls as he hammers into me, his hands spanning my hips as he uses my body just like I wanted.

"She is, and look how well she takes us." Diamond groans. "I can feel her dripping above me. Our greedy queen wants more, doesn't she?"

"Yes, yes, yes," I cry, power flowing through me with my pleasure.

Spade snarls, his fingers bruising my skin as he fills me with each wild thrust, hitting my cervix. The pain only makes me scream for more until neither of us can take it.

We tumble into bliss together, my name on his lips as he fills me with his release, and I drip mine down on him.

I don't get time to recover as he's ripped away, replaced by a grinning Heart with madness in his gaze as he looks at me. "My turn to play, Queen."

Without warning, he impales me on his cock, fighting my fluttering cunt to fill me.

I try to pull away, to fight him, but he drags me down, taking my pussy hard and fast until my screams fill the air, the madness in his gaze growing as he hears it.

"That's it, my queen. Scream for me. Let them all know you belong to us. My body was made to fill yours. I'm going to spend the rest of our lives buried deep inside you."

Whimpering, I nod my head rapidly. "Yours, you're mine." My words make no sense, but they seem to drive him wild.

Pulling from my dripping channel, he slides his slick dick down and presses it against my ass, pushing into me as I widen my legs, accepting him. He presses past my muscles, making it hurt even as it feels good.

My hips roll, chasing pleasure as he fucks my ass with wicked, hard thrusts, my name a constant chant from his mouth as Diamond holds me still for his assault.

The power inside me grows, and unlike usual, I can't control it.

Cards fly from me, but Heart simply grins, fucking me as they embed into his skin, queens sticking from his bare chest.

"Marks of honor," he tells me. "You made me bleed, Queen. Now it's your turn."

My eyes widen as he leans down, digging his teeth into my breast. The pain is so great I almost black out, and when he pulls back, my blood smears his lips and my breast drips with it.

Grinning a crimson smile, he hammers into my ass as he lowers his head once more and bites my other one.

My nails dig into Diamond's skin, cutting him as I scream and writhe, pleasure and pain filling me until it explodes out of me. Cards fly through the room as I come so hard I pass out.

When I come to, Heart is groaning, his cock buried in my ass as he spills his cum, his tongue lapping at the blood across my skin until Diamond kicks him away.

"My turn," Diamond declares.

I'm weak, my body limp as I'm turned once more and forced to my knees. I almost collapse, feeling cum and blood drip down me as I look down at him. He grins up at me.

"There she is: my queen. Now ride your king. I want to watch you claim me."

"Diamond," I warn on a pant, my pussy and ass aching, but he gives me no reprieve. He lifts and drops me onto his waiting cock. With his hands on my hips, he forces me to ride him. My hands fall backwards, gripping his thighs behind me to keep myself up.

He moves me faster, forcing me to ride his cock, and my exhaustion is replaced by desire—desire to see my perfect ringmaster fall apart for me. Moaning, I wind my hips, looking down at Diamond spread out below me. He groans, letting me know he likes it, so I speed up, bouncing on his cock as his eyes drop to my cunt.

His gaze is dark and hungry, his hands sliding over my skin as my power grows. I worry for a moment that I'll hurt him with it, and Diamond reads that.

"Take my flesh. Carve it off with your cards. It's yours, Queen. The cirque has my soul, but you have my heart and body. I am yours until the end," he vows.

That promise releases something inside me, and I give into the power. I ride him harder, faster, taking what I want as my cards cut into him, making him bleed for me. All the while, he urges me on, demanding more.

The power I have over him, over them all, drives me wild as the others surround me. Hands and mouths slide across my skin as I fly higher and higher, soaring toward the abyss of pleasure only they give me.

They work as one to give me what I want, but as I fall into their waiting arms again, it's my ringmaster's gaze I hold. I scream his name, and with his own bellow, he follows me into the waiting darkness, filling me up with his pleasure and love.

Shaking, I roll my hips through the aftershocks as they collapse into my bed, Diamond's softening cock still inside me. Their teeth and hands mark every inch of my skin, and satisfaction pours through me.

It's then I feel the call.

The cirque reaches for us, calling to us.

Lifting my head, I peer out of the tent flaps to the darkness beyond, tasting the menace in the air as I turn my gaze to my collapsed men. "I hope you still have some energy left. We have a call. It's time to go."

Their groans make me laugh.

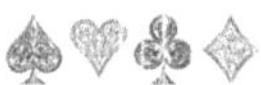

The call doesn't take us too far from Cirque Obscurum, only to the outskirts of town and an abandoned power station where kids have been having parties, which is obvious considering the bottles and trash scattered about. I wander through it, my mask in place and my men behind me. Our souls thrum as one as we answer the call, following it through the darkness and into the building where a young girl is curled into herself, the joker card clutched in her hands.

Her eyes widen when she sees us, and she scrambles backwards, gripping her torn dress to her body. I hold my hand up, and my men step back. I read the truth in her eyes without her needing to say anything, and fury fills me.

Pain recognizes pain. My ghosts match hers, and an understanding passes between us as I kneel before her. She swallows, her tongue darting out to prod her split, bleeding lip. Blood coats her thighs as she tries to unsuccessfully cover herself, and I take off my leather duster and hand it over. Wordlessly, she wraps it around herself, glancing from me to my men.

"Who are you?"

"Your answer to the call," I admit.

She glances down at the card she still holds, her eyes flaring wide with shock. "I heard the rumors, the tales . . . I didn't know if it was true. I hoped . . ." She looks at me as if to assure herself I'm real.

I offer no comfort or words. They won't help.

She doesn't need me to hold her as she cries.

That isn't why she called us.

She needs the monsters.

She needs the hunters.

She wants revenge.

"Tell me your nightmares," I coo as I peer into her terrified, bruised face.

She glances at a busted window, where ripped curtains blow in the wind and laughing voices reach us. "Them. They are my nightmares." She searches my gaze. "I want them to pay for what they did to me."

"We can handle that." I offer her my hand, and she places the card in it. "In return, you have a choice—join us or continue with your life."

"I like my life. It won't be easy, but I want to go home. I can't, though, knowing they are still alive and out there," she admits.

"Then let us rid you of that fear." Standing, I pocket the card as I grin at her. "Stay here."

Whistling to myself, I head out of the abandoned building and around the back where I find a group of three boys passing a joint between them, laughing as they talk.

"Did you try that ass? It was tight—"

My features contort in anger, and I pull my blade, twirling it as I skip their way. "Hi, boys, I heard you like to play. Can I join?"

Their heads whip around, and I giggle. "What the fuck?"

I don't let them say another word. Their actions caused enough pain, and their words won't help them get another chance.

I stab my blade into the first boy's stomach because he's facing us. His scream fills the air as I yank it up and out. I kick him so he falls into the dirt. While the others are frozen in shock, I tilt my head and skip to the next guy. Once I stand before him, I grip his dick through his pants, and with the power of the cards filling me, I rip it from his body, holding it up like a trophy as he howls. "Not much to brag about, is there?" I comment as I toss it away.

He collapses at my feet.

The third turns to run as I laugh. "Run, little rabbit!" I giggle again. "Little rabbit, little rabbit, won't you stay? After all, I thought you wanted to play!"

The power of the cirque still fills me, so I fling my hand out, letting it flow from me. Cards fly through the air like daggers, and they slam into his back, knocking him to the ground with a scream as I prowl over, seeing our suits sticking from his bleeding back. Kicking him over, I grin down at his pale face.

He lifts his hand to ward me off. "Please, God—"

I slice out with my dagger, taking his hand as he screams and gapes at the stump. "No god can save you now," I tell him happily, and then I bring my boot down on his crotch, crushing until he finally passes out. Leaning down, I grip his hair and begin to slice. I carve through his neck, blood squirting across my mask and face, and when his head is finally separated from his body, I turn to see the others watching, letting me take the lead. My eyes land on the first boy. He's still alive and trying to get away.

"Heart, do the honors," I call as we watch the first boy try to crawl away, sobbing and bleeding everywhere.

"With pleasure, Queen." He stalks the boy as he glances back at us, sobbing and screaming louder. Heart feasts on his fear as I watch, and when he finally stops before him, the boy lifts his head.

"Tell me if this hurts," Heart says as he plunges his blade into the boy's chest, carving out his heart while he's still alive. When he falls to the ground again, he's already dead.

Dropping the head with the other bodies, I walk over and check to make sure they are all dead just as the girl stumbles from the building. I expect horror, but all I see is relief and satisfaction in her gaze as she stares at the bloodbath.

"Thank you." She looks at the bodies then us. "Thank you."

"Go home. Heal. Enjoy your life, and remember, if you ever need us, we're here. All you have to do is call."

We watch her go.

We're the shadows in the night, the monsters of this world, the broken and beautiful.

We are the saviors of the weak and the damnation of the strong.

I glance at my men to see them watching me. Diamond steps forward.

With his mask in place, he reaches for me like they did all those nights ago when they saved me. This time, I don't hesitate. I place my hand in his, smiling at the mask and the man underneath.

I chose life all those months ago, and I choose it again each and every day with them.

With my cards and my men, my family and my home.

"Let's go home to where brutal things linger and nightmares thrive," I rasp.

He grins and leans in to whisper in my ear. "Tell me *your* nightmares, Queen."

I smile and lace my fingers with his, but I don't answer. I *am* the nightmare. I am the queen.

And the darkness?

The darkness is home.

ABOUT K.A. KNIGHT

K.A Knight is an USA Today bestselling indie author trying to get all of the stories and characters out of her head, writing the monsters that you love to hate. She loves reading and devours every book she can get her hands on, and she also has a worrying caffeine addiction.

She leads her double life in a sleepy English town, where she spends her days writing like a crazy person.

Read more at K.A Knight's website or join her Facebook Reader Group.
Sign up for exclusive content and my newsletter here
http://eepurl.com/drLLoj

OTHER BOOKS BY K.A. KNIGHT

CONTEMPORARY

LEGENDS AND LOVE *CONTEMPORARY RH*

Revolt

Rebel

Riot - coming soon..

PRETTY LIARS *CONTEMPORARY RH*

Unstoppable

Unbreakable

PINE VALLEY *CONTEMPORARY*

Racing Hearts

DEN OF VIPERS UNIVERSE STANDALONES

Scarlett Limerence *CONTEMPORARY*

Nadia's Salvation *CONTEMPORARY*

Alena's Revenge *CONTEMPORARY*

Den of Vipers *CONTEMPORARY RH*

Gangsters and Guns (Co-Write with Loxley Savage) *CONTEMPORARY RH*

FORBIDDEN READS (STANDALONES)

Daddy's Angel *CONTEMPORARY*

Stepbrothers' Darling *CONTEMPORARY RH*

STANDALONES

The Standby *CONTEMPORARY*

Diver's Heart *CONTEMPORARY RH*

DYSTOPIAN

THEIR CHAMPION SERIES *Dystopian RH*

The Wasteland

The Summit

The Cities

The Nations

Their Champion Coloring Book

Their Champion - the omnibus

The Forgotten

The Lost

The Damned

Their Champion Companion - the omnibus

PARANORMAL

THE LOST COVEN SERIES *PNR RH*

Aurora's Coven

Aurora's Betrayal

HER MONSTERS SERIES *PNR RH*

Rage

Hate

Book 3 - *coming soon..*

COURTS AND KINGS *PNR RH*

Court of Nightmares

Court of Death

Court of Beasts

Court of Heathens - coming soon..

THE FALLEN GODS SERIES *PNR*

Pretty Painful

Pretty Bloody

Pretty Stormy

Pretty Wild

Pretty Hot

Pretty Faces

Pretty Spelled

Fallen Gods - the omnibus 1

Fallen Gods - the omnibus 2

FORGOTTEN CITY *PNR*

Monstrous Lies

Monstrous Truths

Monstrous Ends

SCIENCE FICTION

DAWNBREAKER SERIES *SCI FI RH*

Voyage to Ayama

Dreaming of Ayama

STANDALONES

Crown of Stars *SCI FI RH*

Daddy's Angel *(From Podium Audio)*

Stepbrothers' Darling *(From Podium Audio)*

Blade of Iris *(From Podium Audio)*

Deadly Affair *(From Podium Audio)*

Deadly Match *(From Podium Audio)*

Deadly Encounter *(From Podium Audio)*

Stolen Trophy *(From Podium Audio)*

Crown of Stars *(From Podium Audio)*

Monstrous Lies *(From Podium Audio)*

Monstrous Truth *(From Podium Audio)*

Monstrous Ends *(From Podium Audio)*

Court of Nightmares *(From Podium Audio)*

Court of Death *(From Podium Audio)*

Unstoppable *(From Podium Audio)*

Unbreakable *(From Podium Audio)*

Fractured Shadows *(From Podium Audio)*

Revolt *(From Podium Audio)*

Rebel *(From Podium Audio)* - coming soon

About Kendra Moreno

Kendra Moreno is secretly a spy but when she's not dealing in secrets and espionage, you can find her writing her latest adventure. She lives in Texas where the summer days will make you melt, and southern charm comes free with every meal. She's a recovering Road Rager (kind of) and slowly overcoming her Star Wars addiction (nope!), and she definitely didn't pass on her addiction to her son (she did). She has one hellhound named Mayhem who got tired of guarding the Gates of Hell and now guards her home against monsters. She's a geek, a mother, a scuba diver, a tyrannosaurus rex, and a wordsmith who sometimes switches out her pen for a sword.

If you see Kendra on the streets, don't worry: you can distract her with talks about Kylo Ren or Loki.
#LokiLives #BringBackBenSolo

To find out more about Kendra, you can check her out on her website or join her
Facebook group, Kendra's World of Wonder.
Sign up for Kendra's Newsletter:
https://mailchi.mp/feb46d2b29ad/babbleandquill

facebook.com/AuthorKendraMoreno

x.com/KendramorenoA

instagram.com/kendramorenoauthor

bookbub.com/authors/kendra-moreno

tiktok.com/@kendramorenoauther

OTHER BOOKS BY KENDRA MORENO

SONS OF WONDERLAND

Book 1 - Mad as a Hatter

Book 2 - Late as a Rabbit

Book 3 - Feral as a Cat

Companion novel - Cruel as a Queen

DAUGHTERS OF NEVERLAND

Book 1 - Vicious as a Darling

Book 2 - Fierce As A Tiger Lily

Book 3 - Wicked As A Pixie

Companion Novel - Monstrous As A Croc

THE HEIRS OF OZ

Book 1 - Heartless as a Tin Man

Book 2 - Empty as a Scarecrow

Book 3 - Cowardly as a Lion

Companion Novel - Vengeful as a Beauty

THE LORDS OF GRIMM

Book 1 - Cunning as a Trickster

Book 2 - Bitter as a Captain

Book 3 - Twisted as a Princess

Companion Novel - Hateful as a Sister

THE KEEPERS OF ENCHANTMENT

Book 1 - Charming as a Killer

Book 2 - Ethereal as a Swan

Book 3 - Tricky as a Thief

Companion Novel - Compelling as a Piper

GODS OF UNDER

Book 1 - Golden as a King

PREY ISLAND

Book 1 - Prey Island

Book 2 - Predator Point

CLOCKWORK ALMANAC

Book 1 - Clockwork Butterfly

Book 2 - Clockwork Octopus

THE VALHALLA MECHANISM

Book 1 - Gears of Mischief

Book 2 - Gears of Thunder

Book 3 - Gears of Ragnarök

RACE GAMES

Book 1 - Blood and Honey

Book 2 - Teeth and Wings

Book 3 - Jewels and Feathers

Book 3 - Fur and Claws

STAND-ALONES

Treble Maker

Pharaoh-mones

Philomena And The Seven Deaths

Barbed Wire Hearts

CO-WRITES

FIND AN ERROR?

Please email this information to thenuttyformatter1@gmail.com:

- *the author name*
- *title of the book*
- *screenshot of the error*
- *suggested correction*

www.ingramcontent.com/pod-product-compliance
Lightning Source LLC
Chambersburg PA
CBHW051110300726
48981CB00001B/78

9 781399 988247